THE GIRL DESTINED TO RISE

by Brittany Czarnecki

Books by **Brittany Czarnecki**

The Girl Forged by Fate

The GIRL DESTINED to RISE

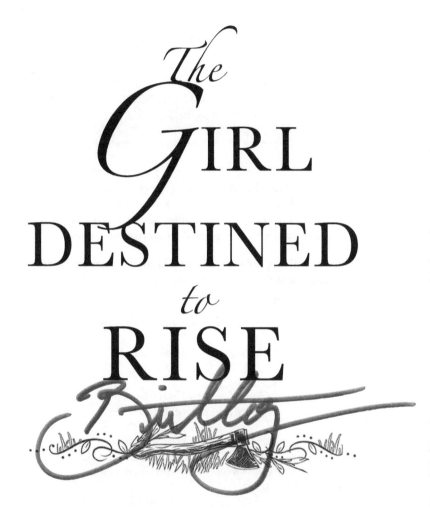

BRITTANY CZARNECKI

gatekeeper press™
Columbus, Ohio

The Girl Destined to Rise: Book Two of the Blackbourne Series

Published by Gatekeeper Press
2167 Stringtown Rd, Suite 109
Columbus, OH 43123-2989
www.GatekeeperPress.com

The cover design and editorial work for this book are entirely the product of the author. Gatekeeper Press did not participate in and is not responsible for any aspect of these elements.

Library of Congress Control Number:

ISBN (paperback): 9781662929175
eISBN: 9781662929182

Cover design by Coco Merwild
www.cjmerwild.com

Book Design by Franziska Stern
www.coverdungeon.com
www.instagram.com/coverdungeonrabbit

Editing by Sarah Grace Liu
www.threefatesediting.com

Map Design by Sheridan Falkenberry
www.instagram.com/ancientmariner115

Published by Gatekeeper Press

To my mom
Thank you for supporting my dreams.

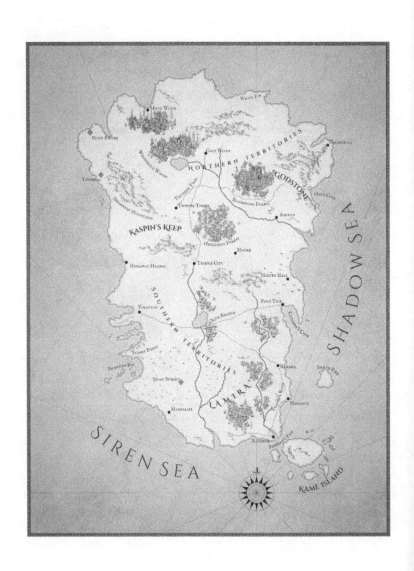

PROLOGUE

Magnus ran along the stone path of the western wall, looking back over his shoulder and losing his breath in belly laughs. The wind whipped his wavy hair back from his brow as he rounded the corner. His little legs ached from running, but he didn't stop. He hopped up onto the wall and began to run along it, stretching his arms out for balance. He could hear him coming; his laughter clawed at the little prince's back. Magnus dared a look back and almost lost his balance.

"Magnus! Get down from there!" someone shouted. He froze and looked over the edge to see his father frantically waving at him to get down. King Erwin stood tall and lean. His auburn hair burned with the dying sun, and his face twisted with anger.

Magnus jumped down from the wall, unaware that Helvarr had caught up to him. He tackled Magnus to the ground, and laughter bubbled up from his core. Helvarr's black hair swept across his forehead and clung to his skin. He was soaking wet.

A few minutes earlier, Magnus had caught Helvarr off guard, standing alone at the practice yard, watching the knights fight. He'd taken a pail of water and dumped it on his friend's head. Helvarr turned around with a scowl on his face, but it brightened when he spotted Magnus. When he reached for his friend, Magnus shrieked with laughter and took off running.

Now, Helvarr couldn't control his laughter as his shaking arms tried to pin Magnus to the ground. They laughed like fools, and Magnus already forgot about his father's scorn. Helvarr was his best friend and brother and always knew how to make Magnus laugh. Though they were only five years of age, Magnus knew in his little heart they would be brothers for life. "Give up!" Helvarr's tiny voice roared.

Magnus tried to crawl away. "A king never gives up!" he said between chuckles.

"You aren't king yet, Magnus," Helvarr retorted.

"Yet." Magnus slipped through his hands and got to his feet. He was looking back to watch Helvarr scrambling to catch up when he ran straight into a sheet of metal.

Magnus was knocked off his feet, and when he looked up, Ser Osmund stood over him, arms crossed, but with a smile on his face. The knight was tall and broad, with long brown hair and a scruffy beard. Helvarr came running up, and Ser Osmund's smile faded slightly. Magnus got back to his feet and stood alongside his friend, ready to be scorned by his father's knight. "Did you enjoy nearly giving your father a heart attack?" he asked. Magnus lowered his head, and Ser Osmund crouched before him. "You can't do things like that, Magnus. You're the heir to Godstone. What if you would've fallen?" His voice was warm, but worry hung heavily in his tone.

"I wouldn't have let him fall." Helvarr stepped up.

Ser Osmund raised his eyes to little Helvarr and gave him a faint smile, but there was something else in his gaze. He turned back to Magnus. "Go find your father. I need to speak with Helvarr." Magnus looked to his friend with concern, but Ser Osmund assured him everything was all right. Helvarr stood still and watched Magnus run off, looking over his shoulder every few feet until he disappeared.

Ser Osmund turned back to Helvarr then got to his feet, motioning for him to follow. They walked silently along the wall until it ended just below the black cliffs that rose above the beaches. "Helvarr . . ." His tone was quiet and careful. Helvarr held his breath. "There's something I need to tell you." He bent down to get eye level with him. He was young, but his face was creased with worry. "You know that your father went off on a special mission."

Helvarr nodded. His father had explained before he left that the king needed his help, and it was his duty to protect his home and the king's family. Helvarr was too young to fully understand, but he'd given his father a hug goodbye with tears in his eyes. His father kissed Helvarr on the head and told him to be good for King Erwin and promised that he would be back soon.

"Helvarr," Ser Osmund repeated. "Your father . . . he died."

Helvarr felt his chest cave in, and tears spring to life in his eyes.

"No," he said, his little voice raspy. "No, Father said he would be back soon. He promised!"

Ser Osmund pulled him in for a hug, wrapping his arms

around the sobbing little boy. He stroked Helvarr's black hair as his tears plopped on the knight's metal armor. "I'm sorry, Helvarr. Your father was a brave man, and he wouldn't want you to be sad."

Helvarr sobbed even louder, and Ser Osmund felt his eyes threatening to betray him. He pulled away and held Helvarr at arm's length. "King Erwin will take good care of you. You and Magnus will be like real brothers now." He tried to smile.

Helvarr sniffed. "Brothers?"

"That's right. Don't you want a brother?" Helvarr nodded and wiped his tears away. "We're your family now, Helvarr, and we'll always take care of you. Do you understand?" Helvarr didn't understand, but he nodded anyway.

"Good boy." Ser Osmund messed his hair. "Come along now, Magnus will be waiting for you in the Hall. I hear the cook made mutton stew." He crossed his eyes and pretended to gag. Helvarr giggled, and Ser Osmund stood up, offering his hand. "Maybe we can sneak some extra apple tarts after supper." Helvarr grinned big and nodded his head. Ser Osmund squeezed his little hand in his as they made their way down the wall of Godstone. He looked into Helvarr's copper eyes that burned in the dying sun but shone with something else.

CHAPTER ONE

GODSTONE

I vy ran the length of the ship to stand over the gunwale as Godstone rose from the Shadow Sea. The black cliffs stood tall and wide, surrounding her home like a shield. Her heart was racing with the wind as she thought about her family again; she couldn't wait to tell Rayner all that had happened while she was away. As the ship pulled into the harbor, Ivy could feel her knees shaking with both excitement and nerves. When the ramp finally came down, Ivy took off in a sprint toward the beach, where she knew her family would be waiting.

Ivy blew past the fishmongers, knocking a basket of clams off one of the booths.

"Hey—" the man started, then stopped when he recognized Ivy. She ran up the small street that had led her in the other direction some months back. She felt the familiar winds running their cold fingers through her hair, and heard the sound of the black waves crashing against the boulders that sat like sentries at the bottom of the cliffs.

A familiar figure walked toward her, and Luna called out from somewhere in the sky. Ivy put all her strength into her legs, running faster as if he might disappear before she could get to him.

Ivy nearly knocked him over as she slammed into her father's chest, and she let tears of pure happiness fall from her eyes. Magnus bent down to kiss Ivy's head, cradling it against his chest.

"I've missed you, sweetling." Magnus seemed to choke on the words.

"I've missed you, Father. I don't ever want to leave again."

"Oh Ivy, your roots are always here." Magnus held his daughter for a long time. Finn and Ronin were still nowhere in sight, and Ivy was grateful for a moment alone with her father. She pulled away, wiping the last of her tears, and looked behind her father. Queen Elana stood tall and beautiful, smiling and waving at Ivy. Elana started to make her way toward where they stood when Ivy realized something.

Her smile faded, and her head swiveled as she looked for the missing member of her family. "Where's Rayner?" she asked Magnus, focusing her gaze on her approaching mother. The king took in a shaky breath and smoothed down Ivy's hair. His demeanor only heightened her nerves.

"Sweetling," he began, "I have something to tell you. Your brother—"

"Rayner!" Ivy interrupted. She took off running toward the figure behind the queen, blowing past her mother.

"Careful! Careful!" the familiar voice called to her, making Ivy slow down as she looked at the man before her. A wooden cane supported her brother, and stitches zig-zagged in a line across his cheek. Rayner's hair was longer and his beard thicker, green spots circled his eyes where bruises were healing, and he held a hand to his ribs. "Well," he began with a smile, "I didn't say to stop."

Ivy threw her arms around Rayner's neck, and he dropped his cane to embrace his sister in return. His beard was no longer scratchy against her cheeks but soft and warm. Ivy didn't let go of him until Magnus and Elana came walking up to them, hand in hand, smiling at the reunion of their children. "Rayner." Ivy finally pulled away and ran her eyes over him again. "What happened?"

"I'm all right, Ivy. It's a long story." Ivy heard someone clear their throat and turned to see Finn and Ronin, leading Cassius and Eclipse up the path. Ivy was grateful that Ronin thought to take Ser Osmund's horse when they fled Helvarr, but it was still an empty saddle.

"Ronin?" King Magnus whispered as if his eyes were betraying him. "What are you doing here? Where's Ser Osmund?" Ivy swayed on her·feet at the knight's name, and Finn stepped forward to steady her. Magnus shot him a glare that demanded he explain himself, but Ivy addressed her father before Finn could trip over his words.

"This is Finn," Ivy said. "He was my sparring partner on Kame Island. He's my . . . we . . . ."

"I've heard much about you, King Magnus, and Queen Elana." Finn stepped forward and bowed before her parents. But Magnus ignored him and again asked where Ser Osmund was, just as Ser Caster was coming up behind them.

Ivy grabbed hold of her father's hand, pulling his attention back to her before she spoke the words that had haunted her for days. "He's dead." Ivy searched her father's face to make sure he'd heard her.

"No," was all he said. Elana covered her mouth with both hands, and Rayner looked at his boots. "It can't be," Magnus continued. "He can't be dead."

"I watched him die, Father. I tried to avenge him, but . . ."

"It's my fault." Ronin stepped forward. Magnus narrowed his gaze on the man as tears welled up in his eyes. "I followed them when they left Kame Island. I got there too late; Ser Osmund was already dead. I'm sorry."

"Why are you here, Ronin? What happened down there?" the king snapped.

"It was Helvarr," Ronin admitted. "He killed Ser Osmund." Magnus dropped to one knee, Queen Elana falling beside him to wrap her arms around his shoulders. Ronin quickly told the king of the Shadow that came to take Ivy, the raiders in Xanheim, and how he spotted Helvarr there, finally revealing the truth of their connection. Magnus kept looking to Ivy as if to confirm that all Ronin was saying was true. Ivy wrinkled her brow and sniffed away her tears as Ronin told the story. Rayner kept a watchful eye on Finn, and Ser Caster stood like a statue in the background. "Where is he?" Magnus demanded, something hateful lingering in his voice.

"I don't know," Ronin admitted.

Magnus stood abruptly, stepping closer to Ronin. "Where is your son?" he roared.

"Father!" Ivy stepped between them; she didn't know why she did it. If someone deserved to be scorned by her father, it was Ronin. "Father, stop. We don't know where he is. Does it really matter right now?" Hot tears stung her eyes as she continued. "Ser Osmund is dead, and we need to mourn him. Please, this isn't Ronin's fault," she said, although Ivy only half believed that.

Magnus looked at his daughter and hung his head, nodding. Ivy knew if her father left to hunt down Helvarr, it wouldn't bring Ser Osmund back. Besides, Ivy had a feeling that Helvarr would be coming to them sooner or later.

Later that evening, as everyone gathered for supper, Rayner told Ivy what had happened that day in the town of Ashton. Ivy listened with wide eyes, looking to Correlyn who sat beside her brother to confirm that what he said was true. Rayner took a moment to gather himself, rubbing his bruised eye before continuing.

"After the attack, I was carried to Magister Ivann's room. I was unconscious when I arrived, and only woke up when the Magister snapped my rib back into place." He flinched as if he was feeling it all over again. "I tried to scream, but nothing but a pathetic yelp came out. Magister Ivann yelled for more men, and they came barging into the room to hold me down while the Magister poured boiling wine over my wound. At that point, I was starting to pass out again, but still, I fought the men that held me down. I couldn't make sense of what was happening, and all I could see was that horned knight . . ." Ivy reached for her brother's hand and squeezed it.

"A few days later, I finally woke up, and though I couldn't speak much, I immediately asked for Correlyn. Magister Ivann wrapped my hand around a small object before fetching her. When she laid eyes on me, Correlyn burst into tears and came to sit by my side. I was sure I looked a mess, but I needed to see her. I smiled and told her that I loved her." Rayner's cheeks blushed slightly as he glanced over at Correlyn, who listened on. "I asked her to marry me then," he said, smiling.

Correlyn smiled and placed a gentle kiss on his cheek. "He only had one request," Correlyn said.

"What was that?" Ivy asked.

Rayner turned to his sister and smiled. "That we wait for you to come home before we tie the knot."

CHAPTER TWO

THE WELCOME

The next night, King Magnus held a feast in honor of Ser Osmund. Ronin sat by his side, and all the knights came to pay their respect to a fallen knight who'd led them and taught them much over the years. The Hall was packed wall to wall with knights and people from the kingdom, every one of them lifting an ale-filled horn to the sky where Ser Osmund now resided with the gods. Ivy sat at the long table upon the dais next to Rayner and Finn. Correlyn was by Rayner's side, and Ivy smiled at the thought of them being married. She was happy for her brother, who, despite everything that had happened, found some sliver of joy.

Ivy sat watching the couple, still unable to believe that her brother was getting married. Even though Rayner's broken rib still wasn't healed, he insisted they continue with the wedding. They would be married in a matter of days, and Ivy couldn't be happier for Rayner, knowing how close he had come to losing his life. She turned to Finn, who was pushing some mutton around his plate. Ivy reached for his cheek and turned his face to hers, placing a soft kiss on his lips.

"What was that for?" he asked, a redness filling his cheeks.

"I'm sorry you didn't get the welcome you deserved. And I want to thank you for staying with me after . . . after Ser Osmund."

"I told you, Ivy"—Finn turned toward her and kissed her knuckles—"I would follow you anywhere." Finn looked past Ivy before releasing her hand. "I'm not sure your family likes me."

Ivy turned and glared at Rayner, who smiled slightly and lowered his eyes to his sister's scorn. "They just don't know you yet. And they're mourning. They'll come around, I promise." The feast carried on through the night, with people coming up to the dais to welcome Ivy home and express condolences for Ser Osmund. Finn instinctively held her hand under the table every time another person came to drag the memory of Ser Osmund up from the grave.

When the feast started to die down, and men were stumbling from their benches in search of a warm bed, Magnus kissed his wife goodnight and moved over to his daughter. The king stood behind Ivy's chair, and Finn scooted away from her, keeping his gaze on the table. "I don't think we properly met," Magnus said as he held his hand out to Finn. "I'm Magnus."

"Finn, Your Grace," he said, and he stood to shake the king's hand.

"Just Magnus. I'm sorry we didn't properly welcome you to our home. How long do you plan to stay?"

"Father," Ivy interrupted. "Finn has nowhere to go. He came here with me . . ."

Magnus searched his daughter's face before realizing what she was saying. "I see," he replied. "Well then, I suppose we'll need to have a talk." Ivy nudged her father in the ribs, but he only smiled down at her before leaving them.

Finn walked with Ivy to the maple tree that sat outside her window. The air was crisp and clean, but a cold wind still blew in from the Shadow Sea. Ivy grabbed his hand and ran toward the tree, her hair sailing behind her. Ivy let go and swung up the lowest branch, leaving Finn on the ground. "What are you doing?" he called to her. Ivy said nothing and kept climbing higher, past the roof of the hall and her bedchamber window. Finn followed her up, snaking his way through the thick branches that now budded with new life. When he caught up to Ivy, she was sitting on a long limb, looking out to the sea.

The night was dark, save for a crescent moon poking out from behind a thick cloud. Ivy closed her eyes, and Finn held her hand in his, letting his gaze fall on her. He couldn't believe that Ivy was his, that only a few months ago, he'd been alone with no family, stranded on an island that he once ran to in search of what he'd lost.

He already loved this place as much as he loved Ivy, but Finn also knew that he felt that way because she was here. It didn't matter where they went or what Ivy's home was like, Finn would love any place that was as dear to her heart as she was to him. He leaned into her and brought a hand to her soft cheek, pushing Ivy's hair behind her ear before kissing her. Ivy angled toward him, bringing her hand up to rest on his chest, making his breath hitch slightly. Finn melted under her touch; his blood pulsed faster as she parted her lips for him. Finn's fingertips slipped under the back of Ivy's shirt and the touch of her soft skin made his pulse beat harder. He could quickly lose himself with Ivy. Every thought was forced from his mind when he was kissing her. Her hand felt hot against his chest, burning through his shirt with a certain eagerness.

Finn didn't want to rush her, knowing that she'd only just come out of the pain-filled fog that surrounded her for the past week. He moved his lips away and leaned his forehead on hers, staring into her eyes. Ivy smiled at him, and Finn felt himself moving back to her lips when a voice called up to them. Rayner stood at the base of the maple tree, craning his neck up to where they sat.

"Finn, was it?" Rayner looked at his sister, then back to Finn. "I'd like to talk to you."

Finn looked back to Ivy for assistance, but she only smiled and kissed his cheek, whispering, "Welcome home," in his ear.

CHAPTER THREE

THE TALK

Finn and Rayner walked side by side through the empty streets of Godstone. Finn glanced back over his shoulder to see Ivy watching from her spot, high in the arms of the maple tree. They walked in silence through the southern gate and out into the open field. Finn noticed a pile of crumbled rocks and looked up to see a statue of a god, missing his head. He stopped in front of it. "What happened?"

"My father destroyed the statue in a fit of anger," Rayner said. "It was after my men brought me back from Ashton. My father thought I was gone and destroyed it himself." Rayner shifted on his feet, not looking at the statue. "He blamed the God of Judgment for taking me away from him and had no one else to direct his anger toward. I think he felt guilty for sending me away and for what happened." He raised his eyes to where the statue's head once sat and visibly shivered. "He'll restore the statue one day, I think."

They continued to walk around the outside of the wall, Rayner leaning into his cane for support against the uneven ground. He finally asked Finn about how he and Ivy met. Finn told the story, careful to leave out any intimate thoughts he had toward his sister, but Rayner saw right through him and grinned knowingly before stopping abruptly and turning to face Finn. They stood eye to eye, though Rayner was slouching a little with the cane. "Do you love her?" Rayner asked plainly.

Finn could think of no other answer but the truth. He didn't care if Rayner was trying to scare him or whether this was a trap to get Magnus to send him away. "More than anything," he answered honestly.

"Will you protect Ivy?"

"Of course. With my life."

"Ivy told me what you did for her when that raider came to take her away. I can't help but think what her fate might've been if Helvarr had gotten his hands on her. You were there for my sister, more than once and in more than one way." Rayner held out his hand to Finn, which he gladly took.

"I can't thank you enough for saving Ivy's life. I can see that you love her as much as you say and that she loves you. If Ivy is happy, then I'm happy." Rayner paused. "She briefly told me about what happened to your family, so I want to welcome you into ours, and I'll talk with my father and tell him to relax." Rayner winked.

"I appreciate that," Finn said, chuckling. They continued their walk on a lighter note. Finn relaxed a little and began telling Rayner how many times Ivy had beaten him in sparring.

Rayner smiled. "I'm not surprised." He stopped and turned to Finn then, mirth in his purple eyes. "How'd you like to spar with another Blackbourne?"

Finn looked Rayner up and down, a grin spreading across his face.

A light drizzle came down over the yard, making Rayner's hair stick to his face and his beard glisten with beads of water. He lifted his cane and held it like a sword, motioning for his attacker to strike.

"Rayner!" Ivy called from behind. "What are you doing?" Rayner ignored his sister and again motioned for Finn to attack him.

It was his second sparring session since he'd returned home. His rib still wasn't healed, but he pushed through the pain as Finn lifted his wooden sword and sent it sailing just over Rayner's head. He narrowed his eyes on Finn and moved toward him, landing a blow on his leg. Finn wore no armor, but Rayner noticed that his attacks were deliberately slow. Their swords crashed together, and Finn shoved Rayner back, forcing him out of the fighting circle they'd dug that morning. He stumbled but didn't fall, leaning back into his heel to launch himself forward.

Finn was almost knocked from his feet as Rayner's sword jabbed into his chest, forcing him back. The two shuffled around the yard, Ivy yelling at them to stop from somewhere outside the circle. Rayner stopped abruptly and winced, clutching his ribs. "Shit," Finn hissed, stepping closer. "Did I hurt you?"

Rayner smirked and swept his cane underfoot, knocking Finn to the ground. He jumped on Finn and smashed his hand to the ground until he let go of his sword. Finn grabbed a handful of mud and smeared it across Rayner's face, obstructing his view. The two laughed like fools as they struggled and rolled in the mud like pigs. They were both covered head to toe in mud as they lay on the soft earth, still trying to catch their breath.

Ivy came up to them and crossed her arms. "What are you doing, Rayner?" she asked again. "The wedding is in an hour, look at you!"

"Relax, Ivy," Rayner said, trying to compose himself. "It's not that bad." On cue, Finn took a handful of mud and squashed it on top of Rayner's head before bursting into laughter again. Rayner pushed him back in the mud, and the two struggled to pin one other.

Ivy smiled but spoke seriously. "Stop it, you two!" she ordered, and she snatched Finn by the arm, pulling him off of Rayner. "Come, we need to get ready too." Finn gave in and helped Rayner to his feet then embraced Rayner before heading off with Ivy.

Finn got to his room, down the hall from Ivy's, and got undressed. A maid had left a hot bath for him, though now it was only lukewarm. Finn didn't mind. The water cleansed him of the mud that caked his skin. He dunked his head, scrubbing at his hair until the mud released its grasp. The water quickly turned murky, so Finn decided he was clean enough and got out.

As he was pulling on his pants, someone knocked on

his door. He called at them to come in as he ran a cloth through his wet hair but then dropped it as he turned around to see Ivy. She stood in his doorway wearing a slim, long gown the color of gold. Orange leaves lifted their way up the bodice, which was cut low and slashed down the middle, while black lace held the two sides together, covering her chest. Ivy had half her hair pinned up in an intricate braid with the gold scarf from her father and had let it fall over one shoulder, loose curls finding their way down her chest.

Finn felt his neck get hot as he stared at her, his eyes running over every part of her.

"What do you think?" she asked shyly. Finn had hardly ever seen her in anything but pants and a loose shirt, and he'd fallen in love with that Ivy, but this one made his heart pound to a different beat.

"You're beautiful," Finn said as he moved closer to her. She brought her eyes down, fussing with the dress and pulling at it. He lifted her chin until their eyes met. Ivy pushed his wet hair behind his ears, running her eyes over his bare chest.

"You need to hurry, Finn. The ceremony is starting soon."

"I don't care," he said with a smile. He leaned in to kiss Ivy, but she pushed away.

"I do," she said. "I don't want to be late."

Finn sighed and pulled away, searching for the doublet that Rayner gave him to borrow. It fit well, but Finn felt silly getting dressed up. He'd never owned a single thing made of silk or fine threads. His whole life, he only wore what was comfortable and was something he could fight in.

Correlyn was sitting in her room while handmaids pinned her hair into place and wove flowers through her thick black braid. She kept searching the sky outside the window, waiting to see those black wings that would bring word from her mother. She expected to see riders approaching sailing the flag of Grey Raven Castle, but the road stayed empty and clear. Correlyn wondered if her mother was indeed so angry with her that she'd miss her only daughter's wedding. Queen Elana had been helpful and happy for Correlyn, but it wasn't the same as having her own mother there.

She had sent a raven carrying the news of Rayner's proposal the day after it happened, asking her mother to come back as they would wed as soon as Ivy returned home. But Lady Oharra didn't answer, and the raven came back a few days later, still carrying Correlyn's letter, though the seal had been broken. She sighed as Queen Elana came in, shooing away the maids and taking a step back to look at her future daughter-in-law. "You look stunning!"

Correlyn stood and let the dress sway around her ankles. It was dark red with long sleeves that flared out around her hands. The bodice was embellished with onyx stones, and the back of the dress was open, thin ribbons weaving down her back to hold the two sides together. White and red flowers stood out against the blackness of her hair that had been pinned up in several braids, all wrapping around each other. Elana walked around her and placed a necklace around Correlyn. It was a thin gold chain that held a blood-red ruby the size of her fingertip. "A gift for your wedding day," the queen told her.

"Thank you," Correlyn whispered. She linked arms with Elana and headed to the ceremony.

CHAPTER FOUR

THE KNOT

The day was bright and sunny, so Correlyn and Rayner had decided to tie the knot on the beach instead of in the Great Hall. Rayner stood under an archway, woven from the twisted branches of the Blackwood trees. Flowers and small bells hung down from the arch, jingling lightly in the breeze. Rayner wore a plain white tunic, slashed with red to match Correlyn's dress, and a light cloak covered his shoulders. Ivy stood next to him, and Magnus stood at the head of the gathering, prepared to say the ceremonial words. Many were already gathered for the ceremony, waiting for the bride to arrive. Ronin stood like a shadow in the back. Rayner's hair was still wet, and he wore it slicked back, his beard combed smooth. He tapped his foot anxiously, waiting for Correlyn to come walking down the black sand.

Rayner didn't bring his cane with him, having decided at the last minute that he wouldn't need it. He tried to stand straight, but his rib began to ache as his heart pounded against it. Rayner noticed Finn staring at Ivy from the crowd and turned to his sister and smiled before giving her a playful look and nodding at her dress. "What?" she asked, annoyed.

Rayner laughed and said, "Nothing. You look different is all." Ivy gave him a playful shove, searching the crowd again for Finn's eyes. "He's very much in love with you," Rayner whispered in her ear. She looked at him then lowered her eyes, hiding her blushing cheeks.

Then Correlyn appeared at the back of the crowd, linking arms with Queen Elana, who began to walk her through the black sand of the beach to where Rayner stood. Magnus smiled at his wife, who wore a plain cotton dress that hugged her body, as her long golden hair twirled in the winds from the sea. Rayner laid eyes on the woman who would become his wife and thought his heart might burst at the sight of her. He took Correlyn's hand and kissed his mother on the cheek before turning back to Magnus, who would say the words that sealed their lives together.

Correlyn and Rayner both wore their swords on their hips, ready for the exchange. Rayner unsheathed his sword and bowed his head as he held it out for Correlyn. She took his sword and then repeated what he did, a tradition expressing that they would protect and fight for one another and the Houses they were marrying into. They then stood facing one another and linked hands, holding them out in the space between them. Magnus stood before them, welcoming family and guests from the kingdom to celebrate the joining of two great Houses. Magnus whistled for Luna, who flew down to land on top of the archway, carrying a strand of ribbon. He took the ribbon from her talons and began to tie it around their hands while speaking the words of the tradition:

"These are the hands of your chosen partner,
The hands of the person you fell in love with,
The hands that will hold you, now and forever.
May these hands help you to build a life together.
May they hold the power to comfort you
with a simple touch,
May they wield a sword against any threat
to the life you've made.
With this ribbon, I bond two souls together for life,
Whether through good or bad, these hands will hold.
And may this bond lay forever unbroken."

As the king tied off the knot, the crowd rose in a cheer, and Rayner and Correlyn shared their first kiss as husband and wife. Ivy kissed Rayner on the cheek and embraced him before everyone set out toward the Great Hall to celebrate and join in the festivities.

To Ivy it seemed the Hall had a certain glow to it, one that had nothing to do with the hundreds of candles hanging from the rafters, their flames dancing to the rhythm of the music. Everyone was laughing, celebrating, and playing drinking games, the entire kingdom in high spirits. Magnus and Elana set up a special table for the married couple, and one by one, Rayner's men came to congratulate him. White flowers lined every table, hung from every lantern, and filled the floor with their petals.

After a feast of many courses, barrels of ale, and wine, men started flooding out of the Hall to join in some of the games. Some men competed in an archery contest, others sparred in the yard. Knights raced one another down the streets of Godstone, and many stood around to watch the games and the drunken men who participated. The music boomed out of the Hall, and many people crowded the streets around the Hall to dance under the dying sun.

Ivy sat with Finn on the dais, next to her father, and watched the people moving around the dance floor and lifting ale-filled horns to the gods. She noticed Ronin go congratulate the couple before leaving the Hall, disappearing into the night. Magnus leaned over and kissed Ivy's hand before turning to his wife and asking her to dance. The king and queen moved seamlessly around the other dancers, smiling at one another as if they were the ones who were just wed. Ivy felt happy looking at her parents. She wondered if they'd loved each other since the moment they met. The way her father told the story was that he was already in love with her the moment he set eyes on his queen.

Finn nudged Ivy, drawing her attention from her parents.

"Would you like to dance?" he asked timidly as if they'd never before shared a dance.

"Oh, I don't know," Ivy answered, moving her eyes back to her parents. Finn stood up and held out his hand to her.

"Come," he said. "You look too beautiful to hide behind this table all night." Ivy blushed and took his hand, letting Finn lead her to the dance floor.

Magnus smiled at his daughter and gave an approving nod to Finn as the couple moved around Magnus and Elana. Magnus leaned into his wife. "What do you think of those two?"

"It seems we had this conversation not long ago, though I believe we were talking of Rayner and Correlyn." Elana smiled as she spotted her son sitting with his new wife.

"I mean, what do you think of *him*?" Magnus responded.

"Finn? I think he's a good man."

"How can you tell?" Magnus asked as he pulled away to look Elana in the eye.

She brushed his hair away and kissed him before answering. "Because Ivy is a smart woman, and she wouldn't have chosen someone who doesn't make her happy. Do you trust our daughter?"

"Of course I do, but—"

"Then stop worrying about her," Elana interrupted. "And stop looking at him like that." Magnus's gaze was on Finn, and she turned his chin toward her with a slender finger. "Ivy's already chosen this man, so we must accept him."

Magnus knew his wife was right. He trusted his daughter in everything she did, and he had to learn to accept that she was a grown woman. A knot formed in his throat as he thought of the decision that he'd made months ago, the choice that would shape the rest of her life. Magnus swallowed the knot, deciding to keep the news from her until after they had celebrated Rayner and Correlyn.

The feast and music were bright and lively around them, but Rayner was in another world. He took his wife's face in his hands, running a thumb over her soft cheeks before pulling her in for a kiss. An approving roar billowed up from the Great Hall, applauding the couple and the hope for happiness that they represented. Rayner never thought that he would have found love in a time of war, never thought he would come so close to death. Even as the God of Judgment tried to snuff out the light within him, Correlyn kept it glowing brightly. "I love you, Correlyn."

She responded by planting a deep kiss on his lips, pulling him closer to her. A single tear worked its way between their lips. Rayner drew back and lifted a finger to wipe away another on Correlyn's cheek. "What's wrong?"

"I wish my mother was here. I'm afraid that she's still angry with me, that she thinks I'm choosing you over her. Or worse—that something has happened to her."

"Correlyn," Rayner said softly. "Your mother is one of the strongest women I know. Lady Oharra is famous throughout the North for her fierce fighting and clever planning. I'm sure she's fine."

"Then why isn't she here?"

Rayner didn't have an answer for her, so offered what words he had. "Enjoy our wedding day, my love. We'll ride to Grey Raven Castle in a few days to check on your mother. I'll ask my father to come if it'll give you peace. They've always had a good working relationship, and I'm sure my father can persuade her if our marriage is the source of her anger."

Correlyn nodded. "Okay." Her shoulders relaxed a little and she leaned her head on Rayner's shoulder and tried to enjoy the celebration.

The night grew dark and cold, and the wind that blew outside and whispered through the crack under the door held a particular bite. As light rain began to fall, a dense fog rose from the sea, creeping ever closer to the kingdom. Many guests had left the feast, retreating to the warmth of their beds for the night, the ale in their bellies rocking them to sleep. Rayner's knights stretched out along the benches and tables inside the Great Hall, their drunken snores creating music of their own. Magnus and Elana bid the newlyweds goodnight before retreating to their room. Finn and Ivy approached the table to congratulate the couple next.

Finn smiled as Ivy hugged her brother and said, "I'm truly happy for you, Rayner."

"Thank you," Rayner said, stepping aside before opening his arms to Finn.

The two embraced, and Finn kissed Correlyn on both cheeks before leaving the Hall and walking to the central tower.

Finn was now staying in Rayner's old room, which was right down the hall from Ivy's. Rayner and Correlyn had a larger room on the fourth floor of the tower, which had been decorated and prepared for their marriage night. Ivy and Finn walked hand in hand up the steps, stealing glances at one another as they approached Ivy's bedchamber. They stood outside her door, and Finn lifted her hand, kissing it softly before turning away and heading toward his room. "Finn?" Ivy called suddenly. "Will you stay?" He stopped dead, turning around to make sure he heard her right. Ivy stood there with a smile on her face, and Finn's heart melted.

"Always," he said, and the two retreated to Ivy's room. She slipped out of her dress behind a curtain and changed into comfortable clothes while Finn unlaced his shirt and slipped it over his head. The two crawled into bed, wrapping arms around one another before falling into a deep, restful sleep.

As Rayner and Correlyn walked the stone steps of the tower, the throbbing of Rayner's heart mimicked the throbbing pain in his rib. He tried to ignore it, not wanting his injury to interfere with their night. Correlyn noticed her husband wincing and took his hand, placing her other one under his elbow to assist him up the last flight. The wooden door to their room was covered in flowers that were threaded through strings and hung up, creating a wall of flowers for them to walk through. Rayner released her hand and scooped her up in his arms, fighting to hide the pain that must be showing in his eyes. "What are you doing?" Correlyn seemed to notice the pain that washed over him, despite his best efforts to push it away. He didn't answer. Instead, he pushed the door open and carried his wife to the bed.

A fire lit up the room from the hearth that sat back in the corner, next to the bed. A small table was placed near the door, spilling over with food, wine, and flowers. A canopy of red roses hung above the bed, which was covered with many different fur pelts. The room smelled of flowers and burning wood, and the scented candles which hung from the stone walls, filling the room with a gentle glow.

Rayner laid Correlyn down on the bed, her eyes lighting up as she gazed at the canopy of red above her. He moved to pour them each a cup of wine, quickly downing his in one gulp to numb the pain. "Rayner, my love." Correlyn sat up to take the cup from him. "You can't hide your pain from me. It's okay." She didn't have to finish. Rayner knew what she was saying but again ignored her and came to stand in front of the bed. She stood up and wrapped her arms around Rayner's waist to pull him closer.

"Do you remember the night we spent together in Hideaway?" she whispered.

Rayner smiled. "It's not the same," he answered. "This night will be different."

Correlyn kissed him and gently lifted his shirt over his head, throwing it into the dark corners of the room. Rayner followed his wife's eyes and looked down at his chest to the place on his lower ribs where the sword had pierced him. Rayner's ribs and chest were still bruised from the horse, and Correlyn ran a finger over them, connecting the bruises one by one. The feeling of her fingers on him gave Rayner goosebumps.

Rayner lifted her and put her back on the bed, then crawled over her, kissing her neck as his hand slid up her thigh. Correlyn fumbled with the laces across her chest with shaky hands, eventually slipping her wedding dress over her head to join Rayner's shirt in the corner. Her nimble fingers then moved to the laces of his pants, and Rayner's whole body flushed with color. He slipped out of his pants and hovered over his wife. The blood in his veins ran hot, but a sudden shiver made his skin prick up. Rayner reached over and grabbed a fur, pulling it over them as Correlyn rolled on top of him. She ran her fingers through his hair, letting the weight of the pelt push her closer to him. Rayner cupped the back of her head and drew her lips to his as his other hand snaked around her bare waist.

Correlyn parted her lips and deepened the kiss, brushing her tongue against his. Rayner's skin was on fire, sparking new flames everywhere Correlyn touched him. He could feel her soft skin pressed against him, the length of her body covering Rayner as his lips moved down her neck and to her shoulders. Rayner smiled against her lips as Correlyn's chest pressed into his. Their bodies wound tight around each other, sealing their marriage and binding their souls together for life. Whether in this world or the next, their lives were tied together, a bond that would never break, even through death.

CHAPTER FIVE

GREY RAVEN

In the morning, Ivy found Ronin just outside the Blackwoods, sitting in a field with his eyes closed. She approached slowly, carefully placing one foot before the other. Ronin didn't move or open his eyes as Ivy lowered herself onto the grass next to him. "Ronin," she almost whispered. "Can I talk to you?"

"You've already begun," he responded with his eyes still closed.

Ivy felt a wave of annoyance at him but pushed it away and continued. "I'm sorry for how I treated you after Ser Osmund's death. It wasn't your fault, and I know that. I lost control of my anger and let it consume me. I went against all the lessons you've taught me. I was blinded by rage . . . but now my head is clear, and I know what I have to do."

"You still mean to kill him?" Ronin wouldn't even say his name.

"Yes," Ivy answered quickly before she could think about it. Ronin let his eyes blink open, and a small sigh escaped through his nose. Ivy felt that she disappointed him again and turned away, getting to her feet. Ronin grabbed her wrist and stood with her, his gaze seeming to look through Ivy down to the thoughts she wouldn't speak. Ivy knew there was no point in hiding what she thought of Helvarr because Ronin saw everything. She felt sorry for Ronin and the pain he suffered through his son, but it wouldn't change anything. Ivy was determined to avenge Ser Osmund's death, and no sharp glare from Ronin would sway her.

"I know you think you have to do this, Ivy. But I worry that you're following your anger, and it'll lead you down a path from which you can't return." Ivy jerked her arm away, and Ronin released her, taking a step back.

"I *do* have to do this," Ivy said sternly. "And it's not anger that fuels me. I let my rage run its course, consume me, and spit me out again. All I want is justice for what he did. I made a promise to my father that I would kill Helvarr if I ever saw him. I won't break that promise again." Ivy turned away before Ronin could argue any further and left him alone in the open field to chew over her words.

Ivy reached her hand out, touching the soft blades of grass as Cassius slowly trotted down the Thunder Trail. A calm breeze moved like a snake through the grass, whispering a cheerful tune as the sun turned the world around her golden and pure. Finn rode beside Ivy, mounted on what was once Ser Osmund's stallion. Eclipse seemed tame, calm even, which made Ivy wonder what Finn had done to win the beast's affection. She smiled at him and moved Cass closer so that she could grab hold of Finn's hand. "Are you all right?" she asked him. The burning sun lit up his soft brown hair, creating a halo of gold around his face.

She knew Finn hadn't been this far north in many years, not since he left his home of Tonsburg when he was nine. It must seem like a different world, but Ivy was sure the same nightmares still haunted him. "I'm fine." He spoke Ivy's common words back to her. Ivy looked back at the group of knights accompanying them. Rayner and Correlyn had only been married a few days, but Correlyn insisted on coming herself to check on Lady Oharra. Grey Raven Castle lay just up the road, and no one was prepared for what they might find. Magnus and Ser Caster rode abreast most of the way, with Luna gliding above her king. They talked in hushed voices, but Ivy knew they were discussing every possible outcome.

Magnus trotted up between Ivy and Finn and asked if he could have a word alone with his daughter. Finn put his heel into Eclipse and rode off ahead of the group, stealing a look back at the two before disappearing behind a bend in the trail. Magnus and Ivy had had long talks over the past week as she filled her father in on everything that had occurred down south. She hesitated when she told the story of the traders and how she killed her first man. Magnus told Ivy that he was immensely proud of her and was eternally grateful for Ser Osmund teaching Ivy at such a young age.

Now, Ivy and her father rode side by side in silence, Magnus rubbing at his beard, seemingly deep in thought. He turned toward Ivy. "I've been thinking," he started. "Do you remember what I told you before you left for Kame Island?" Ivy's heart skipped as she thought of the promise her father had made to her months ago. She nodded and waited for Magnus to continue. "I promised you that I'd reconsider my rules about knighthood, and I thought about it and changed my mind many times when you were gone." Ivy's eyes grew wide, and she realized she was holding her breath, waiting for her father's words to fill her lungs or crush them. Magnus paused and ran a hand through his hair, pushing it away from his eyes. He opened his mouth to speak, but Finn's voice called out from ahead, and Magnus seemed almost grateful for the distraction.

Ivy scrunched her nose and watched Finn trotting toward them, something written on his face that Ivy couldn't read.

"King Magnus," Finn called to him, "you should see this before she does." Magnus followed his gaze back to Correlyn, who was laughing at something Rayner said. The three of them took off ahead of the others around the bend.

The tall grass suddenly ended with the trail, and the Lake of the Dead stood cold and unmoving. A cloud moved in front of the sun, turning everything a sinister shade of grey, but Ivy knew the ground wasn't dark from the lack of light. The field that surrounded the lake had been set on fire, and charred grass crunched under Ivy's boots as she swung down from Cass. Small spirals of smoke rose slowly into the air, creating a fog that enclosed Grey Raven.

Grey Raven wasn't nearly the size of Godstone, but as Ivy, Finn, and Magnus walked under the archway, the town opened up to them. Lady Oharra's castle stood dead in the center of the town, and scorched stone stained its walls. Ivy spun in a circle looking at the charred remains of the houses, inns, and stables that stood deserted. Tall spruce trees stood outside the walls of the town, their limbs now bare and black, showing how high the fire must've been. "What happened?" she heard herself say. Finn placed a hand on her shoulder, but she walked away, deeper into the town.

Vendor booths were overturned, goods lay scattered through the streets, and doors hung limp on their hinges. Ivy drew her sword, Promise, and stepped into the closest house, blinking at the darkness until her eyes adjusted. The house was full of personal relics from the people who once lived there: herbs that hung down from a wooden beam, bowls that still held food ready to be served. A small stuffed doll lay on a bed in the back of the house, and Ivy felt a sickness rising inside her. She stepped out of the house and continued through the streets.

Grey Raven didn't have stone walls as Godstone did. Instead, tree trunks stood upright next to one another, creating a barrier that encircled the town. Ivy noticed that parts of the wall had been pulled down and looked back to see Finn following her from a distance. Something caught her eye from above as it flapped in the wind. Atop Lady Oharra's castle, the flag of the raiders flew in place of hers. Crossed black swords with an even darker raven spread out above on a banner that was the color of blood. Ivy turned to call her father when she heard the rest of their group approaching. She ran past Finn and Magnus to warn Rayner, but she was too late.

Correlyn came pounding through the streets on her horse, fear and panic welling up in her eyes. "Mother!" she called while jumping from her horse, stumbling in the muddy street. Ivy sheathed her sword and went to stop her.

"Correlyn," she pleaded. "You don't want to—"

Correlyn shoved Ivy away and continued to scream for her mother. Rayner came running up and wrapped his arms around his wife before she could get any further.

"Ser Caster," Magnus called out. "Set up a perimeter and look for any trails leading away from the town." Ser Caster obeyed and started commanding his men to spread out around Grey Raven.

"Father." Ivy turned to Magnus and pointed to the banner flying above the castle. The king grimaced and told Rayner to keep Correlyn there while he, Ivy, and Finn searched the rest of the buildings.

Magnus set off to search the main castle, telling Ivy and Finn to follow the wall to the back gate. They walked steadily, staying quiet. It felt wrong to make too much noise in a place that was deprived of life. Ivy drew the dagger that Rayner had given her and walked ahead of Finn, peering around every burnt house and into every broken window. Ivy had battled her brother for the dagger after she returned. Though Rayner had still been hurt, he provoked Ivy to spar with him, letting her win the fight in order to gift her his knife.

The air was filled with the smell of smoke and death, but Ivy didn't smell that familiar metallic scent of blood. It was as if the people torched their own houses and disappeared—but why? It didn't make sense, and the sick feeling returned to Ivy's stomach, making her stoop over, trying to breathe through it.

"What is it?" Finn said while placing a gentle hand on

her lower back. Ivy only shook her head and forced herself to stand upright. Finn moved his hand down, finding the softness of the exposed skin at her side. His electric touch sent a shockwave through her body, but she ignored it and pushed on through the town.

They came to the back entrance and spotted a field of dirt that appeared to be untouched by the flames that had burned everything else. Ivy's pace quickened, and as she came upon the soil, she spotted a small wooden plank stuck into the middle of the ground with one word written on it.

Ivy called to her father, who quickly ran through the streets to where she and Finn stood outside the walls. Ser Caster and a few knights came running as well and stopped in their tracks when they saw what Ivy pointed to. She now realized what the mound of dirt was, but the word still didn't make sense to her. "What does that mean?" Ivy asked her father. The word appeared to be written in blood though the bright red had since faded to a dull brown.

Magnus read the word and let it spill from his mouth in a whisper. "Traitors."

CHAPTER SIX

COLD BLOOD

Correlyn ran through the back gate to stand behind Magnus with Rayner chasing after her. She stopped and covered her mouth when she spotted the mass grave. Correlyn sunk to her knees, sobbing and whispering something under her breath. Rayner dropped in front of her, grabbing hold of her shoulders and pulling his wife into his chest. Rayner stroked her hair and turned his gaze to Magnus, asking what happened without saying any words. The king gave no answer, only lowered his head and rubbed at his eyes that were tired of seeing so much death. "Rayner," Magnus said. "Take her back inside the town."

"No!" Correlyn broke away from Rayner to stand before Magnus. "I need to know . . ." Her voice broke off as tears streamed down her cheeks.

Magnus wiped her tears away and struggled to keep his voice calm. "You don't need to be here, Correlyn." Magnus placed a steady hand on her shoulder. He could feel Correlyn shaking under his touch. He motioned to Rayner, who came and took his wife in his arms, pulling her away from the grave. All the king's knights hung their heads, not wanting to see the pain that emanated from Correlyn's eyes. "You go too," Magnus said over his shoulder to Ivy.

"But I want to help." She stepped toward her father.

"No!" he snapped accidentally. He pinched his eyes shut and turned toward his daughter, whose eyes were wide with confusion at his anger. "No," he repeated calmly. "Go with Finn." Ivy looked at her father for a long moment before obeying and following Rayner back toward the town, Finn trailing behind her.

"Your Grace." Ser Caster beckoned. "What are your orders?"

"Take your knights and keep searching the town. Send a group of them to the Lake of the Dead as well."

"What about this?" Ser Caster motioned to the mass grave.

Magnus unfastened his cloak and dropped it to the ground then unbuckled his sword belt. "I'll take care of this," Magnus said, rolling up his sleeves.

"Your Grace, my men can—"

"I need to do it," Magnus interrupted. "If Lady Oharra is in there . . ." He paused, shaking his head. "I just need to see for myself." Ser Caster didn't argue anymore and turned to leave his king standing over the mass grave.

Magnus sighed deeply before bending down and scooping aside the dirt. Luna sat on the ground watching him with her black eyes. It felt cold and soft in his hands, the death that it covered seeping into every handful of earth that he removed. The world grew darker as Magnus dug deeper until he touched something that made him snatch his hand away. His heart thudded against his chest as he thought of what he might find. Magnus couldn't bear the thought of Lady Oharra lying in the cold ground, buried and forgotten. House Reiburn set their dead afloat on the Lake of the Dead, sending off loved ones in a boat of flames to the gods. Lady Oharra saw the tradition of burying the dead as an insult, saying that the gods wouldn't find their soul if it lay below the earth. Burning the dead allowed their soul to drift up into the sky, carried away by the ash to be placed directly into the hands of the gods.

Magnus dug faster, eager to know whether the Lady of Grey Raven lay below. A limp hand poked up from the earth, and Magnus carefully moved the dirt away, uncovering the first body.

A small boy lay blue and cold under the dirt, and Magnus squeezed his eyes shut, forcing the tears back. But it was too late. The image burned its way through his closed eyes, branding itself in his mind. He wasn't sure he could continue. How could a little boy be marked a traitor and thrown into a mass grave, never to find his way to the gods? As the king continued digging, the bodies rose from the cold depths of the earth. Women clutching their dead children, their fingers stiff with cold blood. Old men buried with their throats cut, faces smashed, or missing limbs. A young girl's face stared up at Magnus, her eyes black with death, her face still holding the fear that she must have experienced moments before her murder. Magnus allowed the tears to burn his eyes and run down his face, dropping silently into the cold grave. He'd dug up the whole mound of dirt with his bare hands, never finding Lady Oharra, only the faces of innocent people.

Magnus sat on the cold ground, looking at his hands when Ivy's voice crept up from behind. He opened his mouth to tell her to leave, but she was already standing behind him. Ivy sunk to her knees beside Magnus and let her eyes travel to every face that lay in the grave. They sat in silence—no words could bring comfort or explanation. Ivy grabbed her father's hand and squeezed it as Magnus turned his head away, not wanting his daughter to see the pain on his face. The two sat like that for a long time before Ser Caster and Rayner came looking for Magnus.

Rayner came to stand next to Ivy, placing a hand on her shoulder as he stared at what Magnus had uncovered.

"Who could've done this?" Ser Caster said under his breath.

When no one offered an answer, Ivy said the only name that made sense to her. "Helvarr," she spat.

"No," Magnus whispered. "Helvarr is cruel, but this . . . this is beyond what I thought he was capable of."

"Perhaps you don't know him as well as you thought." Ivy released her father's hand and stood.

Magnus didn't want to believe that Ivy could be right, though they had all recently witnessed Helvarr's cruelty when he slew Ser Osmund.

"We need to burn them," Rayner stated. Magnus agreed and rose to his feet, wiping his dirt-stained hands on his pants. Ser Caster left to find a wagon to carry the bodies to the lake.

The sky was dark by the time all the bodies had been loaded onto two boats and stuffed with kindling. Ivy tucked a small doll she'd found among the bodies into the lifeless arm of a young girl before stepping away and going to Finn. He wrapped an arm around her shoulder, pulling her close as she leaned her head against his chest. When Magnus told Correlyn that he hadn't found her mother's body in the mass grave, it seemed to do little to ease her worry. They had no way of knowing what took place, and Lady Oharra could be anywhere. Everyone stood silently on the charred grass, waiting for Magnus to give the signal. He nodded his head toward Ser Caster to light the arrow, but Correlyn stopped him. "Wait!" she yelled.

Correlyn broke away from Rayner and went to stand on the dock, looking down at the faces of her people. Tears flowed from her eyes. "I know these people," she whispered, and Magnus felt his heart crack open. Correlyn nodded to an older man and said, "He was our smith." She continued. "The old woman who cared for me when I fell ill, the little boy who lived down the road and always begged me to teach him how to shoot. These have been my neighbors and friends ever since I was a small girl." She sniffed and wiped her face before taking in a shaky breath. "I have to send them away properly," she said. Everyone stayed silent with their heads bowed in respect as Correlyn spoke the funeral prayer of her people.

"Here we gather to honor you,
To send you off to the Hall of the Gods.
May your soul find peace where it once carried pain,
May your body be at ease now and forever.
From the feet that carried you to the hands that fought for
others.

May you rest, knowing your people await you in the sky.
Your lives will never be forgotten,
Your sacrifice . . ."

Correlyn choked on the words as tears blinded her. Magnus stepped forward and continued with the prayer.

". . . will not easily be buried.
You live on through our people.
Your fight has ended, your suffering gone.
You have wielded your last sword and felt your final kiss.
You have fought your last battle and raised your final horn.
Now we celebrate your lives and all that you've done.
May this fire lift you and carry your souls away to the Gods.
Where your old life ended, a new one will begin."

Correlyn broke into a sob as Ser Caster lit the arrow and sent it, cutting through the air above them to find the first boat. The fire caught and quickly grew, rising to lick at the stars in the sky. When both boats were ablaze, Magnus came up behind Correlyn and put his hands on her shoulders. She turned and buried her face in his shoulder, letting herself cry away her pain. Everyone stood in silence, the only noise coming from the crackling of the fire that consumed the bodies and burned the wood that carried them. The knights started to clear out, but Magnus stayed with his family until the fire had turned everything to ash, only a few pieces of wood left bobbing in the dead calm lake.

Ivy sat in front of the fire after they'd set up camp under the stars just outside of Grey Raven Castle. Correlyn refused to go inside, saying that her home was now haunted by the memories of her past and the spirit that once lived there. Rayner handed out some bread and dried venison, but Correlyn passed along the food without taking any.

"Correlyn, you have to eat something," Rayner said to her, but her eyes were fixed on the fire, and she stayed silent. Magnus had gone around to check on Ser Caster and his men who camped nearby in the streets of Grey Raven. Ivy sat quietly next to Finn, nibbling small bites from the bread. He laid his hand on her thigh, startling her. Finn removed his hand and lowered his eyes to his boots.

"Ivy," her father called. "Walk with me." She stood up and followed her father down the street and out the front gate of the town.

CHAPTER SEVEN

KNIGHTHOOD

I vy observed her father as they walked in silence. He looked more tired than Ivy had ever seen him; the thin lines of his face had grown deeper with worry. Ivy fastened her cloak with the maple pin, pulling it tighter around her neck as a cold wind blew through the dead town. The spruce trees swayed in the wind, and Luna flew off ahead and landed on a branch that hadn't been touched by fire. Magnus stopped under a spruce tree and lowered himself into the grass, patting the spot next to him. Ivy sat down, and Luna landed beside Magnus, who reached out to stroke her white feathers. He seemed to be far away, lost in his thoughts, and Ivy reached out to pull him back. "What is it?" Her voice was hushed in the silence of the night.

"I've made my decision," he stated. "I can't keep you from the destruction of this war. Its grasp is reaching farther, and we need to be prepared." He didn't look at Ivy as he spoke, almost as if he was assuring himself of the reality of the war. "I've reconsidered my rules, and, after careful thought, I've decided that I'll allow you to become a knight."

Ivy thought her heart might burst. She had been prepared for her father to deny her knighthood and list all the reasons as to why it was a bad idea. Ivy opened her mouth to speak, but Magnus continued.

"Under one condition," he said, and Ivy's heart slammed to a stop against her ribs. "I want you to wait until you're Rayner's age. He was only just knighted, and two more years isn't that long. If Ronin decides to stay here, then I want you to continue your lessons with him. I need you to be prepared and learn everything you can before I swear you into service."

A small piece of Ivy's excitement died at the thought of waiting two more years to become a knight, but she knew there was no sense in arguing.

"Sweetling?" Magnus said, and Ivy realized that she hadn't answered him.

"Thank you, Father," she said, and she leaned over to hug her father.

Magnus kissed the top of Ivy's head, and they walked back into camp. Rayner and Correlyn were already asleep in their furs, and Magnus went to talk with Ser Caster, kissing Ivy on the head again before disappearing into the darkness. Finn had stayed up to wait for Ivy, and she pulled him away from the fire so as not to wake her brother. Ivy led him down the streets to where Cass was tied up at the stables. "What are we doing?" Finn finally asked. Ivy searched the bag that hung on her saddle and brought out two wooden swords. "Ivy, you should rest," he said, as he lowered her hand that held the sword out to him.

"I don't want to rest." She pushed the sword back into his chest, and he reluctantly took it.

Finn looked at her curiously. "What did you two talk about?"

"My father is going to allow me to become a knight."

"Really?" Finn took a step toward her. "That's great news, Ivy," he said, genuine happiness filling his face, but Ivy frowned slightly. "What's wrong? Isn't this what you wanted?"

She lowered her eyes. "He wants me to wait two years until I've had more training."

"So what? Two years is nothing. This is what you wanted, and I'm happy for you." Finn took another step closer, and Ivy could feel the heat of him washing over her. Ivy smiled and turned her chin up, placing a kiss on his cheek.

"Come on," she said before he could move closer.

They went out the back gate and around the wall to an open field before squaring up. Ivy and Finn hadn't practiced together since arriving in Godstone, and Ivy desperately missed their nightly dance. Finn led the dance as he moved away from Ivy's blows, the soft grass tickling underfoot. The clack of their swords echoed through the empty fields, and their soft laughter surrounded them. Ivy smacked his sword away and jabbed hers forward, but he caught it and pulled her toward him.

Her heart quickened as Finn's hand wrapped around her wrist. She broke free and twirled around him, nudging him in the back. Finn only smiled and threw down his sword, taking small steps towards Ivy. "What are you doing?" Ivy grinned at him, holding her sword between them. Finn didn't answer, only gave her a playful smile before lunging, Ivy just slipping through his grasp.

She turned on her heels and took off, running barefoot through the field, looking back to see Finn following her. Ivy laughed and ran faster, creating her own wind that pulled her hair back to soar behind her. The grass grew taller around them as they ran through the night, the moon peeking out to guide their way. Ivy didn't know where she was going but pushed harder as she heard Finn's footsteps gaining on her. She tore through the waist-high grass before coming to a halt as the world dropped away down a steep hillside.

"Finn, wait—"

Finn was already on her and tackling Ivy to the ground. They rolled over one another, flattening the grass beneath them until the hill spit them out into another field.

Finn saw that Ivy was shaking and crawled over to her. "Ivy?" He turned her over only to see that she was laughing. He let out a sigh of relief and sat back in the grass. "Are you hurt?" he asked. Ivy's laughter only grew louder, and Finn leaned back. "What's so funny?"

"You could have killed me!" she said between laughs.

"That's not funny. You should've warned me." Finn couldn't help but smile.

"I tried, but you plowed into me." Her laugh was contagious, and Finn couldn't resist. He lay down beside Ivy after their laughter died away. The stars flickered in the sky as the moon danced around the dark clouds overhead.

Ivy finally stopped giggling, but her mouth kept a gleeful grin.

Finn turned his head to her and grabbed her hand, running his thumb over the softness of her skin. His pulse quickened and Finn held on to that feeling, never wanting it to leave him. He propped himself up on an elbow and brought his hand to Ivy's cheek. It was hot under his touch, and her skin glistened in the moonlight. Finn moved toward her lips, everything in his body telling him to give in to her, to surrender himself completely.

Their lips brushed together, and Finn felt a shudder move through his body. Moving his hand down her neck, he could feel her pulse quicken beneath his fingers. Ivy parted her lips and let her tongue travel to his, Finn made a small sighing sound, and Ivy sat up. She moved over him to sit on his lap and pushed him back into the cold grass. Finn felt his face grow hot but made no move to stop her.

She kissed him again, this time with a certain eagerness, fighting to get closer to him. Finn ran his fingertips down her back and found that soft patch of skin that made his own skin crawl with excitement. Her fingers were like lightning on his neck, her lips more delicate than any flower petal, and Finn felt himself falling deeper in love with every touch. His hands moved up her shirt, feeling her ribs that expanded with her breath until she stopped kissing him and sat up.

Finn sat up with her, Ivy wrapping her legs tight around his waist. She grabbed his face with both hands and pulled him close, moving her lips to his ear. "I'm yours, always." Her soft voice sent shivers traveling down his neck. Ivy pulled away to look him in the eyes. "There's no need to rush," she whispered. Finn released a disappointed sigh but smiled and placed a hand on her cheek.

"It's difficult for me not to lose myself in you," he admitted. Ivy smiled and kissed him softly on the lips before standing up and reaching for Finn to take her hand. He stood and pulled her in for a hug, and the two stood intertwined under the stars before climbing the hill and going back to camp.

CHAPTER EIGHT

WHISPERS

I vy woke to the whispers of her brother and father.

She sat up, letting the fur pelt fall from her shoulders as she rubbed the sleep from her eyes. The grass was damp under her feet, and small beads of water covered the fields like millions of crystals. Ivy let herself smile at that, knowing that the land wouldn't be scarred forever, the grass would grow back, and the trees would sprout new needles.

Finn came over to Ivy as she got to her feet, brushing a lock of hair behind her ear. "Why did you let me sleep so long?" she asked him.

"I think you needed it," Finn replied with a gentle smile.

Ivy had to admit she was grateful for it—she hadn't been sleeping much since they all left Kame Island, and ghosts haunted her dreams at night, so even when she did sleep, it usually wasn't restful. Ivy placed a hand on Finn's cheek and thanked him before moving over to where her father and Rayner stood.

Correlyn sat on a log beside the cold fire pit, and to Ivy,

she looked like a ghost. Correlyn's eyes seemed far away, glazed over with the sadness that hung so heavily inside them. Ivy took the water skin from Rayner and went to offer it to Correlyn, who took it without looking up at Ivy.

Magnus and Rayner were talking with Ser Caster and drawing out a map in the dirt street. It looked like nothing more than lines and circles to Ivy, but she knew her father must have a plan. She went over and squatted by the markings, studying them until they made sense. "You want to search the nearby fields?" she asked her father.

Magnus sat beside her and started pointing with a stick to the lines and circles. "We're here." He pointed to the first circle, which was meant to be Grey Raven. "Ser Caster and his men will go this way, south around the Lake of the Dead. You'll all come with me west around the lake, and we'll meet here." He tapped his stick into the dirt to show the southern tip of the lake.

Rayner came up behind them. "What are we looking for exactly?" he asked.

"Anything," Magnus answered plainly. "Lady Oharra isn't here, and neither are any of her warriors. They might have been either captured or run out of the town, leaving Grey Raven vulnerable to their attack."

"Lady Oharra is smarter than that," Rayner offered. "She wouldn't leave her people unprotected."

"I agree. Not if she could help it. But we have no way of knowing what happened, and now we need to find her." Rayner nodded and went over to Correlyn to tell her of the plan.

Magnus stood and went over to his horse and pulled off

some leather armor from the saddle. He handed vests to Ivy and Finn. "Here," he said. "This will protect you some, and when we get back to Godstone, I'll talk to the smith about making you both some real armor." Rayner wore a similar leather vest since his armor had been crushed by the horse that trampled him, and Correlyn wore light black leather armor with a raven sewn on the breast.

Ser Caster and the other knights were the only ones wearing proper metal armor. Ivy slipped it over her head, and it pulled heavily on her shoulders. She was surprised by the weight of it. The armor ran halfway down her upper arm, layered like a lobster tail. It was dark brown like her father's, with straps and buckles running down the length of her torso. Finn helped Ivy tighten her straps and check everything, and when he was done, she checked his armor as well, feeling his warm breath on her face as she tightened the strap across his chest.

"How does it fit?" Magnus asked them both.

"It's heavy," Ivy mentioned. Magnus smiled and told her she would get used to it.

Ser Caster and his knights set off south, spreading out in a long line from the lakeshore to the tall grasses and across the road. Ivy mounted Cass and checked her sword belt, touching the hilt of Promise and running a finger over the jewels of Rayner's dagger. Magnus led his family through the black grass and out into a field, leaving the destruction of Grey Raven behind them. The sun was still rising in the sky as they made their way west. Birds could be heard chirping somewhere in the trees, and toads croaked from the tall weeds around the lake. Luna flew ahead of the group but always kept within sight of Magnus.

Cass and Eclipse walked side by side, and Ivy smiled as Finn scratched the stallion behind the ear, making the horse's mouth twitch with delight. "He likes you," Ivy said.

"He's a good horse, just stubborn is all." Finn smiled and patted Eclipse on the neck.

"Spread out in a line," Magnus called back to the group. "Keep your eyes open for any signs that riders might have been through the fields."

Ivy kicked Cass and moved off to the right, putting distance between herself and Finn.

It didn't appear that the land had been touched. The grass grew tall and stood straight, the ground hadn't been torn up by hooves, and Ivy felt a stab of sorrow for Correlyn. She looked down the line, past Finn, Magnus, and Rayner to where Correlyn rode, hugging the shore of the lake. Her eyes stayed on the cold, black waters as if the dead would whisper their secrets to her and tell Correlyn what happened to them. The Lake of the Dead was massive, the other side of it not even visible from where Ivy was. They'd been riding for a while and still saw no signs of life, or Lady Oharra.

Luna called out from ahead and came sailing back to Magnus, gliding through the air to land in front of his horse. The field began to grow thinner ahead of them as large spruce trees rose from the ground. Ivy knew what those woods were and pulled on Cass's reins to move him closer to Finn. Magnus saw it too and called for everyone to come in tighter as the field narrowed, and the spruce trees grew closer to the lake. They all rode in a tight line now, everyone keeping a sharp eye on the trees. Finn looked confused as he read their faces and turned to Ivy to ask what was happening.

Magnus spoke instead. "I don't remember the woods reaching out this close to the lake. Last time I came to Grey Raven, it had been for Lord Asher's funeral. I remember watching him burn on the Lake of the Dead. I'd ridden my horse around the lake afterward to clear my head and get away from everyone, and that was the first time I saw the Whispering Wood. The spruce trees grew higher and darker than any other, and I could've sworn that the woods had been about half a mile from the shore of the lake last time. It's as if the treeline has crept closer to the shore, cutting off the path around the lake."

"Perhaps you remember wrong," Rayner offered. Magnus shook his head and kept his eyes on the woods. The wind seemed to stop where the trees began, and no sounds were coming from the woods. No birds chirped, no branches swayed, not even the faint whisper of grass blowing in the wind. It was as if all life stopped there, and the woods had never heard anything but the screams of the people who entered them.

"What's wrong?" Finn asked again.

"It's the Whispering Woods," Ivy said. "Haven't you heard stories of it?" Finn shook his head and looked over to Magnus for answers. The king stopped his horse, and they all dismounted and stood in a circle, their horses acting as a shield around them.

"There are stories of this place," Magnus began. "It's said that the God of Secrets resides in every wooded area and forest throughout the land, but this one is his own creation. My father used to tell me stories of this place when I was a boy. He said that the woods held power to put people into a trancelike state, leading them into the dark woods and swallowing them up. The trees supposedly uproot themselves and shift around, keeping the person trapped inside the woods forever. The God of Secrets is greedy and uses these woods to get all the souls he can so that they may never find their way to the Hall of the Gods. The God of Secrets created these woods thousands of years ago and has been collecting souls ever since." Everyone sat still, listening to the silence of the world around them grow more prominent.

"Why would a god do that?" Finn finally asked.

"The gods are as complex as we are. They have both good and evil sides. They can give or take away as they please. It's not for us to question their decisions, for you'll never get an answer."

"Should we turn back?" Rayner asked his father.

"No," Correlyn said quickly. "If there's a chance my mother came through here, then we have to push on. I need to know." Magnus seemed to think carefully about how to proceed. Ivy knew her father wouldn't let Correlyn go ahead alone.

"We'll move on," Magnus said. "Form up a line behind me, and we'll stay close to the shore."

Everyone got back on their horses to follow Magnus through the receding field. Rayner brought his horse close to the back of his father's, followed by Correlyn, then Finn, with Ivy last in line. Finn kept looking back at Ivy, likely wary of her father's story about the woods. Ivy kept her eyes off of the woods and watched Luna soaring high above their heads. The sun was high in the sky now, and Ivy had to block it out with a hand as she tried to keep Luna in her sight. Just then, a chilly breeze came out from the woods, blowing her hair over her eyes and obstructing her view. Ivy shivered at the cold air swirling around her, and when she looked back up, Luna was gone. She opened her mouth to call to her father when she heard a faint whisper in her ear.

CHAPTER NINE

THE GOD OF SECRETS

A whisper.

Her skin pricked up, and the hair on the nape of her neck raised as she recognized the voice calling to her. "*Ivy*," it whispered, and suddenly she felt limp all over. It was as if something was controlling her brain, pulling at the wires and commanding her hands to let go of the reins. She felt tears well up in her eyes as Ser Osmund called to her. Ivy slumped over and rolled off of Cass. She stood in the grass with a blank stare at the woods, the breeze blowing harder and cutting through her, down to her soul.

Ivy tried to turn away, but her feet walked her forward. The only thing she could control was the tears streaming down her face. Ivy spotted something moving through the trees. The sun caught the metal of the knight's armor, and Ivy laid eyes on Ser Osmund for the first time since his death.

"No . . ." she managed to say to herself.

"You killed me, Ivy. You let me die. Why didn't you avenge me? You don't deserve that sword!" Ivy felt her hands move to her belt and unbuckle Promise, dropping it in the grass as she continued to walk closer to the dead knight.

Ivy stood only a few feet outside the woods, feeling the numbness of her mind take over and her body violently trembling as she tried to fight it. *"Come, Lady Ivy. It's better here."* Ser Osmund motioned for her to walk forward before he took off running through the trees. Ivy suddenly felt panicked as her feet picked up and broke off into a run, chasing the knight through the dark trees.

"Ivy, no!" Finn cried out as he swung down from Eclipse and ran to Ivy. But Ivy couldn't hear him.

"No!" Magnus screamed.

Finn was only a few feet from her when Magnus snatched his arm and threw him back. Tears burned his eyes as he frantically searched the woods that had swallowed Ivy. Magnus called to his daughter, but the woods were silent. Magnus felt his heart quicken with every second that passed.

"Why did you do that?" Finn screamed.

The truth was Magnus stopped Finn before he could follow Ivy into the woods because he knew the trance was too powerful to be broken. He couldn't let Finn get sucked in also. He had to keep everyone together and come up with a solution. Finn didn't wait for an answer and started to walk toward the woods again, but Magnus grabbed his arm. "You can't go in there, Finn," Magnus said sternly.

"I'm not going to leave her!" Finn's worry was spilling out with his voice. Rayner and Correlyn stood still as statues, not believing what they just witnessed. Rayner shot a panicked look at his father.

"I'll go," Magnus said as he released Finn from his grasp.

"Father, you can't. Let me," Rayner stepped forward.

"No," Magnus said, his voice breaking as he looked at his son. "I won't lose you again." Magnus moved to his saddle to search for a rope so that he could be pulled back out once he found Ivy. His hands were shaking as he searched through his saddlebag when Rayner's cry turned his attention back. Finn was gone.

Finn crashed through the brush, branches clawing at his face as he ran deeper into the woods, calling Ivy's name. He turned to look back, and his eyes widened. The path he'd taken into the woods was gone, and he thought he saw a spruce tree shifting into place, its limbs swaying with movement. His pulse was wild, and his hands were sweating, but he pushed on through the ancient forest. The world was silent around him; even his footfalls seemed to be muffled. Finn stopped and cupped his hands around his mouth, screaming as loud as he could for Ivy, but no one answered. Not one thing in the woods stirred. He ran his shaking hands over his face, trying to think when he spotted someone.

Finn ran as hard as he could toward the woman, but she disappeared around a spruce tree. *"Finnick!"* A loud whisper filled the still air around him, and his hairs stood up on command. Finn ground to a halt. He shivered to hear his full name spoken, only one person ever called him Finnick.

A slight breeze came through the trees, and Finn spun around, searching for the direction of the voice. *"Finnick, my sweet boy. Why did you leave us?"* Tears began to roll away as he listened to his mother's voice, moving through the trees. He bent over and put his hands to his ears, trying to block her out, but the Whispering Woods were working their way into him.

"No, no, no," he muttered to himself, pressing his hands tighter to his ears.

"Finnick, you should have saved us. We died because of you." The whisper was growing louder. *"How could you let that happen? I was protecting Thorman. He was only a little boy!"* The voice screamed at Finn, flooding his head with memories so dense they constricted his breathing. *"He was your baby brother, and you let him die! You should have died with us!"*

Finn dropped to his knees. "Stop it!" he screamed. He pressed his forehead into the dirt as more tears spilled from his eyes. "I—I'm sorry," he sobbed. "I'm sorry, Thor."

Finn lay crumpled by the memory of his baby brother and the slaughter of his family. He had never spoken a word of his brother since that day. The woods seeped into him, raking their cold fingers against his brain and numbing his body. Finn dropped his hands to the dirt and let the tears turn the earth to mud. The woods grew silent again, and his mother's voice disappeared, leaving him numb and broken.

Magnus paced back and forth, letting his panic consume him as he searched the woods, calling for Ivy and Finn. "You two move back!" he ordered Rayner and Correlyn, who obeyed and stepped away from the woods. Magnus unsheathed his sword and swung up on his horse before kicking it into a gallop and taking off into the trees. He could hear Rayner yelling at him from behind but ignored it, hoping his son would stay put until they returned.

His horse swerved in between the dark trees, and Magnus could see that the beast was confused. He raised his hand and hacked away at a low-hanging branch when a loud shriek filled the air, making his horse rear up and throw Magnus from its back. The horse took off in a gallop before Magnus could sit up.

The world spun around him, and he moved a hand to the back of his head, where blood began to trickle through his hair. Magnus stumbled to his feet and snatched his sword up.

"Ivy!" He cried. "Finn!" No answers came. He cut through another branch with his sword, and the shrill cry pierced him again, forcing him to drop his sword and cover his ears. Magnus was horrified at the sound and realized it was coming from the trees that he was cutting. He felt a wave of anger rising in his throat. "Give her back to me!" he yelled at the God of Secrets, but no one was listening, and the woods grew silent and still around him.

The king sank to his knees, feeling defeated as the woods worked their way into his mind. He saw a flash of red hair, and his heart skipped as he launched from the ground toward the woman. "Ivy!" he called as he got closer. The woman turned to face him, and Magnus stopped in his tracks. "No," he whispered to himself. An arrow poked through the front of her neck, and dried blood crusted her chest. Her red hair swirled in the wind, and her green eyes dug a hole into his soul.

"You're dead," Magnus said, taking a step back. "This isn't real." He tripped on a root that hadn't been there a moment ago and fell to his back as Lady Roe came to stand over him.

"You didn't protect me. You let him do this." She pointed a pale finger at the arrow in her neck. *"My blood is on your hands, King Magnus! You killed me! You killed me!"* she screamed over and over again. Magnus squeezed his eyes shut until her voice faded, and the silence crept closer, leaving the king sobbing softly as his eyes glazed over.

Ivy ran through the trees, completely in the grasp of the God of Secrets now. Ser Osmund came in and out of view as he weaved his way through the woods. Ivy felt her heart thudding rapidly, and her lungs screaming at her to stop, but her feet obeyed the god and kept running. She tried to scream, but her mind wouldn't let her. She fought to keep her vision focused on the knight ahead of her when suddenly, her feet stopped.

Ivy dropped to her knees, sucking in air and coughing. Ser Osmund stood in the shadows ahead of her, before slithering behind a tree and out of sight. Ivy spun her head around, trying to find her way out as she could feel the grasp of the woods leaving her mind. She didn't understand what was happening and tried to stand but stumbled back to the ground.

Ser Osmund stepped out from a nearby tree, but this time his appearance made Ivy jump back and start to crawl away. His throat was cut, exposing the bone as black blood seeped from his neck to cover the front of his armor. His eyes were black, and his skin cold and blue as he stepped toward Ivy. Ivy was trembling, and tears fogged her vision as Ser Osmund reached out to grab her. Ivy screamed and yanked her arm away just as a blinding light filled the forest. She held a hand up to block the glow, and when she looked up again, Ser Osmund was gone. The trees groaned and cracked as their limbs bent, as if trying to escape the light. Ivy felt faint as she looked toward it, and without her mind telling her to, she got to her feet and followed it.

Rayner broke into a run as Ivy stumbled out of the woods and fell to her knees. The veil was lifted, and Ivy felt the darkness leaving her mind as Rayner dropped in front of her and grabbed her face in his hands. "Are you hurt?" Rayner's voice was filled with panic, and she suddenly realized it was dark outside.

"How long was I gone?" Ivy asked in a hoarse voice.

"It's been hours, Ivy." Rayner released her and looked deep into her eyes, searching for answers. Ivy felt sick. To her, it had only felt like a few minutes, but she remembered everything.

The trance did nothing to her memory, only controlled

her, and bent her to the god's will. Ivy felt drained and light-headed, her muscles hurt from running, and her voice was raspy from screaming.

"How did you get out?" Correlyn asked. Ivy shook her head, trying to remember how she navigated the woods when the bright light came back to her.

"There was a light," Ivy whispered. "It led me out." She looked around and realized Finn and her father were gone. "Where are they?" she demanded.

Before Rayner could ask what she meant, Finn and Magnus came walking out of the woods. Ivy felt tears form in her eyes, and as she tried to stand up, Finn came running to her.

Ivy felt his body shaking as he embraced her, stroking her hair. "I thought I'd lost you," Finn whispered, his voice hoarse.

"I'm sorry," Ivy responded, hugging him tighter. Magnus stood back, watching the two before Ivy broke away from Finn and ran to her father. He wrapped his arms around her as tears of relief filled his eyes. Rayner, too, came up and hugged his father and sister. They stayed like that for a long moment before Magnus broke away.

Magnus turned, and Ivy followed his gaze to see the trees swaying and bending as a light moved through them. The king's horse burst out of the tree line and ran in circles before calming down. Magnus released his grip on Ivy and walked toward the light that soared down and landed before the king. The bright glow died away to be replaced with pure white feathers as Luna took on her usual appearance.

Magnus bent down to take Luna on his arm. She hopped

up and ruffled the last of the light from her feathers as Magnus stroked her head.

"It was Luna," Rayner said, sounding confused.

"She saved us." Magnus matched his son's level of confusion.

Ivy remembered her father telling her about the day he got Luna and how the man named River told of the bird's powers, but Ivy didn't think this was it. She knew Luna had used her power before when the Tandrycian stag almost mauled her father back in the Hercynian Forest all those years ago. Luna was more mysterious to her than any other creature.

The sound of approaching riders drew their attention as Ser Caster and his men sprinted to where Magnus stood with his family. Luna flew off and landed on his horse's back as Ser Caster swung down from his horse. "What happened? We came around the back of the lake, and you weren't there, so we pushed farther, but the woods cut off our path."

"What?" Rayner stepped forward. "Correlyn and I were standing here the whole time."

"All I know is we came around that bend, and the woods were pushed right up to the shoreline, so we had to double back."

Ser Caster let his gaze fall over the silent woods and visibly shuddered. "I know what these woods are and wouldn't let my men go through them."

"They cut you off," Magnus stated. "The woods cut you off so you couldn't get to us. We were trapped in there for hours it would seem."

"You went in there?" Ser Caster looked shocked. "How

did you get out?" Magnus looked back to where Luna sat atop his horse and motioned for Ser Caster to walk with him. They all headed back toward Grey Raven to spend another night and regroup. Magnus told Ser Caster everything that happened, and the knight kept looking back at Ivy and Finn walking side by side.

Rayner started a fire in their spot from the night before and passed around a skin filled with wine. Ivy willingly took a swallow before handing it to Finn, who gave it to Correlyn without taking a sip. "What did you see?" Rayner asked Ivy from across the fire. Ser Osmund's dead face came bubbling to the surface of her memory, and she snapped her eyes shut at the image.

"It was Ser Osmund," Ivy finally said in a quiet voice. Rayner stayed silent and looked at his boots. Finn looked drained and pale, his eyes blank as he watched the fire dance in the wind.

"Do you want to walk?" Finn asked Ivy.

"Sure."

They strolled through the empty streets, keeping their gaze on the ground in front of them. Ivy didn't wish to go to sleep, knowing she would only have nightmares about what she'd seen in the Whispering Woods. They walked out to the field where they had sparred the night before, and Finn plopped down in the grass with a loud sigh. Ivy sat next to him and opened her mouth to speak before he cut her off.

"Do you remember the story I told you about my home?" Finn began, picking at a blade of grass.

Ivy stayed silent and nodded, recalling his story.

"I lied to you," he said with the same shaky voice from

earlier. Finn drew in a breath to steady himself before speaking again. "I told you my mother was caring for a local boy who was sick." He stopped and looked at Ivy to make sure she was listening.

"I remember," she said quietly.

"That's not exactly true." He ran a finger over the scar on his cheek.

Ivy leaned in closer. "Finn, what did you see in there?"

He closed his eyes. "My mother came to me. She blamed me for leaving them and for their deaths."

"Finn," Ivy placed a hand on his shoulder. "We all saw something that haunts us. It wasn't your fault, you were only a boy."

"That little boy that my mother was caring for," he continued, tears now clinging to his lashes. "His name was Thorman. He was my little brother, only four years old."

Ivy withdrew her hand to cover her mouth as Finn let tears silently flow from his eyes. "I should've saved him," Finn cried, angrily wiping his tears away. "He was only a small child, and I let the raider kill him in his sleep." Finn sobbed and drew his knees to his face, wrapping himself in a protective ball. Ivy felt a tear escape as she watched the man she loved crumble before her eyes.

"Why didn't you ever tell me about him?" Ivy whispered.

"I tried to forget about him. To bury his memory deep in my mind just so I could sleep at night."

"Finn . . ." Ivy didn't know what to say. How could words ever bring him comfort against the pain he'd carried for all these years? She leaned into him as he sniffed away the last of his tears, neither one of them speaking. Ivy couldn't imagine the pain of losing Rayner, especially in such a horrible way. The two sat leaning into one another in the field until the sun started to come up and turn the world grey around them.

As they walked back through the back gate of Grey Raven, Magnus came walking up to them. It looked as though the king hadn't slept either, and black circles hung heavy under his eyes. Finn squeezed Ivy's hand before leaving them.

"Are you all right?" Magnus tried to smile at Ivy but failed miserably. She nodded her head slowly and kept her eyes on Finn's back. "What about him?" He turned to look at Finn.

"I'm not sure," Ivy admitted. Magnus wrapped his arm around her shoulder, and they walked back into the town together.

Rayner and Correlyn were mounting their saddlebags on their horses when Ivy and her father came walking up. "Get some food and mount up," Magnus said, letting go of Ivy. "We're leaving soon."

When they headed out, Ivy nibbled a piece of dried meat as she sat atop Cass. She kept looking over to Finn, but he wouldn't meet her eyes, so she turned around to gaze at Grey Raven growing smaller behind them. This place had taken a chunk of her, Finn, and Magnus, leaving an empty hole in its place. Ivy thought they would all feel broken for a while, and the images from the woods would haunt their dreams for many nights. But the farther away she got from that land, the clearer her head became, and she pushed away the dark memories of the place and focused on getting back home with her family.

CHAPTER TEN

THE STORM

Finn walked over the damp sand of the beach, feeling it give under his boots. A storm was coming, and he had to find his brother before it hit. Early winter storms in Tonsburg were ruthless. The sea rose and fell to the beat of the thunder, hard rains made it impossible to see a hand in front of your face, and thick fog crept down from the Spearhead Mountains to swallow the town whole. The wind picked up and blew Finn's brown hair back from his eyes as he spotted Thorman.

His little brother was standing on a barnacle-covered rock, collecting seashells and small creatures. Finn smiled at his brother, who seemed lost in his own world. "Thorman!" Finn shouted over the wind. His brother lifted his head, and his sandy blond hair was swept back. He smiled and waved for Finn to come over. Thorman handed his big brother a seashell and told him to open it, and when Finn did, his breath caught in his throat. A black pearl the size of his thumb sat inside the shell, rolling around in a puddle of cold seawater. "That's for you!" Thorman exclaimed happily, clearly proud of his find. Finn thanked his brother and rustled his hair before telling him they had to go. Thorman gave a disappointed frown but hopped down from the rock anyway and took Finn's hand.

The brothers walked back through the beach and down the dirt street. Fishmongers had already boarded up their booths and left the road deserted. The rain started falling, and Finn picked up the pace, dragging Thorman behind him. The wind howled around them, and the sky quickly grew blacker than the pearl. As they made their way through the small town, Finn could see people running to their houses, already soaked from the cold rain, while others blocked their windows. Their home was small but comfortable and sat in the back of the town. The log house was overgrown with moss, and small twigs had started to sprout from the logs that made up the roof as if the house was growing.

Finn burst through the door and pulled Thorman in before closing out the rain and setting a long wooden board across the entrance.

"There you are." Finn's mother stood over the cook fire, stirring a pot of stew.

"Finn," Thorman whined in his tiny voice. "Show Mother what I found!" He pulled the shell from his pocket and handed it to his mother, whose eyes went wide. A pearl of that size would be worth a lot, maybe enough to feed their family through the long winter. His mother smiled and closed the shell, handing it back to Finn and telling him to keep it safe.

Their father banged on the door, and Finn quickly went

to remove the plank to let him in. He was soaked head to toe and carried what was once a pile of dry wood. Finn looked much like his father with the same brown eyes and dark wavy hair, while Thorman took after their mother. Her hair was sandy blonde, and her eyes were a deep blue, like the color of the sea on a cloudy day.

The storm raged on through the night. Finn and Thorman sat up in the loft where they slept and listened to the rain beat down on their house. His little brother was antsy and wanted to go back to the beach. He was too full of energy and wouldn't sit cooped up for very long. "We can't go, Thorman." Finn tried to explain to a four-year-old why he couldn't go outside and play.

"But I'll be careful," Thorman persisted.

"Enough Thor. Do you hear that?" Finn paused so they could hear the crack of thunder overhead. "You can't go out in a storm like this, you'll get lost or hurt."

Thorman crossed his arms and turned away from Finn to stare at the wall. Finn sighed and laid his head down, letting the rain lull him to sleep.

He woke in a panic as thunder boomed in the distance and looked over to see that Thorman wasn't in his bed. Finn whispered his name in the dark, but no answer came. He pulled on some boots and a cloak and quietly made his way down the loft, tiptoeing past his parents' bed in the back. The hearth was cold, and Finn knew it must be late. He cracked the door open to the pitch black outside, no stars or moon to light his way. Finn cursed under his breath and stepped out into the freezing rain, pulling his cloak around his face.

Ivy leaned back against the wall and closed her eyes, trying to calm her aching head. Magister Ivann's room was small, and his shelves were lined with glass bottles of herbs and colorful liquids. The stone walls were covered in pieces of cloth with different drawings on them, one depicting the human body with lines connecting to various veins and muscles. Another was an illustration of plants and flowers with descriptions beneath each one explaining their properties. Magister Ivann came through the door, and Ivy picked her head up and stretched her neck.

"Lady Ivy." The Magister sighed. "Please, go home and get some rest. You don't look well." Ivy ignored his plea and moved over to the bed, where Finn had been sleeping for two days. She touched his brow and quickly retracted her hand.

"He's still burning," Ivy said in a worried voice. Ivann came over and felt Finn's head before shuffling over to the shelves, running his finger along the wood until he found what he was looking for.

He grabbed a glass bottle containing a purple liquid and extracted a small amount with a spoon before moving back to Finn. "What are you giving him?" Ivy stood up, blocking Magister Ivann's path.

"It's a mixture of nightshade and herbs, it will help with his fever."

"It doesn't seem to be working," Ivy said with hostility.

"My Lady, there is no quick fix. This will make him more comfortable and keep his fever down some but . . ."

"But what?" Ivy demanded.

"His body must fight the fever off if he's to get stronger. These remedies are only helping his body to do what it must." Ivy looked back at Finn, who seemed deep in sleep, yet his brow was scrunched up, and his face showed signs of pain. She lowered her gaze and sat back down, letting the Magister administer the medicine. He tilted Finn's head back and poured a few drops of the liquid into his mouth. He then lowered his ear to Finn's bare chest and listened to his rattled breathing and quick heartbeat.

They had left Grey Raven about a week ago with no answers as to where Lady Oharra and her warriors might have gone. The ride back was slow and miserable as a steady rain came down on their heads for three days. They camped under trees or built small tents when they could, but the rain made it almost impossible for them to keep warm and dry. Everyone slept huddled together, trying to shiver out the cold that was sinking into their bones. A few of the knights got sick along the way, but Finn's fever had grown worse by the minute. Magnus led the group back to Godstone, and just as they were coming out of the Blackwood Forest, Finn collapsed and fell from his horse.

Ivy swung down and ran to him, lifting his head in her hands. She could see how pale he was. The Whispering Woods had taken a toll on Finn, Magnus, and Ivy, but Finn seemed to have been affected the most. The king rode ahead to warn Magister Ivann to prepare the room while Rayner helped Ivy get Finn back on his horse. Ivy rode behind Finn, wrapping her arms around him to keep him propped up while Eclipse moved gently over the field toward the gates.

Magister Ivann was laying some fresh sheets down when Rayner and Ivy burst through the door with Finn hanging limp with his arms over their shoulders. He was mumbling something that Ivy couldn't understand, and her panic grew worse.

"Get him on the bed," Magister Ivann told them. "What happened?"

"We've been caught in the rain for days," Rayner told him, out of breath.

"He's burning up," Ivy continued.

Since then, Finn had been lying abed, asleep for two days now. She looked at Finn as he twitched and wondered what he was dreaming about, just as she wondered when he would get better or if Magister Ivann knew what he was doing.

Finn held up a hand to block the rain from his eyes as he made his way down the street and through the town. He couldn't even hear the crashing of the waves over the wild winds and the pounding rain. He tripped and fell face-first into the wet sand of the beach, searching the sheets of rain in front of him for Thorman. Finn got back up and started moving toward the water, his heart lurching at the thought of what he might find. He called his brother's name, but it was useless—his voice was only carried off into the storm.

A bolt of lightning brightened the sky for a second, and Finn spotted Thorman on the same rock where he'd found his brother earlier. He broke into a run, the outline of his brother coming into view as he got closer. Finn called up to Thorman, who was squatting down on the rock, filling his pockets with smooth stones and seashells. His brother looked up with an excited expression, holding out the spiral shell he'd just found. Finn reached out his hand for Thorman to grab. His brother stood to bury the shell in his pocket as the sky lit up, and Finn's eyes went wide. "Thorman!" he screamed, but it was too late. The wave crashed down on the rock, sweeping his brother away as it headed back out to sea.

Finn's mind raced, and he fumbled to unbuckle his cloak before throwing it on the beach and running into the sea after Thorman. The frigid water stabbed his skin and took his breath away, but he forced himself to continue. A crack of thunder rattled his bones as Finn pushed through the crashing waves, desperately searching for his brother. "Thorman!" he yelled over and over, but it was no use. He swam as fast as he could out into the raging black waters until the sky brightened up again, turning the world to daylight in an instant.

He spotted his brother's body floating a few yards ahead. Finn slammed his hands into the water, thrusting himself forward. By the time he got to Thorman, he was out of breath and freezing. Finn scooped up his brother under the arms and yelled his name, but Thorman didn't answer. As he started kicking his way back to shore, a wave swept them under the icy water. Their bodies tumbled along the sea's bottom, and then Finn lost his grip on Thorman. A bright flash traveled through the murky water, and Finn saw his brother sinking to the bottom, a column of tiny bubbles escaping his mouth. Finn's lungs screamed for air, and his heart pounded wildly, but he ignored it and dove deeper, stretching his arm toward his brother, whose pockets were heavy with his collection of shells and sea rocks.

"Wake up." A kind voice crept into her ear, and Ivy cracked her eyes to see her mother. Queen Elana wore a light spring dress in the same shade of green as her eyes. Her long blond hair was unbound and hung alongside her face as she bent over to touch Ivy's forehead. "Have you eaten today, darling?"

Ivy shook her head and looked at Finn, who hadn't moved. Some color had returned to his face, but he was still very pale.

"How's he doing?" Elana sat down next to Ivy.

"I'm not sure," Ivy said in a small voice.

Her mother brushed Ivy's hair out of her face and turned Ivy's chin to face her. "You look tired, darling. You should go rest. I'll stay here with him if you like."

Ivy smiled at the gesture, but she couldn't leave until Finn woke up. She was glad that her mother didn't push her any further. "Still no word of Lady Oharra?" Ivy asked, keeping her gaze on Finn.

"I'm afraid not."

"How's Correlyn doing?" Ivy turned to her mother to read her face.

"Correlyn is sad," Elana admitted. "But she's a strong woman, and I know your brother will do all he can to comfort her." Ivy nodded and ran her hands over her tired eyes. "Your father has sent hawks to Earl Rorik and Lord Kevan asking them to return to Godstone."

"When did he send them?" Ivy asked.

"As soon as you got back a few days ago, but there's been no reply yet."

Ivy couldn't even concentrate on what day it was—she'd been sitting beside Finn since she brought him here with Rayner. Her head ached, and her back screamed for a proper bed, but she couldn't bring herself to leave his side.

"So you're to be a knight." Her mother's words startled Ivy back to reality. "I can't tell you how many nights your father sat up, going over this decision while you were away. I think waiting two more years for your dream to come true is a small price to pay, don't you?"

Ivy tried to form a smile, but the effort was exhausting to her, and she turned her face down instead.

"Well, I think you'll make a fine knight," her mother said, getting to her feet. She reached down and caressed Ivy's cheek in her delicate hand. "I'm very proud of you, darling." This time Ivy managed a real smile and rose to embrace her.

"Thank you, Mother," she said. Ivy watched as her mother closed the door behind her, then stood and went over to the window, which looked out to the main street where she could see knights standing guard on the wall in the distance. The central market was nearly empty. The sun was setting, and people made their way in different directions down the streets, heading to their homes. She closed the curtain on the outside world and moved to light the hanging lanterns. The room flickered to life in the dim light.

Ivy stretched her back and chose an apple from a copper bowl and took a bite. Finn made a groaning noise and flinched at some unseen force before lurching his body up and arching his back. Ivy dropped the apple and ran to his side, grabbing his arms so he didn't accidentally hit her. His mouth opened, and a small gasp came out before he took a deep breath and fell still again, deep in the arms of a dream.

He was sweating, and Ivy wet a piece of cloth and wiped Finn's head and chest. She placed her hand on his bare chest and felt the racing of his heart under his pale skin, but as she held her hand there, she could feel his heartbeat start to slow down and become regular. "I'm here, Finn," she whispered.

CHAPTER ELEVEN

THE NIGHTMARE

Finn brushed Thorman's cold, tiny fingers with his hand and quickly grasped them, pulling him from the seabed. He kicked off from the bottom just as his vision started to darken. Finn kept his grip on Thorman as they rose to the surface. He burst through the water and gasped for air, coughing as he lifted Thorman's head above the surface and swam as fast as his tired legs would go, diving under the waves just before they crashed. When he could touch the bottom again, Finn pushed through the water, dragging Thorman's body behind him onto the wet sand. The rain had let up some, but the thunder still boomed in the sky, and the sea raged on behind him. Finn tried to ignore the violent shaking of his body as he laid Thorman down and pressed his ear to his brother's chest. He didn't hear anything and began to cry before remembering what his mother had taught him.

Their mother was the healer of their town, and people came to her for everything from minor scrapes to amputations. Finn wasted no more time and began pushing on Thorman's chest, stopping to breathe life into his lungs. He searched his brother's face as he continued pushing, but Thorman's eyes were shut. "No, no, no, NO! Come on, Thor!" Finn yelled at his brother but mostly at himself. The blame was eating him alive the longer Thorman kept his eyes closed. Finn couldn't help but blame himself for this. Thorman was his little brother, and it was his job to look out for him.

Tears streamed down his face, mixing with the salt of the sea, and Finn slammed an angry fist into Thorman's chest— and his brother opened his eyes. Finn gasped and lifted Thorman's head as he coughed up seawater and gasped for air. He lifted him to a sitting position and pulled Thorman in for a hug, squeezing all the air back out of him. "Are you all right?" Finn asked, immediately realizing what a stupid question that was.

Thorman pushed Finn away and nodded his head before burying his hand into his pockets, searching for the collection that almost drowned him. "I think I lost some." His tiny voice was shaking with the cold, his lips blue. Finn scooped him up in his arms and ran toward their house.

He kicked the door open, and his father shot up from the bed and grabbed a nearby ax. "Mother!" Finn yelled to the back of the house where his mother was just sitting up in bed. Her eyes landed on Thorman, and she leaped out of bed, running past their father.

"What happened, Finnick?" she demanded.

"He must have snuck out while I was asleep . . . I found him on the beach and . . ." Finn finally allowed his tears to come in full force and plopped down on a bench as he watched his mother work on Thorman. Somewhere between the beach and their house, Thorman had passed out in Finn's arms. His father came over to Finn and grabbed ahold of his face in his rough hands.

"Finn, it's all right now. You got him back here, and he's alive," his father said, his voice soothing and calm.

"But it's my fault," Finn sobbed. "I should've watched him." His father hushed Finn and cradled his head against his chest.

Their mother cut off Thorman's shirt, and Finn could see his tiny chest rising and falling with shaky breaths. "Start a fire," his mother commanded, and Finn watched his father start to pile wood into the hearth. The fire was roaring in no time, and Finn moved toward the flames, grateful for their warmth. His father came and draped a fur pelt over Finn's shoulders and hung a kettle over the fire to get hot.

"Is he all right?" Finn asked timidly.

"He's cold," his mother said. "No doubt, you'll both catch a fever, but I think he'll be fine." She looked up and smiled at Finn before going back to mixing herbs. She rubbed something sticky on Thorman's chest before wrapping him in furs as well. Finn fell into a fretful sleep curled up on the floor in front of the fire and didn't rise until the next afternoon.

Thorman was asleep when Finn woke up, and his mother told him that she'd given Thorman an herb mixture that would make him sleep for days. Thorman was still pale, but his skin burned under Finn's fingers as he brushed the hair from his brother's forehead. Finn sat by his brother's side until the world outside grew dark and cold. "I'm sorry, Thor," Finn whispered to his sleeping brother. "I won't let anything happen to you again. I promise." His mother cooked up some soup for supper, and they sat around the fire in silence, everyone occasionally looking over to Thorman, who lay asleep in his parents' bed.

After supper, Finn's father went out to collect some wood, and Finn sat next to his mother, watching her grind up more herbs and checking Thorman's pulse with her fingers. Finn ran the black pearl between his fingers, smiling at the gift from his little brother when he heard a cry from outside.

He shoved the pearl into his pocket and stood up just as his father came crashing through the door. His expression was panicked, and his eyes wild as he yelled at his wife to take Finn and get to the docks. "What's going on?" Finn's mother stood up, while he ran to the window. His eyes grew wide as he saw houses burning and men running through the streets.

"Take Finn and get out of here! I'll grab Thorman and be right behind you," his father ordered.

"I'm not leaving him," Finn's mother said in a stern voice. She moved toward Finn and pulled a fur cloak over his head before pushing Finn toward his father and yelling at them to go. Finn was panicked and confused—he didn't understand what was happening and why his parents were arguing. But then a man came bursting through their door, sending it flying from the hinges and across the room. Finn shot a worried look at Thorman, who still slept peacefully under his furs. Finn's father stood between the man and his family. He wore a large hood that covered most of his face, but Finn saw his mouth open as if he was about to speak when Finn's father tackled him into the wall.

His mother screamed. "Run, Finnick!" But his feet stayed planted where they were, unable to move as he watched the intruder break away from his father and grab for him. His father grabbed the man's cloak, jerking the hand that held a knife and slashing Finn's face. But Finn couldn't feel it. The warm blood trickled down his neck and into his shirt as his father threw Finn aside. He stood shocked, unable to move, as he watched the man stab his father in the heart. Finn tried to scream, but no sound came out, and everything was muffled in his ears. Finn turned to his mother, who appeared to be yelling as she slashed at the man advancing on her.

Finn felt frozen in place, everything moving slowly around him as he watched his screaming mother try to defend Thorman before her throat was slit. Finn felt a punch to the gut as he watched his mother sink to the ground. The man stepped forward and stared at Thorman for a moment. More men could be heard yelling just outside, but Finn's eyes remained on the man who brushed the hair from Thorman's brow and muttered something under his breath before slowly piercing his knife into his chest.

Finn felt as though his own heart had just been stabbed, his breath caught in his throat, and tears spilled from his wide eyes. Before he knew what he was doing, Finn ran out of his house, where his entire family now lay dead. He slipped and fell to the ground, and when he looked down, Finn realized he was covered in someone else's blood. His mind was racing as he looked at the town, blazing with fire against the night sky. The air was filled with screams and smoke, people running out of burning houses only to be met with a sword.

Finn's world came crumbling to his blood-soaked feet. His family was dead, his home gone, and yet he was alive. He couldn't understand why the gods wouldn't protect Thorman, an innocent little boy. Finn ran through the outskirts of the town, sobbing and trying to catch his breath as he pictured his brother lying dead and alone in their house. Finn had promised his brother that nothing would happen to him, but he'd broken that promise, and the full weight of his guilt punched a hole into his soul. Finn couldn't protect his little brother; he couldn't protect anyone.

CHAPTER TWELVE

THE UNDROWNED

The sun rose over the walls of Godstone, streaming in through the sheer curtain and landing on Ivy's cheek. Finn had been awake for hours, sitting in the dark silence of the room, watching Ivy as she slept in her chair. Though he'd been asleep for days, Finn felt utterly drained by the nightmare forcing him to relive the slaughter of his family. He reached into his pocket and pulled out the black pearl that Thorman had given him the day before his murder. It was smooth and heavy in his hand as he rolled it around the center of his palm. A tear fell from his cheek and landed on the pearl with a *plop*. Finn kissed the pearl and put it back into his pocket before swinging his legs over the side of the bed.

He knew he had to let Thorman go and the guilt attached to his memory. Finn was only nine when the raiders came, and over the years, he'd come to the realization that there was nothing he could've done that wouldn't have gotten him killed as well. Finn buried his face in his hands, rubbing out the images of the nightmare that had haunted his sleep for years. They only stopped after he met Ivy, who filled his dreams at night and pushed away his ghosts from the past.

Yet the Whispering Woods had worked their way deep into Finn's mind, bringing to the surface the face of his dead brother. Finn lifted his head and focused on Ivy, who was still sleeping with her head leaned back on the stone wall, and her arms crossed over her chest. He let himself smile, trying to focus his still blurry vision on the rise and fall of her chest or her hair that was messily braided and trailed down her side. Finn let his feet touch the cold stone floor, sending a shock through his body. He stood up and immediately stumbled, knocking over a tray on the bedside table.

Ivy's eyes shot open, and her hand immediately went to Promise strapped at her side. "Are you going to stab me?" Finn teased as she laid eyes on him and moved her hand away from the hilt.

"Finn," she whispered. "You're awake." Ivy stood and went over to him then wrapped her arms around his neck, pulling herself closer. Finn swayed on his feet, but Ivy grounded him. He wrapped his weak arms around her waist and breathed in the scent of her hair. She pulled away and stood back to look at him.

Finn could tell from Ivy's expression that he didn't look much better. "You need to eat something," she told him. Finn didn't dare refuse her and so sat back down on the bed as Ivy poured him a cup of water and started slicing up an apple. Finn suddenly realized how thirsty he was, and he quickly drained the cup, letting the water trail down his neck.

His stomach turned as he lifted the apple to his mouth

and took a bite. "How long have I been asleep?" Finn asked between bites.

"About three days," Ivy said. "You fell off your horse just outside the Blackwoods. Rayner and I carried you here from the gate."

Finn struggled to recall what happened as he slowly ate another slice of apple. "I don't remember the ride back," he admitted.

"You had a bad fever, Finn. It was from the rain." Ivy's voice trailed off as Finn was brought back to his nightmare, running through the rain with Thorman in his arms, his lips blue and eyes shut.

Finn dropped the apple slice and brought a shaky hand to his head, trying to rub the memory away with his palm.

"What is it?" Ivy asked, taking his other hand.

"Just a nightmare," Finn whispered.

"Thorman?"

Finn snapped his head up at his brother's name, and Ivy let go of his hand.

"You were calling his name in your sleep," Ivy told him. "I was worried."

Finn ran his fingers through his tangled hair and let a deep sigh escape through his nose.

"It was the Whispering Woods, Finn. My father and I have had nightmares too since we left, but they go away."

"Not this," Finn said. "I can't erase a memory. But I won't let it haunt me anymore." Finn stood up and reached for his shirt that was hung over the back of the chair.

"Where are you going?" Ivy asked, standing up to follow him to the door.

"Come, I'll need your help."

Ivy helped Finn walk down the street of Godstone, placing her hand on his lower back as they moved along. The sun was blinding to Finn, and he kept a hand up to block its rays as they walked toward the beach. A salty wind came up to greet them as they stepped onto the beach and removed their boots. Finn sunk his toes in the cool sand and closed his eyes against the bright sun, letting himself feel this place.

He moved toward the water and scanned the sand for shells and smooth rocks. He bent over and plucked a small pink shell standing out against the black sand. Finn smiled and put it in his pocket before moving on. Ivy didn't ask what he was doing but instead started filling her own pockets with shells and smooth stones. When Finn's pockets were full and heavy, he moved over to the side of the beach, where a large boulder sat in the sand.

Finn sunk to his knees and started scooping away handfuls of sand and stones. Ivy realized what he was doing and got down in the sand to help him. They dug a deep hole, and Finn began to remove the shells from his pocket, running a finger over each one before placing them into the hole. Ivy did the same, brushing the sand off the stones before carefully setting them around the shells.

Finn felt for the last item in his pocket and pulled out the black pearl. He rolled it through his fingers before bringing it to his lips and kissing it, whispering something only meant for him. Finn gently placed the pearl in the center of the collection, then took a handful of sand and let it slowly slip through his fingers and fall into the hole.

They buried the shells, and Ivy lined the grave with the

smoothest black stones she could find. They moved around the beach, searching for a piece of driftwood that Finn selected and then asked to borrow Rayner's knife. Ivy handed it over and Finn began to carefully carve the wood. He set the piece of wood on top of the grave and stood up, wrapping an arm around Ivy's shoulder and kissing her head.

"Thank you," he whispered. Ivy hugged him close and looked at the spot they created in honor of Finn's brother. They turned to leave, feeling the sand between their toes as they walked hand in hand over the beach. Finn let himself smile for once at the memory of his brother and how excited he would be over the shells that they'd left and how he would've bragged at the name Finn carved into the wood: *Thor the Undrowned.*

CHAPTER THIRTEEN

THE QUIET BEFORE

The world seemed normal, almost at peace. The people of Godstone came and went from the central market, fishing boats pushed out into the harbor, and farmers worked in their fields outside the northern gate, harvesting radishes and carrots from the ground. The day was pleasantly warm with not a single cloud in the deep blue sky, and the wind carried with it the smell of grass and blooming flowers.

Ivy sat on top of a barrel outside the practice yard, watching Ronin teach Rayner how to be silent. Ivy giggled at her brother's efforts and remembered how long it had taken her to learn that same lesson. Ronin sat in the middle of the dirt circle, waiting for Rayner to approach him from behind. Her brother managed to get a few feet away when Ronin, without turning his head, swung his bamboo staff back, knocking Rayner to the ground. Finn came up behind Ivy and wrapped his arms around her waist, making her cheeks flush with color. "How many times has Ronin hit him?" Finn whispered into Ivy's ear.

"Too many to count," Ivy replied, smiling as her brother pushed himself up from the dirt.

It had been a week since Finn woke up from his feverish nightmare, and Ronin had since taken to training Correlyn and Rayner along with Ivy and Finn. They all met in the practice yard at dawn and usually didn't leave until Ronin was satisfied with their efforts. There had been no word from Earl Rorik or Lord Kevan, and Ivy's father was starting to worry. Everything seemed quiet, and she knew the silence unnerved her father.

"Ivy." Ronin waved her over. Ivy pushed away from Finn and took off her boots before she stepped into the pit with her wooden sword in hand. Rayner eyed her from the other side of the circle, stretching his arms above his head and shaking out his legs. "You two will pair up." Ronin pointed to Ivy and Rayner. "Finn and Correlyn, you two are a pair. Move to the other side of the circle."

Correlyn entered the pit and smiled at her husband from across the circle. Her hair was fixed in a black braid that hung down her back. Finn smiled at Ivy and gave her a playful wink before he stood alongside Correlyn.

"Whichever pair can take out the other will be victorious. Understood?" Ronin stood in the middle of the circle with his hands behind his back, waiting for everyone to nod their heads in acknowledgment. Ivy thought she saw Ronin smile as he turned his back and left the pit, throwing up a hand to signal the fight.

Rayner and Ivy stepped forward, Finn and Correlyn mimicked their move before Ivy broke away from her brother and headed toward Finn. Correlyn jumped into Ivy's path and swung her sword, forcing her to fall to her knees and glide under it. Ivy got back to her feet just as Finn's sword was coming down, and she raised hers to meet it. Their wooden swords clacked together, and Finn put all his weight into it, forcing Ivy's knees to buckle. She looked over her shoulder to see Rayner parrying Correlyn's blows, and Ivy rolled her eyes as she noticed Rayner was holding back.

She turned her attention back to Finn and let his weight force her to the ground, moving out of the way just in time. Swinging her sword, she caught Finn in the back of the leg— the force of her swing rattled up her arm. He flinched at the pain and looked at Ivy with surprise written on his face. She half-smiled at him before standing up and jabbing her sword toward his chest. He quickly smacked it away with his blade. Ivy swung at his head just as Correlyn plowed into her from behind, knocking her into Finn and throwing them all to the ground. Rayner ran over and blocked Finn's blow just as he was about to "kill" Ivy.

Finn scrambled back to his feet and squared up with Rayner as Ivy pushed Correlyn off and grabbed for her sword. "Get up!" Rayner yelled at his sister. Ivy let an annoyed sigh escape and narrowed her eyes on her new attacker. Correlyn stood a hair shorter than Ivy, but she was a skilled fighter, and fire ran through her veins. Her cold eyes followed Ivy as she danced around Correlyn, striking blows whenever she could. Ivy stepped into her jab, landing the point of her sword on Correlyn's shoulder.

"Put that arm behind your back!" Ronin yelled to her from outside the circle. Correlyn grimaced but obeyed, now holding her sword one-handed.

Ivy swung, but Correlyn blocked her attack and quickly struck back, slicing Ivy across the ribs. She looked to Ronin, who only raised his eyebrows, and this time didn't hide his smile. Ivy feigned an injury and slowed her movements to match the imaginary blood pouring from her body. They came together in a crash, blocking and shoving one another back until Ivy swung and caught Correlyn across the chest. Ronin smirked as Correlyn dramatically clutched her bleeding heart and rolled her eyes in her head, sinking to the ground with a broad smile across her face.

Ivy giggled at her acting then turned to see Rayner and Finn still fighting one another, both of them laughing like fools. Moving silently across the yard, she jumped on Finn's back, holding her hands over his eyes. Rayner threw his head back, sending his laughter into the sky as Finn desperately swung his sword around and tried to throw Ivy from his back. "Now's your chance!" Ivy called to Rayner as Finn spun in circles. Rayner walked up to Finn and raised his sword to his throat, but Finn swiftly lifted his sword, sending it into Rayner's stomach, killing him. Rayner cackled like a fool as he lowered himself down to the ground, dying of laughter.

"Dammit, Rayner." Ivy threw all her weight back, forcing Finn to stumble and land on top of her. The air was knocked from her lungs, and Finn scrambled away, reaching for his sword in the dirt. Ivy grabbed hold of his ankle and yanked it, fighting off her own laughter as Finn's face dropped to the earth. He turned around and shook his leg, trying to get Ivy to release him, but she dug her nails in until he stopped kicking. Then, sitting up, he launched himself forward, shoving Ivy back into the dirt by her shoulders. Her head slammed into the earth as Finn sat on her legs to keep her from kicking free. Rayner and Correlyn lifted their heads from the dirt to watch as Ronin stood unmoving outside the circle, eyeing the two as they struggled.

Ivy threw up a hand and grabbed a handful of Finn's shirt, forcing him down to her chest. His face lit up with desire as she pulled closer, his eyes moving to her lips. Ivy lifted her hips and thrust Finn to one side, rolling over on top of him. Finn groaned as his back slammed into the ground, and Ivy pinned one of his hands up above his head. He had a surprised look in his eyes, but an approving smile formed on his lips, and Ivy felt herself moving toward them. "Finish him!" Rayner yelled as he sat up. Ivy caught herself before she could give in to temptation. Correlyn got up as well, and Ronin walked closer to throw a wooden sword down near Ivy.

She reached for it, keeping a watchful eye on Finn as her fingers closed around the hilt. Finn made no move and let Ivy grab the sword, smiling up at her as she pretended to stab it into his stomach. Rayner came and picked her up, twirling her around in excitement for her win. Ivy let herself laugh at the childish fight that should've been serious training. Ronin even seemed to be enjoying himself, and Ivy wondered what had given him a change of heart. In the past, their training sessions had been more serious and focused, but now Ronin seemed to relax a little and let his students have their fun.

"Excellent work, Ivy," Ronin said as he stepped into the circle. "And Lady Correlyn for coming to your partner's rescue, though it proved useless in the end." Ronin grinned at Finn, who was still brushing the dirt from his clothes.

"I think that's enough for today. Be back here tomorrow at first light. And Ser Rayner"—Ronin put a hand on his shoulder—"it only took your sister a week to figure out how to sneak up on me." Ronin raised his brow and smiled at Ivy. "It's been a week already. Perhaps that will motivate you to learn quickly." He patted Rayner on the back and walked away. Rayner gave Ivy a playful grimace and smacked her on the arm before taking Correlyn by the hand and leaving the practice yard. Finn scooped up Ivy from behind and twirled her around in the yard, praising her for her skills. He put her down, and Ivy gave him a quick peck on the cheek.

"So." Finn cleared his throat. "What do you want to do now?"

Ivy led Finn to her bedchamber and out the window, to the large branches of the maple tree. She climbed high through its limbs, which swayed underfoot as the wind rocked the tree. They chose a broad branch close to the top of the tree, and they sat down side by side. The tree gave them little privacy as new buds were just starting to form and open up on the ends of the branches, but Ivy loved the tree and was happy to sit within its maze of branches all day.

They sat with their backs to the sea, facing the main entrance of Godstone to the west. The fields outside the walls were bright with new grass, spots of yellow, pink, and blue speckling the land as flowers pushed through the soft soil. Ivy unwove her braid, letting her hair fall around her and pick up in the steady breeze. Finn's gaze was fixed on her, and Ivy lowered her eyes, hoping her wall of hair would hide the redness of her cheeks. Finn smiled at her effort and turned his eyes to the field ahead, letting his hand travel over the branch to find Ivy's. "You and Rayner have become fast friends," Ivy said.

"I like Rayner," Finn admitted with a smile. "And his wife." He turned to look at Ivy, brushing her hair behind her ear. "Do you think they'll start a family soon?" Finn asked.

"I'm not sure," Ivy answered honestly. She hadn't thought of Rayner and Correlyn starting a family anytime soon, not during a time of war. Finn seemed disappointed by Ivy's answer somehow and turned his gaze back to the green fields. Ivy would love to have a niece or nephew to teach things, like how to climb a tree, how to hold a sword, and how to steal food from tables by hiding underneath them. Ivy smiled at the thought and suddenly wished to ask Rayner when he was going to start a family. Maybe their child wouldn't grow up in a time of war and wouldn't need to learn survival skills. They could just play and be a normal child.

They sat in the tree for a long time, holding hands and talking about what the future might bring. They spoke about what Rayner's child would look like, how stubborn they would be, and what a skilled knight the child would make. Ivy talked about serving in her father's army once she was a sworn knight, and how she'd like to travel back south once it was safe again. Finn seemed to cling to every word. Ivy stopped suddenly as she noticed Finn biting his lip, and tapping his foot nervously. "What's wrong?"

Finn stopped bouncing his foot and asked, "Do you see me in your future?"

"Of course, where else would you be?"

"I mean, do you see *us*? Together?" Ivy turned her body

slightly toward Finn, trying to search his face for what he really wanted to ask.

Ivy put a finger under his chin, turning him to face her. "I told you, Finn. I'm yours, and always will be. We belong to each other." Finn brought his hands to her face and pulled her in, placing a soft kiss on her lips. He ran his fingers through her loose hair and wrapped his other hand around her waist to pull her closer. Ivy didn't think she'd ever get used to the way every kiss lit her up like a bonfire. She wanted to hold onto that feeling forever, she needed to keep him forever. Finn pulled his lips away and rested his forehead on hers, then pulled his hand away and started fumbling in his pocket before sitting back to look at her.

"Ivy," he started. "I—"

"Look," Ivy interrupted and stood on the branch, pointing to the field outside the walls.

Finn stood up with her and searched the field ahead. Ivy spotted a group of riders coming in from the west. They flew a blue flag, but Ivy couldn't make out the sigil. "Do you know them?" Finn asked.

"I'm not sure," Ivy said as she began to climb down, leaving Finn on the branch. He sighed and followed Ivy down through the arms of the maple tree until they got to her window.

They climbed through, and Ivy ran out her door and down the stairs of the tower. In the streets, knights from the wall were running toward the Hall, likely searching for her father. Ivy ran past them and looked back to see Finn following her at a distance. Ivy climbed the steps of the turret on the western wall, taking them two at a time and keeping a hand on the hilt of Promise. The riders were coming in fast, and Ivy finally saw the sigil on the flag. A horned eagle gripping a spear between its talons set against a dark blue sky. Her eyes widened, and she turned to peer over the edge as Magnus was walking with Finn toward the wall. "Father!" Ivy called down to him, and when he looked up, Ivy was frantically waving at him to hurry. She turned her focus back to the approaching riders, and as they came near, she noticed that there weren't many of them, and they appeared to be missing their leader. Magnus came up behind Ivy and saw the sigil, rapidly flapping in the wind. "Open the gates!"

CHAPTER FOURTEEN

THE WARNING

The gates opened just in time as the first horse came storming through the archway and immediately collapsed when the rider swung down. The rest of the group arrived, looking tired, dirty, and beaten. A crowd gathered in the streets, and people stopped what they were doing to see who had arrived in the kingdom.

Ivy found Finn standing with Rayner in the crowd and pushed her way through. Magnus and Queen Elana made their way to a woman atop a brown horse, and Magnus offered her a hand down. Her hair was dark brown and cut short above her shoulders, her clothes were tattered and dirty though Ivy could see they were made from the finest of silks. Her eyes were a fierce hazel, and it was clear that she'd been crying. Behind her, a young woman around Ivy's age stumbled down from her horse; her hair was long and so light it almost looked white in the sun. Her frosty eyes ran through the crowd, landing on Ivy for a moment before turning back to King Magnus. As the rest of the knights dismounted, a few more horses collapsed in the yard. Magnus looked confused as he helped the woman off her horse and bowed his head to her.

"Queen Narra." Magnus stood to look her in the eyes. "What brings you to Godstone?"

The queen of Kaspin's Keep looked around at the crowd staring at her before leaning in and whispering something to King Magnus. He nodded his head and led the queen away, the young woman following closely behind as the crowd made way for them.

"Come," Ivy said, grabbing Finn's hand and moving through the crowd.

"Where are you going?" Rayner called to her.

"To listen."

Rayner followed Ivy to the Great Hall, where Magnus and Elana sat in their places upon the dais, and Queen Narra sat with the young woman below them. Knights guarded the doors but quickly stepped aside as Rayner walked up. They let them pass before shuffling back into place. Rayner told Ivy and Finn to stay in the back while he and Correlyn moved closer to the front of the Hall. Rayner took a seat at the long table beside his father as Correlyn sat on the other side of Elana. Magnus waited for a serving girl to set down a tray of food and wine and return to the kitchen before speaking. Queen Narra poured herself a cup of wine and drained it all before taking in a shaky breath and addressing the king and queen.

"King Magnus, Queen Elana," she started, "I come to you seeking refuge for myself and my daughter, Princess Meisha." The princess stood and gave a slight bow before sitting back down and reaching for a cup. She spotted Ivy and Finn sitting a few tables back and focused her gaze on Finn before turning around.

"Why would the queen of Kaspin's Keep need refuge?" Magnus asked. "Where's King Cenric?" Meisha lowered her head as Queen Narra wiped a tear from her cheek.

"My husband is dead." The queen's voice was filled with hate.

Magnus sat back on his throne with a shocked look on his face. Rayner knew that his father and King Cenric had never gotten along and that he'd denied Magnus help years back. Rayner wondered if his father would then lend help to Cenric's family now.

Rayner spoke up. "Your Grace, can you tell us what happened?"

Queen Narra focused her gaze on Rayner while pouring another cup of wine. "Just over a week ago, a vast army of raiders came to our gates. Kaspin's Keep isn't a large kingdom, and we were clearly outnumbered, so Cenric invited their leader to have a meeting. I told him it was foolish, but he wouldn't listen, you know how stubborn he was. We never wished to play a part in this battle for the North, and so we stayed in our kingdom and waited for it to be over.

"Cenric didn't want to risk his men's lives for a fight he knew he couldn't win. King Caato is a cruel king, but he never sent his raiders our way. He and my husband had an understanding. Should King Caato conquer the North as intended, my husband was going to stand behind him and help him protect it so long as we got to stay in control of Kaspin's Keep. Well, I'm not sure what made King Caato change his mind, but when I saw those raiders forming up outside our walls, I knew something was wrong."

Magnus tightened his fists around the armrest of his throne as the queen told her story. Rayner too felt angry by this sudden information. That a king from the North would willingly help the raiders take over their homes burned a hole in his core.

Queen Narra continued. "My husband sent out a small party to bring back the leader of the army, and we all met in our courtroom. The man marched in with a group of his raiders, some in armor, others in leather vests. One knight hid his face the whole time and stood with the leader. I thought he looked like a demon spirit from old children's stories. I'd never seen a helm with horns like that."

Rayner choked on his wine. His eyes went wide, and his heart began to jump and leap through his ribs. His palms started sweating, and he instinctively put a hand to the scar at his side. Rayner had had nightmares of the horned knight ever since that day in Ashton, though he tried to hide his fear on the surface. Magnus seemed to notice his son's reaction and turned back to the queen with fire in his eyes.

"Describe this knight," Magnus demanded.

"Like I said, his face was hidden, but the armor was expensive, black as night, and the helm had horns forged on it that ran down the back," Queen Narra ran her hands over her head to show how long the horns were, then turned to Rayner. "Do you know him?"

"Not yet," he said quietly, then got up to fill his cup.

"Please, continue with your story," Queen Elana persisted.

"Their leader demanded that my husband give up Kaspin's Keep in the name of the true king. My husband, of course, was baffled, as King Caato had promised him that we would stay in our kingdom. The man said that there had been a change of plans and a new deal. They argued for a long time, back and forth until the man grew impatient. He signaled to his knights who quickly barred the door of the court and formed up behind him.

"The man came up to Meisha and me, eyeing us with a wry smile on his face before telling us to step down from the dais. I grabbed Meisha and moved to one of the lower tables as the man took my seat beside Cenric. He pulled a dagger from his boot and began picking under his nails with the blade as he spoke. He told me I had to deliver a message and that it was crucial. I told him I'd do whatever he wanted as I feared for my family. He said, 'You will ride for Godstone tonight and warn King Magnus the Mighty of my arrival. He won't know when I'm coming, but I want him to know *who* is coming. I am inevitable.' I asked him who he was, and he stood up, smiling at me before sinking his blade into my husband's neck and dragging it across his throat."

Queen Narra put a hand over her mouth and shut her eyes, forcing her tears back.

Princess Meisha stood up, anger covering her face like a blanket. "This man knows you, and your quarrels with him cost my father his life!" she snapped at King Magnus. "As my father struggled to die on his own throne, that man came toward me and wiped his blood on my dress and whispered his name into my ear before telling us to run."

Magnus sat forward on his throne, waiting for the princess to utter his name. "He called himself Helvarr the Banished and said that he was the true king of the North, and he's coming to take his seat."

The king turned to his wife with a worried expression as Queen Elana placed a hand on his shoulder. Rayner wasn't shocked but angry.

Ivy abruptly stood, and Meisha turned around to look at her. "You know him too?" she asked.

Ivy walked closer. "I watched him kill someone important to me too," Ivy said.

"I'm going to kill him," Meisha declared, glancing back at Finn, who was coming toward Ivy.

"Not before I do." Ivy turned around just as Finn walked up. She grabbed his arm and led him from the Hall, Meisha keeping her eyes focused on him the whole time.

"Magnus." Elana gently shook his shoulder until he sat back up. "What should we do?" Everyone stayed silent in the Hall, waiting for the king to answer. Rayner remembered asking his father what he'd do the next time he encountered Helvarr, and that his father didn't really have an answer. Magnus then stood up and ran his fingers through his beard.

"Queen Narra, Princess Meisha, I'm sorry for your loss. And I'm sorry that you were forced from your home, but there is only so much protection I can offer you. I have written to my allies and heard nothing in return, and I fear for their safety. You may stay, but you also saw the army with your own eyes, and you know what's coming."

"Where else are we to go?" Queen Narra asked. "This needs to end, and you can have my knights that managed to escape with us."

"Very well," Magnus said. "I'll send new hawks out to my allies and warn them of the news." Queen Narra let out a sigh of relief and thanked the king and queen for their help. Rayner pushed out of his chair and walked out of the Hall, not saying a word, Correlyn following behind.

After Queen Elana took Queen Narra and Princess Meisha off to their rooms to settle in, Magnus sat on his throne for a long time, listening to the chaos inside his head. He couldn't imagine seeing Helvarr again after all these years, and the guilt of his actions weighed on his mind. He couldn't help but blame himself; if he hadn't banished Helvarr, then maybe none of this would have happened. He wouldn't have needed to send his daughter away, Ser Osmund would still be alive, and Rayner wouldn't have been targeted. King Caato might have never gotten as far in this battle if he didn't have a leader who was bloodthirsty for revenge. Helvarr would do anything to win back his place here, and Magnus knew Helvarr would kill him and his family to take what he wanted.

Magister Ivann wrote down every word that Magnus spoke, then sealed the letters with the king's maple leaf seal before tying them to the hawk's legs. They walked along the northern wall as the sun was setting, and lifted the first hawk, letting him jump and fly away toward Tordenfall where Earl Rorik lived. "Do you think they're still there?" Magnus asked as he watched the hawk flap it's way higher into the darkening sky.

"We need them to be," Magister Ivann said softly.

They walked around to the west side of the wall to send off the other hawk to Lord Kevan at the Twisted Tower. Magnus rechecked the binding before thrusting his arm up and letting the hawk soar away. The king stood there watching the hawk as Magister Ivann made his way down the stone steps of the wall. The bird appeared as if it were ablaze in the dying sunlight, its long brown feathers swiftly carrying it through the sky. Magnus was about to turn his back away when he noticed the bird diving toward the ground. His eyes widened as the hawk crashed into a field of flowers.

He ran down the stairs, past his knights who yelled something at him from behind but didn't follow. He mounted the first horse he saw and ordered the gates open as he galloped through the yard. The horse squeezed through the wooden doors and burst out into the dark field. Magnus scanned the ground around him, searching for the fallen hawk. He spotted the patch of blue flowers that held the bird and pulled back on the reins to stop his horse. Magnus jumped down and swiftly walked over to the hawk and picked it up.

Ser Caster came trotting up with a few knights who quickly surrounded their king and drew their swords, not knowing what was going on. "Your Grace?" Ser Caster dismounted and went to stand next to the king. An arrow pierced the hawk through the chest, the point coming out of its sternum, and the king's letter was still bound to the bird's leg.

"Our letters haven't been getting out," Magnus told Ser Caster. "We haven't heard from Rorik or Kevan because they never received our messages." His voice was growing hot with anger. Magnus took the letter from the hawk and dropped it back into the flowers. He lifted his head and scanned the Blackwoods and surrounding fields but saw no one.

"Why wouldn't they attack if they've been lurking around the kingdom?" Ser Caster said as he put a hand to the hilt of his sword.

"Because there is no 'they.' It must be a scout who's been killing my hawks." Magnus balled his fists and commanded the knights to search the grounds for the rest of the hawks and collect the letters they carried.

"What will you do now?" Ser Caster asked.

"I have no choice but to go in person. I need my allies, and if I can't get a message out, then I need to go get them."

"But, Your Grace, I'm sure that's precisely what the raiders want, for you to be exposed. Why else would they have killed your hawks?"

"I have no choice. They either shot down my messenger birds to get me to leave my walls or because their army is already coming, and the raiders know they can take Godstone if I have no allies to help me hold it. What does it matter which one was their plan? It worked, and I must leave to bring back men if we have any hope of keeping our home."

Ser Caster lowered his eyes and nodded before kicking his horse and joining his men in the search. As Magnus held the arrow in his hand, running his fingers over the feathers, a sick feeling rose from his stomach, but he pushed it back down and broke the arrow in half, scattering the pieces into the sea of flowers. He got back on the horse, who was eating the blue flowers, blissfully unaware of the situation. Magnus pulled on the reins and trotted back toward Godstone, looking back over his shoulder to make sure he wouldn't find an arrow embedded in his back.

CHAPTER FIFTEEN

SEPARATE PATHS

The steady thumping of the supply wagons over the rocky street echoed off the walls of Godstone. Horses whinnied and stomped their hooves, anxious to get on the road. All able-bodied knights were assigned to either Rayner's group or the king's, and they would be setting off in opposite directions today. Ser Caster insisted he stay by the king's side and had put together a small army of his best men to accompany Magnus west to the Twisted Tower. Magnus told Rayner to choose the men he wanted and to ride for Tordenfall and bring back Earl Rorik and his army.

Rayner was securing his new armor while Correlyn checked her horse's saddle as they prepared to leave. Ivy and Finn were chosen to go along with Rayner, for which her father had seemed grateful and relieved.

As promised, Magnus had armor made for Finn and Ivy after they returned from Grey Raven, though Finn respectfully declined, preferring the lighter leather armor over metal. Ivy was happy to wear her armor, which was light and sleek. The black metal formed precisely to her body and ran halfway down her arms. She also had metal shin guards that strapped on over her boots. The weight wasn't as bad as Ivy had expected it would be. She fussed with the leather straps of her shoulder plate as Finn came up behind her. He wrapped an arm around her waist and turned Ivy to face him.

The army was getting ready to leave, and Rayner was already mounted on his horse, talking with Correlyn and Ronin, who pointed to a map. Ivy leaned in to kiss Finn, but he pulled away and closed his eyes. "I'm not going with you," he said quietly. Ivy stepped back, furrowing her brow.

"What do you mean you're not coming with me?"

"I want to go with your father," Finn answered. Ivy crossed her arms and said nothing, demanding an explanation with her stare. "I've been looking at your father's maps, and the Twisted Tower lays directly below the Spearhead Mountains, only twenty leagues from the shore." Ivy let her arms hang down as she realized what Finn was telling her.

"You want to go home?" Her voice felt constricted.

Finn placed his hands over the cool armor that covered Ivy's arms. "I need to see it. If there are people there—"

"I'm going with you, Finn," Ivy interrupted.

"No," he answered quickly. "You have to stay with Rayner; you'll be safe with him."

"And what about you? You think my father is going out there because it's safe? Finn, let me come. Please."

Finn shut his eyes and hung his head but again told Ivy that she shouldn't come.

Ivy felt tears starting to form in her eyes as she looked at Finn, who wouldn't meet her gaze.

"Ivy, Finn!" Rayner called to them from his horse. "Are you ready to go? I want to get there by tomorrow morning."

Ivy moved away from Finn and started walking toward her horse Cassius. "Finn isn't coming," Ivy told Rayner before tugging on Cass's saddle and checking the straps as a tear fell from her eye.

Magnus came up behind her. Queen Elana stayed in the crowd that was forming to see them off. "Are you set to go?" Magnus asked his son. Rayner shrugged and looked at Ivy for confirmation, but she wouldn't take her tear-filled eyes away from the saddle.

"Ivy, please," Finn said, placing a hand on her shoulder, but she shook it off.

"What's going on?" Magnus asked.

"King Magnus," Finn began, "I want to come with you instead."

"Why?"

"My childhood home sits close to the Twisted Tower, and I want to go there to see if there are any people left. I can't leave them again."

Ivy had told Magnus the story of what happened to Finn's family, and she felt great sorrow for him at that moment. Finn tried to catch her eye, but Ivy looked back down, pulling at the straps of her saddle. "Very well," Magnus said. "You can come with me, but we will all go to Tonsburg, you won't go off on your own." Finn thanked the king and moved around the horse to say goodbye to Ivy. Rayner moved his horse away, giving them some privacy, and went to form up at the head of the group.

Finn stood before Ivy, his russet eyes warm as she finally looked up at him.

"Ivy." He took a step toward her.

Ivy sniffed her tears and turned away from him, not wanting Finn to see the fear in her eyes. She felt his presence behind her, and then his arms gently slid around her waist and his chest pressed into her back as Finn brought his lips to her ear. "I'll be all right," he whispered. "Your father is King Magnus the Mighty. How do you think he got that name?" Ivy didn't answer him as she stood still within his arms. "If there were survivors then I need to help them, I need to see what has become of my home."

Ivy lowered her head, not knowing what to say. She didn't want to be separated from Finn, and what if something happened while they were apart? Ivy shoved those fears down before they could take over. Finn squeezed her tighter and rested his chin on her shoulder.

"Do you really think your father would let anything happen to me? Knowing he would have to face your wrath upon his return?" His tone was playful and light. "Ivy the Feared." Finn deepened his voice and shook her slightly. "Ivy the Vengeful, Ivy the Slayer." She stifled a giggle as he continued, lowering his voice further and turning her around. "Ivy the Beauty, Ivy the Honorable, Ivy of the Maple Tree." Finn wiped her tears as a small smile started to form on her lips.

"I know you have to go," she finally said. "Promise me you'll be careful?"

"I promise, my beautiful Ivy. I'll come back to you."

Ivy threw her arms around Finn, burying her face in the crook of his neck, and breathing him in, locking in the scent— forest and rainwater. Rayner called to Ivy, telling her they had to go. "I love you, Finn," Ivy whispered in his ear.

He turned his head and kissed her cheek, speaking as his lips lingered on her skin. "I love you so much." Finn pulled back just enough to find her lips with his, kissing her deeply. Ivy grabbed his leather chest armor, crushing herself against him as Finn's hands cupped her cheeks, and his lips moved slowly over hers, in loving, tender sweeps. When they came apart, Finn brought her hand to his lips, kissing her knuckles.

"I'll see you soon, my Ivy."

Finn lowered her hand, hesitating before letting go of her fingers and turning to join Magnus' group.

Ivy mounted Cassius as her mother came over, placing a hand on Ivy's leg. "Stay safe, my darling, and look out for one another." Elana looked over to Rayner and Correlyn sitting in the front of the line.

"We will," Ivy replied, bending down to kiss her mother on the cheek. Magnus came over and kissed Ivy goodbye, running his fingers over the golden fabric tucked into Ivy's belt.

"Stay safe, sweetling. And don't worry about Finn, I'll look after him."

"Thank you, father."

Magnus smiled up at Ivy, then patted her boot and moved over to where Elana stood.

Ivy watched her parents say goodbye to one another as Ser Caster's men started to move out through the gates.

Rayner brought his horse alongside Ivy's as they watched their parents embrace one another. Elana pulled Magnus in and placed a soft kiss on his lips before moving to his ear, and Magnus's eyes lit up. Ivy turned to Rayner, who had the same wondering look on his face. When Ivy turned back, her mother was glowing with happiness, and Magnus kissed his wife again before kneeling down in front of her. Ivy felt her heart skip as she watched her father's hand rest on the queen's still-flat stomach. Rayner grabbed Ivy's shoulder and squeezed it, a broad smile forming on both their mouths. Magnus turned toward his children and smiled as Queen Elana wrapped her hands around her stomach and gave a slight nod to Rayner and Ivy.

The two groups forked apart outside the walls of Godstone. Ivy and Rayner waved to their father and Finn as they turned their party west and watched them disappear into the Blackwoods. Rayner, Correlyn, and Ivy rode abreast at the front of the line as Ronin traveled alone in the back.

"How long do you think Mother has known?" Rayner leaned forward to see his sister, who sat on the other side of Correlyn.

"I don't know. She must have waited to tell Father until she was sure," Ivy said, taking an apple from her saddlebag and tossing it to Rayner before reaching for another one to offer Correlyn.

"I hope it's a boy," Rayner said as he chewed a chunk of apple.

"It'll be strange to have a baby sibling so much younger," Ivy admitted.

"Mother has always wanted more children, and it seems

the gods have finally answered her prayers." Rayner motioned his hand toward the sky above.

Ivy leaned closer to Correlyn so Rayner couldn't hear her. "Perhaps it will be good practice for Rayner to take care of a baby." Correlyn smiled, looking over her shoulder at her husband.

"We've talked about it," Correlyn replied in a hushed voice. "But I think we will wait; there's no rush."

They rode all day, hugging the coastline until the sun was pushed from the sky, and they found a spot next to the beach and made camp. Rayner commanded his knights to unload the wagon and set up the tents while he gathered some wood for a fire. Ronin went with Rayner to help gather wood as Ivy walked through the tall grass that led to the beach. She took off her boots before stepping into the cold sand, letting her feet sink into it. The beach was narrow, and tall weeds hid their camp from the view of the sea. Ivy heard the distant rolling of thunder as heavy clouds moved in from the north and the wind picked up. She braided her hair and tied it off with a leather cord before pulling Promise from its scabbard.

Ivy squared up with an invisible attacker and started dancing her way through the sand, kicking up clouds of it as she slid and twirled around. Her thoughts went to Finn, and Ivy pictured him standing before her, smiling as he swung his sword and blocked her blows. His light brown eyes sunk deep into Ivy, pulling her closer until they were inches apart. "Ivy!" a voice called to her from up the hill. Ivy opened her eyes and realized she was standing still, Promise hanging heavily in her hand.

She turned her gaze and saw Correlyn making her way

down, her black hair swirling like smoke around her face. "Would you like a partner?" she asked as she came closer.

"Where's Rayner?"

Correlyn waved her hand away dismissively and started to unlace her boots. "He and Ronin are busy craning their necks over maps," Correlyn said with a smile. She wore light black armor as well, and so they decided to keep their real blades and fight until one of them managed to touch the other's armor with a sword. Ivy waited while Correlyn pinned her hair back in a knot and drew her sword. They tapped their swords together and squared up, each waiting for the other to attack. Ronin had taught them his style of fighting, and they knew not to strike first, to let their attacker come to them. But Ronin wasn't watching, and the anticipation ran through Ivy, moving her legs forward to jab at Correlyn.

She smiled and slid out of the way, piercing her sword at Ivy's chest plate. Correlyn had been taught to fight from a young age and was more experienced than Ivy. Correlyn stepped closer and leaned into her sword as Ivy turned her body just in time and smacked Correlyn's blade away. The two danced around each other, twirling their blades in the cold night air until Correlyn drove hers into the sand and kicked up a cloud, forcing Ivy to snap her eyes shut. She backed away, holding her sword out in front of her as she tried to wipe the sand from her eyes. Ivy could hear Correlyn laughing and couldn't help but smile as the sand fell from her eyes in salty tears. Ivy was glad to have Correlyn as a sister.

When she could finally open her eyes, Ivy spotted Correlyn running away down the beach, looking over her shoulder and laughing. She took off in a sprint, letting the wind push her from behind. Correlyn bolted left and ran into the tall grasses, still holding her sword as she ran. Ivy jumped into the grass and pushed her way forward, keeping her eyes peeled for any movement. After a moment, she slowed to a walk and crouched down deeper into the grass, keeping Promise tight at her side. The wind snaked its way through the grass, forcing Ivy to swivel her head in every direction. A sea bird called out from above, and Ivy tilted her head toward the sky, taking her eyes off the parting grass beside her.

Correlyn leaped onto Ivy's back, knocking both of them down and rolling them out into the sand. Correlyn kicked Promise from Ivy's hand. They were both laughing as Ivy got to her feet, staying in a crouching position and eyeing Correlyn, who stood with her sword between them. Ivy quickly looked to where Promise lay in the sand and grabbed a handful, keeping her eyes locked with Correlyn's. In one swift motion, Ivy flung the sand at Correlyn, who instinctively threw up her hands and rolled away before scrambling to get to her feet. The sand was slick beneath her bare feet, and Ivy slipped and crashed down right in front of Promise. She reached her hand out but heard the clap of metal against her back and turned to see Correlyn standing over her with a wide smile.

"Nice move." Correlyn offered a hand to Ivy. "I think you might be better than Rayner," Correlyn said with a playful wink. Ivy gave her a gentle punch in the arm, and the two walked back toward camp, laughing about nothing and talking about everything.

CHAPTER SIXTEEN

FALLING THUNDER

S ometime late the next morning, their party ascended a
hill, and Ivy laid eyes on Tordenfall for the first time.
Rayner moved the group along, but Ivy sat still as a
statue, taking in the view. Tordenfall sat pushed back from
the sea in what looked like a bowl. The land rose around the
town in rolling hills that resembled the choppy water of the
sea. Rayner had thought he heard a storm approaching as they
climbed the hill, but now Ivy saw that it was not thunder, but
a massive waterfall.

The water cascaded down a rocky cliffside and seemed
to disappear before touching the ground, carried off by the
constant winds from the sea. The waterfall enveloped the
town in a thin mist, and Ivy could see small pools of water
that pushed a dense fog up into the sky. As Ivy kicked Cassius
to continue forward, the constant thunder of the water
echoed off the many surrounding hills, and Ivy wondered
if the people still heard the rumble of the falls after living
here their whole lives. All the buildings were made from pale

driftwood or dark logs from trees that must have been felled further north. The land had no trees surrounding it, but the hills were rich with the greenest grass Ivy ever saw.

As their party entered the bowl that held the town, Rayner swung down from his horse and offered a hand to Correlyn. Ivy jumped off Cass and led him by the reins through the wooden archway of the town. Strange markings were carved into the wood that Ivy couldn't make sense of.

Ronin moved silently alongside Ivy as they walked deeper into the town. People rose from the hot pools of water to see their guests, and others came out from their homes while children pushed past them to run alongside the knights in the street. Ivy studied the people, recalling how silly she felt at the Feast of Winter wearing that gown when Earl Rorik and his people dressed so plainly. Their clothes were various shades of dark green, black, or brown, and Ivy noticed that most of them had light-colored hair. A man stepped out into the street and crossed his arms as Rayner approached. Ivy squinted her eyes before recognizing the red-bearded man with blond hair that stood towering over Rayner.

"Rayner Blackbourne," Grimm said coldly.

"Grimm Roriksson," Rayner replied, the same frosty snap in his voice. Grimm took a step forward then cracked a smile and held out a hand for Rayner. The two shook hands and patted one another on the back. "Welcome, Blackbournes." Grimm nodded to Ivy, who made her way to Rayner. "To what do we owe the pleasure?"

"I need to speak with Earl Rorik immediately," Rayner said.

"Where's King Magnus?" Grimm searched the sea of knights standing in the street.

"We're here on my father's behalf. He's traveling west to the Twisted Tower to retrieve Lord Kevan and his people." Grimm stroked his beard and eyed Correlyn. "Surely you remember Correlyn Reiburn?" Rayner said, placing a hand on the small of her back. "She's my wife." Grimm smiled and angled his head to her.

"Welcome, Lady Reiburn," then, to the rest of the group, "come. I'll take you to my father." Rayner ordered his men to water the horses and set up camp outside the town.

They followed Grimm through the dirt streets, Ronin keeping silent and watching everything as they went. Ivy leaned closer to Ronin, whose gaze was focused on the back of Grimm's head. "Relax, Ronin," Ivy whispered. "Earl Rorik and my father have been friends for years; our families are bonded through them."

"I'm not your family," Ronin said coldly and walked ahead of Ivy. She scrunched her brows together and glared at him from behind. Ronin had been even quieter after the news of King Cenric's murder, and Ivy knew he was thinking of his son, Helvarr, and the monster he had become. She sighed and let the comment go, knowing that it was hard for Ronin to face the inevitable reality of his son's fall.

They came upon a massive wooden building, far grander than her father's Great Hall back home. The building towered over all the others, and the doors were tall enough for a horse to walk through with Grimm standing on its back. Two wooden swords crossed above the door, and elaborate carvings in the wood of the doors depicted a man fighting a giant serpent, which was thrashing its way under the waves of a small boat. More strange markings lined the door frame, and the carvings were painted red or white. As Grimm opened the massive doors, Ivy's breath caught in her throat.

The walls were covered in beautifully stitched rugs, and banners with intricate patterns or depictions of different animals, some of which Ivy recognized, and some she didn't. From the large, vaulted ceiling hung deer antlers, bound together and fixed with metal plates on the tips that held white candles, their wax dripping down into the antlers. Wooden pillars parted the two sides and created a walkway that led to the dais. Lines of tables and benches sat on either side of the hall, and a stone firepit rose from the wooden floor just in front of the dais.

Earl Rorik stood up as Grimm approached and announced the arrival of the Blackbournes. The earl was just as Ivy remembered, with chestnut hair that was woven into cords and fell down his back. The sides of his scalp were shaved and he had tattoos that looked similar to the ones Grimm had on the sides of his head. His beard fell over his chest, and a small cord pulled it together halfway down, with tiny silver balls hanging from the ends of the string. The earl had come to Godstone at the start of winter, and Ivy never saw his people in anything but heavy furs. Now they wore lighter clothing, and the earl had his sleeves rolled up, revealing blue tattoos that crawled up both arms and poked out of his neckline.

Queen Ingrid sat beside her husband's throne, wearing a long moss-colored dress, and her same rope-like hair was tied back. Ingrid smiled at Ivy as they came closer to the dais, and Earl Rorik spread his arms out and welcomed them. He signaled to a young woman to bring wine and food over and asked Rayner and his group to have a seat. It was customary for the northern clans to offer food and drink before any business was done, showing that you are under the protection of their house and sealing trust in one another. Rayner motioned for everyone to take a sip of wine and eat a bite of food before beginning.

"Now." Rorik's voice boomed in the empty hall. "Welcome to Tordenfall, Ser Rayner, Lady Ivy, Lady Correlyn, and who is this?" Rorik motioned to Ronin, who was seated at the end of the table.

"This is Ronin," Rayner said. "He's our trainer and an old friend to my father."

"Why does my friend Magnus not grace me with his presence?" Rorik asked, taking a seat on his throne, which was modest and plain with a tall back.

"You offered my father your services when you left. I'm here on his behalf to request that you keep your word and come back to Godstone with us." Grimm took a seat beside Ivy, helped himself to a cup of wine, and listened as Rayner told a brief version of what had happened in Kaspin's Keep.

"My father has been trying to get a message to you, but someone has been shooting down our hawks," Rayner explained.

"King Magnus the Mighty, the last king in the North," Rorik said, his gaze focused on the liquid in his cup.

"Earl Rorik," Rayner said, standing up. "My father isn't only asking for your help; he fears for your safety as well. The raiders have a massive army, and they could be on their way to Godstone right now. My father is rallying his allies and asking that they come to Godstone for their own protection. We can't hope to defeat them alone, and if you stay, then you will be exposed." Rorik turned to his wife, whose eyes told him a message only he could read.

"Who else is your father gathering?" Ingrid directed the question to Rayner.

"Lord Kevan of the Twisted Tower," he answered, sliding his eyes to Ingrid.

"And House Reiburn, surely?" Ingrid nodded her head to Correlyn, who averted her gaze and stared down at her empty cup. Rayner looked at his wife and placed a hand on her shoulder, giving her a gentle squeeze.

"House Reiburn is gone," he said, his voice constricted.

"The Lady Oharra?" Rorik asked.

Correlyn grabbed the flagon of wine and poured herself a full cup. "I don't know where my mother is," she admitted before taking a long swallow of the red wine. Rorik said nothing and took another sip of his wine.

"Earl Rorik," Ivy began, "I know this isn't your fight, and you don't know the man who has caused my family so much pain. But we need your help. Helvarr . . ." Ivy choked on his name and balled her fists before continuing. "Helvarr is a monster, but he's powerful and strategic." The words tasted of bile in her mouth. "He sent a raider to capture me when I was in the South, he sent an assassin to kill my brother. I watched him murder someone who was like a second father to me. Who knows what he might have done to Lady Oharra?" Ivy stopped herself and looked at Correlyn, who gave Ivy a reassuring smile and nodded for her to continue.

"He's been moving his men around the land like pieces on

a Taffl board. He's been one step ahead the whole time, and now he's closing in on our home. He means to take Godstone and crown himself king. What do you think will become of your lands should we let that happen?" Ivy lifted her chin and stared right at Earl Rorik. He didn't seem upset but rather nodded his head slowly, taking in what Ivy said. Rayner sat back down and gave Ivy a prideful smile as she continued. "Will you sit on your throne and allow the world around you to burn? Or will you keep your promise to my father and help us put out the flame before it can catch?" Ivy's hands were shaking as she sat back down, running them over one another.

Ingrid lifted her brows and turned to her husband with a smirk on her lips. Grimm gave Ivy a reassuring pat on the back, rattling her bones with his forceful touch. Rorik stood abruptly and eyed Ivy as he descended the two steps and stood on the other side of the table, looking down at her. Out of the corner of her eye, Ivy saw her brother shift in his seat, but she refused to look away from Earl Rorik. He put his large hands on the table, leaning down to look into Ivy's purple eyes.

She stood to meet his gaze, feeling the pounding of her heart and wondering if she had insulted him. Rorik stared into her before his lips curled into a smile, and he tilted his head back, sending a burst of loud laughter from his belly into the rafters. Ivy looked at Grimm in confusion and balled her fists again, waiting for the earl to mock her. "You've got a fire in your belly," Rorik exclaimed. Ingrid grinned at Ivy from her throne and tilted her head as if seeing Ivy for the first time. Ivy released her fists and felt a wave of relief. Rorik held up a cup for Ivy to take and clacked it against his own before downing the wine in one gulp. Rorik settled his laughter and sat down across from Ivy, red wine dripping down his brown beard.

"I will help you," he said. "We will come to Godstone and help protect it against this monster of a man." Rayner relaxed his shoulders and looked over at his sister, raising an eyebrow at her and smiling. Ivy looked at Ronin, expecting to see his stern face boring a hole in her, but a thin smile formed on his lips, and Ivy smiled at her trainer in return. "But I will not leave my other clansmen exposed," Rorik continued. "If it is like you say, then no one is safe, and I must protect my other allies as well."

"How many more clans are in the North?" Correlyn asked. Ingrid stood and went over to one of the fabric hangings on the wall. She pulled it down, and Grimm cleared away the cups so his mother could set down the fabric. Everyone stood to get a better look, and Ivy saw that it was a map. Ingrid ran a slender finger over the cloth and up to Tordenfall before moving it north along the coast.

"There is White Fin," she said, tapping her finger on the edge of the land. "And west of that is the people of the Moon Wood," she said, following the shoreline with her finger. Ivy let her eyes keep going and found Tonsburg at the edge of the western coast. She felt a stab of pain as she feared for what Finn might find there.

"What about Moat Birger?" Ivy asked, pointing just above Tonsburg.

"Those people were wiped out years ago," Grimm said, coming to stand over Ivy. "Right after the fall of Tonsburg." Ivy snapped her eyes shut and pictured Finn walking through the ruins of his home. If Moat Birger was gone as well, then Finn had no hope of finding survivors. Rayner put a hand over Ivy's, and she opened her eyes again and plopped back down on the bench.

"How quickly can they get here?" Rayner asked the earl.

"I can send out hawks right now, but the people of the Moon Wood will take at least a week to get here."

Rayner ran a hand through his hair and studied the map.

"It will take my father at least a week to get to Lord Kevan, perhaps another day or so to rally his men," said Rayner. "We should all be back in Godstone before my father's party arrives."

"You will wait here until the clans arrive?" Grimm asked Rayner.

"Yes. We're stronger in numbers." Rayner turned to Earl Rorik. "Are you sure they'll come?"

"They will come," Rorik answered plainly.

"Then send your hawks, and we'll wait."

CHAPTER SEVENTEEN

THE CLANS

Over a week later, Rayner led the last three clans of the North back to Godstone. The White Fin clan arrived within days, and Rorik explained everything to them in detail while they waited for the people of the Moon Wood to arrive. The White Fin people were mostly fishermen and farmers who weren't equipped to hold their land against an attack, and Rorik feared that if they didn't come, they would suffer the same fate as Tonsburg and Moat Birger. They had no leader but a council who advised on behalf of all their people. They looked much like Rorik's people with long fair hair and some with similar tattoos on their skin.

A few days later, the Moon Wood clan arrived at Tordenfall, and they set off that same day. The Moon Wood people were led by a woman whom Ivy thought at first to be an old woman, but as Ivy got closer, she saw that the woman was only a few years older than she was. Her name was Kyatta, and she was beautiful.

Kyatta had a blue tattoo in the center of her forehead that was an upside-down crescent moon with small blue dots falling from the moon down the bridge of her nose. Her hair was stark white, and her eyes were such a light shade of blue that Ivy thought for a moment they were as white as her hair. Her hands were covered in blue tattoos that went up into her sleeves. No one else in the clan had white hair, save for the elders. Many dressed in various shades of blues from the deepest blue to the brightest, but their clothes were similar styling to Rorik's people. They rode on white horses and carried spears and bows instead of swords.

Rayner rode with Correlyn and Grimm at the front of the army while Ivy stayed back with Ronin and kept catching Kyatta staring at her out of the corner of her eye. "Your father will be proud," Ronin told Ivy.

Ivy shrugged. "Rayner would have convinced the earl just as well."

"But he didn't, you did," Ronin said through a smile and placed a hand on Ivy's shoulder. She lowered her eyes and twisted the reins in her hands.

"What will you do if you see Helvarr again?" she asked, keeping her gaze off of him.

"I don't have an answer for that, I can't know what I'll do in a moment that hasn't happened yet."

"Are you going to tell him you're his father?" Ivy lifted her head to Ronin.

"Perhaps, that is if he doesn't kill me first."

"You think he'll kill you?" Ivy furrowed her brow, not wanting to think of someone else dying at the hands of Helvarr. Ronin didn't answer and focused his gaze straight ahead. Ivy swallowed a lump in her throat and asked, "Do you think he'll fight my father?"

"I think he'll do anything to get what he wants," Ronin said, meeting Ivy's gaze. Ivy sighed, and they rode in silence the rest of the way home.

As soon as they entered the gates of Godstone, Ivy swung down from Cass and took off running toward her mother, who was walking down the street. Ivy hugged her mother and told her how happy she was about having another sibling. They came apart, and Ivy asked after her father and Finn. "They aren't back yet," Elana said, placing a gentle hand on her daughter's cheek.

Elana and Rayner coordinated sleeping arrangements for the earl's family and the leader of the Moon Wood people. Godstone was a sizeable kingdom, but there wasn't sufficient room for the army that had come back with them. Rayner guessed that their numbers had grown by the thousands with the three clans. The people of White Fin were happy to make camp on the beaches, which allowed more room for the Moon Wood people and those of Tordenfall to stay within the walls. Rayner and Correlyn moved to the room just under the king and queen's within the central tower, and Elana asked Ivy if it would be all right to move Finn's bed into her room. Ivy agreed, and Finn's room, which was Rayner's old room was given to Kyatta. The rest of the tower was packed with Earl Rorik's family and Kyatta's most trusted advisors, while the remainder of their clans spread out around the kingdom.

Ivy spent her days on the western wall of Godstone, carefully watching the horizon for her father's banner. She stayed late into the night, any hope for sleep drifting off in the occasional wind. A full moon lit the field in front of her, and Ivy felt her eyes burning from lack of sleep. She rubbed them and looked up to see Kyatta coming down the wall toward Ivy. She looked like a ghost in the pale moonlight with her dark clothes and white hair blowing around her face.

Kyatta stood alongside Ivy and said nothing at first, turning her head back to look at the moon. Ivy didn't know what to say, so stayed silent as well. "Did you know that my people have not fought a battle in over one hundred years?" Kyatta's voice surprised Ivy. It was warm and friendly. Ivy shook her head and waited for Kyatta to speak again. "We don't like to leave our land or get involved with others' bloodshed."

"Then, why did you come?" Ivy asked.

"I saw you in a dream." Kyatta turned to look at Ivy, her icy eyes lit up in the moonlight. "I was guided through my dream by the gods, and they led me to you."

Ivy furrowed her brow. "I don't understand."

"Neither do I," she admitted. "I can't always read the signs of the gods, but I know what one looks like."

"What did you see?"

Kyatta sighed and twirled a lock of white hair between her inked hands. "I saw a maple tree pushing into your back and an army at your feet. I saw a bird falling from the sky and an eagle with an arrow piercing its heart before it burst into flames. Thunder and fire fell from the sky and consumed everything around it." Kyatta's voice drifted off as if she saw it. Ivy's palms were sweating, and her heart sped up, but she kept her composure.

"Is that a riddle?" she asked.

"It's no riddle," Kyatta said, focusing her gaze on the empty field.

"But it doesn't make any sense," Ivy persisted.

Kyatta smiled slightly and raised her eyebrows, shrugging her shoulders. "Perhaps not." Then she turned on her heels and walked away before Ivy could say anything else. The words scrambled in her head as Ivy stood on the wall through the night, watching the horizon and saying a silent prayer to the gods for her father and Finn.

CHAPTER EIGHTEEN

THE TWISTED TOWER

Finn rode beside the king as Eclipse's hooves squished in the mud underfoot. A light spring rain fell from the grey clouds above, and Finn pulled his hood tighter around his face. The rain was cold against his cheeks, and he feared that it would make him ill again. It had been a few weeks since Finn's bout with the fever and since he buried the memory of his brother's murder. After eight years, Finn couldn't believe that he was finally returning to his childhood home. His mind had been clouded with thoughts since they left Godstone, and he feared what he might find when they arrived.

Magnus handed a small leather pouch to Finn, who took it without saying anything and grabbed a large piece of dried venison. He tore off a piece of meat with his teeth and let his mind wander to the thought of Ivy. Finn tried to push away the guilt of leaving her. He didn't want Ivy to worry about him, and though she saw how much it broke Finn to bury Thor's memory, he knew that whatever he found back home would only bring more demons. Yet he needed to see it; his past was calling to him.

The Twisted Tower came into view on the horizon, its massive tower standing like a sword to the sky. The king called out to Ser Caster, who then ordered a few knights to ride out ahead of the group to clear the field before they crossed. Their group came to a halt as the knights rode off, growing smaller before disappearing into the misty rain. Magnus moved his horse closer to Eclipse and tried to catch Finn's eye, while Finn tried to bury his face deep in his hood. "Are you feeling well?" Magnus asked.

"I'm fine," Finn replied, with as much conviction as he could muster.

"You've been quiet for the whole journey," Magnus started but then didn't speak again. To Finn, it seemed that Magnus had been too preoccupied with what was happening to get to know Finn, though now the king seemed to be making an effort.

Finn let his hood fall away and buried his hands in his pockets.

"I don't know you very well," Magnus said. "And that's my fault. I've watched you and Ivy together, and I can see in her eyes how happy she is."

Finn smiled at that. Since their departure, he'd been counting the seconds until he could see Ivy again.

"I welcomed you into our family, and I need to start treating you as a member." Magnus's voice grew quiet. "My son has taken a liking to you, and that should be all the assurance I need, but I would like to spend my own time with you when we return."

Finn lifted his eyes to the king but didn't know what to say. Finn never expected Ivy's father to show any interest in him, let alone welcome him into their family from the start. The silence grew between them, and Magnus cast his glance down to his horse's mane.

"I'm honored that you want to get to know me," Finn finally managed.

Magnus sighed and turned his horse so that it stood in front of Eclipse. "You don't need to be so formal when speaking to me." Magnus let a wry smile cross his lips. "I want you to feel at ease, and please just call me Magnus."

"In front of your own men?" Finn asked, looking around at the knights.

"They're my men, sworn to me. You aren't, and I want you to feel as though you can talk to me like any other man. I think you'll find that I'm not like other kings." Magnus caught Finn's eye and held him there for a long moment.

"Thank you, Magnus," Finn replied. Magnus opened his mouth to speak again, but Ser Caster called the all-clear to the king and started to move the group along.

The walls of the Twisted Tower rose much higher than those of Godstone, and as the portcullis was drawn up, Magnus led his men under the stone archway and into the city. The streets were cobblestone of various colors, and the buildings had a uniform look of tan stone blocks and rounded rooftops. Finn's gaze wandered in every direction from the stained glass of one roof to the jousting lanes to the left of him.

White trees grew in front of every building, and their slender limbs were speckled with new leaves. The streets were crowded, and one of Lord Kevan's men led them to the stables to feed and water their horses. The stables were massive, holding too many horses to count, and Finn wondered why they were even here. Lord Kevan's walls were higher, and he had an enormous army of his own. Surely the Lord of the Twisted Tower could hold his own city. But then Finn glanced over at Magnus and remembered that he desperately needed Lord Kevan's help. Finn had listened to the knights talking about Lord Kevan on the trip over, and it seemed as though the man had no taste for war. Though he was sworn to King Magnus and had come to his aid before, Lord Kevan preferred to stay safely behind his walls.

They were led through the streets while most of the king's knights stayed behind in the stables or wandered off in search of ale. Lord Kevan's tower rose before them in the center of the city. The tower's stones were the color of charcoal rather than the light tan of the other buildings. It spiraled up into the sky, and Finn craned his neck up as they approached. An unkindness of ravens circled the tower above. The base was broad, and the tower slimmed out as it grew higher.

Magnus led them up the few stone steps to the massive wood doors, which swung open to greet them. The room echoed their footsteps as they approached Lord Kevan. Finn took in the low-hanging chandeliers made of wagon wheels, each holding at least twenty tall candles, their white wax creating sharp daggers that hung from the wood. Round tables were set throughout the room, and fluffy cushions sat in every chair. A burgundy and gold carpet ran down the center of the room and crept up the stone steps where Lord Kevan sat on his throne. The chair was made to resemble the tower in which they stood, the back of it rising high above the lord's head and coming to a point. His wife, Lady Laila, sat beside him in a similar chair, and their son Piotr sat opposite his father on a simple chair with a red cushioned back. Lord Kevan stood as Magnus approached and gave a slight bow of his head down to the king. Finn and Ser Caster stood beside Magnus, who greeted his friend.

"Your Grace," Lord Kevan started. "When my scouts brought word of your arrival, I thought they must be joking. I've been sending you messenger ravens for weeks now." Lord Kevan's voice bounced off the smooth walls of the room.

Magnus drew his brows together as Lord Kevan stepped down and ushered the king to the nearest table. "I didn't receive any of your birds," Magnus admitted.

"And for a good reason. I've had an army of raiders lurking around my city for some time now. How is it that you arrive in my city without knowing I needed your help? And how did you get here, unscathed?"

"We saw no army on our journey, but I've come to ask for your help. I also tried to get a message to you and Earl Rorik, but my hawks were shot down just outside my walls."

Lord Kevan tapped his finger on the wooden table nervously. "What happened?" he asked.

"King Cenric is dead," Magnus said, and Lady Laila gasped from her seat. "His wife and daughter came to Godstone to warn me of the army that's coming. I've sent my son and daughter to retrieve Earl Rorik from Tordenfall, and I come to you now asking for your help to protect my home and keep the North."

Lord Kevan stared at Magnus in disbelief. He seemed unnerved by this news, yet admitted that he'd never liked King Cenric, which is why he swore his loyalty to House Blackbourne.

"Has this army attacked?" Magnus asked.

"No," he admitted. "Only circling my land and burning my crop fields."

"Do you know how many?"

"A few thousand at least," Lord Kevan said as he ran a hand through his blond hair.

"You must leave and come with me," Magnus urged. "It's only a matter of time before they attack your city. Surely they saw my men riding in, and they may attack now that they know the only living king in the North resides within your walls."

Lord Kevan's eyes grew wide. Finn was surprised that Magnus had spoken with such force, but perhaps Lord Kevan needed a bit of fear to act.

"You want us to leave our home?" Lady Laila stood from her chair. "What about the people here?"

"They need to come too," Magnus said, and Finn wondered where Magnus planned to keep all those people. "Everyone needs to leave and come back to Godstone. We're safer in numbers." Magnus sat back in his chair as Lord Kevan seemed to be contemplating.

Piotr scoffed from his chair as he sat lazily against the cushion with one leg hung over the armrest. "And you'll protect us, will you, my king?" Piotr asked sarcastically.

"Piotr!" his mother snapped at him. Finn crossed his arms and narrowed his eyes on the blond boy who questioned Magnus.

"You'll be safe within my kingdom," Magnus said, keeping his voice calm.

"And if I won't go?" Piotr retorted. Lord Kevan sighed and lowered his head.

"You will come, or I'll drag you behind my horse," Magnus answered, putting some depth back into his voice. Finn smirked and lowered his head to hide his smile.

"You think that's funny?" Piotr snapped at Finn. "Who are you?" he demanded.

Finn uncrossed his arms and put them behind his back before giving Piotr his name and bowing with a hint of sarcasm. Piotr rose from his seat and walked down to where Finn stood. He looked up at Finn, who stood a few inches taller, his blue eyes staring into Finn's. Piotr looked over the leather armor and sword that hung from Finn's belt before smiling back up at him. "You're no knight," Piotr pointed out. "So, what makes you think you can laugh at me?"

Finn scrunched his brow and looked over to Magnus, who rolled his eyes in return, then spoke up before Finn could. "He's with my daughter," Magnus said. "Just because he's not a knight doesn't mean he isn't important to me." Finn let himself smile but kept his eyes focused on Piotr.

"Him? With Ivy?" Piotr chuckled, and Finn felt his cheeks growing hot. "Well, I don't know what I expected. She never knew how to dress like a lady so she couldn't possibly attract the eye of a decent man," Piotr said as he flicked his finger under Finn's chin.

Finn caught his finger and bent it back until he saw the pain in Piotr's eyes. "Don't touch me," Finn growled. "And don't speak another word of my Ivy." Piotr shot a look to his father, who only glared back at him with a stern look. Finn released his finger and crossed his arms again over his chest, waiting for Piotr to step away. Magnus smiled at Finn and turned back to Lord Kevan, urging him to leave immediately. Piotr went back to his chair and stared at Finn as if trying to intimidate him, which only made Finn want to laugh at him again.

"We're traveling to Tonsburg from here, but if you lead your men straight to Godstone, we'll be only a day behind you." Finn turned his head at the name of his home, but Magnus scooched closer to Lord Kevan and hushed his voice, no doubt explaining the reason for their detour. Lord Kevan looked up at Finn and nodded his head as Magnus spoke.

"Very well," Lord Kevan said quietly. "We'll leave today. Give me some time to alert everyone and allow them to pack." Magnus nodded, and Lady Laila walked out of the room with tears in her eyes.

"Why is Lady Oharra not with you?" Lord Kevan asked.

Magnus cast his eyes down at that. "We don't know where she is. Grey Raven is gone."

Lord Kevan lowered his eyes to the floor, chewing his lip. "I'll come with you to Tonsburg," he said. "I'll order most of my men to accompany my wife and son to Godstone along with the rest—"

"I'm coming with you, Father," Piotr interrupted.

"You'll go with your mother," Lord Kevan ordered, but

Piotr wasn't listening to his father as he strolled over to Finn again.

"What could go wrong? After all, Tonsburg is a ghost town with nothing there to hurt us." His words were like a snake, slithering their way into Finn's ear and crawling deep into his mind.

They set out later that day before the rest of the city had left. Magnus rode alongside Lord Kevan and kept looking back at Finn, with a concerned look on his face. The Twisted Tower disappeared behind them as they headed west through a valley that cut through the Spearhead Mountains. Piotr rode just to the right of Finn and slightly behind him, but Finn could feel his stare at the back of his head. He'd argued with his father until Lord Kevan finally gave in and told Piotr that he could come. Finn didn't know why Piotr wanted to go or what Finn had done to get under his skin so quickly. Finn could tell that they were about the same age, though Piotr's childish demeanor sliced the years off him.

The valley was many shades of green, from the thick moss that blanketed the black rocks to the grass that grew high above their heads. The ground was rocky underfoot, and sharp, jagged stones rose into the sky all around them. The spearlike rocks surrounded them on both sides, creating sharp black shadows that crept in as the sun started to dip behind the mountains. They would save a day of traveling by going through the mountains, which would have been next to impossible if it were winter.

The Spearhead Mountains were known for their many avalanches and for the thick fog that made them difficult to traverse and had sent many men down to their deaths. Finn remembered hearing the distant thunder of the avalanches during the long winters in Tonsburg. Now the mountains looked beautiful, and Finn felt a shudder of guilt at telling Ivy that she couldn't come. He knew she would have loved to see the mountains with their sinister rockfaces and the yellow wildflowers that managed to grow on the steep cliffsides. He reached into his breast pocket and closed his eyes, just as Piotr's voice echoed off the walls of the canyon. Finn snapped his eyes open and put his hand to the small ax on his belt.

After waking from his fever, Finn had gone to see the smith's apprentice, a young woman named Arleta. He knew she was discrete, so Finn had sought her out to create the few items he envisioned. The ax reminded Finn of his father, and he explained it as best he could to Arleta, but what she presented him with was nothing like his father's ax. It was better—the handle was made from a Blackwood tree, and the head of the ax shone like no blade Finn ever saw. Finn remembered mentioning his brother to her and how he loved shells and the pearl that Finn buried, but he never thought Arleta would be able to incorporate anything into the weapon. Where the head of the ax met the wood was a small spiral shell skillfully etched into the dark metal. It was small and simple, but it meant a great deal to Finn to have something new to remind him of his brother.

Finn ran a thumb over the handle and stopped at the black pearl embedded there. Finn had reacted poorly when he first saw it. He'd assumed that Arleta had dug up the pearl that Finn buried for Thor, and when she saw the look on his face, she quickly explained that it wasn't the same pearl. "What do you mean?" He'd asked. She'd opened a small leather pouch that hung from her neck and poured the contents into his palm. Small black pearls bounced out and rolled around in his hand. "These beaches are not only dark with sand and stone. If you know what to look for, you'll be surprised at the treasures hidden under the surface."

Finn relaxed his shoulders and looked at her. "I'm sorry. I shouldn't have assumed you'd do such a thing."

She waved away the apology. "No need for that. As for the second item you requested . . ."

"I'll be back tomorrow to pick it up," Finn said, excitement fluttering in his chest.

Arleta smiled and bowed her head. "I'll have it ready."

"Thank you."

Finn relaxed his grip on the ax and looked again at the black pearl within the wood. It had been a rare and precious object to Finn years ago, though it seemed it wasn't a rare thing in Godstone. Finn wondered how many black pearls his eyes passed over when he was digging for shells with Ivy.

Now, Finn touched the cold metal of the ax and glared back at Piotr, who sat smiling at him from atop his white horse. "What did you say?" Finn demanded.

"I said, do you think Ivy will be happy to see me?" His grin grew wide and garish. Finn hadn't heard much about Piotr back in Godstone, but what he had heard came from Rayner's mouth, not Ivy's. Rayner had only briefly mentioned Piotr one night, recalling the last time he had seen him and laughing at what Ivy said to Piotr. Finn had gotten the impression that Piotr was a thorn in her side and decided not to ask her about the boy she'd insulted.

"Seeing as she's never mentioned you and from what her

brother tells me, I'd say she isn't looking forward to your arrival," Finn said with what he hoped was an insulting tone. Piotr narrowed his eyes and dug a knife from his jacket. Finn's eyes followed the blade as Piotr began using it to pick under his nails. Finn could see why he wasn't well-liked. He even seemed to despise Ivy, so Finn couldn't figure out why Piotr insisted on pushing him by talking about her. Finn turned away and ignored Piotr, trying to keep his eyes forward and his mind clear.

They camped in the middle of the stony valley. Magnus and Lord Kevan both sent scouts to keep watch from the cliffs while Ser Caster ordered more men to set up a tent for King Magnus. "Don't bother," Magnus called out to him.

The night was clear, and the sky seemed full of light as the stars twinkled above. A semi-full moon hung within the field of stars, and a steady breeze blew its way through the valley floor. Magnus came to sit by Finn, who was setting up his furs against a rock and watching while Eclipse nipped at Piotr's white stallion. The king sat down in the small tuft of grass as Finn leaned back on the rock and pulled a skin of water from his bag. Magnus offered up his own skin, and Finn took it, smelling the fruity wine inside before it hit his lips. Finn gave the skin back, and Magnus took a long sip before also leaning back and letting his eyes dance around the stars.

"Don't mind, Piotr," Magnus said softly. "He's always been a mouthy little boy." Finn smiled at Magnus's use of the word 'boy.'

"I didn't do anything to him," Finn responded. Magnus handed Finn the skin of wine again and let out a deep sigh. "I think he's jealous that's all," Magnus said.

"Jealous?" Finn questioned. "Of what?"

"Piotr has often teased Ivy. Any time he was in my kingdom, any chance he got, Piotr would follow her around or seat himself near her during feasts. He poked at her and insulted her, and the more I watched him, the more I saw how he watched her." Finn swallowed some wine and put the skin down.

"It became clear to me that Piotr was teasing Ivy because he liked her, though I don't think she knew that at the time. Any time Ivy would walk away from him, I watched his eyes follow her, and his smug smile disappear. Ivy insulted him the last time he was there, and I watched Piotr follow Ivy to the beach. I watched him for a long moment, but he never went to her. Instead, he watched her from the back of the beach before turning around to leave. I mentioned it to Ivy sometime later, but she said nothing about it, so I left it alone."

Magnus looked over at Finn, whose brows were scrunched together. Now he knew why Ivy never mentioned Piotr. Finn remembered what he did to Prince Kal out of jealousy, but Kal was nice to Ivy and was once Finn's good friend. He tried not to be jealous of Kal's feelings for Ivy, but he couldn't help it. Piotr seemed cruel, and already Finn didn't like him, but he would try not to let Piotr's words get the better of him.

Finn looked at Magnus and realized he hadn't responded to the king's story. Magnus spoke again before Finn could think of what to say. "I never worried about Ivy when it came to Piotr because I knew she could stand up for herself and make that boy cry if she wanted to." Magnus smiled as he spoke. "And now I've seen you stand up for her when she's not here to do it herself. I sleep better at night knowing you've made Ivy happy and that you'll always protect her." Magnus lowered his eyes to the skin of wine in his hand. "I can see why she chose you and why she loves you." With that, the king stood up and left Finn before he could say anything. He rolled over and pulled his cloak over his head before falling asleep. He dreamed of Ivy and her soft smile, and the purple fire that burned in her eyes just before he kissed her.

CHAPTER NINETEEN

Far From Home

Finn's heart pounded steadily in his chest as they emerged from the valley the following morning. The salty spray of the sea came up to meet him, blowing his dark hair behind his ears. The sound of crashing waves filled the morning air, and Finn laid eyes on the sea that he once loved so dearly, the sea that almost took his brother's life. The sun danced off the pale blue waves, and the light sand stretched out north and south, as far as the eye could see.

Their group turned north and stayed close to the shoreline, Magnus riding alongside Finn and observing him carefully. Finn didn't meet the king's eye; he was too focused on what might lay ahead. As Eclipse climbed a small sand-covered hill, Finn spotted a small structure up ahead. His eyes widened, and Magnus said his name just as Finn put his heel into the horse and took off. "Finn!" Magnus called from behind, but he ignored Magnus and snapped the reins driving Eclipse farther away from the group. He'd promised not to go off on his own, but Finn wanted to see his home before anyone else did. The horse pounded through the beach, splashing through the cold water that seeped in and out with the motion of the waves. Finn glanced back and didn't see Magnus chasing after him.

He slowed Eclipse to a trot as the wooden structure came into view. Finn jumped down, splashing through the water, and ran up the beach, pulling his ax free as he crested the hill. The structure was in ruins, and what Finn thought may have been a house was only the framework of a small shack. His breath fogged in the crisp morning air as he continued past the structure. Finn stopped when he spotted a large rock protruding from the sea, covered in barnacles and seaweed. He walked closer and recognized the rock immediately.

Finn saw a four-year-old Thorman standing atop the boulder, happily picking at the shells that lay in the little water-filled holes. His finger ran over the black pearl in the handle of his ax, and Finn reached out his other hand to touch the rock. It was cold and wet under his fingertips, and he felt his eyes begin to burn. He forced himself to let go of the rock and turn away. Finn walked up the beach back through time. The fishmonger's shacks sat along the beach, the dirt road stood before him and led through the town, to all the wooden houses with smoke coming from the stacks on their roofs. Finn let himself smile before shaking the memory from his head and looking at what his town had become.

Gone was the only word that came to his mind. Finn walked up the overgrown path that was once a road. All around him lay piles of wood, empty frames that once held families but now grew weeds. Trees sprouted from the ground in places Finn didn't remember, and wildflowers grew at their trunks.

The land had healed and now worked away at the town, covering the carnage that took place there and burying the memory of its people. Finn hung his ax heavily by his side as he made his way to the back of the town where his home once stood. A large mound of grass sat where his house had been, and as Finn walked closer, he could make out the wooden pieces of the roof. Moss still clung desperately to the wood as grass and tall weeds grew around it. Finn sunk to the ground and let his hand run over the wood, feeling the softness of the moss under his fingers. He lowered his head and pinched his eyes shut as a fat tear rolled down his cheek. Finn didn't know what he was expecting to find, but he always pictured it much worse than what it was.

He thought of what he saw the last time he ran through his town, the puddles of blood, overturned wagons, and people lying dead in the streets as the fire consumed their homes. But none of that was here. The town lay still, almost peaceful, and the ground had swallowed the bones of the slain. This wasn't his home anymore; it was a graveyard. Finn felt the damp grass that covered his home and thought of his family's bones that lay just underneath. Finn had always thought he angered the God of Lost Souls for saving his brother from drowning and wondered if the god had brought the raiders' ships to Tonsburg in his wrath. Finn blamed himself for many years for the death of his brother and even wondered that if he'd failed to save Thorman if the god would have sunken the raiders' ships or created a storm to persuade them to sail away. Stealing back life from the God of Lost Souls was unheard of, and Finn even prayed for the god to take him when he fled his home and sailed south. Of course, no storm came, and the god remained silent, forcing Finn to live with his guilt.

Finn sat back and let out a deep breath. He said a silent prayer to the gods for his family's souls and wondered if they could see Finn. A strong wind came up from behind, and Finn turned his head to see Magnus and the rest of the group following but hanging back at a distance. The king swung down from his horse as Finn turned away to wipe his tears. Finn stood up and turned his head to look at the rest of the town. Magnus stood beside him and rested a heavy hand on his shoulder, looking down at the mound of moss-covered wood. "This is your home?" Magnus asked quietly.

"It was," Finn answered, his voice flat. "But not anymore." He moved away from Magnus and walked back to where he'd left Eclipse on the beach. Ser Caster gave Finn a sorrowful look as he passed, and Lord Kevan averted his eyes. Finn hoped he didn't look as broken as he felt and picked up his pace toward the beach. Piotr sat on his white horse, looking around at the ruins until he spotted Finn. His lips curled into a smile, but Finn kept his eyes forward, tightening the grip around his ax handle. He could hear Ser Caster start giving the men orders to move on through the town.

"So this is home, huh?" Piotr asked as Finn passed his horse. Finn's palms started sweating, and he slowed his pace, waiting for Piotr to say something else. Piotr seemed to sense the challenge and turned his horse to face Finn's back. "What's the matter," Piotr sneered. "No one was home?"

Finn didn't remember turning around, but suddenly he was on Piotr, dragging him from his saddle and slamming him to the ground. Piotr tried to remove the knife from his coat, but

Finn caught his hand before he could reach it, and snatched the knife. He tossed the blade off into the grass and drove the head of his ax deep into the ground right beside Piotr's head. The smile left Piotr's mouth as his face transformed into pure fear. Adrenaline coursed through Finn's body, and he knew it was apparent by how Piotr was looking at him. Terrified. Finn grabbed a handful of Piotr's shirt and put the other hand around the handle of his ax.

"Finn!" Magnus shouted as he came running up. Lord Kevan dismounted his horse, but Magnus stopped him from getting closer. Finn leaned down closer to Piotr's face, whose hot breath came out in shaky gasps.

"Say it again," Finn growled.

"What?" Piotr asked, honestly. Finn lifted his shirt and slammed him back into the ground.

"Say it again!" Finn screamed in his face. The dark tendrils of rage wrapped around his soul as Finn stared into Piotr's wide blue eyes.

"No one was home?" Piotr said in a timid voice, clutching at Finn's hand that held his shirt.

"Again," Finn said through his teeth as he lifted the ax from the ground. Piotr's eyes danced back and forth between Finn and the sharp blade of the ax head. "No one was home," Piotr's voice cracked in a wave of panic.

"Again!" Finn ordered. He could feel Piotr shaking beneath him, and his hands were sweating against Finn's

"No one was home," he cried. "No one was home. No one was home. No one was home!"

Finn screamed in Piotr's face before lifting the ax into the air and sending it down with all his force.

It sunk deep into the earth beside Piotr's head. A lock of blond hair fell loose, blowing away in the wind. Finn released Piotr's shirt and leaned down to his ear to whisper something. Piotr's eyes went wide, and Finn stood up, yanking his ax from the ground and storming off toward Eclipse. Finn could hear steps following him, but his red-rimmed eyes stayed locked on the beach ahead.

Magnus caught up to Finn on the beach and turned him around. Finn was shaking with adrenaline and hate as he put his ax back in his belt and tried to climb on Eclipse. Magnus grabbed the back of his leather armor and thrust him back down into the sand.

"What are you doing?" Finn demanded, taking a step toward Magnus.

"I know you're angry, Finn. But don't let him—"

"He dishonored my family!" Finn snapped. He brought his shaky hands to run through his hair. "He's lucky I only took a lock of his hair instead of his fucking head." Finn's eyes were wild, his pulse thundering with rage. Magnus stepped back and drew his sword. Finn furrowed his brow. "What are you doing?"

"Draw your sword," Magnus told him. Finn stood still but put a hand to the hilt of his sword. "You're angry?" Magnus asked, stepping forward. "Then show me. Draw your sword and get it out of your system. Remember what Ronin taught you," he said as he lunged at Finn.

Finn stepped away and drew his sword in one swift motion before sending it crashing into Magnus's blade. The king smiled at him and attacked, driving Finn back and slicing at his chest. Finn parried the king's blows and advanced, using his adrenaline to fuel his swing. Magnus ducked as Finn's blade came sailing overhead, and then he shot forward, plowing into Finn, who drove his elbow down into the king's back, but all he hit was armor. Magnus shoved Finn back until he tripped, and they both went down in the sand.

Magnus rolled off him and stood again, waving at Finn to attack. He got to his feet and pulled his ax with the other hand. He came at Magnus and caught the king's sword with his ax, waving it around and kicking Magnus's wrist, forcing him to let go. Finn stepped over the king's sword and threw his own into the air, which Magnus caught. Magnus swung the sword, almost slicing Finn's arm, but Finn smacked the sword away with his ax before Magnus lifted his foot and sent it into Finn's stomach, making him crumple over in pain. Finn felt his own blade come to rest beside his ear and quickly jerked his head away and threw up a cloud of sand toward Magnus's face.

Finn turned his ax around and swung it, catching Magnus in the back of the knee and forcing him down. The king tried to wipe the sand from his face, but it clung to his sweat. He managed to get one eye open and turned the sword and swiftly sent it to hit the back of Finn's foot, sweeping him off his feet. Finn crashed down on his back, and Magnus grabbed his hand that held the ax, slamming it into the sand. Finn sent a punch up and connected with the weak spot in the king's armor. Magnus grunted from the blow and slammed Finn's wrist until he opened it. Finn shifted under the weight of Manus and buried one foot in the sand then thrust his hips up while grabbing hold of Magnus's chest plate. He flung Magnus from him and lay back down in the sand, out of breath. Magnus lay beside him breathing heavily and smiling at Finn's skills.

"Now," Magnus said between breaths. "How do you feel?"

Finn didn't want to admit it, but he did feel better. He even caught himself smiling during the fight and wondered if Magnus had seen it. "Better," Finn admitted. Magnus sent a fist down on Finn's chest, startling him. "What was that for?" Finn demanded.

"I was just checking. If you were still angry, you would've hit me back." Magnus looked over at Finn with a wide smile. Finn gave in and smiled, resting his head back in the sand and trying to catch his breath. "You're a good fighter," Magnus admitted. "Ronin has taught you well." Finn put a hand to his stomach, where the king had kicked him, and smiled at the dull pain. He'd never felt anger like that in his life, and he was grateful Magnus had snapped him out of it before he'd done something foolish. It wasn't what he'd imagined when Magnus had said he wanted to spend more time with him, but it was a start.

The two got to their feet and put their weapons away. Magnus put an arm around Finn's shoulders and walked back toward Eclipse, who was patiently waiting, nibbling at seagrass. Magnus released Finn and turned to him as he was shaking the sand from his damp hair. "What did you say to Piotr?" Magnus asked. Finn stopped what he was doing and cast his eyes down at the sand. "It's all right. Tell me," Magnus insisted. Finn looked up and searched the king's eyes, trying to find the trick in them, but he seemed sincere.

"I told him if he keeps pushing me that I'll show him what pure terror feels like. I told him that if he bothered Ivy when we return if he did anything to make her feel the way I do now, I'd kill him." Finn gave the king a worried look, but Magnus let out a quick chuckle.

"I'll tell you this, Finn. You certainly scared me, and I was only watching. If that wasn't pure terror for Piotr, then I don't think he's too eager to find out what that feels like."

Finn smiled at Magnus and mounted Eclipse before walking through the streets of Tonsburg to join the rest of the group. Finn stopped his horse as Magnus gave him a nod over his shoulder and continued walking. Finn took one last look around his home and at the ruins that now covered the land. He felt a weight lift from his chest and filled his lungs with the smell of the sea as the wind picked up from behind him. Finn turned around to look at the rock on the beach, but this time he didn't see Thorman, only a rock covered with barnacles.

He let his guilt blow away with the wind and released Thorman from the darkness of his mind. Finn wasn't going to forget his brother—he was only moving the memory of him to a better part of his mind. One that wasn't damaged with bad memories and nightmares. He turned and trotted through the town of Tonsburg, a place that was once his home. He looked ahead to Magnus and the group who was already heading east, where Finn's true home now resided. Ivy and her family were his home now, and Finn let himself smile as Eclipse picked up speed to join Magnus, who was waiting for him at the edge of the town. "Are you ready?" Magnus asked.

Finn didn't even look back. He kept his eyes on the horizon ahead. "I'm ready. Let's go home."

CHAPTER TWENTY

PERMISSION

It had been six days since Finn left Tonsburg behind him, and with every step, he felt the dark memories leaving him. The sun had just set, and Finn sat atop a hill, watching it disappear, and the world grew dark around him. Piotr hadn't tried anything more with Finn, but he made sure to keep his hateful stare and crooked smile painted on his face. Finn had a feeling that Piotr meant to challenge him on the threat, he just didn't know when.

He sharpened his ax on a stone and watched lightning bugs floating in the fields below. Magnus came to find him sometime later, bringing with him a bowl of stew. Finn's stomach growled at the smell, and he gratefully took the bowl and began to devour it. "We'll cross through the Blackwoods tomorrow," Magnus said. "Perhaps another day's ride until we get home." Finn's heart fluttered at the thought of seeing Ivy in only one day, but even that felt like years. The king and Finn sat on the hill and watched the camp come to life with fires and listened to men laughing and yelling at one another.

Finn knew they had brought ale with them and thought they must be relaxing now that they were within King Magnus's land. He wondered how long the rest of Lord Kevan's men had been waiting in Godstone.

Magnus had kept his word and ridden with Finn for most of the trip home, talking with him and getting to know him. Finn talked briefly about his childhood in Tonsburg and his journey south. He told Magnus how he met Ronin and how Ronin had helped Finn, taking him under his protection and gaining him a room with the king's permission. Mostly Finn found himself talking about Kame Island and what his life had been like before Ivy and Ser Osmund arrived, when Finn had spent most of his day's training with Ronin and Kal or wandering the island alone, searching every cave and beach until he knew the island as well as his room.

Finn spoke of Ivy, and how fierce she was when they first fought. He admitted that he hadn't wanted to train with her at first and even told Magnus of the time he injured her. Magnus's face never faltered, and he listened intently to everything Finn told him. Finn was sure Ivy had told him these stories already, but Magnus seemed happy to hear them from Finn's perspective. Magnus asked about the raider who tried to take Ivy, and he explained everything, fearing if he left out a detail that Magnus would know. Finn told Magnus of what he did to Prince Kal when he saw him kissing Ivy, and Magnus chuckled at the image of Finn punching the young prince. Magnus had never met Prince Kal, but Finn painted a good enough picture for him.

They talked like that for days, Magnus waving away Ser

Caster every time he came to speak with the king. Finn increasingly let down his guard with each story, every time Magnus gave him a reassuring smile or laughed at something he said. Finn was beginning to look at him the way Magnus wanted, like any other man. But Finn never forgot that he was Ivy's father, and that seemed more important to Finn than Magnus being king. Finn felt himself blushing as he told Magnus of Ivy's name day celebration, and how stunning she looked even dressed in her normal attire.

It was after that story that Magnus asked Finn when he knew that he had fallen in love. Finn tightened the grip on his reins and looked away from Magnus, unsure of what to say. Magnus was patient and stayed silent until Finn felt comfortable answering.

"The moment the raider took her and I thought she was gone, that I would never see her again," Finn reluctantly admitted. He'd never told Ivy how strongly he felt back then, he never even admitted it to himself until now. Finn had only told Ivy of his feelings the night Kal kissed her and still held back even then. He didn't want to scare her if she didn't feel as strongly. Finn remembered the night he'd finally summoned his courage and told Ivy that he loved her. He remembered a wave of relief as the words passed his lips, but even that didn't seem to sum up how he felt. Maybe nothing could.

Now, Magnus and Finn sat on the hill listening to the bugs chirping in the grass and men getting drunk in the camp. "So," Magnus began. "Would you like to train with me when we return? Surely you could use a break from Ronin's eternally blank stare," Magnus joked.

"I'd like that." If it was anything like their fight on the beach, he wouldn't need to hold back his strength like he still secretly did with Ivy.

"Good," Magnus said, and he got up to leave. Finn felt his heart sink and put his empty bowl aside, touching his pocket.

He stood up, hands sweating and heart racing, but it was now or never. He had to ask before his courage left him for good. "Magnus," he called, and immediately regretted it. The king turned back and waited for Finn to continue. Finn took a deep breath and forced himself to stand up straight, digging his nails into the soft tissue of his palm.

"Yes?" Magnus took a step back toward Finn.

"I need to . . . there's something I want to ask you." Finn felt a wave of sickness churning his stomach. Magnus's eyes went to Finn's hand touching the outside of his pocket, and he cocked his head to one side, raising an eyebrow at Finn. "Magnus," Finn began though it still felt strange to call the king by his first name. Finn cleared his throat and tried to make his voice not sound so terrified. "I want to ask you for something." He was surprised at the calm voice that left his mouth. Magnus smiled and nodded his head, waiting for Finn to ask.

"I want to ask your permission to marry Ivy," he spat out a little too quickly. At first, he thought Magnus didn't hear him as the king just stared at Finn with his light purple eyes. Finn felt a trickle of sweat run down his neck as Magnus stood there in silence.

"Why?" Magnus finally asked.

"Because I love—"

"No." Magnus waved his hand through the air. "Why are you asking me?"

"What do you mean?" Finn was falling into a trap, he could sense it.

Magnus sighed and looked away, focusing on the lightning bugs in the field. "I mean, what makes you think you need my permission?"

"You're her father and the king. I didn't think it would be right to ask her without letting you know first, but . . ." Finn stumbled to tell Magnus the truth now that he'd asked for permission.

"But what?" Magnus cocked his head.

"I almost asked her a few weeks ago," Finn admitted and cursed himself for trying to hide it. "Right before Queen Narra and Princess Meisha arrived with their news."

"I see," was all Magnus said, stroking his wavy beard. "Let me see it," Magnus held out his hand to Finn and looked down at the pocket that Finn was continually touching. "If you meant to ask her some weeks back, then surely you already have a ring." Magnus again cocked his head to one side and grinned. Finn dug deep into his pocket, then lifted the ring and handed it over.

Magnus studied the ring, turning it over in his hands and admiring the smith's skills. Finn had returned the day after the smith made the ax to retrieve Ivy's ring. He'd given Arleta precise instructions and even drew out a picture of it and bought the stone himself. When Finn laid eyes on the ring, he willingly handed over the last of his coins from Kame Island to the smith. The band was solid gold with small, delicate maple leaves etched into the metal and wrapping around the band, ending on either side of a small amber stone.

The more Magnus looked at it, the more worried Finn grew. He'd put a lot of thought into the ring and knew Ivy would love it. She didn't wear much jewelry, and Finn thought a gold band with a small stone would fit her perfectly and still be sleek enough to wear even when sparring. Finn bounced his foot up and down as Magnus took his time, running his finger over the small maple leaves. When he finally looked up, Finn was surprised to see tears in his eyes. He stayed silent and waited to see if they were happy or sad tears.

Magnus handed the ring back to Finn and blinked away his tears before letting a broad smile form across his face. Finn felt his heart skip as he realized Magnus was happy. He was happy for his daughter and Finn and that they found one another. "Though you didn't need it," Magnus said softly. "I give you my permission to ask Ivy's hand in marriage." Finn thought his heart might burst through his shirt, but then Magnus continued. "But," he said, "you're both very young still, and Ivy has agreed to wait two more years until I will swear her into my service as a knight. I ask you to wait until that happens."

Finn's heart slowed down at the king's words. "I'm not telling you not to ask her. I'm only asking that you two wait to be married until you're twenty. Two years may seem like a lifetime, but until Ivy is knighted, I would prefer that you wait." Magnus studied Finn's expression, as if trying to read his mind. Finn put the ring back in his pocket and ran a hand through his hair, brushing it behind his ear.

After a moment, Finn held out his hand to Magnus, and they shook on it. "I'll wait to ask her," Finn said.

"You don't need to wait to ask her, Finn. Only hold off on the wedding," Magnus explained. Finn shook his head but let a faint smile form.

"It will be better to wait until she's knighted like you said. Thank you, Magnus." Finn released his grip and got to his feet, and headed back to camp.

The next day Magnus led his men into the Blackwood Forest with the thought of home dancing around in his mind. Finn seemed quiet but not unkind toward Magnus. He hoped Finn wasn't upset by his decision and wondered if Ivy would be engaged right now if Queen Narra and her men hadn't interrupted Finn's proposal.

Magnus couldn't help but feel bad. Perhaps his conditions were too much, and he should ease up. He only wanted what was best for Ivy and thought that waiting would give them more time to truly get to know one another. Finn and Ivy met only months ago, but even Magnus agreed that it felt like another lifetime since he'd stood at the docks of Godstone and watched his daughter board the ship to Kame Island.

Magnus had decided to marry Elana on the spot, but he still waited many months for the wedding as a lot of preparations had to be made for a king's wedding. He ran his hands over his face, trying to decide if he should run after Finn and tell him he'd changed his mind. Magnus knew they were happy and felt that Finn was deserving of her, but he still couldn't grasp the idea of his only daughter getting married. Perhaps Magnus didn't want to let go of the image of Ivy as a little girl, which he knew was selfish, but he couldn't help but be protective of her. Magnus let his mind wander to Elana and the child that she carried. He was still overjoyed at the news and couldn't wait to get back to his pregnant wife and be with his family.

Ser Caster sent men to flank their group, two on either side, and Magnus watched them disappear into the dark forest. A few men went ahead as well, looking for signs of raiders or to call back when they spotted Godstone. Their group would spend the entire day just gettingthrough the forest. They stayed on a lesser-traveled road that cut straight through the woods. It was only wide enough for three men to ride abreast, and Magnus kicked his horse to move up to where Finn was riding alone. He had Ivy's ring in his hand when Magnus pulled alongside him but quickly shoved it back into his pocket.

Piotr rode ahead of Finn, occasionally glaring back and smirking. Magnus looked at the gold band around his ring finger and smiled at the thought of his wife. Finn noticed and asked Magnus if he was excited about another baby. "I couldn't be happier," Magnus said to him.

"Well, I'm happy for you and Queen Elana," Finn responded. "Do you have a preference?"

Magnus had thought about it nearly the whole trip as to whether he wanted another boy or another girl. But in the end, he decided that it didn't matter. "It makes no difference to me," Magnus answered with a smile.

The woods grew dark as the sun hid its face behind storm clouds. Finn pulled on his cloak, preparing for the rain as a distant rumble of thunder rolled in from the north. They stopped around noon to eat and stretch their legs. Finn went off and sat beneath one of the black trees. Their dark purple leaves were unfolding, making the trees appear to be encircled in shadows. He gnawed on a piece of dried meat and watched the rest of the knights gather around each other, passing around a skin of what Finn assumed was wine.

Magnus sat with Ser Caster at the edge of the road, talking while they ate bread and cheese. Finn finished his piece of meat and again took out Ivy's ring, running his fingers over the cold metal. Finn still intended to ask Ivy to marry him, but after his talk with Magnus, he thought that he should wait to ask. If he asked Ivy when he returned, he feared she'd want a wedding soon, and he didn't want to deny her that. Of course, she had to say yes first. He also didn't want Ivy to talk Magnus into changing his mind and have Magnus thinking that Finn put her up to it. He was starting to feel comfortable around Magnus and didn't want to do anything to jeopardize his new relationship with Ivy's father. Finn leaned his head back against the twisted trunk of the Blackwood tree and closed his eyes.

His eyes opened when Luna called out from above, and Finn realized he must have dozed off. Men were still sitting around, but many were starting to move back to their horses. Finn stretched his arms above and turned his neck, spotting one of Lord Kevan's scouts off in the distance. The man was riding his horse slowly through the dark trees. Finn stood up to stretch his legs. The man disappeared behind a tree and when his horse emerged, the saddle was empty. Finn strained his eyes to see if the man had fallen off and took a step forward just as the man's body came crashing down through the branches and jerked to a halt from the noose tied around his neck.

Finn's eyes went wide, and he drew his sword, but before he could yell to the other scout in the distance, Finn saw a rope drop over the man's head, and the scout was whisked away into the canopy. He dropped back down, and the violent jerk of his body made Finn's stomach turn as the man's neck snapped, and his body went still. "Magnus!" Finn screamed as he turned on his heels and bolted through the brush.

CHAPTER TWENTY-ONE

GHOST IN THE FIRE

Magnus looked back in confusion as Lord Kevan came up behind the king. "Lord Kevan," Finn breathed, "your scouts—"

But just then, an arrow flew past Finn's head, taking his words with it as it embedded itself into the back of a knight. Magnus spun around with a panicked look in his eyes as a flock of raiders came running through the forest. Ser Caster broke off in a run, shouting commands at his men as he unsheathed his sword.

Magnus looked back at Finn and drew his blade before running to his horse. Finn did the same and swung up onto Eclipse as the shouting of the raiders echoed through the trees. Magnus could see the raiders closing in, but many of them were on foot. An arrow came down near Finn and landed just beside Eclipse, who stomped at the ground frightened. Magnus looked up and saw people moving through the thick branches of the trees. His stomach turned, and his pulse quickened just as Finn yelled, "They're in the trees!" Turning his gaze to the darkening sky, Magnus yelled at his men to run as another arrow flew down and caught a knight through his throat.

Finn kicked Eclipse and took off through the trees, looking back to see Magnus coming up alongside him. "Stay with me!" Magnus ordered over the pounding of hooves. Finn nodded and galloped alongside the king as the raiders' screams clawed at their backs. Some of the raiders broke off and managed to get in front of the group as more flanked them from the sides. Magnus pulled on the reins of his horse as his knights fought the raiders that cut off their path. A mounted raider came at Magnus, and he quickly slid his blade into the man's stomach and shoved his body from his horse. Finn slew a raider who had come running through the bushes toward him, screaming with the thrill of battle. Beside Magnus, Finn lifted his sword to another raider when someone jumped out of the tree, knocking him from Eclipse.

"Finn!" Magnus bellowed as his body hit the ground. The raider got up and swung his blade, but Finn rolled out of the way and threw his sword up, catching the raider in the thigh. Thick blood seeped down his leg and filled the air with its metallic scent. Magnus swung down from his horse as Finn stumbled, touching the back of his head where a trail of blood trickled down his neck. Another raider attacked, clearly a knight, and Finn crumpled under the man's powerful blow, forcing him down to one knee as he tried to hold the knight's weight.

Magnus drove his sword through the knight's neck, spraying Finn with blood as the man coughed, then crumpled.

He offered his hand, and hauled Finn to his feet, scanning him for more injuries.

"Are you alright—"

An arrow flew past the king and embedded in Finn's chest. His eyes went wide as Finn dropped to one knee, Magnus catching his arm as he fell. He spun around and spotted the archer nocking back another arrow. Magnus curled his body over Finn's and took the arrow in the back, letting it scrape against his metal armor. Whipping around, Magnus charged the low branch that held the archer, throwing his weight up and slicing at the man's ankles from behind. The archer fell from the tree, and Magnus stepped on his chest before plunging his sword through his neck. He looked around to his men, who were desperately fighting back and keeping many of the raiders at bay. The trees rattled with the running of archers, and Magnus ran back to Finn, dragging him into the brush and off the road.

His eyes were open, and Finn's hands turned red with blood as he pressed on the wound. Magnus cut away his leather armor to see that the arrow had only just gone through and stuck about an inch deep. "I'm going to take it out," Magnus warned him. Finn said nothing and nodded for him to do it. He cried out as Magnus quickly snatched away the arrow and threw it off into the dark woods. A crack of thunder startled Magnus, and when he looked up, a raindrop plopped on his cheek.

A cold rain started to fall on the blood-soaked earth as Magnus lifted Finn to his feet. Finn drew his ax and held his sword with the other hand, and the two stepped back out into the path. The screams of angry raiders and dying knights filled the air, only to be drowned out by the thunder above. Ser Caster was fighting with his men to keep the raiders from advancing on Magnus. They ran to their horses, Finn struggling to lift himself with the fresh wound. Magnus and Finn heard Luna call out again and they looked toward the branches above, but Magnus couldn't spot the bright white bird against the black trees. As Finn held up a hand to block the rain, another arrow came down and sliced his forearm.

Finn cursed and dropped his ax in his lap as fresh blood ran down his arm. Eclipse seemed to smell the blood and reared up, forcing Finn to use both arms to grab the reins. He snatched his ax before it fell and put it back in his belt as Magnus came over and yanked Finn's sleeve up to look. "I'm fine," Finn insisted, and they both moved toward Ser Caster and his men. Magnus knew there were too many and yelled at Ser Caster to gather his men and retreat. They would have to make a run for it back to Godstone and hoped they reached the gates in time. Just as Magnus gave the order, more raiders came charging through the darkness to join the group that Magnus already thought was too many.

"Get out of there!" Magnus called to Ser Caster, who turned to see the rest of the raiders charging through the woods. Ser Caster yelled at his men to get the king and go. Magnus tried to yell back, but Ser Caster was already running through the sea of fallen knights to a wagon that held their supplies. Knights came up to Magnus and Finn.

"Your Grace, you have to leave!" one knight urged. Magnus looked at the fear in his eyes, then turned to Finn while addressing the knight.

"Take him and go. I'll be right behind you."

"No!" Finn argued. "I'm staying by your side." The crashing of steel rang loud in his ears as Magnus gave in and nodded for Finn to follow him.

Just ahead, Ser Caster ran to the wagon, throwing open the doors and tossing bags out into the bloody puddles of the road. He grabbed a small barrel and thrust the point of his knife into the base, letting a thick black tar ooze out from the hole. He then ran across the road and into the brush as the remainder of the raiders joined the group ahead of Ser Caster. Magnus watched as Ser Caster sparked a flintstone over the tar, and a wall of fire rose just as a handful of raiders jumped their horses over the growing flames.

Magnus galloped to the raiders and sliced through one before moving to the next. He glanced back to see Finn burying the point of his sword in a man's shoulder, knocking him from his horse. Ser Caster ran back to where Magnus was mounted as a cloud of thick smoke filled the air, and the fire crackled behind them. Another crack of thunder split the sky open above them. They needed to leave.

"Let's go!" Magnus called to Ser Caster, who was running to his horse. He turned around to see Finn slicing a raider's throat, sending a spray of blood onto his face. Ser Caster's horse ran from him just as he tried to grab the reins, the horse galloping past Magnus to join the knights ahead.

Finn came up beside Magnus, blood dripping down his face and his eyes wild with adrenaline. Magnus held a hand down and bellowed, "Run, Caster!" The knight took off in a sprint toward his king. The wall of fire held back the raiders, giving Magnus and his men a better chance of escaping. Their flames licked at the low-hanging branches, cracking the wood with their heat. Magnus looked back at Ser Caster and turned his horse to help the knight swing up behind him. Ser Caster stretched his arm out, reaching for Magnus just as the point of an arrow tore through his eye.

Magnus felt his friend's fingertips brush against his just before he fell, revealing the long arrow that protruded from the back of his skull. Finn cried out to Magnus, but his gaze was focused on Ser Caster, his most trusted knight who now lay dead, just before Magnus could save him. Magnus ground his teeth together as hot, angry tears pooled in his eyes. He couldn't blink, couldn't look away as his friend's blood began to pool beneath him. The chaos around him died away, leaving nothing but a searing ringing that echoed in his ears. After a moment, Magnus lifted his eyes to the wall of fire and smoke creeping down the road.

The woods were lit up by the flames, and the noise of fire crackling, of dying men came crashing back into him. Magnus searched the hazy group of raiders beyond the fire until his eyes fell on a ghost. A black knight moved seamlessly through the sea of raiders, all of them parting before the knight who stood just beyond the flames. Magnus felt his heart sink, and then a wave of pure rage burned through him. A ghost, a demon, a spirit from a bad story stood behind the flames, and though Magnus couldn't see his eyes, he knew they were focused on him. The knight's helm grew a pair of black horns that ran down the base of the skull with his face fully concealed.

Magnus looked at the knight that tried to kill his son, his only son, and heir to his throne. The knight that stomped over Rayner's bleeding body after he'd already fallen. The knight that almost cost Magnus everything and now he was there, likely smiling under that black mask. Magnus tightened the grip on his sword and charged the wall of fire, his vision blurred with rage as his pulse rushed blood through his veins. He would walk through the fire himself to slay the knight if his horse wouldn't carry him. The horned knight made no move, standing there like a ghost in the flames, urging Magnus to run him down.

His path was cut off by Finn, and Magnus's horse slammed to a stop, almost tossing Magnus over its head. "Move!" Magnus ordered. Finn looked shocked but quickly recovered.

"No," he said sternly, then more gently he added, "Think of your wife and the child she carries. Remember what you did for me on the beach." Magnus's gaze was still focused on the horned knight. The flames were starting to die down, and Finn pressed harder, some of his worry creeping into his next words. "Is it worth dying to avenge a son that still lives?" Magnus finally peeled his eyes away from the knight and looked at Finn. "I know you're angry," Finn said, throwing the king's own words back at him. "But don't give him what he wants. You'll die before you even reach him." Finn glanced up as the branches shook with more archers.

Magnus ground his teeth together but released his tight grip on the hilt of his sword. Finn didn't move from the king's path until Magnus reluctantly turned his horse away and broke off into a gallop. Magnus took one last look back at the horned knight as he rode away. He stood like a demon beyond the flames, the heat making his image dance and wave with the flickering fire.

They rode hard for Godstone, exhausting their horses and

never looking back at the carnage within the dark world of the Blackwoods. Thunder clapped overhead, and lightning touched down beyond the walls of Godstone. The kingdom lit up before them as they came bursting through the trees and across the wet fields. Though the king felt Finn's gaze, he wouldn't look at him.

The gates opened, and Magnus spotted Ivy jumping the last steps of the stone stairs that snaked their way up the wall. Finn swung down from Eclipse, grimacing at the pain in his chest as Ivy ran to him. The look of horror painted on her face was well placed as she ran her eyes over Finn. She stopped in front of him and put a hand over her mouth. "It's not mine," he blurted out. "Well, most of it." Before Ivy's question could leave her lips, Finn grabbed her by the shoulder and pulled her in, wrapping his arms around her and burying his bloodied face into her hair.

A crowd formed around the king and his men, and Magnus spotted Rayner standing with his wife. Magus noted the presence of Earl Rorik's men standing with Rayner and Correlyn. His eyes roamed the crowds but stopped on Princess Meisha, who seemed to be staring at Finn, with an unreadable expression on her face. A young woman with white hair stood like a ghost within the mass, her light eyes rested on Ivy and Finn before she turned away and disappeared into the crowd.

Ivy pulled away and brought her hands up to Finn's face, running her fingertips over the crusting blood. "Where are you hurt?" she asked in a small voice.

"I'm fine," Finn said as he placed a hand on his wound. Ivy snatched his hand away and pulled back the armor that Magnus had cut.

"Come on," Ivy said, pulling him away. "Magister Ivann can stitch you up, and you can tell me what happened." Finn didn't argue and allowed Ivy to lead him away, but his eyes turned back to the king once before the crowd swallowed them.

As Magnus swung down from his horse, Elana pushed her way through the crowd and made her way over to her husband. He brought a shaky hand to her soft cheek and pulled her into him. Elana's dress turned red with the blood that covered the king, but she didn't seem to mind. She whispered something in his ear, and Magnus nodded his head, pulling away and planting a gentle kiss on her forehead. Rayner walked up with Earl Rorik, and Grimm followed closely behind. Magnus nodded at his old friend but didn't have the energy to properly welcome him. Not with Ser Caster's death fresh in his mind, and the image of the horned knight. Magnus squeezed Elana's hand and moved over to where Rayner stood before pulling him close.

Magnus whispered into his son's ear, and Rayner's eyes flickered with panic, instinctively traveling to the gate as if the knight would appear. Rayner backed away and looked at Magnus, whose eyes held nothing but pain and guilt. Rayner snapped his eyes shut and backed away, his breathing becoming more labored. Ser Caster had been a good mentor and friend to Rayner. He'd fought hard to save Rayner's life, and if it weren't for him, Magnus might have lost his son.

Magnus put a steady hand on his son's shoulder, grounding him. "There's something else." Magnus's voice didn't sound sorrowful anymore but angry. "The raiders who attacked us, they were led by the horned knight. He's the one that killed Ser Caster."

Rayner looked up into his father's eyes. The color drained from his face as he clutched the ribs that had been broken. Magnus touched his son's shoulder as Rayner bent over, a fresh coat of sweat coating his brow. "Rayner?" He didn't answer. Rayner was hyperventilating as Magnus grabbed his son by the shoulder, trying to meet his eye. "Rayner!" he said more urgently. Rayner's eyes were wide with panic, his entire body shaking as he crashed down to his knees. Magnus knelt before his son, searching his eyes but all he saw was the horror that he'd lived through, the pain that had been brought upon him. A moment later, Rayner's eyes rolled back in his head and he fell forward into Magnus's chest.

CHAPTER TWENTY-TWO

BROKEN

A few weeks ago, everything had seemed calm and at peace. Finn was hoping to be engaged to Ivy, they trained with Ronin every day, and things were normal. But the news of King Cenric's death had rattled the kingdom and set off a wave of events that rippled through the calm like a stone dropping into a pond. Finn could feel the tension building, and with the kingdom packed with people, it was a perfect recipe for chaos. The more time that passed, the more he could see his new family starting to crack.

Magister Ivann had just been finishing stitching the wound in Finn's chest when Magnus had carried Rayner into the room. Rayner had collapsed at the news of the horned knight, and he looked pale as a ghost. Magister Ivann tried to give him some sort of clear fluid, but Rayner smacked it away and stumbled back out the door. Finn worried for Rayner. Rayner was strong and resilient, but the horned knight had taken a piece of him, and Finn knew that if Rayner gave in to his fears, it would break him.

Finn snapped out of his thoughts as the wooden sword came down on his hand, bloodying his knuckles. He looked at Magnus with a hint of anger, but the king advanced on him, ignoring the blood dripping from Finn's hand. Magnus swung his practice sword at Finn, who stepped away just in time as the wood kissed the sleeve of his shirt. Rayner was nowhere in sight, but Ivy had come to watch them practice, and soon, a crowd began to form behind her. Ronin stood in front watching the fight. Finn tried to ignore the eyes on him and focus his own on the king. The expression on Magnus's face wavered between anger and pain. Magnus wore his worry on his face like a mask. Finn understood a father's protective nature, especially for his heir, but Magnus was letting it eat him alive, and Finn watched it take a bite with every angry blow that came his way.

Finn lunged, thrusting his sword at the king's belly, but Magnus swiftly slapped Finn's sword aside and thrust his own back. It caught Finn in the shoulder, and he grunted from the pain, quickly glancing down to make sure his stitches didn't tear. Magnus had been the one to pull the arrow from his chest, so the king knew precisely where his weak spot was. Finn twisted his mouth into a frown and pressed on, throwing his blade up just before the kings came down on his shoulder. Finn struggled against the king's power, and his arms began to shake under the weight. Magnus noticed and let a wicked smile cross his lips before he drove his foot into Finn's stomach. He crumpled over, coughing from the blow, and clutching his stomach. Magnus had told Finn not to let his anger win, but now it seemed as though the king couldn't follow his own advice.

Finn dropped his sword and stayed low, plowing into Magnus and forcing him back. His feet tore through the dirt as Finn pushed him back until Magnus tripped and grabbed hold of Finn's shirt. They both fell to the ground, and Magnus quickly elbowed him in the ribs and tried to get to his feet. Finn felt the anger rising in his chest and dug his fingers into Magnus's leg as he tried to crawl away. Magnus threw back his foot, nearly kicking Finn in the face, and the final wave of anger washed over him.

Finn slammed his fist into the back of his knee and clawed his way onto Magnus's back. He tried to throw him off, but Finn pinned down his hand and drove a punch into his ribs. Magnus grunted into the dirt, and Finn thought he heard Ivy's voice call to him, but he ignored it. Magnus threw back an elbow and caught Finn in the eye. His vision blurred, and he let go of Magnus, bringing a hand to the throbbing pain behind his eye. Magnus threw Finn from his back and quickly stood, snatching up his sword and holding it to Finn's throat.

Magnus relaxed his arm as he looked at Finn's bloodshot eye which was quickly turning black. Finn thought he saw a hint of regret in his eyes, but as Magnus opened his mouth to say something, Finn stood up and glared at him before turning away and storming out of the practice ring. He couldn't ignore the whispers of the crowd or their eyes following him. Ivy stepped into his path, but he brushed past her, the crowd's constant gaze filling him with more anger.

"Finn!" Ivy called to him as he picked up his pace, heading toward the tower. Ivy cut him off again and her gaze drifted to Finn's eye. She tried to reach out and touch it, but he put her hand down and looked away. "Finn." Her voice was gentle and soft. "My father didn't mean it. He's just—"

"Angry," Finn finished. "I know. Everyone is." Ivy stepped back at the tone of his voice.

"Ser Caster's funeral was only hours ago," she said. "What did you think his mood would be?"

Finn didn't have an answer. He'd watched the king and Rayner both during the funeral that morning, and Rayner's countenance was disturbing. He was coming apart at the seams, his hair was unkempt, his beard had grown wild, and dark circles hung lazily under his eyes. There was to be a feast that night to celebrate Ser Caster's life rather than mourn over him.

Finn was hopeful that the feast would put people back into a cheerful mood while trying to remember that this battle wasn't over. If everyone fell apart now, then they would surely lose everything. Finn said nothing more and walked toward the tower, Ivy following him closely. They reached their room, and Finn took off his shirt after noticing a bloodstain. He cursed as Ivy walked in after him and sat down in silence on her bed.

Elana had moved Finn into Ivy's room after Queen Narra, and Princess Meisha arrived. At first, Finn was glad to come home and find that he now shared a room with Ivy. But since he'd decided not to propose to Ivy, he found it challenging to be so close to her and fought not to give in to temptation. His bed was on the opposite side of the room, but he could still feel the pull at night to slip into Ivy's bed. They had shared a bed before but had never done so much as cradle one another or kiss. Finn felt Ivy's eyes on him as he threw his bloody shirt on his bed and moved over to a small table.

He rinsed his hands in a bowl of water, then wet a cloth and started wiping away the blood on his chest. He flinched at the cold touch and let the water run down his chest and stomach. No stitches were ripped, and Finn was grateful for that. He moved to the trunk at the end of his bed and pulled out a clean shirt and slipped it over his head. He noticed Ivy's eyes traveling over his chest from across the room and turned away so she couldn't see his blushing cheeks as he buttoned the shirt.

The feast would begin early that evening, and everyone would pile into the Great Hall to celebrate the fallen knight. It seemed almost wrong to Finn, but he hoped it would change the tense mood that hung throughout the kingdom like a thick fog. He picked up a mirror and noticed how dark his eye had already turned, and wondered if he looked just as undone as everyone else seemed to be. Finn turned around to see that Ivy was gone and let a disappointed sigh escape his lungs.

The sky was on fire as the sun dipped below the horizon, turning everything bright just before it would grow dark. Finn waited for Ivy in their room, but when she didn't appear, he decided to walk to the feast alone. Finn wore a cotton doublet the color of blood in case his wound reopened. His pants were black and tucked into the tops of his boots.

The Great Hall boomed with the sound of people, and Finn felt his heart lift a little as he opened the massive wooden doors. The walls were lined with hundreds of candles, and even more hung down from the dark ceiling, creating a constellation of light above. Some of the tables had been removed and sat outside the hall to make more room for dancers. The place was packed with bodies, and Finn felt the heat wash over him as the doors closed behind him. Magnus sat with his family on the dais, drinking and talking as the music echoed through the Hall. Finn scanned the crowd and saw many of Earl Rorik's people sitting in the back of the hall, drinking ale-filled horns and laughing. He walked through the sea of people, turning his head to look for Ivy when he felt a cold hand grab his wrist.

Finn turned to see Princess Meisha holding him at bay. Her light blond hair bounced around her shoulders in loose ringlets, and her sharp blue gaze held Finn in place. She wore a gown the color of her eyes with a plunging neckline only covered by a sheer fabric the color of her skin. Finn kept his eyes on hers as she smiled up at him and released her cold fingers from his wrist. He had to look down to make sure she wasn't touching him anymore, the coolness of her grip lingered on his skin. "I'm Meisha," she said, holding her hand out between them.

"I know who you are," Finn said, not taking her hand.

She snapped it back to her side, but her smile never faltered. "You're Finn, right?" she asked innocently. Finn nodded his head impatiently, waiting for her to explain the reason for stopping him.

"Well," she said and stepped closer. Finn could feel her breath on his neck as she spoke. "I just wanted to say hello, that's all. Perhaps I'll find you later for a dance?" Finn felt a prickle on the back of his neck, but before he could answer, Meisha twirled in her blue dress and snaked her way back through the crowd.

Finn walked up to the dais, searching for Ivy. His eyes landed on Rayner, who was tilting back a cup, letting the red wine run into his beard. Beside him, Correlyn gave Finn a brief smile. Finn walked up behind Correlyn's seat and leaned in to be heard over the music. "Where's Ivy?"

"I thought she would have come in with you," Correlyn answered. Rayner didn't turn away from his wine, and Finn opened his mouth to speak but snapped it shut again as the doors of the Hall opened. Ivy turned more than a few heads as she walked through the center of the Hall, people parting before her.

Finn snapped up straight and felt his heart flutter as he ran his eyes over Ivy. Her hair was loose and fell in waves down her back. Her dress was the darkest shade of scarlet with black stones running down the bodice. Her pale skin stood out against the dress, and Finn caught himself as his eyes wandered to her chest. The sleeves fell from her shoulders and dipped in the middle of her chest, and as she turned slightly, Finn could see her bare back as the dress dipped down to her hips in a V shape. Everyone was dressed up for the celebration, but they all looked to be in rags compared to Ivy. She gave him a shy smile as she came up the steps.

Finn left Correlyn and walked over to Ivy, fighting to keep his mind from other things. He slipped a hand around her waist and pulled her in. His fingertips traveled over her smooth skin as he brought his lips to her ear, their cheeks brushing. "You are dangerously beautiful," he whispered to her. Finn felt his mind fogging as his hands slid across her back, and he gave in to the feeling.

He pulled Ivy in and buried his other hand in her hair. His lips crashed into hers, and Ivy put a hand on his hip, trying to pull herself closer. His kiss was eager like he needed it to live. As if he would have dropped dead right there if his lips didn't touch hers. Finn's tongue brushed against Ivy's, and Ivy let a small whimper out. Finn had never kissed her like that in front of so many people, and Ivy pulled away from him, seeming to be aware of the eyes on them.

Finn smiled and let his eyes slowly run down the bodice of Ivy's dress. "Have you been drinking?" Ivy asked, trying to catch his eye. "Your eyes look glassy."

"No." Finn blinked, meeting her eyes. "I just got here."

Magnus's voice interrupted Ivy's thoughts, and Finn grabbed her hand, pulling them to their seats beside Correlyn and Rayner. Magnus gave a small speech about Ser Caster and all of his heroic accomplishments. A silence fell over the crowd as they listened, and when Magnus was done, a cheer rose from the people and ale sloshed over horns before being swallowed in one gulp. The music picked up again, and the food started pouring out from the kitchens. Ivy felt someone watching her during supper and scanned the crowd, searching for that white hair. Kyatta stepped out from behind a pillar and caught Ivy's eyes. She shuddered at the words Kyatta had spoken to her up on the wall. *Thunder and fire fell from the sky, consuming everything around it.* Ivy had gone over her words again and again but still couldn't decipher their meaning. Kyatta smiled at Ivy before turning her back and vanishing into the packed crowd of people.

She noticed another pair of blue eyes on her and narrowed her gaze as Piotr lifted his cup to Ivy. He wore a white doublet with gold thread twisting around the sleeves, and his blond hair seemed to glow in the low candlelight. Ivy twitched her mouth and averted her eyes, turning back to Finn, who was running his fingers over his wrist. Ivy looked past him to see Rayner drinking wine from a large cup as his full plate sat in front of him, the food growing cold with every sip that passed his lips. "I'm worried about Rayner." Ivy leaned into Finn and seemed to startle him. He turned to look at her brother and furrowed his brow.

"Rayner is just enjoying the party," Finn said.

"Will you talk to him?" Ivy pleaded. Finn turned toward her and brought a hand to her cheek, but his eyes said no. "Please, Finn," Ivy persisted. "He'll listen to you."

Finn withdrew his hand and took a gulp of wine before pushing up from his chair. Correlyn seemed to sense what was happening and offered her seat to Finn as she went down into the crowd dancing around the Hall. Finn sat down with a sigh as Rayner kept his eyes on his wife. "Are you well?" Finn asked. Rayner answered by downing his cup of wine and reaching for the flagon in front of him. Finn caught his hand before he could reach it, and Rayner snapped his head in Finn's direction. His eyes were bloodshot and glazed over, Finn could smell the wine coming off him. "Rayner," Finn started, "your sister—"

"Yes, yes," Rayner interrupted and waved a hand at Finn. "I'm fine, so go away and let me drink in peace."

Finn touched at a sudden throbbing in his black eye as Rayner snatched the flagon away from him. "I understand your fear toward the horned . . ." Finn stopped himself before finishing his sentence, and Rayner paused, letting the cup hover inches from his lips.

Finn didn't know what to say, he didn't want to upset Rayner any further, but Finn had to admit that he was worried about him too.

"I'm not afraid of him," Rayner snapped and took a sip of wine.

"Ser Caster saved all of us from certain death, Rayner. His death won't go unavenged."

Rayner closed his eyes at the mention of Ser Caster's name and tightened his grip around his cup until his knuckles were white.

"Rayner, you have to stop this. Your family is worried about you. I'm—"

Rayner slammed his cup down and grabbed Finn by the collar. Magnus and Elana looked up as Rayner leaned closer to Finn. "Do not tell me how to deal with my fears." Rayner's eyes widened a little, and his grip relaxed some. "And stop treating me as if I'm a broken little boy." Rayner sneered and thrust Finn back in his chair. Magnus started to rise from his seat, but Finn shook his head, and the king sat back down, keeping his eyes on his son. "I don't want your pity," Rayner said as he turned away and gulped down the rest of the wine. Finn lowered his eyes and pushed back the chair, leaving Rayner to drown his fears in wine.

CHAPTER TWENTY-THREE

ENCHANTED

I vy watched Finn go to her brother just as someone blocked her view and plopped down in his seat. Meisha looked back to where Finn sat down at the table, and Ivy tapped her foot as she followed her gaze. "He'll be right back," Ivy said, and Meisha turned around wearing a smile.

"Oh, I have no doubt." Her eyes ran over Ivy's dress. "How could he stay away?" Ivy sensed the sarcasm in her voice and felt her cheeks growing hot. She'd noticed Meisha watching Finn ever since she arrived with her mother. "This is a lovely feast," Meisha said, turning her smile to the dancers. "Did you know the knight well?" she asked.

Ivy nodded her head in response and followed Meisha's eyes out into the crowd and felt a wave of annoyance as she caught Piotr's eyes on her once again.

"What do you want?" Ivy looked back at the princess.

"Who said I wanted anything?" she said innocently. Meisha turned to look at Finn again, and Ivy balled her fists.

"Why do you keep looking at him?" she asked with hostility in her voice.

"Why wouldn't I look at him?" Meisha turned back, but the smile faded. "He's delicious," she said, slightly licking her lips. Ivy dug her nails into her palm and twisted her lips tight. She opened her mouth as Finn came walking back, his eyes immediately going to Meisha, who sat in his chair.

Meisha stood up as Finn reached for a cup of wine and gulped it down like water. Ivy stood up and grabbed Finn's hand, turning him toward her. "What happened?" she asked. Finn shook his head and was about to speak when he looked out into the crowd. Ivy followed his hateful gaze to where Piotr sat, watching them. Finn reached to pour more wine, turning away from Ivy. Meisha caught his wrist, and Finn seemed to freeze under her touch.

"Are you all right, Finn?" Ivy asked as she tried to read his face.

"I'm fine," Finn replied as Meisha's grip tightened. He tried to pull away, but she held him there, staring into his eyes and smiling her wicked smile.

"Would you like to dance, Finn?"

Meisha turned to Ivy as innocent as a little girl. "You don't mind, do you?" Ivy looked at Finn, but his gaze was lost in the crowd, and she slowly shook her head as Meisha was pulling Finn along behind her. "Besides"—she leaned in close to Ivy—"I think someone else wants to dance with you." She winked and pulled Finn down to the dance floor.

Ivy could feel the anger making her blood hot as she watched Finn being dragged along. The two wove into the crowd, and Ivy struggled to keep an eye on them as other dancers created a wall around them. She plopped down in her chair and drank some wine as she narrowed her gaze on the princess. Finn had acted strange, and she wondered what Rayner said to him. She looked down the table and saw her parents leaning in close to one another and Ronin sitting at the end with Earl Rorik. Correlyn had returned to her seat and was talking to Rayner, though he seemed lost in another thought. Luna ruffled her feathers above the king's head, where she sat perched on a twisted branch of the throne.

Ivy was startled by Piotr's voice in her ear. She whipped around, cracking him across the face with the back of her hand. Piotr grabbed his cheek which was already turning red and gave Ivy a horrified look. "What was—"

"I know what you did to Finn in Tonsburg." She spat the words at him like venom. Ivy pushed back her chair and stood to leave, but Piotr caught her arm and flinched, preparing for another strike. He held his other hand up in submission as Ivy snatched her arm free.

"I'm sorry," Piotr said as he stood to face Ivy. His eyes traveled down her neck, and Ivy shifted uncomfortably at his lingering gaze.

He took a deep breath, and Ivy felt its warm touch release on her neck. "I'll apologize to him as well, but I'm afraid he'll kill me," he joked, but Ivy wasn't smiling. "I was jealous," Piotr blurted out. "All right? I'm sorry."

Ivy looked at him like he had just spoken another language. Piotr jealous of Finn? Piotr had consistently teased Ivy every time he came to Godstone, and though she had her suspicions, to hear him admit it made her feel uncomfortable. Piotr looked down to his polished boots, and Ivy turned her gaze to Meisha, who was running her hands up Finn's arms. She balled her fists again and snapped her head back at Piotr.

"So you want to dance?" she asked. Piotr didn't answer, but something twinkled in his eyes. "Isn't that why you came up here?"

"I came to apologize and to—"

"And now you have," Ivy grabbed his hand. "So, let's dance." Piotr didn't dare argue and gladly followed her onto the dance floor.

Ivy shifted closer to Meisha and Finn and snapped her skirts at Meisha's feet as they passed. The princess gave Ivy a surprised look, but Finn didn't even look up at Ivy. Piotr placed a hand on Ivy's back and gripped her hand in his. His fingers pressed into her spine, and Ivy hoped he wouldn't feel the dagger she concealed back there. Ivy thought having Promise strapped to her side would take away from the dress, so she had settled on Rayner's knife and kept it tucked safely away.

Piotr pulled her in closer, and Ivy could feel his breath on her cheek. He smelt of wine and roses, not something Ivy was expecting. The music swirled around them as they glided across the wooden floor. Ivy lifted her eyes to the many candles dangling above, looking as if suspended in midair. Piotr followed her gaze and smiled. "Beautiful, isn't it?" he whispered against her cheek. Ivy barely heard him as her eyes came down to see Finn lost in Meisha's cold blue stare. His hands were around her waist and hers around his neck. Ivy tightened her grip on Piotr's hand. Finn seemed to be stumbling, but Ivy knew he only had one cup of wine.

She twirled around Piotr, trying to look into Finn's eyes, but Meisha kept spinning him around, moving deeper into the crowd.

"What's wrong?" Piotr asked.

Ivy strained her eyes, searching for the princess. "Something feels wrong," she said half to herself. The song ended, and dancers broke apart to clap and cheer, but Piotr kept his hand on Ivy's back.

The Hall boomed with the sound of applause, and the music started up again, but it was much slower. Ivy noticed her parents moving to the dance floor, leaving Rayner and Correlyn at the table. Earl Rorik and his wife were dancing as well, and more people seemed to pack in tighter. Ivy bumped into someone behind her, and Piotr pulled her in closer as the soft music drifted up to the rafters. "You look beautiful by the way," Piotr said as his eyes fell to Ivy's dress.

"Thank you," Ivy replied coolly. She caught a glimpse of Finn still dancing with the princess, her head gently laid against Finn's chest. Ivy couldn't help but be jealous. Meisha was gorgeous, and she had swept Finn away so quickly. Finn always danced with Ivy at feasts, and she felt like he had tossed her aside. It wasn't like him, but Ivy knew everyone was suffering a little after what happened, each one of them a little broken. Still, it was no excuse, and Ivy grew angrier as she met eyes with Meisha, who gave her a small wave of her fingers. This must be how Piotr felt if his confession was to be believed.

As if he read her thoughts, Piotr turned her chin toward him, away from Meisha and Finn. "Stop watching them," he said quietly, his lips hovering above hers.

"He's not even looking at me." Ivy glanced away from his blue eyes.

"Then he's a fool," Piotr said and planted his lips against her cheek. They were surprisingly soft, and Ivy was surprised by the sudden blush on her cheeks. She pushed him away, and by the look on Piotr's face, Ivy could tell he was hurt.

She turned away before he could say anything and pushed through the crowd, trying to find Meisha. Ivy spotted Kyatta standing in the back of the Hall watching Ivy with those cold eyes. She heard the sound of the large doors shutting and craned her neck to see who just passed through. Ivy spotted a wave of blue fabric as the doors closed and pushed harder to get through the thick sea of bodies.

Outside, a drizzle was coming down, and fog crept in the streets, swirling around Ivy's skirts as she stomped through the road. Her bare shoulders grew slick with rain as it ran down the bodice of her dress. Ivy turned the corner of the Great Hall, where the maple tree stood just outside the tower. Her eyes lifted to the leaves as she rounded the building but quickly snapped down as something caught her eye. Ivy ground to a halt.

Finn's lips were pressed against Meisha's, and her hands ran through his soft brown hair as he pulled her waist closer to him. Ivy's heart drummed in her ears, and the rain on her skin began to boil. She felt hot tears threatening to come as she reached back and felt the cold metal of Rayner's dagger. Ivy grabbed the knife, pulled it out, and took aim.

Their kiss was broken up by the loud *thump* of Rayner's dagger sticking into the trunk of the tree, just above Meisha's head. The princess shot a startled look toward Ivy and backed away from Finn. He stood there like a statue and followed Meisha's gaze. Ivy looked at a stranger wearing Finn's face. His eyes were glassy, and his expression unreadable. Meisha curled her lips into a thin smile as Ivy stormed across the grass toward them. Finn didn't say anything or try to stop Ivy as she balled her fist and sent it sailing toward Meisha's face.

Someone caught her by the wrist, and she turned to see Piotr holding her back. "Let me go, or I'll turn this punch on you," she growled. Piotr let her arm go and backed away, shooting a worried look at Meisha. The princess stood with her hands behind her back with an easy smile on her lips.

"I told you he was delicious," Meisha said, taking a step closer. Ivy fought every instinct in her body telling her to knock her out or to strangle her. But she was a princess as Ivy was, and Queen Narra would likely fight to punish Ivy should she lay a hand on her precious daughter. Meisha leaned into Ivy's ear, her breath as cold as a corpse. "I just wanted a little taste," she whispered.

Ivy threw up her balled fist just as Meisha snapped her fingers, and Finn dropped to the ground. Ivy froze and turned to see Finn lying lifeless in the grass. She ran over and dropped to Finn's side, shaking his shoulder. "Finn," Ivy croaked. He stayed unmoving against her touch, and Ivy glared back up at Meisha as Piotr stood shocked behind Ivy. She got up and rushed Meisha before she could get away, grabbing her by the throat and squeezing. "What did you do to him?" Ivy demanded

"Ivy, stop!" Piotr pleaded.

Meisha choked under Ivy's grip but didn't answer. Ivy

searched her eyes but saw nothing. She thrust the princess back who fell to her knees, gasping for air.

"Why did you do that?" Piotr directed this toward Meisha. Ivy could sense panic in his voice.

"Isn't it what you asked for?" She smiled as she got to her feet.

Ivy whipped her head around to Piotr, who crumpled under her glare. "What does she mean?" Ivy demanded, taking a step toward Piotr.

"I . . . she . . ."

Ivy turned her back and walked over to the tree, drew the knife out of the trunk, and stormed back toward Piotr. "Ivy, wait—"

Ivy's blade cut off his words as she held it to his throat and pinned him up against the wall of the Great Hall. She was only inches from his face and could feel his breath coming out in shaky puffs. "I'll ask you again, and maybe this time you'll be smart enough to answer. What does she mean?"

"I . . . I told you I was jealous." Piotr sounded like a little boy.

Ivy furrowed her brow—she didn't understand. "What did she do to Finn?" Ivy pressed the blade a little harder.

"I don't know!" His voice was panicked. "She was just supposed to break you away from him, I don't know why he dropped like that. I swear!"

Ivy turned back to Meisha, but she was gone. Finn still lay on the ground, not moving, but Ivy could see the rise and fall of his chest. "You did this." Ivy turned her attention back on Piotr.

"You were supposed to find them kissing and be heartbroken. Then I . . ." Piotr trailed off mid-sentence. Ivy couldn't stop the sharp laughter that came shooting out, and Piotr narrowed his eyes on her.

"You thought you could sweep me away? Just like that?" Ivy leaned in closer, hovering above his lips, and she watched something like desire come into Piotr's blue eyes. "You're pathetic," she hissed and removed the blade from his throat.

Ivy walked over and tried to shake Finn awake. The cold rain was seeping into her bones, and she knew she had to get Finn out of the weather. Something caught her eye, and Ivy lifted Finn's wrist to see the imprint of a hand. It shimmered like silver before her eyes, and Ivy's breath caught in her throat.

Finn had been enchanted.

She had only ever read about it in stories, not believing that such powers could exist in her world. If Meisha was an enchantress, Ivy knew whatever hold she had on Finn couldn't be broken until she released him, or...

She turned back to Piotr, and her eyes went wide, dropping Finn's lifeless arm and reaching for her dagger. Meisha was gripping Piotr's wrist in her cold hands, and Ivy could see the same look that Finn had start to wash over his face. "Ivy," he managed to say. "I'm so . . ." Piotr's voice broke off as his eyes glazed over, and his arm relaxed.

Meisha released him, leaving a silvery handprint on his arm, and leaned close to Piotr. "Get her," she commanded Piotr.

Ivy stood up, gripping her dagger in her hands. Her eyes frantically searched Piotr's face, but nothing was there. A blank stare, a puppet for the princess. "Piotr," Ivy said as he crossed the grass toward her. "Don't do this! Fight it!" But it was no use, Piotr closed the space between them, and Ivy threw up her knife in defense as he grabbed for her. He didn't even flinch when Ivy cut his arm, and she paused long enough for him to grab her by the throat.

She lifted her blade again, but Piotr caught her arm and twisted it until she cried out in pain. He turned the knife around and sent it crashing into the back of Ivy's head. She saw stars dancing in her eyes as she went down, and the world grew dark. Meisha stood over her with that wicked smile and placed a hand on Piotr's shoulder. Ivy's vision blurred as she sank her head to the grass and then nothing. Cold darkness swept around her and swallowed her whole.

CHAPTER TWENTY-FOUR

PUPPETS

I vy woke up on the cold stone floor of a room she didn't recognize. The air was damp and smelt of dirt and blood. Her vision blurred as she tried to open her eyes, and a wave of nausea crashed over her as she sat up. She realized her hands were bound behind her back and instantly panicked, her last memories coming back in pieces.

Ivy looked around the dim room and realized she was under the tower. Her father had built a holding cell below the central tower before Ivy was born. She never asked why since the knights' barracks had their own cells for criminals. This cell was different than the ones at the barracks, and being underground made Ivy's heart race a little faster. Suddenly she felt like she couldn't breathe, and the roof was closing in on her. She looked around the stone room and noticed there wasn't any furniture or candles. Only a dim light coming from under the door where a set of stairs led up to the main floor of the tower. Ivy tried to scream, but the pain in her head forced her mouth shut before she could do it. She remembered Piotr hitting her and Meisha controlling him and . . . *Finn!*

Ivy spun around the room as tears came to her eyes, but Finn wasn't there. She scooted closer to the door and pressed her ear against it, listening to muffled voices outside. She kicked the door, and the voices stopped before a key turned, and Piotr walked in.

Ivy felt a sudden relief, but when he held the torch up in front of him, she could see that he was still enchanted. Ivy moved away from him as he called over his shoulder to someone outside. Meisha stepped into the dim light from the torch and smiled down at Ivy. "Bring me a chair," she commanded Piotr, and he turned to leave as Meisha grabbed the torch from him. She strolled into the cell and looked around just as Piotr came back in and set a chair in the middle of the room. Meisha put the torch into a metal ring on the wall and lowered herself into the chair. Piotr closed the door behind him and stood guard with a blank stare. "Where's Finn?" Ivy said through gritted teeth.

"Ah, your dark-haired beauty," Meisha answered while twirling a lock of blond hair. "He tasted just as I'd imagined." Ivy spit at the princess, who seemed more amused than anything. "If you want him returned, then you better not test me," Meisha said in a sharp tone. Ivy rounded her shoulders and lowered her head as it continued pounding. Meisha turned her eyes on Piotr, her puppet. "He really does like you." Meisha sounded as if they were two friends gossiping about boys. Ivy looked at Piotr, but his gaze remained on the stone wall across the room. "You can't blame him, he had no idea what I planned to do. But after he arrived with your father, I began to notice how often he watched you." Meisha turned back to Ivy.

"His eyes followed you everywhere, and I thought"— Meisha raised a finger in the air as if she'd just now come up with her plan—"what a perfect way to get what I want by using his feelings for you. I was going to use your brother, but Piotr seemed like a safer choice. It's so easy to persuade someone in love." Her grin turned sinister, and Ivy turned her attention back on Piotr.

Love?

Piotr couldn't love Ivy. After everything he said to her all those years. The way he treated Finn in Tonsburg. But then Ivy remembered the way his hands slid over her back, how close he held her when they danced as if she might slip away. The look in his eyes as Ivy leaned closer to his lips and called him pathetic. She felt a stab of guilt and lowered her eyes from Piotr, sniffing back her tears.

"Oh, don't cry for him," Meisha said softly. "He was powerless before I even enchanted him." Ivy snapped her head up at Meisha and realized she was still in her blue dress. It was still the night of the feast, which meant no one was likely looking for her as everyone was still enjoying themselves above ground.

"What do you want?" Ivy sneered.

"We want Godstone," Meisha said as if it were obvious. Ivy's mind raced, and then she thought of Queen Narra, likely still at the feast. Ivy pulled on the rope binding her hands, rubbing the flesh of her wrists against its coarse bristles.

"Where's your mother?" Ivy demanded.

Meisha waved her hand up at the ceiling. "Somewhere up there, likely keeping your family distracted."

"You and your mother think you can take Godstone from—"

"Don't be stupid," Meisha interrupted. "We're just here to report back now that your father has rounded up the northern Houses for us."

Meisha clicked her fingernails on the armrest of the chair. Her blue eyes seemed to glow in the dim room. Ivy couldn't make sense of her words. The queen and princess had come here for refuge, King Cenric had been killed, and they'd come to warn Magnus. Why would they willingly wait until Magnus gathered all the forces he could? A cold chill crept over Ivy's body as Meisha smiled at her from her chair. "Your father isn't dead, is he?" Ivy asked.

"Oh, he's dead, I can assure you. I watched it happen just like I said." her voice sounded amused.

"You let Helvarr kill your father?" Ivy asked in disgust.

"My father was weak," she snapped. "He deserved what he got."

Ivy sat back further at Meisha's words and the mad look on her face. Ivy's palms were sweating as she tried to loosen the bonds behind her back. "Let Finn go, you don't need him anymore." Ivy tried to make her voice sound stern, but it came out as pleading.

"I'll let him go as soon as our deal is done. Though he'll likely die with everyone else anyway."

Ivy grimaced at the thought. "What do you want from me?"

"I'm going to deliver you to Helvarr, of course," the princess said plainly.

Ivy felt the wave of nausea again and tried to keep calm, but her heart sped up, and the aching in her head intensified. If Helvarr got his hands on Ivy, she knew her father would do anything to get her back, including opening the gates to his kingdom. Ivy swallowed down her panic as Meisha leaned on her knees, hovering closer. Ivy couldn't let that happen. She would rather die than see her father's kingdom fall, and all her people be slaughtered. Ivy thought of her pregnant mother, her brother, and his new wife. She thought of Finn and how upset she was with him, though now she wished she could kiss him one last time.

Ivy forced herself to meet Meisha's cold eyes. "What are you getting out of this?" Ivy was genuinely curious. Meisha looked bored and sat back in her chair, twirling another lock of blond hair.

"We get to rule our kingdom the way we want. Helvarr will be the High King, of course, but he's promised my mother and me our lands back with the freedom to rule."

Ivy snorted. "And you really believe he'll keep his word?"

"Of course." She smiled wide. "Before Helvarr came into our walls, my mother and I snuck out to meet him. My mother explained to him what I was and so we devised a plan to put my powers to use. He told me to enchant Rayner and bring him, but like I said"—her gaze turned back to Piotr— "this poor boy made it too easy to choose you instead. I saw him watching you during the feast and went to talk to him. At first, he didn't believe that I could really enchant your man Finn, but he watched me do it and quick as a snake came to sweep you away on the dance floor. He wasn't supposed to follow you out of the building—one of my guards failed to grab him, but he'll be taken care of." Meisha stopped to look at Ivy, her cold gaze sending shivers down her spine. "Anyway," she went on as if the story bored her, "I'm sure Helvarr will understand and be equally as pleased that I have you, though someone else will be disappointed."

Ivy felt sick at the thought of Rayner being enchanted by Meisha and willingly handing himself over to Helvarr. Rayner had been through so much, and it pained Ivy to think of how close he came to being captured. Ivy tried to remember Meisha's story about her father's death. She was a good actor, Ivy had to admit, and her lies flowed out so smoothly that it's possible she even believed them. Everyone believed their story when the queen and princess first arrived. Magnus had rounded up more people than he ever had because of their warning, and now Helvarr was going to come and destroy them all in one fell swoop.

Helvarr would be tickled to have Ivy, especially after he'd sent a raider to capture her on Kame Island and failed, then came himself to slay Ser Osmund in front of her. When Ivy ran at him, something in his eyes was eager to see what would happen. As if he was urging her to do it, to kill him.

Ivy snapped out of her thoughts and recalled what Meisha had just said. She felt goose flesh crawl across her skin as she shifted on the cold ground. Meisha gave an approving smile as if she knew what Ivy was going to say even before Ivy did. "The horned knight," Ivy said, half to herself.

"Ah, clever girl." Meisha seemed delighted.

"You know who it is?" Ivy asked.

"Well, of course. The horned knight badly wants your brother, but they'll get their chance eventually."

"Who is he?" Ivy yelled, the pulse in her head growing faster. Meisha started laughing and Ivy scrunched up her nose in anger. She moved closer to Meisha as she continued to laugh. Meisha snapped her finger, and Piotr rushed at her, kicking the heel of his boot into Ivy's chest. The wind was knocked out of her as she slammed back onto the stone ground.

"You'll find out soon enough as well." Meisha wiped away a tear from her laughter. "Piotr," she turned toward him. "Be a dear and fetch Finn for me." Piotr turned on command and left the room.

Ivy's heart pounded against her chest as she sat back up and watched the door. "Please," she said, not caring any longer how timid her voice sounded. "I'll go with you. Just let Finn go. You said you'd let him go!" she screamed.

Meisha bent down in front of Ivy, her eyes pulsing with excitement as the words left her mouth like a cool breeze. "I lied." Ivy struggled harder against her restraints as Finn and Piotr walked into the room.

"Finn!" Ivy called to him, but his eyes were still as glassy as a doll's, and he stood with his gaze fixed straight ahead. Ivy let her tears burn her eyes as she tried desperately to squeeze her wrist free. She could feel the warm blood trickling down her hands as the rope cut into her.

"Now." Meisha clapped her hands together. "The feast should be winding down, everyone well drunk at this point. We'll go out of the southern gate where my mother should be waiting with some horses. It's a long ride, plenty of time to mourn for your loss." Meisha brushed the top of Ivy's hair as if to comfort her. She sobbed as Meisha touched her head, and she could feel the cold from her fingers even through her hair. Meisha turned to Finn and brushed her cold hand over his cheek. "Perhaps I'll keep him after all." Meisha turned to look at Ivy. "He is very handsome." Meisha placed her cold lips against Finn's, and he melted under her enchanted kiss, bringing his hand to caress her face. Ivy turned away, not wanting to see what had been done to her Finn. "I could use some company at night," Meisha said to herself.

"So." She twirled back to Ivy, her blue skirts swirling around her ankles. "I'll take Finn to the horses and make sure everything is set and ready to go." With that, she twirled around and looped her arm through Finn's. She turned back to Piotr, who stood behind the chair Meisha was using. "If she tries anything"—her crooked grin slipped back into place—"kill her, and we'll go back for Rayner as planned."

"If you touch my brother, I'll kill you," Ivy snapped at her back. Meisha only turned her head back and winked before walking off with Finn and closing the door behind her. Piotr stood still as a statue, and Ivy listened for the footsteps to disappear before speaking. "Piotr." Ivy rolled around to her knees. "Please, it's me. I know you're in there." Ivy got to one knee slowly. Piotr didn't look at her until she stood up. He pulled Rayner's dagger from his back and held it close to his side. Ivy's blood ran faster as she spotted the knife and tried to force her bloody wrist out of the rope. Ivy took a small step forward, and Piotr finally met her eyes. They were hauntingly blue and empty. His stare unnerved her as she took a small step forward. Piotr tightened his grip on the knife, and Ivy stopped moving, beads of sweat running down her back.

"You don't have to do this, Piotr," she continued. "I know you're being controlled, but please." Her voice cracked. "Try to fight it."

She took another step and pulled at the rope as Piotr came around the chair to stand in front of her. He was close enough to strike her with the knife if she made the wrong move. Her mind raced with the beating of her heart as she opened her mouth to speak. "Piotr . . ." She tried to make her voice as gentle as possible. "I know how you feel." She took the tiniest step toward him, the blood on her wrists making the rope slick. "I know you love me." The words tasted strange on her tongue, but she had no choice, she had to try. Ivy thought she saw something flicker in his eyes just as she slipped a wrist free.

Ivy plowed into him, slamming his back up against the wall as she tried to reach the knife. Piotr grunted in pain and punched Ivy in the gut. She crumpled over and backed away from him, focusing on the dagger in his hand. "Piotr, please—"

He swung the knife at her face, and Ivy nearly lost her balance as she stumbled back. His eyes showed no emotions as he came at her, thrusting the blade toward her heart. Ivy grabbed his arm and sent her elbow into his chest as she reached for the blade again. He drew it away, cutting Ivy across the palm of her hand. She snatched it away and watched the blood pool in her palm. "Piotr!" she yelled at him, but he ignored her, as she wildly tried to catch a glimpse of the real Piotr in his dead eyes.

He slashed at her in a rage as Ivy twirled around him and grabbed the chair. She lifted it and sent it crashing into Piotr's side as he turned toward her. One of the legs splintered on contact and went sailing across the room. Piotr stumbled, and Ivy took her chance, plowing into him and knocking them both to the ground. They struggled to pin one another as Ivy wrapped her hand around his silver wrist. She slammed it into the stone ground with all the strength she had left, again and again. Piotr's grip was firm, and Ivy let go with one hand and sent it crashing into his face. His head slammed against the stone floor, and Ivy gave his wrist one last thrust. He let go of the knife, and it went skidding across the floor. She crawled off him and reached for the blade as he grabbed the skirts of her dress, tearing them.

Piotr slammed his fist into her back, and Ivy dropped to the floor, grunting in pain as he climbed on top of her. She shifted under his weight, turning to look at him just as his hands gripped her throat. Ivy gasped for air as his strong hands closed off her airways, white lights beginning to form in her vision. She punched him in the ribs, and he sneered with every punch but didn't lose his grip on her. Piotr lifted her head and slammed it down on the stone floor, and Ivy felt her strength leaving her. Ivy couldn't think straight; her head pounded fiercely as Piotr desperately tried to squeeze the life from her. She had to try something, she couldn't let Meisha take Finn and her brother. Godstone would fall if Helvarr got his hands on either one of them, and she couldn't let that happen.

Ivy swung the rope still attached to her wrist around the back of Piotr's neck and grabbed it with her other hand. He continued digging his fingers into her throat as she used all her strength to pull him down. His eyes stayed focused on her, but Ivy felt him resisting and craning his neck up against her pull. Ivy grunted and yanked him down to her until he was hovering just above her face. His breath was hot, and Ivy could see how different his eyes looked up close. They held nothing of the real Piotr in them and only showed hate toward Ivy. Ivy remembered reading about enchantresses like Meisha when she was younger. In all of those books, Ivy only found one sure way to break a trance, such as the one holding Piotr, but it was a gamble, and she had to trust what Meisha told her. *It's so easy to persuade someone in love.* The room was turning dark around her as she gave him one last pull and pressed her lips against his.

Piotr's lips were tight against hers, but she felt his grip on her throat lighten up. Ivy watched his eyes looking into her before she closed hers. She pulled him in closer and parted her lips to deepen their kiss. Piotr's mouth seemed to loosen along with his fingers as Ivy brought her hands to his face. She kissed him the way Finn had kissed her earlier that night. She kissed him like she needed it to live as if she would drop dead without it, except in her case, it was true. Piotr's fingers let go of her throat and slowly moved to her shoulders as his lips finally gave in and parted against hers.

She heard him make a small moan as he returned her kiss, and Ivy could feel the enchantment leaving him as he ran his fingertips over her bare shoulders. Blood ran down his face from where Ivy had punched him and worked its way between their mouths. It tasted metallic and felt warm against her lips, and she felt her cheeks grow hot as Piotr grabbed her head, cradling it as his lips moved against hers. Her heart was hammering, and she felt lightheaded, though she told herself that it was her injuries, not Piotr. Ivy pushed her hands into his chest, separating their mouths, and looked into his eyes. They were brilliantly blue, like before, and intensely focused on hers.

Piotr seemed to recognize her at that moment and looked down at himself as he straddled Ivy's body. He looked confused, and Ivy brought her fingertips to her throat which still burned with his touch. Piotr untangled his hands from her hair, and they came away bloodied. His eyes went wide as he took in the blood and the imprint of his hands around Ivy's throat. Ivy propped herself up on her elbows, and Piotr's eyes flickered as their faces came close together. His eyes traveled to her lips, and he instinctively brought a finger up to her throat. Ivy shuddered at his touch, and he withdrew, looking hurt.

"Ivy." Piotr's voice was shaky as he looked at her. "Did I do this?" His finger raised to point at her neck again.

Ivy pushed back and slid her legs out from under him, his cheeks growing red with sudden embarrassment, forgetting that he was on top of her. Piotr brought a hand up to the cut above his brow and looked back at Ivy. She tore a strip of her shredded dress and began to wrap it around the slice to her palm. Piotr's eyes fell to her wrists, and his face crumpled. "Let me help." Piotr moved toward her, but she was still shaken up and drew away from him. "Ivy, I . . ."

"We don't have time for this," Ivy said more sharply than she intended. "And I don't have time to explain. We need to get to the southern gate." Ivy stood up and grabbed Rayner's dagger from the floor. The sudden movement sent a rush to her head, and she swayed on her feet. Piotr caught her by the arm, genuine worry dancing in his eyes as he looked her over. She pulled away from him and put a hand on the stone wall to steady herself.

"I'm sorry," Piotr said as he let go of her. She cut away the bottom of her skirts so she wouldn't trip on them as Piotr stepped closer. "How did you know it would work?"

"What?" Ivy asked, standing up straight to look at him. He ran a nervous hand through his blond hair.

"The kiss, how did you know it would work?" Ivy felt her cheeks blush and looked away.

"I didn't," she admitted. She couldn't tell Piotr that she knew of his true feelings, not when he'd never revealed them to her himself. There was something else she remembered reading in those books, but she couldn't think of that. Not now.

"You must have known something." Piotr stepped closer still.

"Just something I read in a book." Her eyes met his as he hovered over her. "You were killing me, Piotr. I did what I had to."

His blue eyes looked down, filling with new pain. Ivy cracked the door to make sure the stairwell was clear before turning back to Piotr. His eyes were cast down, looking at his empty hands as if he couldn't believe what he'd done. Ivy grabbed his hand, and Piotr raised his eyes to hers. Ivy thought they looked shiny with tears. "We have to go, Piotr," Ivy urged. His hand closed around hers, and they went through the door and up the stairs.

CHAPTER TWENTY-FIVE

BETRAYAL

A s they stepped outside, Ivy saw the moon still lingering in the sky, and the rain had stopped. Ivy led Piotr through the streets, making sure to keep to the darkness and hug the buildings. She could still hear laughter coming from the Hall but fought the urge to go inside. There wasn't time to explain everything, but Ivy quickly filled Piotr in on Meisha's plan and Helvarr's promise of power. She poked her head around a corner and spotted the southern gate. There were no guards on the wall, and Ivy felt a sudden cold sweat wash over her as she imagined the knights who were likely dead up on the wall. Ivy stepped out into the street, but Piotr grabbed her around the waist, pulling her back. "Wait," he said in a hushed voice. "What are you going to do?" His hand was still firmly wrapped around her hip. Ivy didn't have a plan, she just knew she needed to get to Finn before Meisha discovered they were gone or the princess would kill him and go back for Rayner.

"I don't know," she admitted. "But I have to do something, go back if you want."

"I'm not leaving you." Piotr stepped closer. If he did indeed love Ivy, then he would likely do anything for her, and she couldn't let him risk his life again.

"Go back, Piotr, your feelings already got you in trouble." She tried to sound stern but regretted it the second Piotr took his hand from her. His face looked pained and hurt at her words, but still, he wouldn't budge.

"You can insult me all you want later, but I'm not going." At that moment, Ivy liked him more than she ever had. A faint smile fell across her face, and Piotr returned it.

They stepped out of the shadows and ran to the wall. Ivy could hear voices coming through the open gate and took out her dagger. She looked back at Piotr, who kept his eyes on her, and noticed he didn't have a weapon. There was no time to go back. Ivy handed her dagger to Piotr, who looked at her with a new worry in his eyes. "Take it," Ivy whispered. Piotr took the knife, never taking his eyes from hers. "I'm going to step out and try to lure Meisha this way. When I do, grab Finn and run." She took a deep breath and turned away, but Piotr grabbed her hand, holding it tight.

"You can't do that," he whispered.

"There's no time to argue, Piotr," Ivy said. Piotr shook his head and opened his mouth to argue, but Ivy cut him off. "Just get Finn and get out of here, please." Piotr didn't say anything but lowered his eyes to the ground. Ivy raised her hand to cup his cheek, and Piotr snapped his eyes back up to meet hers. "Promise me if you get the chance you'll take Finn and run." Ivy studied his face, staring deep into his eyes until he finally gave a small nod of his head. Ivy let her hand slide away and tried to steady her breathing before she stepped around the wall.

Meisha had her back turned, talking with one of the guards, and Ivy quickly took in how many there were. She only counted four, and Ivy didn't see Queen Narra anywhere. Finn stood still beside a horse as one of her guards spotted Ivy and quickly drew his sword. Meisha spun around and laid eyes on Ivy, turning her mouth into a tight smile. Her eyes traveled over Ivy's bloody wrists and torn dress before going back up to her throat. "Where's Piotr?" Meisha asked as if she really cared.

"I killed him," Ivy said, trying to keep her voice from shaking. Meisha raised an eyebrow and brought her hand to twist around a lock of hair.

"That's too bad." She sounded disappointed. Ivy could see Piotr in her peripherals, and knew his eyes were on her. "What a sad way to die. By the hands of the woman you love," Meisha mocked. Ivy felt her heart stutter. She was sure that Piotr heard that, and now he knew that Ivy learned his secret. Ivy pushed the panic from her mind and stepped forward. Meisha didn't seem concerned and let her do it as her guards stood by, ready to kill her.

"Let Finn go, Meisha." Ivy held out her hands as if to show she was unarmed. "I'll go with you."

Meisha studied her face and narrowed her eyes, taking a few quick steps toward Ivy. "You know," she said, looking down at Ivy's dress, "I have to admit I was jealous of you tonight. That dress certainly caught both Finn's and Piotr's eyes. Though I had already slightly enchanted Finn before you arrived." She waved her hand at Ivy. "Piotr wasn't enchanted until after we were outside. What did you say to him again?" Ivy felt her neck growing hot and balled her fists. "Ah! Pathetic was the word I believe." Her wicked smile beamed at Ivy. She already felt guilty about what she said to Piotr. If only she'd known how he felt before.

Meisha's eyes turned wide as she looked beyond Ivy. Ivy turned just as Rayner's dagger came flying past her head and buried itself into one guard's throat. The man's head whipped back, and he fell to the ground. Ivy turned around and threw a punch to Meisha's gut as Piotr ran past her and grabbed the knife from the guard's throat. Piotr ran to Ivy just as Meisha was getting back to her feet. A guard slashed at Piotr from behind, and Ivy watched him quickly drag the dagger across another guard's neck. The blood spurted out, covering Piotr's face in a red mist.

Ivy turned on her heels and ran for Finn, who still stood beside the horse. A guard cut her off, and Ivy ducked as his sword flew over her head. "Ivy!" Piotr yelled and tossed the knife into the air. She reached for it as the guard grabbed a handful of her hair and thrust her head back. Ivy was pulled to her feet, and she kicked back as hard as she could, making contact with the guard's shin. Piotr plowed into the man, and he let go of Ivy's hair. She fell to the ground, crawling for the dagger. Grabbing the handle, she spun around and jumped on the guard's back, who was strangling Piotr from behind. Ivy lifted her arms and drove the blade down into the back of the man's neck, and his knees buckled under her. Ivy quickly got off of the dead guard and ran for Finn as Piotr gasped for air behind her. She reached out her hand just as she came up behind Finn, then she heard the snap of cold fingers.

At Meisha's snap, Finn came to life and immediately threw up a fist, punching Ivy as she reached him. The last guard ran to Piotr, and Ivy watched the two struggling against one another as Meisha strolled over to Ivy. Finn stood above her, showing hate and anger in his eyes. She reached for Finn's shirt and pushed him back until he was pinned against the horse. Meisha seemed amused by Ivy's efforts. She sent a panicked look over to Piotr, who was driving the point of Rayner's dagger under the guard's armor. The guard managed to punch Piotr in the face before the blood started pooling around him. Piotr scrambled to his feet, clutching a bloody hand around the knife. Meisha turned to him with a sinister smile, and Piotr stopped moving. Ivy's heart stopped as she thought perhaps he was still enchanted, and their kiss hadn't fully brought him back. Piotr eyed Meisha and slowly started making his way to Ivy, not taking his glare off the enchantress.

Meisha snapped her fingers again, and Finn kicked Ivy in the stomach and shoved her to the ground. She heard Piotr snarl in anger as he watched Ivy fall and quickly broke into a run. Meisha stood by as Piotr slid under the horse and knocked Finn to the ground. Rayner's dagger went sailing off into the grass as Ivy brought a hand up to her face. Hot blood covered her hands, and Ivy felt a surge of anger. She got to her feet as Finn and Piotr struggled in the grass and stormed over to where the dagger landed. Grasping it in her hands, she ran back and threw Finn off of Piotr and held the blade to Finn's throat. Piotr quickly recovered and shot Ivy a look of panic.

"Stop this, Meisha!" Ivy's voice was trembling with anger and adrenaline.

Meisha scanned Ivy's face and looked around at her guards, who lay dead in the grass outside the walls. She turned her attention back on Ivy and smiled while Ivy began digging the blade deeper into Finn's neck. "What happens to you if I spill his blood?" Ivy asked through gritted teeth.

"Do it and let's see," Meisha returned, putting her hands behind her back. Ivy looked over at Piotr, but his face was unreadable. Finn wasn't fighting her anymore, and she felt his body go stiff against hers. She wasn't sure what to do. She couldn't kill Finn, and her threat clearly hadn't shaken Meisha like she hoped it would.

The princess wasn't attached to Finn and had only taken him to anger Ivy. Her hand was shaking as she held the blade against his skin. "Ivy," Piotr began in a small voice. She turned to look at him—his face was covered in blood, but his blue eyes shone through the carnage on his face. "Kiss him." Piotr let the words fall from his mouth. Ivy saw the pain in his eyes as he said the words, and she felt her heart skip a beat. "Do it," he urged.

"You believe it will work?" Meisha asked as she took a step forward. Ivy's head was swarming with too many thoughts and feelings. She remembered what she'd read long ago in those books, and her heart broke at the thought. Enchantresses had power, but they weren't as strong as the legends told. They could easily manipulate someone who was in love, that part Meisha hadn't lied about. But there was also something from those stories that stuck out to Ivy. Running her mind over the events within the past few hours, she couldn't help but believe it. The love trance that Meisha had used was difficult to break and could only be done by someone they truly loved.

Piotr's trance was broken within seconds when Ivy kissed him, and her heart broke at the thought of his love for her. Piotr didn't need to be enchanted to kiss her the way Finn had, the trance was already broken, and yet Ivy felt all the love and desire pouring out of Piotr when he kissed her. There was an eagerness to it like he desired it more than anything. When Finn kissed her at the feast, he was already partially under Meisha's power, and Ivy just happened to be the first girl he saw. Her heart felt as heavy as lead. Those stories always mentioned that if someone were more willing to be enchanted, whether they knew it or not, then it would be easier to control them. Ivy took her blade from Finn's neck and moved toward Meisha instead.

She removed her hands from behind her back and stepped away as Ivy advanced on her. "And what happens if I spill your blood?" Ivy asked through gritted teeth. Meisha's eyes, for the first time, showed signs of fear, and she shot a pleading look to Piotr, but she would get no help there. He wasn't her puppet anymore.

"You don't want to do that." Meisha's voice was as cold as the wind.

"Oh, but I do," Ivy returned with a sinister tone in her voice. She continued stepping closer to Meisha. Meisha lifted her fingers to snap again, but Ivy was on her. She could hear Piotr tackling Finn to the ground behind her, but Ivy's eyes were focused on Meisha's cold stare. Ivy grabbed her as she tried to run and pinned her to the ground, holding her wrists above her head and putting the dagger to the enchantress's throat. Meisha's blue eyes seemed to go dull at that moment as Ivy pressed the blade in harder. "Why isn't your mother here?" Ivy asked. Piotr grunted in pain behind her, but Ivy couldn't take her eyes off of Meisha.

"I'm sure she's on her way here," the princess answered coolly.

Ivy's hand was still shaking as she gripped the handle harder. "Tell me why I shouldn't kill you." Ivy leaned in closer. Meisha might not have planned to take Ivy initially, but she had undoubtedly underestimated her. Ivy doubted that Rayner knew anything of the legends that told of enchantresses, and Ivy was grateful that Meisha changed her mind. No matter how much pain it was causing Ivy, physically and mentally.

Now it was Ivy's turn to smile as she held the power to end this in her hands. Meisha seemed delighted by Ivy's amusement and chuckled under the blade digging into her throat. Ivy narrowed her eyes on her and asked what was funny. Meisha lifted her head from the grass, forcing the knife in deeper. Ivy saw that what she had thought were beautiful blue eyes that glowed with desire now more resembled burning cold eyes, filled with madness. Meisha was insane, and she didn't seem to care for her own life. "Go ahead and kill me," Meisha urged. "You clearly know more than I thought, so surely you know what will happen to your man Finn when you kill me." Ivy loosened her grip on the handle and tried to think, but her head was clouded, and the throbbing returned in full force.

She stole a look back at Piotr, who had Finn pinned on his stomach, forcing his head into the grass. Though he looked concerned for Ivy, she had no doubt that he was enjoying overpowering Finn. When Piotr was straddling her, Ivy could feel the weight of him, his muscles, and the power of him as he pressed into her. She shook the thought from her head and turned back to Meisha, who no longer wore a smile. Ivy had to hurry. Queen Narra would be coming, and she might have more guards with her.

"You would let me kill you?" Ivy asked, edging the knife back into Meisha's pale skin. Her eyes lifted to look behind Ivy, setting her cold gaze on Finn.

"A part of him will die with me," she said, and Ivy sensed no emotion in her voice. "So go ahead." Her gaze found Ivy's eyes again. Meisha lifted her head until their faces were a mere inch away.

"Perhaps he doesn't love you like you thought," Meisha whispered. "Why do you think it was easy to manipulate him? Piotr fought me, I could feel it as I worked my power into his mind."

Ivy's hand was shaking so bad that she saw a trickle of warm blood flow down Miesha's neck, but she didn't flinch at the cut. "Ivy?" Piotr's voice called to her from behind.

Meisha smiled her wicked grin and pressed her neck harder into Ivy's blade. "He loved me more in that kiss than he's ever loved you," she snickered.

Ivy sat frozen on the enchantress, her head raced with her blood as Meisha lifted her head even closer, bringing her frozen voice to Ivy's ear. "You'll never taste the desire that I did on his tongue. His lips quivered under mine, and I'll take that love with me to the grave." Meisha licked her tongue against Ivy's ear.

"Ivy!" Piotr pleaded with her from behind, but it was too late.

Ivy steadied her hand and felt the fog lift from her mind as she slashed the blade across Meisha's throat. The blood turned black under the moonlight, and Ivy watched Meisha's eyes turn dark. Her body went still under Ivy's as the life drained out from her, taking a part of Finn's love with it. Ivy sat atop Meisha's body, trying to swallow back her tears. Meisha had almost taken everything from Ivy and her family. She had manipulated Finn and Piotr and trusted in their feelings toward Ivy to get what she wanted. Ivy felt sick at the thought and closed her eyes, trying not to picture how Meisha had kissed Finn.

She squeezed the handle of the knife until the cut across her hand began bleeding again. Ivy lifted it into the air and sent it through Meisha's eye. Her teeth ground together as she lifted the dagger again before Piotr's hand wrapped around her wrist, and pulled her off. She slumped her shoulders over and began to let the tears fall freely. Piotr wrapped her in his arms and took the knife from her grip. She let herself cry against his chest as he cradled the back of her head, running his bloody hands through her hair. She could feel his heart beating against hers, and at that moment, she felt lost. Her head raced with too many thoughts, her heart was dragging her down, and Piotr was desperately trying to hold her together.

Finn sat up in the grass and looked over at Ivy. Piotr turned the knife around, searching Finn's face as he stood up. Finn furrowed his brow and looked around the field at the bodies turning the earth red. He ran a hand through his hair, and Ivy saw the moment he realized what was happening. Ivy took in a shaky breath before pushing away from Piotr and standing. Finn looked angry and confused all at once as Piotr stood behind Ivy, and he placed a gentle hand on her shoulder.

"Ivy?" Finn stepped closer, and Ivy could feel Piotr shifting on his feet, preparing to fight. Ivy followed Finn's eyes as they went to Meisha, who lay cold and dead in the grass.

Finn snapped his head back up, a frightened look dancing in his eyes. "What happened? Are you all right?" Finn stepped closer until he stood in front of Ivy. Her dress was torn and bloody, along with her hands and wrists. Blood stained her hair, and Piotr's enchanted hands had left their marks around her neck. Piotr put a protective hand around Ivy's waist, and Finn scrunched his nose in anger. Ivy didn't know how to answer Finn. Of course, she wasn't all right, but she was sure he didn't remember much of when he was in a trance. Ivy wanted to scream at him, she wanted to kiss him, but most of all she wanted this to be over.

Finn lifted his hand to Ivy's face, but she quickly smacked it away. She no longer held back her pain-filled tears, and they mixed with the blood on her face as they fell. Ivy felt the anger wrapping around her like Piotr's secure grip. Finn stepped even closer, and Ivy shoved her hands into his chest, pushing him away. Piotr let her go and stepped back. Finn looked hurt but stepped away from her as she punched him in the chest. Her head pounded, and her eyes burned with the sting of tears. Ivy lifted her hand again, but Piotr caught it, and she crumbled. Her knees buckled, and she sank to the ground in a pile of scarlet grief as her dress pooled around her. Piotr held her close as Finn stood shocked above them.

"Ivy," Finn's voice broke as tears came to his eyes.

"Get away from me!" Ivy screamed at him. It didn't seem as though a piece of his love had died with Meisha, but Ivy still couldn't be sure. Everything was confused in her head, and she felt her brain twisting.

"Ivy," Finn persisted. "I didn't mean . . . I didn't know . . ."

"She almost died tonight," Piotr broke in.

Ivy opened her mouth to speak as the sound of a horse's whinny carried her gaze to the west side of the gate. Her eyes grew wide as she saw Queen Narra sitting alone on her horse, watching them. Ivy shot a panicked look at Princess Meisha lying dead in the grass, and Queen Narra surely saw it as well. The queen was alone, but Ivy guessed she'd been sitting there long enough to see everything. With no guards around her, the queen wouldn't have risked her life, not even to save her daughter. She turned her horse and rode off into the dark fields, never looking back. Ivy had to stop her. She rose to her feet, and the world turned upside down. Ivy fell to the ground as her vision blurred, and the grass came up to kiss her cheek.

Piotr dropped beside her and tried to shake her awake, but Ivy had lost a lot of blood. His eyes filled with worry as she lay there unconscious. Finn dropped to his knees and placed a hand on Ivy's cheek, tears falling from his eyes. "Ivy," he pleaded. Finn leaned down to her ear and brushed the hair from her face. "I'm sorry, my Ivy." Piotr didn't make a move to stop him, seeing the pain cross over Finn's face. They didn't have time to argue about their feelings or who did what, Ivy needed to get inside.

Piotr wrapped her arm around his neck and slipped his hands under Ivy's legs, picking her up in his arms. Finn stood up with him but kept his gaze on Ivy's closed eyes. "We need to get her to her room," Piotr said, turning away and walking back through the gate of the kingdom. Finn hung his head and rubbed his fingers against the skin of his wrist. The silver handprint was gone, but he still felt strange. He followed closely to Piotr through the empty streets as people were still gathered within the Hall. The sky was still dark, but it would be morning soon, and Finn felt a twitch of pain at having to tell Magnus what had happened, although Finn was still unclear on that part. Piotr climbed the steps with Ivy hanging limp in his arms and kicked her door open. Finn followed him in, as Piotr was gently laying Ivy down in her bed, brushing the hair from her face. His fingers lingered a little too long, and Finn stepped forward.

"We have to tell Magnus," Finn said.

"She needs the Magister first." Piotr raised his voice slightly before putting a gentle finger to his handprints across Ivy's throat. A tear threatened to fall, and Piotr snapped his eyes shut. "I'll go," Piotr said after a moment. He stood up and walked over to Finn, standing face to face. "Stay with her," Piotr commanded and turned to look back at Ivy before turning his back.

CHAPTER TWENTY-SIX

THE ENCHANTED ONES

I vy remembered the day she picked up the leather-bound book in her parents' room. It was low enough on the shelf for her to reach, and the silver words drew her eye. *The Enchanted Ones.* The words swirled across the binding and seemed to twinkle in the candlelight. Ivy was only nine years old at the time, but she read better than her brother Rayner. Ivy ran her hands over the soft cover, tracing each letter with the tip of her finger before opening the book. The book told the legend of one enchantress and the history of her family. Her powers passed on through generations, and some think their bloodline went back to the beginning of the gods. It was told that the God of Secrets, who was known to be a trickster, gave one young woman more power than any other enchantress or enchanter. Her name was Elowyn, and she was the daughter of a simple farmer.

Elowyn prayed to the gods every night; she prayed to fall

in love and be swept away from her life. A man named Prince Amon had stolen her heart when Elowyn's father brought her to the royal palace for a celebration. Her father supplied the kingdom with crops, and Elowyn pleaded with her father to take her. When they arrived, Elowyn went off to explore the kingdom on her own. The feast started, and everyone was dressed in their best gowns, silk doublets, and jewels that held every light from the flickering candles. Elowyn wore only a simple brown dress and pinned up her golden hair to better fit in with the crowd, though she noticed right away that she stood out. People snickered and laughed as Elowyn made her way around the room. She didn't let that bother her though. Her eyes were darting in every direction, taking in the beauty of the palace when she spotted Prince Amon.

The prince stood tall, leaned up against a pillar, and looked rather bored at the festivities. His hair was the color of midnight, and his pale skin seemed to shimmer in the low flames dancing above his head. Elowyn thought her heart would burst when he cast his gaze in her direction and smiled. She quickly turned around and pushed her way through the crowd, looking over her shoulder to make sure the prince wasn't following her. Elowyn had no idea what to say to such a highborn man, and suddenly everyone's mocking glare started to upset her. She kept her eyes down and wove through the crowd until she slammed into someone.

Elowyn was knocked to the ground, and when she looked up, Prince Amon stood above her. His emerald eyes ran over her dress before coming back up to her face. He reached his hand out, and Elowyn hesitated before taking it. His cold fingers wrapped around her wrist as he lifted her to her feet.

"Thank you," Elowyn muttered and tried to slip past him. Amon put a hand on her shoulder and held her back.

"What are you doing here?" Amon's eyes again went to her dress.

"I'm here with my father." Elowyn remembered who she was talking to and dipped down into a curtsey. "I should be getting back." She tried to push past him again, but his steady hand slid down her arm and took her hand. His fingers felt like ice against her skin.

"Would you like to dance?" the prince asked. Elowyn looked at him as if he had horns growing from his head. The prince wanted to dance with Elowyn, and she couldn't come up with an excuse to refuse him. She nodded her head slowly, and his smile grew wider as he led her to the dance floor. People turned their heads to watch as Amon parted the sea of people and pulled Elowyn into him.

Her cheeks flushed with color as his arm slipped around her waist, and he brought her closer. His raven black hair shadowed his eyes as he twirled her around the marble floor. Elowyn's heart was beating through her chest, and she felt a fog of desire start to creep into her mind. Amon didn't take his eyes off her as he gently traced his finger over her jawline. The music slowed around them, and some people started to leave the dance floor, but Amon kept a firm grip on his partner.

"I really should be getting back," Elowyn said, her voice a little shaky from how he was touching her.

"What if I don't want to let you go?" Amon whispered

against her ear. His fingers wrapped around her wrist again, and suddenly, Elowyn didn't want to leave either. Her breathing picked up as Amon smiled down at her and ran a cold finger down her neck to her collarbone. Her vision blurred slightly, and she felt lightheaded in his arms. Amon's green gaze bore into her, and he moved her body closer to his. She was pressed against his muscular chest as his lips hovered above hers. Elowyn couldn't think; her mind went blank leaving nothing but a hollow shell. She felt it the moment she stopped fighting and leaned into his lips.

Amon tasted of darkness and misery against her mouth, but Elowyn was too far gone to realize it. His lips parted against hers, and Elowyn felt herself melting. He ran his frosty hand up her neck and into her golden hair and grabbed hold of it as if she might slip away. This was everything Elowyn ever wanted. To be swept away by a handsome highborn man. Someone to take her away from her dull life and transform her into someone new. A wave of desire hit her, and she knew she would do anything for this man that she didn't even know. Elowyn slid her arms around his neck as his lips slid over hers, his tongue pushing into her mouth. Her heart stopped when she heard the snap of fingers, and a burst of loud laughter filled the room around them.

Amon pushed her away and joined in the laughter. Elowyn frantically looked around the room before realizing they were laughing at her. Amon ran a sleeve over his lips and looked at her like she disgusted him, like her mouth against his was the vilest tasting thing in the world. Elowyn felt tears burning her eyes as she realized she had been enchanted in front of the whole kingdom. Amon took a step toward her and leaned in to be heard over the laughter. "No one will ever willingly love you," he said, and his voice grew colder with every word.

Elowyn prayed to the God of Secrets after her humiliation by the prince. She wanted him dead, but the god wouldn't obey her wishes. Instead, he came to her in a dream and offered her something better. Elowyn woke the next day and rode for the kingdom in search of Prince Amon. She could feel the gift from the god within her, its power coursing through her veins. *With this, you will be the most powerful enchantress who ever lived. You will have the power of a god, the power to control those around you with nothing more than a simple touch.*

The prince had humiliated her, and Elowyn was hungry for revenge. She stormed into the palace, and once she found the prince supping with a group of people, she casually walked over to him. Amon noticed her and stood up, anger written on his face. His hand rose to strike her, but Elowyn reached out a cold finger and simply touched his arm. The power worked much faster than his had, and Amon instantly lowered his hand and smiled down at her.

It's said that Elowyn enchanted the whole kingdom and married the prince. All of her daughters possessed the same powers as she, though they faded some over centuries. Elowyn used her power to seek revenge and get what she wanted. Though some say, she was even lonelier than before because she knew the prince never truly loved her, and with a snap of her fingers, it could be over. But she never did. Elowyn thought he deserved a life of control. A hollow puppet for her to play with.

CHAPTER TWENTY-SEVEN

HOLLOW

I vy tried to open her eyes, but the throbbing in her head was still there. She felt like she couldn't move, like her muscles were paralyzed. Her head swam with thoughts as she recalled what happened. Ivy wanted to fall back into sleep as soon as she realized she was awake. The pain that coursed through her body was all-consuming. From the bruises to her throat, the cut to her head, and the slice across her palm. Her hearing was still muffled from her head wound, but her ears pricked up as she heard voices in the room with her. Both were male, but Ivy struggled to place them. "Already gone . . ."

"I can . . . the queen . . ."

"Ivy needs . . . someone to . . ."

"I don't . . . when she wakes . . ."

". . . don't know that . . ."

The slam of a door finally pried Ivy's eyes open a crack, and the light in the room flooded her vision. Ivy tried to lift a hand to her face, but her muscles were weak, and her arm violently shook as she tried. Ivy blinked until her vision was a little clearer before opening her eyes all the way. She was in her room, she realized, and someone was standing at the door. Ivy looked down and noticed someone had changed her out of the bloody dress and into something comfortable. She looked down at the bandage wrapped around her hand and suddenly became aware of her heart beating in the center of her palm. Ivy tried to push herself up, but her body screamed at her to stop.

The figure approached Ivy and came into her blurry vision. "Take it easy."

Rayner looked awful as he came to sit on Ivy's bed. The dark circles under his eyes were ever more present, and his beard grew wild around his jaw. Ivy tried to sit up again, and Rayner slipped a gentle arm under her to prop her up against the pillows. Ivy touched the back of her head with a shaky hand and felt the stitches under her hair. Rayner poured her a cup of water and lifted it to her lips. She took a few swallows, but her throat was still swollen from Piotr.

"How long have I been here?" Ivy's voice sounded foreign in her ears. It came out raspy and restricted.

"Only a day," Rayner said quietly. "The feast was last night."

Ivy noticed the sky was black outside her window. A gentle fire roared in the hearth, and Ivy realized Finn's bed was empty. Rayner was checking the wrapping on her wrist when he noticed Ivy's gaze.

"Where is he?" Ivy asked, something else restricting her voice.

"Finn left with Father this morning after Piotr came to tell us what happened."

"Where did they go?" Ivy asked, still trying to recall every detail of the night.

"They went to hunt down Queen Narra." Rayner's tone was sharp. Ivy felt the memories rushing back to her as she recalled trying to go after the queen before she collapsed. She couldn't believe that Queen Narra had sat there while Ivy killed her only daughter. Meisha had deserved to die, and Ivy felt nothing as she recalled slitting her throat and stabbing her corpse. The anger that fueled her had washed away the last of her strength and a piece of her soul. How could her heart feel heavy and hollow at the same time?

"Ivy." Rayner's voice was soft again. "Piotr told us everything. He told us that Meisha planned to take me but . . ." His voice fell away as he looked at his sister, lying beaten and bloodied instead of him. "I know you risked your life to save Finn and Piotr and almost gave it away for me. I can't take back what has happened to you, and I'm so sorry I wasn't there to protect you. It should've been me." Rayner's eyes grew wet with tears, and Ivy felt a pang in her heart. She would never blame Rayner for anything. Ivy knew exactly what she was doing by sparing her brother, and she would do it again.

Rayner leaned over her and gently wrapped his arms around Ivy as a few more tears fell. Ivy knew Rayner was feeling broken after learning that the horned knight killed Ser Caster, and she couldn't imagine what this might have done to him. Though from the look on his face, Ivy guessed it pained him just as much to see her broken as well. Ivy wished she could forget everything about that night. She wanted to go to sleep and wake up with no memories of it. She wondered if Finn really had lost a part of his love for her. Or whether Piotr meant everything he confessed, though Ivy didn't need an answer to that. Not after the enchantment was broken, and she felt all of Piotr's confessions in his kiss. Ivy sat back against the pillows and sipped more water as her mind wandered. "Why did Finn leave me?" Ivy asked.

"He wanted to help track down the queen. After what her daughter did to you, after what she put you through, Finn felt like he was somehow responsible even though we explained to him that he was enchanted. When he looked at you lying in bed like this, I could see the hurt weighing him down. He just seemed . . . lost." Ivy closed her eyes and felt guilty for pushing him away last night. She'd been filled with anger and disgust, but deep down, she knew it wasn't his fault, and she shouldn't have treated him like it was.

"Who was here if Finn left?" Ivy asked, suddenly remembering the other voice. Rayner looked at the closed door as if someone might still be there.

"It was Piotr," Rayner admitted. Ivy hoped her cheeks didn't flush at the mention of his name and to think he was here while she slept. She wanted to be angry with him for what he did. For keeping his feelings a secret from her and using them to get what he desired. But a part of her felt bad for him. Meisha had used him to her advantage, and it made Ivy sick inside. Piotr had always treated her as if he disliked her, but now, thinking back, Ivy realized he was probably hiding his feelings from himself. He buried them under harsh words toward her and scolded her every time they were together. Ivy now knew that when he discovered that Ivy and Finn were together, it made him admit to his true feelings. Ivy wondered what he thought at that moment.

Rage, jealousy, loss, regret, broken.

"Why was he here?" Ivy's raspy voice grew quieter.

Rayner got up and went to sit in a chair at the foot of her bed. "He's been here the whole time. He only just left before you woke up when I came in to check on you. He seemed upset that Father left without him, I guess he wanted to help track down the queen, but it was too late." Ivy looked down at the furs covering her legs and ran a finger over the bandage on her palm. Piotr had been sitting in her room for an entire day, likely still dressed in his ruined clothes covered in blood. A part of Ivy was glad he wasn't there anymore. She didn't know what she'd say to him and was afraid of what he might say to her.

Rayner got up and poked at the fire, averting Ivy's eyes. She wondered how much Piotr had told them and felt her cheeks growing warm as she recalled the way Piotr kissed her. Ivy was sure he left that part out, but Rayner had seen the way Ivy reacted to his name.

"Rayner," Ivy said, but he kept his eyes on the fire. "I don't want this to weigh on your mind. I'm fine." She tried to smile, but it seemed like too much effort.

Rayner sighed and stood up. "Everyone in this kingdom owes their lives to you, Ivy. You put your life at risk to save Godstone from being taken, and that's a debt we can never repay." Rayner's voice sounded sad and filled with regret, and Ivy opened her mouth to speak again when the door opened.

Elana walked into the room and instantly glided over to

Ivy. The queen still didn't look like she was carrying a child. She was as beautiful as ever in a slim green gown with her golden locks tangled in a braid atop her head. Rayner smiled at Ivy before slipping out of the door without another word. Elana sat down on Ivy's bed, and suddenly, she felt like a little girl again. Ivy sniffed at the tears forming in her eyes as she leaned into her mother. Elana stroked her head and let Ivy cry away her worries. Her whole body was shaking as she finally let herself sob about what had happened to her and everything she almost lost. The queen held her daughter for a long time, not trying to tell Ivy that it was all right or that it was over. Elana could see the defeat in Ivy's eyes the second she walked into the room.

Ivy suddenly feared what her mother might think of her after she killed Meisha. Ivy knew she lost control and would have stabbed Meisha until she couldn't raise her arm anymore, but Piotr had stopped her. Ivy choked back the rest of the tears begging to fall and pushed away from her mother's embrace. Elana smiled, but Ivy saw worry lurking in her eyes as she brushed an auburn lock from Ivy's face. "You gave us quite the scare, my darling." Elana's voice was warm as she spoke. "Your father nearly dropped when he saw you."

Magnus was strong and tried to hide his emotions, but his weak spot was his family. Ivy had only seen her father openly cry once when he said goodbye to her at the start of winter. Ivy could picture how her father's face must have looked when he walked into her room, and she lay abed, bleeding, and bruised. She didn't want to think of her father that way, and more guilt piled on top of her at her family's pain. Ivy knew they all cared about her, but she didn't wish for them to suffer along with her. Ivy had been debating going to the feast at all after she watched her father and Finn fighting one another. They both seemed so angry, and Ivy could see everyone coming apart at the imminent threat to their home. Ivy felt as if she had to bottle up her own worries and try to keep everyone together, or it would all keep piling up until they exploded. But if she hadn't gone to the feast last night, Rayner would likely be gone, under Meisha's spell as Helvarr planned his final move.

It was too much for Ivy to think about, and the pounding in her head returned. She grimaced at the pain and brought a hand up to cradle her head. Elana reached for the water and handed it to Ivy after pouring a purple liquid into it. "What's that?" Ivy strained to talk as the pounding continued.

"It's from Magister Ivann. It'll help you sleep." Elana pushed the cup at Ivy.

"But I just woke up," Ivy said as she watched the purple liquid dissipate into the water.

Elana brought a gentle hand up to caress Ivy's face. "You need sleep so that you can heal, darling. I'll be back to check on you later." Ivy gave in and tilted the cup to her lips. The water tasted bitter with the sleeping potion, and Ivy only managed a sip.

Elana got up, and Ivy quickly put the cup down as Elana leaned over and kissed Ivy atop the head. Her mother left, and Ivy felt the hollow room closing in on her. She didn't want to be alone with her thoughts, but she also didn't want to go back to sleep anymore. No amount of sleep would erase her memory of the night before, and Ivy accepted that. She nestled back into the pillows and stared up at the ceiling, listening to the fire crack and pop in the hearth. The window was open, and a gentle breeze washed over her, and Ivy closed her eyes.

The night air calmed her, and she felt the pounding in the back of her head ease up as she breathed in the fresh air. She heard the door to her room shut and opened her eyes then shot up to a sitting position. Piotr seemed equally as startled, probably hoping to find her still lost in dreams. He stared at her for a long moment as Ivy ran her eyes over him. He had changed into a fresh shirt and dark pants. His hair looked clean, and Ivy noticed the cut above his brow from where she punched him. Piotr's face drained of color, and he turned to leave, reaching for the doorknob. "Wait!" Ivy's voice came rattling out, and she snapped her eyes shut at the pain, bringing a hand to her throat.

Piotr stood frozen with his hand on the door as Ivy lowered her head, trying to hide her pain. Piotr slowly released the handle and moved toward her. When Ivy lifted her eyes back to his, he stopped moving, and Ivy could see the same shade of worry in his blue eyes as in everyone else's. This must be how Rayner felt—everyone looking at him like he was broken. Ivy felt a wave of nausea and turned her head back down until it passed. Piotr sat in the chair at the end of her bed, wringing his hands in his lap. "Ivy." Piotr's voice was soft in the silent room. "I'm so—"

"Don't tell me that you're sorry again," Ivy snapped her head up, but her expression was soft. "Please." Her voice grew quiet. "I'm tired of everyone being sorry." Ivy rubbed the bruises on her neck and flinched at the pain. Piotr didn't speak again, but Ivy could feel his eyes on her. She lifted her gaze and tried to sit up more. "Why are you here?" Her voice sounded crueler than she'd meant it.

"I just wanted to make sure that you were—"

"All right?" Ivy cut in. "I'm not. So why are you really here?" Piotr sat up straight and held her gaze with his crystal eyes. "Because I wanted to be here," Piotr admitted.

"You know," Ivy started, still holding his stare. "When we were younger, you would never look me in the eye like this when you insulted me. Now I know why. You couldn't look at me and manage to say something terrible, could you?"

"No," Piotr said. "I couldn't look you in the eye and lie about how I felt."

Ivy sat back even further. Piotr's eyes told the truth, and Ivy still couldn't believe how he felt about her and the way their kiss still lingered on her lips. Ivy silently cursed herself and pushed the thought from her mind. "Do not lie to me again," she said, voice harsh. Piotr smiled a little. She and Piotr had always been at each other's throats, and now Ivy wondered if that fire she threw back at him only added to his feelings for her. Ivy leaned forward, waiting for Piotr to acknowledge what she said.

"I never wanted to lie to you, Ivy. But I promise I won't ever do it again."

Ivy held out her hand, and Piotr's eyes fell from hers. He got up and stood over her bed, taking her hand in his and sealing his promise.

"Sit down." Ivy moved her eyes to the edge of her bed. Piotr's cheeks flushed, but he stayed standing. "Don't lie and tell me you don't want to." Ivy managed a smirk. Piotr lowered his head to hide his smile and sat down beside her. He kept his body turned away from her as Ivy pulled her legs up to hug against her body. "I have some questions, and you're going to answer them honestly," Ivy said. Piotr nodded his head but didn't meet her gaze. "You used to tease me about the way I dressed. Why?"

Piotr turned to her and let his eyes run over Ivy as she sat curled in her furs. He smiled warmly and returned his gaze to the stone wall in front of him. "You always dressed differently than other girls, especially for the daughter of a king. I was so used to seeing women in my father's city dressed in flowing gowns with jewels hung from their necks. But you were different." Piotr turned to look into her purple eyes, and Ivy felt her heart skip. "You don't need a fancy dress to look beautiful." He smiled shyly.

Ivy looked away and asked another question before she could decide against it. "Why did you treat Finn the way you did?"

Piotr lost his smile. "I think you already know the answer to that."

"Tell me," Ivy said, leaning forward. She did know, but she needed to hear him say it.

Piotr let out a breath and rested a hand inches from Ivy's on the fur pelt. "I told you I was jealous. After your father explained who he was, all I felt was regret and anger and I turned that anger on him. I didn't want to accept that you had found someone to love when I could have had you." Piotr stopped for a moment and ran a hand over his eyes. Ivy realized he must be tired if he'd stayed up the whole time while she slept. Piotr likely hadn't slept since the night before the feast, and Ivy could start to see it in his eyes. She had never seen him like this, being open and honest was not something Ivy thought him capable of. Yet she could hear the raw confession in his voice as he continued.

"I could tell how much he loved you, and I knew I'd lost my chance. I wanted to hurt him, and he could have killed me for what I said, but he didn't." Piotr looked into Ivy's eyes and smiled. "He's a good man, and I can see why you chose him."

Ivy's heart felt heavy as Piotr looked at her. She didn't know how much of the legend was real or if Meisha indeed had taken a part of Finn's love with her. Ivy hugged her knees tighter to her chest. "I'm not sure how much he still loves me," Ivy said half to herself.

Piotr shifted closer but stopped himself before he put a hand on Ivy's arm. "Don't believe what Meisha told you when you had your blade to her throat. She knew she was going to die, and she would have said anything to provoke you." Piotr gave in and rested his hand on her arm. She could feel the warmth of him through her shirt and it sent shivers down her spine. "Finn is still as much in love with you as he was." Piotr's voice sounded restricted as he spoke the words. "What's not to love?"

Ivy raised her eyes to his. Piotr slid his hand down her arm and went to remove it, but Ivy snagged his hand before he could take it away. "Piotr, I . . ."

He stopped her. "Please. I have to tell you this, I might not get another chance." Ivy felt her heart fluttering nervously. She didn't need him to confess everything, but something inside her wanted to hear his words. "Ivy, I'm the fool. I had so many chances to tell you how I felt, but I buried them instead. I was afraid you would reject me, laugh at me for being honest for once. I didn't know how to tell you, so I stayed silent. I teased you, insulted you, and hurt your feelings for years, and for that, I'm genuinely sorry." His blue eyes seemed to glow with every word that passed his lips. "I've thought you were beautiful since I laid eyes on you. I watched you, I thought about you, and at night I dreamed about you. You're smart and fierce. You're elegantly beautiful in a way that many women need tricks to obtain. I wish I could go back and change it. I wish I would have told you sooner that I would die for you, I would lose my sword hand if it meant I got your love in return." Piotr's eyes left Ivy's and looked down at their joined hands. "I have loved you for many years, Ivy. And I know I won't soon stop."

Ivy loosened the grip on his hand, and edged closer to him, bringing a finger under his chin. His eyes danced as she brought her face close. Ivy searched his eyes for any hint of a lie, but all she saw was pure, raw desire and love. "That was all you wanted to tell me?" Her voice was no more than a whisper.

"I could go on forever, but I don't think it would do me any good." Piotr's voice was low, and Ivy shivered at his breath on her neck as his eyes found her lips. Ivy believed Piotr was being truthful, which only made her heart hurt all the more. She didn't know why she did it. Maybe at that moment, she needed to find her own truth. She needed to know if any part of her felt the same way, but she knew it was a bad idea the moment she leaned into him.

Ivy watched Piotr's eyes widen as she pressed her lips against his. For a moment, he sat unmoving against her touch, and then in an instant, his hands were caressing her cheeks. She felt Piotr shift and turn toward her as his lips slid over hers, and he trailed a hand down her neck. Piotr kissed her the same way he did when Ivy brought him out of the enchantment. The eagerness and desire radiated from his body as he pulled Ivy in closer. Ivy tried to focus on what she was feeling, but then Piotr's tongue was in her mouth, and his hand moved down her side to touch her skin just under her tunic. He smelt of roses and dark desires, but Ivy struggled to sense something else.

She placed a hand on his cheek and felt him tense up at her touch. Piotr parted his mouth and kissed her deeper, taking in every part of her at that moment. Ivy spoke against his lips, and he stopped kissing her. Their faces were still together, and Ivy felt his shaky breath against her lips as his golden hair brushed against her forehead. Piotr let out a sigh and pulled away from Ivy, removing his hands as he did. Ivy struggled to say the words that she was thinking. But her head had never been more clear, and she knew what she felt.

"Piotr," Ivy said, still holding his face close. "I'm sorry. I shouldn't have kissed you." Piotr didn't look disappointed like Ivy expected. It was as if he already knew what the kiss meant before Ivy did, and he let her do it.

"I know," Piotr said. "You don't have to explain." He raised his hand to Ivy's cheek. Ivy closed her eyes and leaned into his palm. "Finn is a lucky man," Piotr whispered as he came closer and kissed Ivy one last time. But it wasn't filled with desire like the other one. Piotr's kiss was soft and gentle, only lasting a moment before his lips left hers.

One last kiss to the woman he let slip through his fingers.

Ivy let him do it, knowing their previous kiss hurt him more than it had her. Piotr smiled and ran a thumb over her cheek before pushing back and getting to his feet. Ivy cradled her knees again, and as Piotr reached the door he turned back to her. His blue eyes were bright, but a sad smile formed on his lips. "I'll always have a hollow space in my heart for you, Ivy." With that, he turned and left before Ivy could say anything. She sunk back into the bed, letting the furs swallow her up as she drifted off to sleep with the hopes of seeing Finn in her dreams.

CHAPTER TWENTY-EIGHT

THE QUEEN & THE HUNTER

Finn never wanted anything more in his life than he wanted Ivy. His mind was racing through all the foggy memories of the night before, but Finn was missing some of the pieces. Months ago, when the raider came to take Ivy away from him, he thought he'd lost her forever. He would have killed anyone in his path, crossed the world, and given his life for her. When Meisha tried to enchant Finn the first time, it hadn't worked. At least not in the way she wanted it to.

Finn felt the powers working through his brain, but they seemed to release their cold grasp the second he spotted Ivy at the feast. She was the most beautiful woman in the room, and she only had eyes for Finn. When he kissed her, he felt the dark veil of the enchantment lifting from his mind. Ivy always grounded him and brought him back to where he needed to be. It didn't matter what he was feeling, Ivy could snap him out of it the moment she kissed him. He was utterly powerless to her. That night, he felt Meisha's power leaving him as he kissed Ivy. He kissed her in a way that he hoped would express more than his words could. Finn sensed that Meisha had lost her grip on him and used all of her strength to force him into her enchantment. He never thought that Meisha would use her powers in front of Ivy, but she had, and it almost cost him everything.

Finn felt it the moment Meisha touched his wrist a second time, he tried to warn Ivy, but his lips wouldn't let the words pass. His body went slack, and his mind blank as the trance consumed him. Finn had so many things he wanted to tell Ivy. There was so much that he regretted that he wished he could have changed, but no amount of dark power could ever take a piece of the love that he held for Ivy.

Finn only knew what Piotr managed to tell him before they left, which wasn't much. He knew what Meisha had done and what her plan with her mother was, and that Meisha used Finn and Piotr to get to Ivy. The thought made him sick, not only the thought of Meisha using him as a puppet, but that Piotr had feelings for Ivy. Piotr had treated Finn like the enemy ever since they met, and now he knew why. Piotr didn't have to say that he was in love with Ivy, Finn could see it in the way he looked at her. Finn was afraid to ask any more questions because he was afraid of the answers he might get.

As he watched Ivy passed out in her bed, he wondered what she thought of him when she had shoved him away. He worried that perhaps she'd lost some love for him because of what happened, and it broke his heart. He didn't want to believe it, but he could see the pain in her eyes from the moment he came back to her. Finn didn't know what to say at that moment. He didn't know any other way to prove his love had not weakened toward her. So, when Magnus left in a fury to hunt down Queen Narra, Finn was the first to offer help. It was one of the most challenging decisions to leave Ivy in that state and risk not being there when she woke up. But he needed to do anything to prove his love for Ivy, even if it meant hunting down a queen.

The sun rose to meet them as Magnus and his group topped the hill and set off toward the Blackwood Forest. Finn rode beside the king but kept his eyes peeled on the horizon. Earl Rorik and his son Grimm stayed close behind with Lord Kevan and a few of his knights. As they reached the forest edge, Magnus suggested they split up to cover more ground. Lord Kevan and Earl Rorik headed into the woods with half the knights while Magnus, Grimm, and Finn stayed in the fields with the rest of Kevan's knights. Finn snapped the reins of Eclipse and took off ahead of Magnus. The wind whipped at his face as Eclipse's steady gallop pounded on the earth. Finn felt so many things that he couldn't focus on one emotion. He was angry and sorry. Hurt and tired. Enraged and worried. They all swirled around his mind like a fog in the night. His heart felt like it had split in two from the way Ivy looked at him, but he figured carrying a broken heart was better than an empty one.

They rode for hours, but it felt like days. Finn watched the sun clawing at the sky, pushing itself higher and higher, as if it was mocking Finn, telling him he was running out of time. They were trotting alongside one another in a line spread out across the field, keeping the Blackwoods to their right side. Finn felt a sudden cold wind as he glanced in the direction of the dark trees. Ser Caster had given his life in those woods not long ago, and Finn shuddered to think what would have become of the kingdom if he hadn't stopped Magnus. The horned knight was as eager as Helvarr to get what he wanted, but Finn's mind went blank whenever he tried to figure out who he was. He knew Magnus would do anything for his family, even if it meant giving up his life to protect them.

Magnus hid his anger well as they continued hunting the queen, but Finn still saw the pain in his eyes. "What will you do if we catch her?" Finn called out to Magnus. The king kept his gaze stern, not letting on to whatever he was thinking. He turned to Finn but quickly averted his gaze.

"I think the question is, what will you do?" Magnus retorted. Finn had thought of so many things during the hunt, but not that. Honestly, he had no idea what he'd do. He knew what the penalty for traitors was, though the king held a certain amount of discretion in what happened, and he couldn't imagine Magnus permitting Finn to do it. They both wanted revenge, and acting on the punishment for treason seemed to fit the category of justice and revenge.

Revenge was something Finn wasn't used to. Ronin had always taught him to control his anger and not to let it fuel him. But how could anyone stay completely devoid of anger when someone you love had been hurt? Finn thought it impossible, and instead of pushing it away, he let it warm him from the inside. He wouldn't let his anger control him but instead use it. Revenge can be dangerous, cold, and swift with quick relief. But at that moment, Finn felt equally as dangerous. He couldn't think about what he'd do if they caught Queen Narra; first, he had to focus on finding her.

The sun was on its descent in the sky. A spring rain began to fall, light and pleasantly warm against Finn's cheeks. He let it wash over him, hoping it would take some of the doubts that plagued his mind. He lifted his head to the sky and closed his eyes against the raindrops. Finn said a silent prayer to the God of Judgment and hoped he wouldn't judge Finn for his next thought. Magnus's voice cut through the twisted vines that encircled his thoughts, and Finn opened his eyes. The king was pointing his finger ahead, and Finn followed his gaze. A lone rider disappeared over the hill in front of them, and Finn's grip tightened as he spotted the queen.

"Finn, wait!" Magnus called to him, but Finn was already breaking into a full gallop, snapping the reins and leaning forward behind Eclipse's neck. His blood raced through his veins and made his skin grow hot. The wet wind ran their warm fingers through his hair and caressed his face. Finn narrowed his eyes against their touch and tried to spot the queen as Eclipse reached the top of the hill. Her horse was tired and started to slow down as it reached the bottom. Finn stole a glance back to see Magnus and Grimm falling behind with the knights, and there was no sign of Lord Kevan or the earl. He pursued the queen down the hill and was quickly gaining on her. She shot a look of panic back at him but then twisted the corners of her mouth into a spiteful smile. Finn heard himself growl and pulled his ax from his belt.

The queen still wore the gown from the feast, covered by a thin black cloak that sailed like a flag behind her. Eclipse was almost on her, and Finn steered him to ride just off to the left of Queen Narra's horse. He took a deep breath and thought of Ivy before standing in his stirrups and hiking on leg up, placing his foot in the center of the saddle. He held his ax in one hand and slowly released the reins with the other. He felt his heart leap with him as he jumped the distance between the horses, crashing into the queen. They had been at full gallop, and Finn felt the speed as he and the queen crashed to the ground.

They tumbled over one another, rolling through the field to a stop. Finn let out a cry of pain and brought his hand up to his shoulder. His breathing was labored as he tried to take in every breath that had been pushed out of him. Queen Narra looked to have a broken leg as she tried to crawl away. Finn cursed at the pain in his shoulder and sat up, reaching for his ax. He crawled a few paces in the grass, feeling the anger working its way through his mind. He thought of all the pain that Ivy had been put through, and what it must have done to her. Finn gritted his teeth and sent his ax down into the queen's broken leg. She cried out in pain and tried to turn around, but Finn pinned her down. He withdrew his ax and slammed it down into the earth as he turned the queen on her back.

Finn heard Magnus and Grimm coming down the hill, but he wouldn't release the queen from his gaze. His pulse pounded behind his eyes as he put a hand to her throat. Ivy had killed Meisha the night before, releasing him from her grip, but the queen had gotten away. She sat on her horse and watched her daughter die and did nothing. She was cold and devoid of any emotions that didn't get her what she wanted. Finn wondered if she ever loved her husband or just his title. Any parent that would stand by and let their child die deserved nothing better. Finn thought she deserved far worse. He wanted to choke her like Ivy had been strangled. He wanted to cut her again and watch the blood pool out into the grass. He wanted to break her heart, but he knew he wouldn't find anything beating inside her chest.

Finn tightened his hands around her throat and leaned down closer to her face. Her hazel eyes pleaded with him, but Finn pretended not to see it. "Tell me why, or I'll kill you now," Finn growled at her. The queen choked, and Finn reluctantly let her go to get the answers he wanted. She brought a hand up to her throat and tried to push away, but Finn shoved her back to the ground and grabbed his ax.

The queen seemed to relax underneath him and returned the same wicked smile that Meisha wore. "Why do people do anything in this battle?" Her tone was mocking. "We all want more power, and Meisha would have given me that."

Finn sat up and searched her eyes for anything other than a terrible queen and mother. "You speak about your own daughter as if she was nothing more than a soldier to do your bidding," Finn said.

"Why else do people have children?" Queen Narra asked as if she were actually curious. Finn furrowed his brows and squeezed the ax handle. Magnus stood back and watched, waiting to see what Finn would do.

"Do you not care that she died because of your plan?" Finn raised his voice. "You knew what she was, and you used her powers for your own benefit." Queen Narra stayed silent and kept her smile. Finn knew enough about Helvarr to realize he couldn't be trusted. He must have offered the queen something that King Cenric couldn't. She was already a queen and had no part in the battle, so why rope herself in? Piotr filled in Finn before he left about what Ivy learned of the queen's plan. Piotr said that Helvarr offered the queen power to rule her kingdom, but that didn't seem right to him. Finn grabbed the collar of her dress. "What did he really offer you?" Finn snapped.

"I never obtained the powers of my ancestors, it seems it skipped a generation and went straight to Meisha." Her voice was drifting away as if she was lost in thought. "I always wondered what it would be like to have a man fall in love with just one touch." She raised a fingertip to Finn's face, but he smacked it away.

"Tell me!" Finn roared, shaking her. In the end, it didn't matter what Helvarr offered the queen. He just needed to hear it. He needed to know the reason why she and Meisha had been so willing to take everything from him. Finn couldn't think of anything in the world worth giving up someone he loved.

"Helvarr had spent many years wandering this land after his banishment." Finn thought he saw Magnus shift out of the corner of his eye. "He promised me more than the power of a kingdom. He promised me the power that coursed through Meisha's veins. He knew of a way to transfer it to me. She was always going to die." Narra broke off as Finn released her and sat down in the grass beside her.

Finn's hands were shaking. His mind couldn't comprehend what she said. What kind of person would sacrifice their only daughter for some ancient power? Magnus didn't take his eyes off Finn as he sat there, thinking about what to do. "He lied to you," Finn said.

"That may be so, but I couldn't live with myself if I didn't try. Who would give up a chance for such a power?"

Finn turned to look at the queen, his eyes seeing nothing more than a monster. "You couldn't live with yourself?" Finn asked. He leaned into her until they were face to face. "You're disgusting," he said through gritted teeth. "You'll never have the power or love you desire. Who could love such a monster?"

Queen Narra spit in his face, and Finn felt his skin heating. The rain continued to fall as Finn grabbed the queen by the throat and pulled her to her feet. Magnus took a step closer but made no move to stop him. Finn looked at the king for guidance, but Magnus's expression was stern. He was going to let Finn take his revenge in any way he saw fit.

Finn pushed the queen away and pulled his sword from the scabbard. Grimm stayed silent and crossed his arms over his chest, eager to see what would happen. Finn tried to steady his shaky breathing and kept reminding himself that she deserved to die. Ivy suffered at her hand and almost died to save Finn's life. The penalty for treason came to the surface of his mind, and he looked back at Magnus one last time. The king stood clasping his hands over one another and gave Finn a firm nod of his head, waiving the king's discretion and giving Finn full power.

Finn steadied his grip on the hilt and turned to stand before the queen. She was slumped over, trying to stand on her broken leg and the ax wound. She was losing blood fast, and Finn thought she would die anyway if they turned around and left. He held his blade to her neck and watched her eyes light up with panic. "For the crime of treason against King Magnus the Mighty," Finn's voice was stern and serious, "I sentence you to die by beheading." Queen Narra shot a pleading look to the king, but Finn kept his eyes on her. He returned her wicked smile that was often part of her mask, which was rapidly slipping from her face. Her knees began to shake, and she tried to speak, but her fear constricted her throat. "Kneel," Finn commanded her.

"Please." She knelt but focused her attention on the king. "Hold me as a prisoner . . ."

"What makes you think I want to waste food on you while you rot in my cells?" Magnus snapped back. "Helvarr used you, and you let him. Will you go to your death a coward?" Magnus's voice held all the authority of a king at that moment. Queen Narra let a single tear fall as she lowered her head. Finn didn't look back at Magnus. He held on to the anger and used it to lift his sword into the rain and send it down with all the force he could muster.

Queen Narra's head came off in one swing and rolled off into the grass. A spray of blood mixed with the rain covered Finn's face. His heart was pounding and his hands shaking as he lifted his sword and put it back into the scabbard. Magnus came up and placed a heavy hand on his shoulder. Finn looked at the head of the queen but saw no sign of fear etched on her face. In the last moment of her life, she must have accepted her fate and given into death. Finn had prayed to the God of Judgment for the strength to be able to do it, and it seemed the God answered.

CHAPTER TWENTY-NINE

To Die For

W hen they got back to Godstone, it was late, and Magnus immediately called a meeting with Lord Kevan and the earl, but Finn didn't go. He felt as fragile as a piece of paper, his muscles ached, and his mind was tired. Magnus didn't argue with him and even embraced Finn before letting him retreat to the tower. Finn stood outside of his door for a few moments to listen for any movement. He wasn't sure if he was ready to face Ivy, but against any doubts, he pushed the door open.

He was relieved to find her asleep in her bed. Finn quietly moved to his side of the room and removed his shirt. He took a cloth and dipped it into the copper bowl filled with fresh water and washed the queen's blood from his face. His clothes were wet, and he quickly changed into a dry pair of pants and was rummaging through his trunk for a shirt when he heard Ivy. He snapped upright at her voice and dropped his shirt back in the chest. Her purple eyes were clear and bright in the low light of the candle beside her bed. Ivy's hair fell over her shoulders, and she looked more rested than she should have been.

Finn felt his cheeks flush and wondered how long she'd been awake. "Is she dead?" Ivy's voice was small. Finn was lost for words and only managed to nod his head. Ivy looked down and twisted the furs in her hands before beckoning him to come sit. She patted the bed beside her, and Finn felt his legs moving toward her.

His mind was racing, and his hands were sweating as he came closer to Ivy. Her eyes bore a hole into him and ran over his bare chest. Finn felt naked under her gaze as he sat down on her bed. He couldn't read what she was thinking, her eyes shielded him from her thoughts. Finn felt as nervous as the first time she touched him, or the first time he kissed her. Ivy always had that effect on him, and Finn willingly gave in to her power. Finn turned toward her and dug for his courage before speaking. "Ivy, I'm so sorry," he started. "I tried to warn you, but—"

"Warn me?" Ivy drew her brows together.

"Last night, at the feast, when Meisha grabbed my wrist at the table. I knew what was happening and tried to warn you, but I could already feel the fog covering my mind."

Ivy sat back in her pillows and watched him carefully. "You mean when you kissed me last night. That was really you? You weren't under her spell?"

"It was me." Finn moved closer to her. "She tried to enchant me before that, but it didn't work. I could feel it, but I didn't realize what was happening until she did it a second time. When you walked into the Hall, I could feel my mind fighting the trance. You brought me out of it, Ivy."

They stared at each other for a long moment, and Finn hoped that Ivy could understand, that she could see the sincerity in his eyes. "Ivy," Finn leaned closer and took her hands in his. "Piotr told me what Meisha said, but I promise you, no part of me died with her. I know you risked your life for me, and I can never repay that. You're the only thing in the world that matters to me." Finn's voice grew constricted.

"I love you more than anything, and I'll spend the rest of my life trying to prove that to you. I never want to see you hurt, and I would die to protect you." Finn's heart was beating faster with every word. Ivy leaned in closer, running her eyes down his chest that held his beating heart. She pulled a hand free and brought it to rest against his cheek, and Finn melted under her touch.

"Finn," she whispered while moving closer. His eyes traveled to her lips as she spoke. "I don't want you to die for me." She ran her thumb over Finn's lips. Her electric touch made him shiver, and he was eager for her to continue. "But I want you to kiss me like you need it to live."

Ivy closed the space between them and pressed her lips against his. They were familiar and warm, and Finn edged closer to her, feeling the heat coming off her body. Finn felt the broken pieces of his heart stitching themselves back together as Ivy's kiss brought him back to life. Wrapping his hands around her waist, Finn pulled her onto his lap. Ivy locked her legs around his hips, struggling to get closer to him. His hands went to her cheeks and then slowly ran down her neck as their lips glided over each other. Ivy trailed her fingertips down his bare chest, and Finn felt himself flush all over. Ivy lowered her hands and let them travel over the smooth skin of his lower back. Finn arched under her touch and moaned against her lips.

He couldn't take it anymore, and a second later, Finn scooped her up and laid her on the bed as he crawled on top of her. Ivy's eyes were glowing with desire as Finn moved toward her lips. They crashed together again, and Finn let himself give in to the power she held over him with nothing more than a simple touch. Ivy didn't need magic to control Finn; he'd given himself to her a long time ago.

Ivy's hands traveled to the buttons on his pants, and Finn shot up from her. Ivy's cheeks were red and her lips bee-stung as she stared up at him. Finn composed himself and ran his thumb over her bottom lip then onto her cheek. "Are you sure you want this?" he whispered. Ivy pulled him back down on top of her and brought her lips to his ear.

"I only want you." Her words set his skin on fire, and Finn surrendered. He lowered his head and kissed her neck as Ivy's hands fumbled with his pants. His hand ran up the length of her body before he slowly started unlacing her shirt and slipped it over her head. Ivy visibly blushed as Finn's eyes slowly roamed over her body. Moving his eyes back to hers, Finn cupped the back of her head and dove in. His breathing became erratic, and Ivy's kiss grew more eager and hungrier as his hands explored her bare skin.

It was soft and smooth against his rough fingers, and Finn pressed his chest into hers, eager to feel more. Finn felt like his heart might explode when Ivy's fingers continued to gently work at the buttons of his pants. In an instant, their bodies were together, and no amount of fur pelts could stop Finn from shaking. He craved Ivy in a way that he'd never felt before. The way her hands ran over him, how her lips parted against his, her tongue exploring his mouth. Finn might have let out a moan as Ivy bit his bottom lip. He moved his lips across her jawline and down her neck, then up to her ear and kissed her lobe before whispering to her. "I've wanted you for a long time." He didn't recognize his own voice; it was deep and hoarse. Ivy wrapped her legs around him, pulling him closer. Finn hovered above her lips, and she brushed the stray locks of hair from his eyes so he could see her. Finn caught her hand and kissed the center of her palm, moving his lips up and kissing each fingertip. "I have loved you long before we first kissed, and I will love you forever, my Ivy. No enchantment will change that." Ivy stared at him for a long moment, as if letting his words seep into her skin, to her soul. Then she smiled and kissed him again, pulling him into her. Finn smiled against her lips. He never wanted this moment to end, though as they came together, it felt like time stopped.

After, Finn lay with Ivy wrapped tight in his arms. He cradled her head against his chest as Ivy slept peacefully. Finn didn't dare close his eyes. He ran his mind over everything that happened, everything he felt, and how deeply he had fallen for Ivy. He thought about giving her the ring so many times last night, but Magnus's conditions stopped him every time. Finn wanted nothing more than to have Ivy be his wife, but after the night they shared, he knew that they belonged to each other already. Finn watched the sun work its way into their room. He tilted his head to Ivy and watched the furs rise and fall with every breath. He kissed the top of her head and gently moved out from under her, laying her head on the pillow. Finn grabbed up his clothes and quickly dressed before he looked back at Ivy and slipped out the door.

CHAPTER THIRTY

A LULL IN TIME

I vy never wanted to wake from her dream. She wanted to get lost in it, to let it consume her and transport her to a different world. She knew that the perfect world didn't exist. Ivy dreamed of her night with Finn. Everything was crisp and clear as if she was reliving every moment of it. Every touch tingled her skin, every brush of his hair against her face felt like the softest feathers. Every raw emotion that passed between them felt like a lull in time, and she never wanted that moment to end.

Ivy woke up alone. The spot where Finn should have been was cold, and the furs tangled around her bare legs as she sat up. She rubbed her eyes and looked around the room, wondering if last night was, in fact, a dream that lived in her head. She got up from the bed and dressed in the clothes from yesterday. They were in a pile on the floor, and when Ivy slipped her shirt on, she could smell Finn. It hadn't been a dream. She and Finn had spent the night together, and suddenly Ivy's heart was racing as it came back to her.

She was just pinning on the maple tree cloak from her father when the door opened. Finn strolled in on a breeze, and his eyes immediately smiled when they caught her across the room. "I thought you'd still be asleep," Finn said as he came closer. He held a tray piled with food and set it down beside Ivy's bed. Ivy finished lacing up her tunic, and Finn's eyes intensely watched her fingers. He rubbed the back of his neck and moved closer, giving her a shy but sweet smile. Their night had been something Ivy wanted for a long time, and she knew Finn had wanted her for even longer than he admitted. Ivy could feel herself being pulled back into him as his eyes rested on her lips. He ran a nervous hand through his hair and looked away.

"Are you hungry?" He motioned to the tray of food and sat down on the bed.

"Thank you," she replied, taking an apple from the tray. It was filled with more food than Ivy could ever eat, and she smiled at him as she took a bite from the apple. The corners of his mouth lifted as he watched the juice run down her chin. Ivy could sense he wanted to reach out and wipe it off, but he made no move to touch her. She could sense his nervousness from the moment he set the tray down and stood in front of her. Ivy felt it too but was trying to keep her composure. She had never felt anything so intimate with someone and wasn't sure how to react.

"So," they both said in unison. Finn turned his head down to hide his smile and blushing cheeks.

"I have to find Kyatta," Ivy quickly said before he could say anything about last night. His smile faded, but his face remained warm.

"The woman with white hair?" Finn asked.

"Yes." Ivy took another bite of the apple. "I saw her watching me at the feast, and I need to know why she didn't warn me of Meisha."

"What makes you think she knew anything?" Ivy hadn't told Finn about the dream Kyatta had. She didn't like to keep it from him, but she was afraid that if she told anyone that somehow it would come true. Ivy still didn't understand the meaning behind the words, but she wasn't very anxious to find out either.

"Just a feeling I have," Ivy lied. Finn wrinkled his nose and studied her as she finished the apple.

She stood up and strapped on Promise then twisted her hair into a loose braid. Finn stood with her and strapped on his sword and cloak as well. "What are you doing?" Ivy asked.

"I'll come with you."

"That's all right. I should probably talk to her alone." Ivy tried to keep her voice indifferent. Finn took a step closer to her, filling the air with his warm scent. He smelled of the forest and rainwater, and Ivy felt herself moving closer. Finn tried to catch her eye, but Ivy was focused on his lips that quirked slightly when he was thinking. She couldn't help but smile. When Ivy first met Finn, she thought he was the most handsome boy she'd ever seen, with his dark brown hair and matching eyes, yet they always appeared light when he looked at her.

Finn placed a finger under her chin and turned her head up to his. "Are you sure you don't want me to come?" His voice sounded more curious than hurt.

"I'm sure," she said before she could change her mind and stay in her room with him all day. "I'll find you later."

Finn only managed a tiny smile in return. He brought his lips to hers and kissed her in a very different way. Last night their kisses had been electric and eager, filled with hunger and lust. But when Finn kissed her this time, it was light and loving. His gentle lips moved against hers until Ivy felt a heat coming from her core. She pulled away before she could get lost in him again.

Ivy pulled her cloak tighter to try and hide the bruises still lingering on her neck. She could still feel the stitches in her head if she turned too quickly, but the pain in her palm was nothing more than a dull throb now. The sky was bright and warm, but a cold wind came off the Shadow Sea and swept through the kingdom. Ivy walked to the western wall where Kyatta had found her that first night. Only knights lined the walls, but when Ivy peered over the edge, she could see men digging a moat. It was no more than a few feet deep, but Ivy had the feeling it wasn't going to be filled with water.

As she moved along the wall heading south, her heart caught in her throat. Suddenly Ivy was back at the southern gate with Meisha, Piotr, and Finn. She blinked her eyes, but all she could see was an image of herself sitting on top of the princess and running her blade across her throat. Ivy expected her blood to be silver or shimmering, but it came out blacker than anything Ivy had seen. It made her sick to think about it, and she desperately tried to push the image from her head.

She reached out to steady herself on the wall while her heart slowed back to a regular beat. Ivy leaned over the wall and closed her eyes. The wind picked up her cloak, flapping it in the wind, and muffling the sound of approaching footfalls. Ivy snapped her eyes open, and instinctively put a hand on the hilt of Promise. Kyatta seemed to glide over the stone walkway toward Ivy.

Her white hair was filled with small silver beads that captured the sun, giving them the appearance of glowing. Her cold blue eyes held on to Ivy's as she came closer. Ivy ran her eyes over Kyatta, whose clothes were a rainbow of every shade of blue Ivy could imagine, from her dark boots to her twilight blue pants and the sky-blue tunic she wore covered by a thin cloak the color of her icy eyes. Ivy could see more of the woman's inked arms against her milk-like skin. Kyatta noticed Ivy's gaze and held out her arms as she came closer.

Kyatta's right arm was covered in black inked flowers. As she studied them more closely, Ivy could see they were all flowers of the moon, ones that only bloomed under the moon's light and curled up against the sun. They seemed to run all the way up her arm, disappearing under her blue sleeve. The other arm was every face of the moon encircled by a tangle of knotwork and swirls of black ink. Both hands were wrapped in intricate knots and wove their way through the flowers on one arm and the faces of the moon on the other. Ivy had never seen such well-done tattoos like hers. Earl Rorik and his people had many tattoos, but none so detailed and real as Kyatta's. Ivy felt drawn to them and reached out a finger, but Kyatta quickly pulled her arms away and hid them behind her back.

"You were looking for me?" Kyatta's tone was casual as she turned away to look south over the wall.

"How did you know that?" Ivy asked. Kyatta didn't answer, but Ivy saw her lift the corner of her mouth to an almost smile. "Why didn't you warn me about Meisha?" Ivy demanded.

"Who said I knew anything about it?"

"But you said you saw me in your dream. Doesn't that mean you have some sort of connection to me?"

"A dream is only a set of images the gods give us. They can hold our most desired thoughts or the darkest secret."

Ivy balled her fists. "I don't have time for another one of your riddles. Finn could have been killed, and this whole kingdom would have—"

"Finn." Kyatta was standing right next to Ivy, but her voice sounded far away. "The boy who resisted the powers of the enchantress." Finn had told Ivy that he knew he'd been enchanted after it was too late and that Meisha's powers didn't work on him the first time. He claimed that Ivy brought him out of the fog and broke the trance.

"So you did know?" Ivy asked.

"I knew enough about what she was. I could see her powers radiating from her body. People with particular skills tend to have a connection to one another, even if their powers aren't the same." Ivy didn't like the way Kyatta said *skills,* as if Meisha should have been praised for her powers. Instead, Ivy made sure she could never use them again.

"Why didn't you warn me? I nearly sacrificed my life to save Finn, to save everyone here, and you could have stopped it!" Ivy's voice was booming with anger as she thought of what could have happened. That night felt like a bad dream, and Ivy couldn't shake the feeling of it. Not until last night when Finn had stayed with her.

Kyatta turned to face Ivy, and her eyes seemed to have

changed color since they began talking. They were almost white as they looked into Ivy's eyes. "Perhaps the gods were trying to show you something from that experience."

"What does that mean? What the hell kind of screwed up lesson is that?"

Kyatta stepped closer until she was hovering over Ivy. "Is there something you doubted that night that you've since accepted? Is there something you believed that forced you to act differently than what your heart was telling you?" Kyatta leaned in until all Ivy could see were her steel-blue eyes. Even her breath was cold against Ivy's face as she spoke. "The gods rarely give someone such a test. Be glad that you passed and that no one you loved died in the process." She ran a cold finger against Ivy's cheek before turning to leave. Ivy couldn't think of what to say, and Kyatta was already disappearing around the bend before Ivy could open her mouth to speak.

Ivy huffed a breath of anger and turned to walk in the other direction. Her mind was spinning with Kyatta's words as she made her way back to the central tower. What kind of game were the gods playing with her? Kyatta said she'd passed, but Ivy didn't feel like she'd won anything. She couldn't think of a reason for the gods to toy with her, especially in such a way where she could have lost everything.

She wondered what Kyatta had meant by *skills* and knew she wasn't only referring to Meisha. Ivy could sense something more in Kyatta and doubted that her only *skill* was interpreting the messages of the gods. Ivy had never met anyone like Meisha or Kyatta before, but she could feel what Kyatta had described. It was as if their powers were swirling around them, waiting for someone to notice that they were different. Ivy couldn't allow herself to fully trust Kyatta. Maybe her words were hollow, and she didn't know what the gods had in store for Ivy. But if she did, then Ivy needed to figure it out before her fate was sealed.

All her life, Ivy felt like she was destined to remain in Godstone, never to become a knight or travel the world. She could never feel anything about her future when she thought about it. One thing she always felt attached to was her family as if she could feel their souls even when she wasn't with them. That's why Ivy never felt the loss when Rayner was thought to have been killed by the horned knight. Her father had chosen not to send a letter about what happened, and Ser Caster had promised not to mention it when he came to retrieve Ivy from Port Tsue. Ivy knew she would have felt it if Rayner had died. It was a connection she couldn't explain, and she was starting to feel it with Finn.

CHAPTER THIRTY-ONE

THE SNAP

I vy got back to the room only to find it empty. The tray of food was gone, but something else sat in its place. Ivy smiled as she walked to the table and lifted a single orange tulip to her nose. Her mind instantly erased the words Kyatta had spoken and instead focused on Finn. A piece of paper sat under the flower, and Ivy picked it up and read it.

My Ivy,

Meet me on our dance floor when you're done interrogating the white-haired woman.

I can't wait to see you.

All my love, Finn

Ivy's heart fluttered at the note. She tucked the tulip into her braid and quickly made her way to the sandpit near the front gate. Ivy spotted her father in the hall, talking with Earl Rorik. He smiled as his daughter approached and waved away the earl with a flick of his hand. Magnus pulled her in and kissed Ivy on the top of her head. "How are you feeling?" His pale purple eyes fell to the bruises on her throat. Ivy pulled her cloak up higher, not wanting to see the worry in her father's eyes.

"I'm all right, Father. I feel fine." Magnus hadn't seen Ivy since the night of the feast, and she wondered if he knew what happened with her and Finn. Her cheeks grew hot as her father looked at her. It made her feel like a little girl again, but she knew he was just giving her time to heal and rest.

"You look better." Magnus smiled down at her. "I'm sorry I didn't come to check on you last night when I returned."

Her father definitely had no idea what had happened.

"I thought you could use some rest, time to heal," Magnus said.

"That's all right, Finn checked in on me." It wasn't a total lie, but something in her father's eyes shifted. Whatever he was thinking, he kept inside his head. He rested a hand on Ivy's shoulder and returned his smile.

"Good. Finn's a good man."

"I know."

Magnus hugged his daughter quickly and left, saying he was late for a meeting with all the leaders. They'd been building defenses around the kingdom all morning, and though her father hid his fears well, Ivy could see it in the new lines around his eyes.

When Ivy turned the corner, she was slightly disappointed to find more than just Finn waiting in the sandpit. Ronin stood off to the side while Rayner and Correlyn sparred in the center. Ivy was surprised to see that Rayner had trimmed his beard, and his hair looked freshly washed. Perhaps he was done letting his fear control his looks. Finn had his back turned to her as he watched the two fight. His arms were crossed against his chest, and his wet hair clung to the back of his neck.

He turned just as Ivy came up behind him, and a broad smile instantly formed over his lips. He was always happy to see Ivy, and she knew that they were fated to be together. Finn snaked a hand around her waist and pulled her in, sniffing at the tulip in her braid. He pressed his lips against hers in such a tender way that Ivy thought she might melt. She brought a hand to his face and let him pull her in closer. His fingers brushed against the skin under her tunic, lighting that patch of skin on fire. He gently caressed her cheek then traced her jawline with his fingertips, running them slowly down her neck. Someone cleared their throat loudly from behind, and Ivy snapped her eyes open and pulled away, but Finn's eyes stayed locked on her.

"Are we going to practice, or would you two like to be left alone?" Rayner's mocking tone filled the air, and Ivy felt her heart rising again. Her brother seemed to be back to normal. She forced herself to back up and look past Finn to where Rayner stood. He was dressed in plain, loose clothing and held a metal practice blade in his hand. Correlyn smiled at Ivy and raised an eyebrow as she looked from Ivy to Finn and back again. Ivy felt her cheeks blush and was sure she'd just given Correlyn the answer to the question her eyes were asking. Ronin even seemed to be in a good mood and gave Ivy a slight nod as she removed her boots and cloak and stepped into the pit.

Finn stood beside her and leaned in close. "I didn't know they would be here. I was hoping for a private dance session." His grin turned wicked.

"Maybe later." She winked and squared up with Rayner. Ronin threw her a dull blade and asked Correlyn and Finn to step out of the circle. Ivy and Rayner eyed one another with a teasing grin while they waited for Ronin's command. He snapped his fingers to signal the fight, and Ivy hesitated at the sound.

It filled her ears and blurred her vision. Her palms started sweating, and her eyes went wide as she saw the image of Meisha, lying dead in a pool of black blood. The bruises on her throat pulsed intensely as Ivy fell to one knee. "Ivy!" a faraway voice called out. Ivy dropped her sword and buried her shaking hands in the sand, trying to catch her breath. She felt hands on her face as her vision was lifted to Finn. "Ivy?" He no longer wore his charming smile; his face was lined with worry as Ivy tried to blink the image out of her head.

Rayner knelt next to her and placed a hand on her back. "It's got to be her head wound. It's too soon for her to fight," Rayner argued with Ronin as he came up behind him. Ivy felt her body stop shaking, and her vision return to normal as Finn ran his thumbs over her cheeks.

"I'm fine," she said, taking her hands from the sand and sitting back on her heels.

"You're not fine. I'm taking you back to bed." Finn's voice was stern as he helped Ivy to her feet, but she stepped away from him, trying to stand on her own.

"What happened, Ivy?" Rayner asked.

"I don't know," she answered as she bent over to pick up

the sword. She had the same image in her mind when she crossed over the southern gate where she'd killed Meisha. Ivy couldn't explain it, but it was as if somehow her ghost was haunting Ivy, making her feel the pain and fear that Meisha must have felt at that moment.

"Ivy, my love." Finn's voice was soft and warm again. "Please, let me walk you back to our room so you can rest." *Our room.* It still felt strange to Ivy. Finn seemed to be growing more comfortable around her family and no longer tiptoed around the fact that they were together.

"I'm fine, Finn. I want to fight."

He smirked. "I know you do, that's what worries me."

She placed her hand against his cheek, and he leaned into her touch.

"It's up to you, Ivy." Ronin's voice broke into the conversation. She looked over to her trainer and nodded her head. Finn kissed her hand and stepped back out of the circle, but he never took his eyes off her.

Rayner squared up on Ivy again, and this time Ronin only gave a firm nod of his head to signal the fight. Ivy lunged and jabbed her sword at her brother's chest, but he swept it away with his blade and swung at her feet. Ivy leaped back in the sand and sent her sword crashing into his. She could feel her muscles already starting to strain with every blow. Ivy had taken a beating from Piotr and Finn, but she tried to push those thoughts far from her mind. They moved around the pit, striking and blocking. Ivy sensed that Rayner was holding back, but she knew it was out of love. Ivy landed a blow to his side as he was turning away. Her eyes locked on someone standing out of the circle, just beyond Rayner. She hesitated for a moment when she met Piotr's stare, and Rayner landed a blow to her leg.

Ivy winced at the pain and thrust her sword forward, jabbing at his heart. Rayner stumbled back from her blow and looked at Ronin.

"You're dead," their trainer called. "Switch with someone else."

Ivy saw Finn start to enter the pit when Piotr's voice called out from the other side. "I'd like to go," he said as he began to remove his boots. Ronin didn't argue, likely curious to see what was going to happen. Ivy had only seen Piotr fighting the night of the feast. From their own fight together, she knew he was strong. Piotr took the practice sword from Rayner, who met Ivy's stare before he left the pit. She didn't want to look back at Finn, so she kept her gaze on her next opponent.

Piotr gave her a shy smile as he approached and ran his eyes over her. "You look better," he said.

"I feel better."

"I'm glad to hear that." There was no usual mocking tone to his voice. Piotr seemed genuinely happy to see her, and it made Ivy feel odd. She was so used to their encounters being a battle of insults, but after he admitted his feelings to her, Ivy sensed a change in him. She could feel Finn's eyes at her back, but she refused to look. Ivy had decided not to tell Finn about her kiss with Piotr because, to her, it didn't matter. If anything, it only proved to Ivy that her heart was in the right place with Finn. She couldn't explain it, but Ivy knew that the gods had brought them together and that she was never fated to be with Piotr.

Her eyes went wide as she recalled Kyatta's questions from

earlier. *Is there something you doubted that night that you've since accepted? Is there something you believed that forced you to act differently than what your heart was telling you?* Perhaps her words weren't just empty riddles. Ivy and Finn both always felt like the gods brought them together for some reason, and if that night had been a test, perhaps it was a test of their love. Ivy had doubted Finn's love for her after killing Meisha. She'd believed in the legends instead of what she knew. Finn even said that the enchantment didn't work on him the first time, so had Miesha lied when she said Finn didn't fight her?

Perhaps Finn fought harder than Piotr did, and Meisha only lied about it to make Ivy doubt his love for her. Finn would always love Ivy, she knew that now. No power could take away what he felt toward her. But she still didn't understand why the gods would put Ivy through such a test just to prove that Finn was in love with her. There must be another reason the gods brought them together, but Ivy wasn't sure what it could be.

"Are you all right?" She realized Piotr was looking at her, and Ronin was waiting for Ivy to let him know she was ready.

"I'm sorry." Ivy turned to Piotr. "I have to go."

"Oh." Disappointment hung in his voice and on his face. Ivy turned to leave, and Finn gave her a curious look. Rayner walked up to her and motioned to the practice blade she still held in her hand.

Ivy's mind was running over Kyatta's words when Rayner snapped his fingers to try and get her attention. Ivy felt instant panic and collapsed just in front of Finn. The throbbing in her head returned, her heart sped up, and the blood drained out of her face. She felt light-headed as a cold sweat came over her. Ivy's whole body was trembling with fear as she saw a vision of Meisha again, bleeding from the cut across her throat. This time the image was clear, and Ivy's vision didn't blur. She reached out to touch Meisha, but the enchantress vanished before she could feel her. A crowd formed around Ivy, and she realized she was lying in the sand. Piotr, Rayner, Ronin, and Correlyn all stood over her as Finn scooped her up in his arms. "What's wrong with her?" Rayner demanded.

"I don't know," Finn snapped back. Piotr's face was white with horror, and Ivy wondered if he'd felt it too. She felt limp and weak as Finn pressed her into his chest. Ivy buried her face against his chest and breathed in the scent of him as he carried her away.

Ivy opened her eyes again as Finn gently set her down in her bed. He moved over to the copper bowl on his side of the room and wet a cloth for her. The cold water felt refreshing on her face. "Ivy." His voice was no more than a whisper. "You have to tell me what's going on." Ivy propped herself up on the pillows and took the cloth from his hands and held it to her neck. His eyes followed her hand to the bruises around her throat. "I'm worried about you," he persisted.

"I'm fi—"

"Fine. I know. You always say that. But Ivy, something is going on—you collapsed twice." She could see that it pained him to watch her fall apart like that, but Ivy didn't have an answer. She needed to talk to Kyatta again and find out more.

"I'm sorry," she said and placed a hand on his cheek. "I need to find Kyatta again."

Finn's mouth turned to a frown, and his brows pushed together. "No. I don't think that's a good idea."

"She knows something she's not telling me. I can feel it."

"What if she's the one who did this to you?" Finn grabbed hold of her hands as if she might slip away.

"I don't think she did this. It happened this morning, too, when I went searching for her."

Finn's mouth opened to speak, but Ivy continued before he could comment. "It happened right above the southern gate, where I killed . . ." Ivy didn't want to say her name. She felt a cold tingle at the back of her neck and was afraid uttering her name would throw her into a panicked state again. Ivy felt like she was being triggered by the memory of what she'd done. When Ronin had snapped his fingers, Ivy felt fear and pain wash over her like a wave. Then again, when Rayner snapped his. "I need to talk to her, Finn. I know she can tell me what's happening."

Finn scrunched up his nose and let go of her hands. He grabbed at the back of his neck and cast his eyes down from hers. "Fine," he said after a moment. "But I'm coming with you this time."

Ivy knew there was no point arguing. Finn was very protective of her. He always had been.

CHAPTER THIRTY-TWO

TRANSCEND

It was late afternoon when Ivy relented and agreed to let Finn accompany her to find Kyatta. The sun was still lingering in the sky, reluctant to give away its spot to the moon. The days were beginning to grow longer as summer was approaching. Spring and summer always seemed to bleed into one another in the North. The only seasons that lasted long were autumn and winter. Ivy loved autumn. The maple tree outside her window burned with a fiery orange for months. She loved the way the tree held onto its leaves even well into winter before finally giving into its frosty surroundings. Now, however, it was green with new leaves. She couldn't wait to see those green leaves transform into their fall colors.

Finn had changed his shirt into a lighter cotton one as Ivy pretended not to stare from across the room. The day only seemed to be getting hotter and hotter as the sun crept across the blue sky. Ivy dug through her clothing and found a light skirt that fell to her knees. She'd never been one for dresses or skirts, but the weather forced her to wear something lighter.

She pulled it out and watched Finn's eyes light up. He loved her in whatever she wore, but Ivy could see the look on his face change every time she wore something out of the usual for her.

"Turn around." Ivy twirled her finger at him.

Finn's eyes narrowed, and a playful grin formed on his mouth. "Ivy, I've already seen you." His eyes sparkled as if the memory of their night were playing through his head.

Ivy gave him a playful glare and twirled her finger again.

"You're serious?"

"Turn around," she told him again. Finn smiled wider and reluctantly turned his back. Ivy felt her blood rushing as she remembered the way his skin pressed against hers last night.

She quickly unlaced her pants and slipped on the skirt. It was dark blue and flared slightly at her knees. Ivy changed her tunic as well to a fresh tan-colored one and untied the braid from her hair. "Can I turn around now?" Finn asked over his shoulder.

"Yes." Finn's face lit up at the sight of her. She lifted her tunic to tuck it into her skirt, and Finn's eyes traveled to her exposed skin. His gaze made Ivy feel nervous and excited at the same time. He closed the space between them and picked up the tulip that had fallen from her hair. He kept his eyes locked on hers as he lifted the flower to his nose and breathed it in.

"You look beautiful," he said, his voice low and deep.

Ivy smiled as he turned her around and began to weave the tulip into her hair. His fingers were gentle as he untangled the knots and pulled half of it back, braiding it around the stem of the flower. Ivy didn't expect to still feel nervous around him after they had shared so much the night before, but Finn had that effect on her, and she hoped it would never go away.

The two held hands and moved through the halls of the tower. Ivy occasionally caught him staring at her as they walked. She didn't know where to look for Kyatta, but it seemed she'd sensed that Ivy wanted to talk to her earlier that day. They moved through the streets and decided to check inside the Great Hall. Grimm stood leaning against the door frame with his arms crossed, chewing on a twig. His eyes fell on Ivy and Finn as they walked up, and he smiled a warm greeting to them. "Have you seen Kyatta?" Ivy asked.

Grimm took the twig from his mouth and asked, "The Moon Wood lady?"

"Yes, the Moon Wood lady," Ivy responded.

"With the white hair?"

"Yeah."

Grimm ran his hand up one of his arms. "And the odd tattoos?"

Ivy crossed her arms, annoyed. "Yes, Grimm. Have you seen her or not?"

He put the twig back in his mouth, smirked, and said, "No."

Ivy narrowed her eyes on the giant man as Grimm smiled to himself. "I have been here all day," Grimm said, gesturing to the Hall. "Your father is building many defenses to prepare for Helvarr's arrival." Ivy shuddered at his name and felt her hand grow hot in Finn's. She'd seen the moats being dug earlier but thought that was all her father was planning.

"What sort of defenses?" Finn asked.

"Everything he can think of." Grimm spat out the twig

and continued. "Tar filled moats, spikes around the walls, barrels of tar on top of the walls in case people try to climb over. He is closing off the eastern gate to the sea, though I doubt Helvarr would try to come that way."

"What makes you say that?" Ivy asked.

Grimm shrugged. "I do not know the man, but from all I have heard, it seems he is confident in what he is doing. I imagine he will march right up to the walls and demand the kingdom be handed to him."

"That's not going to happen," Ivy said.

Grimm flashed his teeth. "I did not say it would. But he is welcome to try." Ivy turned her attention to the people inside the Hall and saw that Ronin was seated beside her father, along with Earl Rorik, Lord Kevan, and their wives. Rayner and Correlyn were sitting on the other side of Magnus as well. Ivy recognized a few people from the other clans of the North, but no sign of Kyatta. Ivy's mother was nowhere in sight, and she guessed the baby must be making her sick still.

"Why aren't you in there?" Ivy turned back to Grimm.

"Why aren't you?" he countered. "You are the one who assembled the northern clans, I imagined you would want a say in how we will help protect your home."

"I trust my father. It isn't just our home that needs protecting, it's the entire North."

Grimm smiled even wider and patted Ivy on the shoulder. "My father likes your fighting spirit. I believe it is why he put his trust in you."

"I was there on behalf of my father," Ivy admitted.

"Yes, but it was you who swayed him. It was not your father's words that came from your mouth that day." Ivy didn't want to think that Earl Rorik wouldn't have come only at her father's request. He wasn't a sworn ally to House Blackbourne, but he was a friend, and Ivy had to have faith that he would have helped.

"Why isn't Kyatta in there if she's the leader of the Moon Wood people?" Ivy turned her gaze back to the table of people.

"I do not know," Grimm answered. "But I am sure you will get your answer." With that, he pushed off the door frame and strolled back into the Hall.

Finn and Ivy continued walking through the streets of Godstone. They went back to the eastern gate, and Grimm had been right. Only a low wooden wall lined the back of the kingdom where the beach met the streets, and the gate had always been open. Now it was closed, and knights stood guard at the door and along the wall. The couple turned back and headed north, where the wooden wall met the stone wall that enclosed the majority of Godstone. They slowed their pace as they walked through the apple trees that grew behind the central tower.

Finn let go of her hand and reached into the tree to snatch an apple from a branch. The apple trees in Godstone seemed to be in harvest almost all year round. The only time their branches were bare was in the dead of winter, but as soon as spring started to melt the ground, the trees bloomed, and the apples began to grow. The soil there had always been fertile, and everything seemed to grow beautifully all around the kingdom, though they still bought crops from surrounding villages.

Finn took a bite from the apple and wiped away the juice with the back of his hand. Ivy snatched the apple out of his hand and took a bite. Finn's eyes watched her mouth as she sunk her teeth into the flesh of the apple. He reached for it, but Ivy slid away and walked around a tree. His eyes followed her every move, and his smile grew wider with every step.

He lunged for the apple again, and Ivy quickly twirled away and darted behind another tree. Finn let out a small laugh and came after her. She ran through the twisted apple trees, stealing a look behind her to see Finn happily chasing after her. Her skirt flowed with her movements as she ran through the orchard. Finn caught her by the arm and whipped her around. His breath on her neck sent shivers down her spine. He wrapped his hands around her waist and pushed her back until she was pinned against a tree. Ivy dropped the apple and brought her hands to run through his feathery brown hair.

He traced a line with his finger from her back and up around to her collarbone and neck. Finn knew how to tease her with his touch now that she'd made it clear she was still shy around him. But Ivy knew he felt the same way, no matter how confident he looked on the outside. Ivy lowered her hands to his pants and pulled him closer. She watched his eyes dance with desire and knew she held more power than he did. She smiled up at him and pressed her lips to the scar on his chin. Finn's breath hitched, and she felt his body growing tense against hers. His hands tangled in her hair as he pressed his lips against hers. She could taste the apple on his tongue as it slid into her mouth. She slipped a hand under his shirt and ran a finger over his back. Ivy could feel him arch his back at her touch. He kissed her with the same hunger from last night, and Ivy craved him in a way that she couldn't explain.

Ivy cracked her eye open when she heard the crunch of a twig and spotted Kyatta's flowing white hair stalking toward them. She put her hands against Finn's chest, and he stopped kissing her and turned around. Kyatta's eyes followed Finn as he stepped aside and grabbed hold of Ivy's hand. She was still dressed in her swirling blue clothing from that morning with the silver beads dangling in her pale hair.

"You summoned me again," Kyatta stated as she stood before Ivy, but her focus was on Finn.

"I didn't *summon* you, I was looking for you."

"And so I am here." Her eyes finally found Ivy's. Finn ran his thumb over her hand in a reassuring way to let her know that he wasn't going anywhere.

"I have more questions."

"Yes, I thought you might."

"This morning, before you found me on the wall, I had an image of Meisha." The enchantress's name tasted foul on her tongue. "I can't explain what happened, but I was overcome with pain and fear."

Finn spoke up. "She collapsed twice during a sparring match with her brother."

Kyatta returned her eyes to his and lifted a brow. Ivy watched as she ran a pale finger over the moon markings on her arm. "Interesting," Kyatta responded. Ivy felt Finn's grip grow tighter around her hand, but she spoke up before he could argue with Kyatta.

"You know what's happening to me, I can feel it."

"In what way can you feel it?"

Ivy didn't know how to answer that or explain everything that was happening to her. She felt drawn to Kyatta and knew she had some sort of power that she was keeping secret from Ivy. "I can just sense it," Ivy managed to say.

"These images you see, something is triggering them, is that right?"

Ivy furrowed her brow. "How did you know that?" she demanded.

Kyatta stayed silent and waited for Ivy to answer her question. She let out a sigh and told Kyatta it was the place where she killed Meisha, and when people snapped their fingers. Even admitting it out loud gave Ivy a cold chill. Meisha's snap was powerful enough to control Finn and Piotr that night. Kyatta studied Ivy as she explained all that she could, and when she was done, Kyatta moved closer. Ivy was afraid she might snap her fingers to see if it was true, but her hands stayed tight at her sides. "Do you remember what I told you about people with specific skills being drawn to one another?" She observed Ivy as she recalled their earlier talk.

"So? What does that have to do with my visions?"

"I believe you hold some sort of power."

Ivy felt her knees go weak and waited for Kyatta to tell her she was joking. "I'm not an enchantress." Ivy lowered her voice.

Kyatta shook her head. "I didn't say that. I said I think you have something within you that you weren't aware of."

Finn turned to Ivy, but she kept her gaze on Kyatta.

"I believe Meisha cursed you when she died," Kyatta went on. "I think she attached herself to you, and now she's suppressing your ability. When an enchantress is killed, they can hold onto this world through the person who slew them, and that's you."

Ivy couldn't fully grasp what Kyatta said. It didn't make sense. Ivy couldn't have any *skills,* or she surely would have figured it out by now.

Finn stepped forward. "What does that mean?"

"How did she seem when you killed her?"

The question was so direct it knocked Ivy off balance. She leaned back against the tree and tried to remember. "She seemed calm, she mocked me and pushed me to kill her."

Kyatta gave her a knowing smile. "That's because she transferred her fear and pain into you the moment she died. When you spill the blood of an enchantress, you take their fear upon yourself. It's a simple curse, but it can be crippling." Kyatta spoke as casually as if they were talking about a storybook. But this was real. Ivy could feel that something was wrong after she passed out that night.

"Can you fix it?" Finn asked, and his eagerness cut through the silence of the orchard.

Kyatta crossed her arms and nodded. "I can. But I can also give you a gift. I can transcend you."

Ivy didn't like the sound of that. "I just want the images to go away," Ivy said, trying to keep the curiosity out of her voice.

"I think you want to know what power lies within your blood." Kyatta stepped closer.

Ivy's mind was racing with thoughts. She'd only ever read about people with powers such as Meisha's in books. She never imagined meeting one, let alone having powers herself.

Kyatta still hadn't revealed what her powers were, but Ivy had a guess.

"Why don't you tell me what power lies within yourself first." Ivy pushed away from the tree and stood face to face with her.

Kyatta smiled and twisted a lock of white hair between her inked fingers. "I think you know."

Ivy narrowed her eyes. "I think you draw power from the moon. I know you receive messages from the gods in the form of dreams. That's why you came to Tordenfall, because of the dream you had about me."

Finn tilted his head toward Ivy, and she knew she had to explain. She quickly told Finn about Kyatta's dream and her vision. Finn watched her intently, and she could see worry creeping over his face as she spoke. Ivy hadn't told him because she hadn't wanted it to be true. Whatever vision Kyatta had didn't sound good, and Ivy wanted to forget it. Finn stayed silent, crossed his arms against his chest, and leaned back into the apple tree.

"There's something else you aren't telling me." Ivy turned her attention back to Kyatta, who flashed her teeth in a crooked smile and again touched the faces of the moon that crept up her arm.

"You're correct," Kyatta said. "I do interpret messages from the gods."

"And the moon?"

"I was attached to the moon from birth. I was born during a blood moon, and the people of my village knew it was a sign from the gods. I've always felt a pull to the moon, and it allows me to see things that others can't. I can read people in a way you read words on paper. I can see their emotions in their eyes."

Ivy recalled how closely she watched people's eyes and felt a cold shiver down her spine.

"During a full moon, I can even persuade people to do as I wish." Kyatta must have read the fear in Ivy's eyes as she quickly added, "Don't worry, I have never used that power unless it was crucial."

Finn was growing impatient and stepped closer to Kyatta. "Can you fix Ivy or not?"

"I can, but I won't unless she agrees to be transcended."

Ivy tilted her head curiously. "What does that even mean?"

Kyatta shrugged. "Just as it sounds. You will become what the gods intended for you to be."

Finn shook his head. "Ivy is who she is, you can't just change a person."

"Not change, transcend."

Ivy chewed on this for a moment, then finally asked Kyatta, "Why do you care?"

"Because I believe it will be of use to you in the future."

"Do you know something more you're not telling me?" Ivy could hear the worry in her own voice.

"No, I only know what I told you that night. But I still don't have a clear picture of your future. I can only read what the gods give me."

Ivy considered everything she said. She was afraid of what her powers might be, but she desperately wanted to be rid of Meisha's fear. Finn gave her a worried glance, and Ivy reached for his hand and squeezed it. "Fine, I'll do it."

"Ivy." Finn turned her toward him. "You don't even know

what you're agreeing to." Ivy placed her palm against his cheek. "I can't live with her fear forever, I need to get her out of my head."

Kyatta looked back and forth between them, but Ivy tried to shield her eyes so she couldn't read the fear within them. "What do I need to do?" Ivy turned to face her.

Kyatta tilted her head toward the sky and closed her eyes. "It's a full moon tonight. Come meet me on the southern wall at midnight." She turned to leave before Ivy could ask why. She didn't like the idea of being transcended, and she didn't understand what that meant. But Meisha's fear and pain were weakening her, she could feel it taking hold, and she needed to get rid of it before it broke her.

CHAPTER THIRTY-THREE

THE DREAM

The full moon lit their path as Ivy and Finn made their way through the streets. A halo of gold encircled the moon, which seemed to glide across the sky as dark clouds desperately tried to cover her shining face. The moon seemed to glow with a brightness that Ivy had never seen. Ivy had asked Finn not to come, but he couldn't stay away. Ivy knew he would do anything to keep her safe, and while that gave her comfort, it also made her worry. Her father was the same way. He would give up anything in a heartbeat to make sure his family was safe and happy. Ivy didn't like the idea of anyone giving their life for hers. This was her problem. She was the one who had killed Meisha, and now she was paying the consequences. She had to fix it no matter what the cost.

Kyatta was already on the wall when Ivy and Finn arrived. Ivy tried to keep her gaze straight forward and not look down to the spot where she'd killed Meisha, but she could feel it crawling on her skin like spiders. Her heart quickened its pace, and Ivy reached for Finn's hand to steady herself in case she became faint again. Kyatta turned her attention away from the moon as they approached. She'd changed clothing since earlier, and Ivy ran her eyes up the woman's bare arms. Despite the chill in the air, Kyatta seemed to be radiating heat. The tattoos on her arms ran to her collarbones and disappeared under her clothing.

"Are you ready?" Kyatta's voice was soft and pleasant like the first time they had talked. Ivy nodded her head, released Finn's hand, and stepped forward.

Kyatta pulled out a dagger, and Ivy's eyes immediately snapped down to the cold steel that seemed to glow in the moonlight. Kyatta must have sensed her hesitation, for she quickly threw up her hands as if to say she wasn't going to hurt Ivy. Somehow Ivy thought that was a lie.

"I just need a little blood is all," Kyatta said innocently.

"Why?" Finn demanded.

"This's how it's done," Kyatta answered simply and turned her attention back to Ivy. "If you want the pain gone, then I must take your blood." Ivy still didn't know whether she could trust Kyatta, but she saw no other way. The longer they stood on the wall, the more Ivy started to feel Meisha's pain clawing its way back into her mind. Her hands were beginning to sweat and shake with fear, so she reluctantly nodded her head.

Kyatta held out her hand for Ivy to take and pulled her in closer. The blade was slim, with a pale blue stone embedded in the black handle. As Kyatta sliced it across Ivy's palm, the stone seemed to glow. Ivy winced at the pain but stayed silent as Kyatta brought her lips to the warm blood and licked it up. Ivy wanted to ask what she was doing, but suddenly her vision changed.

She was lying on her back outside the southern gate, staring into her own eyes. She tried to move or scream but could do neither. The image of herself looked furious, and she didn't recognize her own eyes. The purple in them seemed to take on a greyish color, and Ivy felt a bolt of panic as her mirror image held Rayner's dagger to her throat. Ivy finally let out a terrified scream, but she couldn't move her body.

"You're hurting her!" Finn's voice sounded miles away.

"She has to relive the death through Meisha to be rid of the fear that haunts her." Kyatta's voice was calm and in control. Ivy watched with panicked eyes as her mirror image slid the blade across her throat. She pressed her hands to her neck, and when she felt the warm blood leaking through her fingers, Ivy immediately thought Kyatta had betrayed her and was killing her. She tried to think, but her strength was leaving her with every black drop of blood. It pooled around her, and Ivy gave in, closing her eyes to let death consume her. If she truly was dying, she only hoped Finn could get away and save himself.

When Ivy opened her eyes, the first image she saw was the full moon overhead. Its pale face greeted her with a warm light as she sat up. She was lightheaded and drenched in sweat from the vision. Ivy looked at Kyatta, who stood over her wearing an expression that she couldn't quite make out.

Finn ran to her side and pulled her face close to his. "Are you all right?" He didn't bother to keep the fear from his voice. Ivy looked at the wound Kyatta had given her, but there was no cut. "What did you do to me?" she asked. Ivy lifted her gaze.

Kyatta's eyes seemed shiny with tears, and she hugged her arms close to her body. "I took your pain for you and transcended you." Her voice sounded on the verge of breaking.

"Why would you take Meisha's fear?"

"I told you the gods showed me something of your future in that dream. I believe I had a part to play, and this might have been it."

She couldn't feel Meisha's grip on her any longer, and the pain and suffering the enchantress had felt was now as dead as she was.

"Ivy." Finn's voice brought her back. "How do you feel?"

"I'm not sure. I don't feel anything different."

"It may still take time for you to discover your ability, I only helped to unlock it," Kyatta said, then leaned back against the wall.

"So you don't even know what it is? You can't feel anything different about me?" Ivy asked. Kyatta pushed off from the wall and came over to Ivy. She bent down and took her face in her hands and stared into her eyes.

"There has always been something different about you." Kyatta pushed up from the ground and left.

Finn walked Ivy back to their room in silence. Ivy could feel his gaze on her, but she didn't want to look at him. She was afraid that she would have the same ability as Kyatta, and Ivy didn't wish to read people like that. Ivy collapsed on her bed, exhausted from the encounter with Kyatta. Finn sat next to her and ran his fingers through her hair while Ivy closed her eyes.

"Do you think you might actually have some sort of power like she said?" Finn asked in a quiet voice.

"I don't know. If I do, I need to discover it before Helvarr and his army come. If I can help in a different way, then I need to use what Kyatta unlocked."

Finn stared at her but said nothing more. Ivy could sense his concerns, but she didn't want to talk about it anymore. "Surely he's discovered Queen Narra's body, and if so, then Helvarr is close, and we all need to be ready," Finn continued.

Ivy propped herself up and placed a hand against Finn's cheek and gave him her most reassuring smile. "How can anyone prepare for what's coming?" she asked.

Finn had no answer for that. Ivy knew her father could build his walls higher, set traps, and close off every gate, but none of that would keep Helvarr's wrath from falling upon them. It filled Ivy with dread. She kept it bottled up, not wanting to worry Finn anymore. If their fates were already sealed, then all Ivy could do was try to accept that the gods had a plan. Ivy might not be able to interpret their messages as Kyatta, but she had faith in her father and her family. Helvarr existed on revenge and hate, and Ivy couldn't imagine that the gods would favor him in this battle.

Her father's choice to banish Helvarr had set him on a path of destruction that was making its loop back to Godstone. Ivy knew her father must have realized that his decision had shaped their future and everything that had happened to his family. Her heart broke for what her father must be feeling. If Magnus hadn't banished Helvarr, maybe things would have turned out differently. Since he had, that one decision had changed everything. Their fates were already sealed the moment her father had cast Helvarr out.

Finn snaked his arm under Ivy's neck and crawled into bed with her. Ivy's mind was cleared of all negative thoughts as Finn cradled her in his arms. They didn't speak about Kyatta again, or Helvarr. They fell asleep, wrapped up in each other, and Ivy met Finn in her dreams.

They stood in the practice yard back on Kame Island, where they had first met. It felt so real—even as Ivy reached out to touch Finn, her skin pricked up, and his warmth washed over her. He looked at her curiously, and Ivy tried to imagine her family. Rayner seemed to appear from a fog along with their pregnant mother, but something was wrong.

Their mother looked distressed and sad. Her belly had grown, and she looked closer to giving birth than she should. Ivy spun around, searching for the two missing members of her family when Finn's voice cut in.

"Ivy? Are you doing this?" The sky grew black, and storm clouds hovered overhead.

"I don't know what's happening. Where is—"

"This is your dream, Ivy," Finn cut in. "Just picture them, and they'll come."

"I'm trying." Ivy's voice was growing constricted. Tears began to burn in her eyes, but no one else appeared. No matter how much Ivy tried, she couldn't conjure up their images, and she began to panic. She sank to her knees and buried her hands in the sand. "This isn't a dream. This isn't a dream. This isn't a dream," she muttered to herself over and over.

"It is a dream, Ivy." Finn dropped down in front of her. "It's all right."

"No, Finn. Something's wrong. I have to wake up." Ivy squeezed her eyes shut, but when she opened them, she was still in the sandpit.

Ivy sprang up to her feet and began to run. She didn't know where she was going, but a sudden realization hit her like a punch to her chest. Ivy had always had vivid dreams in the past, some that meant something and others with messages she didn't understand until it was too late. She didn't get the sense that they were messages from the gods like Kyatta's dreams, but something else. They were—

Ivy slammed her bare feet against the cobblestone road, her breath faster and faster as she ran down the hill. She stopped at the docks that she first arrived at with Ser Osmund. One of her father's ships sat in the port, his Blackwood tree sigil flapping in the wind. Ivy's body began to shake as sweat ran down her neck.

This isn't a dream.

Ivy pressed her hands over her ears and sank to the ground. It all felt too real, but none of that had happened. Ivy had come to Kame Island with Ser Osmund to train. Her world spun, and Ivy yelled at herself to wake up. Finn came running up behind her just as she felt herself waking. He disappeared before he could reach her, and Ivy sprang up in bed to the sound of thunder.

Finn was still asleep by her side, and as Ivy heard another rumble of thunder, her heart skipped. She ran to her window and realized the sun was up and the sky clear. It wasn't thunder, and that wasn't a dream. Finn sat up in bed with a confused look on his face and turned to Ivy. "What is it?" he asked in a sleepy voice.

"He's here."

CHAPTER THIRTY-FOUR

THE LAST KNIGHT

I vy sprinted from the room before Finn could even get out of bed. She bumped into some knights in the hall who were dressed head to toe in shining steel plates. They called to her to stop, but Ivy kept running. She didn't have time to explain; she just needed to find her father. Ivy burst through the door of the Central Tower and into the streets. People were scrambling, horses ran loose, and knights were running toward the wall. Ivy took off after them, hoping to find her father there giving orders.

"Ivy!" Finn's voice clawed at her back, but she didn't stop.

At the top of the stone steps, Ivy could see knights filling barrels with arrows and lighting fires in the braziers that lined the wall. When her father wasn't there, Ivy braved a look over the wall, and her whole world came crumbling down. The colorful fields of flowers and rich green grass were covered like thick snow with raiders. Everywhere Ivy looked, men were lined up in ranks that stretched farther back than Ivy could see. Their red raven sigil violently flapped in the wind, bringing with it the smell of death. But it wasn't only the men that made Ivy's heart drop, it was the sound that she had thought was thunder. Five catapults sat nestled between the sea of raiders. Ivy froze, her feet encased in the stone wall she stood on as a boulder ablaze with fire launched into the air toward Godstone.

"Get down!" a voice called from behind her, and Ivy was tackled and thrown to the ground as the boulder sailed overhead. The noise shook her down to her bones. Rayner jumped off his sister and helped her back to her feet. "Come on." He pulled her along by the arm. Finn joined them as they made their way back down the steps. Ivy had never seen so much chaos and terror. They spotted Earl Rorik with his wife and their son Grimm as they all laced on leather armor. Finn had grabbed their armor as well and pulled it over Ivy's head. The thin black armor suddenly felt like boulders resting on her shoulders; the armor felt like the weight of the gods forcing Ivy's fate on her.

Rayner ran to Correlyn and hugged her close before helping her strap on her armor and double-checking it. Ivy surveyed the destruction. Only a few boulders had been sent over the wall, but already Ivy could see buildings crumbling and the market burning. She squeezed her fingers into a fist to try to stop her hands from shaking. Finn worked with swift hands as he used the maple leaf pin from Magnus to pin Ivy's cloak around her. The morning was windy, but the sky was devoid of any clouds. The wind swirled through the streets, pushing the maple tree cloak into Ivy's back. Finn took her cheeks in his hands, drawing her attention back to him. "Ivy, stay with me." His voice was warm, but she could sense the fear in it. Ivy checked her sword belt and ran a finger over the hilt of Promise as her mother and father came into the yard.

Magnus looked like a warrior king. His armor wasn't polished, his wavy hair blew carelessly in the wind, and his black cloak sailed behind him. Her father had never worn a crown atop his head. He didn't need it; he was everything a good king should be. Lord Kevan and Piotr came up behind him, and Piotr let his gaze fall over Ivy. Something in the way he looked at her gave her more chills than she already had. Ivy ran to her father, and as soon as he saw her, his eyes lit up. He wrapped her in a hug that felt like he never wanted to let go. Magnus's rough hands ran down her hair as Ivy pressed her face into his shoulder. "It's all right, sweetling," he whispered against her head. Ivy always thought that she was brave and tough, but when her father called her that, she felt as defenseless as a little girl. She didn't mind, though. Ivy imagined her father still saw her as his little girl and always would.

She hugged him tighter before pulling away. "Father, I have to tell you something." Ivy expected him to brush her off, to say not now or that there was no time, but instead, he smoothed back the wild hair that fell over her face and stayed silent. Elana too watched with curiosity behind her green eyes. Ivy quickly spit out everything she knew about Meisha and Kyatta, what she had told Ivy about her dream. She told him that Kyatta had unlocked some ability that, at first, Ivy wasn't aware of until her dream last night. Ivy told him about the dream and her suspicions as to what it meant.

Magnus listened to every word his daughter had said, but when she was finished, he couldn't believe it. Magnus had known something was different about Kyatta and had also read about enchantresses along with other people that held abilities, but at that moment, he couldn't believe it. Maybe he just didn't want to consider it. Ivy eagerly waited for him to say something. He opened his mouth to speak just as another flaming boulder shot over the wall and crashed through a local inn. Magnus snapped his attention to the fire, and it was as if he had just woken up. He turned away from Ivy and began shouting orders to Lord Kevan and Earl Rorik. Piotr left with his father toward the southern gate, and Earl Rorik led his family and people to the western gate where the main threat was. Elana was stopped in the street by the knights who were assigned to protect her, but Magnus waved them off. "Your Grace!" a knight called down from the wall. Magnus turned his attention away from his wife and ran toward the wall.

When he reached the top, the knight was pointing down the wall to where one man stood. Magnus's heart dropped to his boots, and his stomach twisted into knots. He took in the black armor, the red cloak flapping against his back, and the crooked nose. Helvarr's hair was shorter than the last time Magnus had seen him. He wore it slicked back, and his black beard grew tight to his face. Magnus felt a surge of anger as Helvarr spotted him and flashed his white teeth in the same crooked smile he had given Magnus over nineteen years ago.

"I think it's time to talk, old friend!" Helvarr called up to Magnus. Helvarr stood alone in front of his massive army as if he genuinely wished to talk and work it out, though Magnus doubted their encounter would be anything of the sort.

Magnus made his way back to his family. His head was on the verge of bursting as he tried to think about what to do. Magnus caught Ronin's eyes from within the crowd and was sure he could see something different in them. Luna circled above and landed on a nearby horse, keeping an eye on her king. Magnus wrapped his arms around Elana, who had tears in her eyes. "I have to go talk to him," Magnus said against her cheek.

"No!" Elana couldn't keep the worry from her voice. She pushed away and put a hand over her belly. "You can't go out there."

"She's right, Father." Rayner stepped forward. "You really believe Helvarr wants to talk? After everything he's done?"

Magnus looked from Elana to Rayner, but Ivy stood silently beside Finn. What could he do? If Magnus refused to go and face Helvarr, he would only continue to open fire and eventually tear down the walls. Magnus couldn't risk everyone's life for his mistake. It was his job to try to correct it. He only hoped that some shred of the old Helvarr lay buried in the new one.

"I'm coming with you." Ronin stepped out from the crowd. His hair was pulled back in a small bun, and he wore his two swords across his back. He didn't have the same calm look on his face that he usually did. "He's my son, and I might be able to get through to him."

"You're going to tell him?" Ivy asked.

"It's time I fixed my own mistakes as well," Ronin said, and his face shifted to something that resembled calm, but fear crept under it.

Another boulder flew over the wall and crashed just behind where the group stood. Helvarr was likely growing impatient, and the longer Magnus waited, the more of Godstone would crumble. A sick feeling grabbed hold of Magnus as he looked over his family and his men who stood by for orders. Magnus forced a smile and pulled his wife in. He held her cheeks gently and slid one hand into her golden hair before pressing his lips against hers. Magnus always got the same feeling when he kissed his wife. Every sensation was intensified, and his blood raced through his veins. Elana wrapped her arms around his neck and pulled Magnus in closer. The king and his queen stood surrounded by the kingdom. Their love was radiant, like the sun against a pool of water.

"I love you, Elana," Magnus said against her lips, then he felt a tear roll down her cheek. He pulled his face away and ran his thumbs over her cheeks, catching her tears. Elana cradled her belly that held their child and kissed Magnus on the cheek.

Magnus turned to Rayner, who stood with his wife. "Father, please don't do—"

Magnus placed a hand behind Rayner's neck and pulled him in. He wrapped his arms around his father. Rayner had always tried to guard his emotions the way Magnus did, but it was as if something in their hug made him weak. Rayner squeezed his father tighter until he crushed himself between their armor. Magnus gave Rayner a firm pat on the back and kissed him against his auburn hair.

Ivy's whole body was shaking with fear. Although she had told her father of the dream, he hadn't seemed concerned. Perhaps he felt that this was the only option. Ivy wasn't sure if she believed everything Kyatta had told her. Maybe she hadn't really transcended Ivy, and last night was only a dream. She'd always had vivid dreams that felt real, so why would that one be any different?

Ivy had to convince herself of this because if she didn't, she knew she couldn't let her father walk out that gate. When Magnus turned to Ivy and Finn, the two exchanged a look that Ivy couldn't read. Like some secret code that was only meant for their eyes to unlock. Ivy was about to speak and demand to know what it had meant when a flaming barrel came over the wall. This time, when it hit, it exploded like a clap of thunder and sent fire raining down from above. *Thunder and fire fell from above and consumed everything around it.* Kyatta's words echoed in her head. People screamed and ran from the burning building, but Magnus held Ivy's gaze and stepped in front of her.

"I love you, sweetling," Magnus said as he kissed Ivy on the cheek. The king looked at Finn again with the same secret look before pulling his sword. "Kneel," Magnus directed to Ivy.

"What?" she asked, genuine confusion snaking around her mind and squeezing until it popped.

"Kneel, Ivy," Magnus repeated, smiling warmly. Ivy felt her heart begin to flutter as she looked to Finn for answers, but he only gave her a nod. Behind Magnus, Ivy could see Rayner walking closer as he suddenly realized what was happening. Tears burned in his eyes as he watched his sister kneel before their father, who would have the honor of knighting his daughter.

Ivy didn't understand why this was happening. What happened to waiting two years like Magnus had wanted? Why now? Ivy couldn't think as she sank to the ground and kept her eyes locked with her father. Magnus stood tall above her, and nothing but pride burned in his eyes. He lowered his sword to Ivy's left shoulder and instructed her to repeat the oath of the knight after him.

"With these words, I take on what the unfit might call burden, but I call an honor.
I will hold my honor as close as a promise.
I will shield those who can no longer fight.
I will show mercy when it is needed and
Never take a life without just cause.
I will serve loyally for the rest of my days
And follow my morality wherever this oath may guide me.
I will wear my bravery as armor
And never give in to fear but use it to drive me.
With these words, I promise to defend my family and their lands.
To sacrifice everything for those I love.
And to serve my king until his reign should end."

Magnus lifted the sword above her head and rested it on Ivy's right shoulder, sealing the promises of a knight. "Now," Magnus's voice boomed in the yard, and everyone stood up a little taller. "Rise, Lady Ivy. Knight of Godstone and daughter of King Magnus the Mighty."

Ivy rose to her feet, and a roar lifted from the crowd. Rayner stepped forward and wrapped his sister in a hug. Magnus turned to Finn and gave a small approving nod of his head, yet another secret look that Ivy couldn't read.

Rayner pulled away and gave Ivy a playful punch against her shoulder. Finn wove his arms around her waist from behind and buried his face in her hair. "I'm so proud of you, Ivy," he whispered. Ivy couldn't pinpoint what she was feeling. She was beyond happy, past overjoyed, but she also felt the tug at her heart, telling her that this wasn't the end. Ivy always dreamed of being a knight, but it tasted bittersweet on her tongue, and it wasn't the way she had imagined it. Magnus kissed his daughter on the head. "You'll make a fine knight, Ivy Blackbourne."

Ivy stared at him for a long moment, and finally managed to utter a few words. "Thank you, Father." Magnus smiled at his daughter, then turned and headed to the gate. The crowd cheered her and shouted her name, but Ivy couldn't peel herself away from her father and Ronin as they headed outside the walls to meet Helvarr.

CHAPTER THIRTY-FIVE

THE MIGHTY

A few knights lifted the wooden post and opened the gates for their king. Magnus paused to take a deep breath before stepping outside the walls of Godstone with Ronin at his side. Helvarr's army was like nothing Magnus had ever seen. It stretched far into the horizon, and though Magnus had gathered everyone he could from the North, he knew it wouldn't be enough. Helvarr surely knew that as well, which was why he used Queen Narra and Meisha to get everyone to Godstone so that he could defeat them all.

Magnus felt nervous but kept his composure and his face stern as he walked across the grass. Ronin stayed slightly behind Magnus as they closed the distance between themselves and Helvarr. He stood tall and lean with his wry smile and crooked nose. He still looked the same as the day Magnus had banished him, and Magnus wondered who had truly suffered more from that decision. The king turned as he heard a commotion behind him and saw that his army had followed him outside the gates. Ivy stood in front with

Finn at her side. The knights at the gate wouldn't close out their king, and Ivy wouldn't leave her father. She still had a promise to keep.

Helvarr smiled as Magnus came to stand before him, his eyes never crossing over Ronin. "Magnus." Helvarr's voice sounded like a snake hissing. Luna called out and continued to circle Magnus from above. He turned his head up and realized something was flying above Luna from higher in the sky. Helvarr's horned eagle, Arne, was circling Luna like she was prey, waiting for her to make the wrong move. "You look well, Magnus," Helvarr continued. "I can't say the same for her, though." He brought his hands out from behind his back and lifted a head from a bloody bag. He threw Queen Narra's head at Magnus's feet and let the smile on his face fade away. "You beheaded the queen of Kaspin's Keep." Helvarr shook a disapproving finger at Magnus.

"It wasn't me," Magnus replied.

"No? Then who?" The king stayed silent. He would never tell Helvarr that it had been Finn who killed Queen Narra. Helvarr seemed indifferent and rolled his eyes. "It won't matter soon, anyway."

"Helvarr." Magnus shuddered at speaking his name. "You have to stop this. It's gone too far—"

"I think I haven't gone far enough." His voice chopped off the king's words. "If I had, your son would have died when I sent my assassin, and I would have killed your daughter after taking Ser Osmund's life." His smile returned, and he flashed his white teeth at Magnus.

The king balled his fists but held back his anger.

"You should be thanking me for sparing her life."

Magnus looked past Helvarr and saw the horned knight standing like a shadow in the crowd. He put his hand to the hilt of his sword and eyed the man who tried to kill Rayner and who succeeded in killing Ser Caster. "Let's not do something stupid, Magnus," Helvarr said. "You'll die before you reach the first line of my men."

"Give me the horned knight, and I'll let you go," Magnus demanded.

Helvarr tilted his head back and sent his laughter into the blue sky. "I can't do that I'm afraid. But I can give you something else." He took a step toward Magnus and held his gaze captive. "I can give you the chance to save your family. You can hand your kingdom over to me and leave with your people."

"How about you turn around and leave, and I won't kill you in front of your men." Magnus's voice grew heated with rage. Helvarr seemed to enjoy it even more and chuckled at the king's empty threat.

"Magnus, my friend, we all know you aren't capable of bloodshed the way I am. I know your weakness, and I know you would never kill me." Magnus felt his heart skip. He always tried to live by the words he'd just spoken to Ivy. He was a king, but he was also a knight, and Magnus felt the binding of those words ever since he spoke them years ago with Helvarr. But Helvarr hadn't taken them seriously. He killed for pleasure and took what he wanted. He killed to enjoy the silence of death around him.

"People change," Magnus replied.

"Ah, yes. But not you, Magnus. You're still the same man I once knew." Magnus could have been mistaken, but he thought he saw a flicker of regret in Helvarr's eyes. However, it was gone in a flash and burned away with anger as Helvarr finally looked at Ronin.

"What is he doing here?" he snapped.

Magnus glanced back at Ronin, whose expression looked pained with regret, yet he took a step closer to his son.

"Helvarr." Ronin's voice didn't falter. "I know you think I was only a trainer to you. That I never cared for you when you were a boy. You had a difficult life as a child, and that's my fault." Ronin lowered his gaze.

Helvarr watched him curiously, but the amusement that usually painted his face wasn't there. "I was consumed by anger and rage toward you, and that's why I left you in the woods when you were only a baby."

Helvarr now looked furious and confused at the same time. "What are you rambling about, Ronin?" he asked, but there was a certain eagerness in the question. Ronin stepped closer and stared into Helvarr's eyes, as if seeing a ghost.

"You're my son, Helvarr."

Magnus could've sworn Helvarr swayed a little on his feet. He looked to be sweating, and his eyes shook with anger as he balled his fists. He either didn't believe Ronin, or he didn't want to. Helvarr was raised by a man who claimed to be his father, but he soon died in battle and left Helvarr alone.

Magnus was his only family, and Ronin had tried to take on the role of his father, and now Helvarr knew why. "You have your mother's eyes," Ronin continued. "She died giving birth to you, and I couldn't control my anger. I blamed you for taking her away from me. I know it was wrong, and I'm sorry, son." Ronin studied his face, but Helvarr quickly covered what might have been sadness with anger. Magnus didn't think Helvarr knew how to be sad. His emotions had always been so rapid-fire and strong, but never did Magnus see real sadness in him. That was until the day he banished Helvarr and watched his mask slip.

Magnus quickly tried to keep it going, hoping to see that look come back into his eyes that proved he was a real man with feelings. "It's true, Helvarr. Ronin is your father." Helvarr snapped his head back to Magnus and gave him a look that radiated disgust. "He's wanted to tell you for a long time now." Magnus didn't know if that was true, but he had to try something. "Ronin was there for you when the man who you thought was your father died. He trained you, he taught you everything you know. Ronin and I were your family, and we can be that again." Magnus took a small step toward Helvarr, who surprisingly didn't step away. "I know I made a mistake when I banished you, brother." The word brother tasted as bitter as blood on the king's tongue, but he forced himself to continue. "I've regretted it every day, and I know I'm to blame for everything that's happened to my family."

Magnus was actually relieved to finally say it out loud. For a while now, he'd been feeling guilty, not about banishing Helvarr, but what it led to. Magnus had always done whatever it took to protect his family, and he had let them down the moment he banished Helvarr. He never could have imagined what Helvarr would turn into by casting him out. Had he known, Magnus would have broken his rule and killed Helvarr nineteen years ago. Magnus had always believed in showing mercy and giving someone every available opportunity to change, but Helvarr was unchangeable. His wrath was inevitable.

Helvarr didn't seem to know how to react. His face desperately tried to hold up the mask, but Magnus saw it slipping. He'd always been jealous of Magnus and his right to rule Godstone and claim the throne. Helvarr only had his knighthood to be proud of, and even that wasn't enough. He'd always wanted more. More power, a family as Magnus had, and the ability to rule people without having to use fear. But Helvarr wasn't a king, and he had to fight for everything he wanted. The day Magnus threw him to the side had killed a part of Helvarr. He had lost his only family and a chance for another one.

"Son, please," Ronin spoke up.

"Don't call me that!" Helvarr roared. He looked back at Magnus and drew his dagger, but Magnus didn't avert his eyes. Magnus heard Ronin take a step forward, but he held up a hand to stop him. Ronin couldn't help anymore; he'd tried and failed. Magnus ordered Ronin to go back and looked over his shoulder to see Ronin stepping back but not as far as where the army stood at the gate. Magnus had to try and get through to Helvarr before it was too late. A fire burned in Helvarr's eyes as he clutched his dagger and eyed the king. Magnus held up his hands as if to say he wouldn't hurt Helvarr. He scrunched his brows together and watched as Magnus unbuckled his sword belt and dropped it to the ground.

"Would you kill a man who is unarmed?" Magnus asked.

Magnus could see that Helvarr didn't know how to react. Magnus was giving him full power over the situation.

"Father!" Ivy's voice made Magnus turn his head. Ivy stepped forward with his army at her back. He could see she was crying, and her eyes pleaded with him to come back. Magnus made a fist and placed it across his chest, just above his heart. It was something Magnus only did with Ivy. It was meant as a promise that everything was going to be all right. It was the promise of a king but, more importantly, the promise of a father. He watched Ivy mirror him, and he tried to force a smile for her sake.

When Magnus turned back to face Helvarr, he thought he saw a tear roll down his cheek and disappear into his black beard. "Brother, please stop this and come home." Helvarr blinked at the word home. "You can end all of this, you have the power to end this war, this battle for the North. Too many people have died already." Magnus stepped even closer until they were face to face. Helvarr's copper eyes shined with something close enough to sadness. Magnus placed a hand on his shoulder and continued. "My love for you has never died, and you'll always be my brother." Helvarr lifted a hand on the king's shoulder and studied his purple eyes. Magnus pulled him in and embraced Helvarr. He could feel Helvarr's long arms wrap around him and return the embrace.

Magnus let a tear roll down his cheek as he hugged his oldest friend, the only brother he ever had, but the tear wasn't only for him. He felt Helvarr's body relax and give in. Helvarr squeezed Magnus tighter and brought his copper eyes up to rest on Ronin, who stood back by the gate behind Magnus. His eyes shifted, and he brought his mouth close to the king's ear, still holding him in the hug. Helvarr kept his eyes locked on Ronin as he spoke. "My father died long ago." The words felt as cold as ice against Magnus's ear. "And it's like you told me so many years ago," Helvarr hissed. "You're not my brother."

Helvarr shoved his dagger through the weak spot of the armor, piercing the king's heart. He felt Magnus shaking against him as the blood spilled out around him. He dropped the dagger and caressed Magnus's head, stroking his hair. Helvarr could feel the life draining from Magnus as he held up his weight. He leaned into the king's ear once more as he held the back of his head. "And you were never my king." Helvarr let go, and Magnus's body dropped to the grass, which seemed to shimmer in the sun with fresh blood. The blood of a king. The blood of King Magnus the Mighty.

CHAPTER THIRTY-SIX

THE PROMISE

I vy couldn't believe what she was seeing. She blinked her eyes shut, but when she opened them again, her father and Helvarr were still embracing one another. She was too far away to see Helvarr's expression, and her father's back was turned, but Ivy had hoped that he could end this. Ivy's father never did anything without thinking it through. He considered every option before making a choice and never backed down on his decision. Magnus wasn't like other kings. He ruled in a way that no other could hope to live up to, but Ivy knew Rayner would make a great king someday as well.

She looked at her brother and saw he had the same shocked look on his face. Ronin was standing just ahead of the army, observing his son. Ivy turned around and was surprised to see Kyatta standing within the ranks of men with a bow in her hand. The look she gave Ivy was somewhat haunting, and as Ivy opened her mouth to call to her, a piercing pain struck her heart.

Ivy felt her heart bursting with pain and desperately

clutched at her chest. She turned back to her father, who was still wrapped in Helvarr's arms. Ivy's heart began to slow, and the pain blurred her vision. Finn looked at her with concern, and Rayner only seemed confused because nothing had struck Ivy, but she could feel the stabbing pain in her chest. Tears welled in her eyes, and when she lifted her gaze back to her father, Helvarr let him go, and Magnus dropped to the ground.

Ivy fell to her knees and felt the hole in his heart searing its way into her chest. Ivy couldn't move, she couldn't think. Everything seemed blurred, and time slowed down as her father's body lay in the grass in front of them. She heard her brother scream and tried to peel her eyes away from their father, but she couldn't do it. It had to be a dream. Her father couldn't be dead, not when they were so close to ending this battle before it began.

Finn lifted Ivy to her feet, and she finally turned her eyes to Helvarr, who stood above Magnus as if he were a prized buck that he'd been hunting for years. Ivy was shaking so badly that she thought her bones might snap. Finn grabbed her arm and was yelling something, but Ivy couldn't hear it over the chaos in her head. It wasn't supposed to happen like this. Luna's shrill cry shook Ivy back to reality, and when she looked up, her father's bird was falling from the sky.

Helvarr's horned eagle dove for Luna, and the two birds latched talons, twirling through the sky and plummeting toward the ground. Ivy knew that Luna too must have felt it the moment her king fell. Her eyes grew wide as she watched Luna falling to her death. The birds snapped at each other, and feathers fell loose. The sun caught Luna's brilliant white feathers, and Ivy thought she looked like a falling star. Just as Ivy thought the birds were about to crash to the ground, an arrow pierced the horned eagle through the heart. It let go of Luna, and she spread her wings and took off.

Ivy snapped her head back at Helvarr, who was screaming for his fallen eagle. As swift as the wind, Luna came down and clawed Helvarr's face, leaving three large scratches down his cheek. Ivy turned back and saw that Kyatta had stepped forward. It was her arrow that had pierced the eagle's heart.

Everything was happening too fast. Ivy's father had only fallen a moment ago, Luna almost died, but Ivy knew what she had to do. She drew Promise from its scabbard, rubbing a finger on the silk scarf her father had given her as Ivy's cloak pushed onto her back. She was running before she knew what was happening. Ronin attempted to grab her, but she slipped through his hands and ran faster. Helvarr ordered his archers to shoot down Luna, and Ivy's heart began to beat faster. Helvarr turned toward her and drew his sword, an absolute fury burning behind his copper eyes. Ivy felt tears being pulled from her cheeks as she ran across the field. Helvarr made no move to run. He stood there with his sword held in both hands and eyed her, begging her to try and kill him.

Ivy jumped over her father's body and swung her sword with everything she had. It caught Helvarr in his side armor, but Ivy didn't give him a chance to lift his sword before she swung again. He ducked, Promise just missing the top of his head, and Ivy thought she saw something change in his face. Helvarr shoved her and brought his sword down as Ivy rolled away. It struck the grass just beside her with such force, that Ivy felt it shake the earth.

"You've got more fight in you than your father ever had!" Helvarr yelled over the noise of the two armies running toward each other. Ivy was too angry to speak. Too hurt and broken to waste energy on forming words. She heard herself growl and jabbed her blade at Helvarr's leg. He kicked it away and grabbed Ivy by the neck of her armor, and lifted her into the air.

He was stronger than he looked, and Ivy desperately tried to kick him. Promise lay in the grass beside his feet, and his eyes followed her stare to the ground. Ivy headbutted him while he was distracted, and as soon as he let go, she reared back and threw all her force into a punch. It caught him just under the jaw, and Helvarr staggered slightly. His anger swelled in his eyes, and just as he lifted his sword, the thunder of horses came up behind Ivy and blew past them to Helvarr's men. Helvarr and Ivy stood in the center of raging horses and screaming men, but his eyes never left her. He smiled and lifted his sword into the air as Ivy tried to reach Promise. An arrow pierced Helvarr through his shoulder just as he was about to swing, and Ivy turned to see Correlyn standing there with the string of her bow still quivering.

The two armies blended into one another, and the battle for the North began. Rayner ran up to Ivy and pulled her into a hug as she watched her father's knights carry away his body. Ivy fought back her tears as she watched her father, the king of Godstone, lie limp in the arms of his men. She pulled away and turned around. Helvarr was lost in the sea of men, and the flaming barrels started to fly again. Ivy heard each crash as they exploded against the walls, and their flames ignited the tar-filled moat around the wall. Smoke swirled up into the air, creating dark clouds in the perfectly blue sky.

Her father's knights formed a circle around her family and were fighting off Helvarr's men. Ivy got a sick feeling in the pit of her stomach as she realized what they were doing. The knights weren't only protecting Ivy and her family, but more importantly, Rayner. He was the heir to Godstone, and he would be the next king.

Rayner seemed oblivious to this as he shouted commands to the other knights. Kyatta loosed arrows behind them, dropping the charging raiders mid-run. The wall of knights was slowly letting in a trickle of raiders to be slaughtered. Ivy's mind was spinning as she picked up Promise and eyed her first raider. He came barreling through the wall of knights, but Rayner stepped in front of his sister before she could slay him. She watched as Rayner slit the man's throat and shoved his body back through the wall of knights. Finn grabbed Ivy by the arm and turned her to face him. His eyes were filled with as much pain as Ivy felt, but if there was any fear inside him, he did well to hide it from her. "Stay with me!" he bellowed over the screams and explosions. Ivy gave him a firm nod, and they went back to back as more raiders streamed into their circle. Ivy skewered a raider who wore no armor and kicked his limp body off her sword. She could feel Finn's body against her back as he fought off men. Correlyn and Kyatta stood on opposite ends of the circle, firing arrows as the knights parted to let in more raiders.

Earl Rorik and his family stood within the circle, along with Lord Kevan and Piotr. Ivy had never seen Piotr fight in a battle, but she knew how strong he was. She watched as he nearly sliced a man's head from his body and dropped another with a punch to the face. Ivy sliced at another raider when he suddenly collapsed in front of her. Ronin stood behind the man's body, and Ivy saw something different in his eyes. Ronin was always calm and in control of his emotions when he fought. But now, Ivy could see pure anger burning in his eyes, and before she could say anything, Ronin turned and jumped over the wall of knights and into the sea of raiders. "Ronin!" she called after him, but it was too late.

Ivy watched in amazement as Ronin took on a group of raiders all at once. His sword cut through their flesh like it was cutting through the air. He was a ghost, slipping from their path. Another explosion drew Ivy's attention to the wall behind them. The catapults were firing boulders again, and Ivy watched in horror as a large portion of the western wall fell. They couldn't let the raiders get into the kingdom. Innocent people were still inside, along with their mother. But all Ivy could think about was the promise she made to her father months ago. She needed to find Helvarr and kill him. It wouldn't bring her father back, but she could stop him before more innocent people died. Ivy turned to Finn, who was slicing a raider's throat with his ax. The smoke was beginning to fill the air, and from the thick grey fog, a demon appeared.

The horned knight charged the wall of knights on his black horse. Ivy yelled to Rayner, but he couldn't hear her over the commotion. She pulled Finn by the collar of his leather armor as the horned knight jumped the wall of men. Kyatta shot an arrow at the horned knight, but the arrow bounced off the armor. "Rayner!" Ivy shouted again, and this time he turned, and Ivy thought his eyes glazed over with pure terror. The horned knight spotted him just as Ivy called to her brother, and he charged on his black stallion.

Rayner didn't move, but he didn't run either. He tightened the grip on his sword as the knight charged. Suddenly, Correlyn was in front of him, pulling back an arrow, and didn't hesitate as she shot the arrow and watched it bounce off the knight's armor. She quickly reached back to her quiver and pulled another arrow as the knight slammed his stallion to a stop. Correlyn let the arrow fly, and it caught the horse in the chest just as he reined back. The horned knight fell from the horse, and Rayner pulled Correlyn back by the waist until they were standing together.

The horned knight rose to his feet and drew his sword before storming across the grass toward Rayner. Correlyn stepped in front of her husband again and drew another arrow, but the knight didn't swing his sword. Instead, he threw back his armored arm and backhanded Correlyn across the face. Rayner watched his wife fall and then turned his eyes back to the knight. Finn stood in front of Ivy as another raider made its way through the wall. He cut the man down, spraying Finn's face with warm blood. Ivy watched her brother fighting the horned knight, but Rayner couldn't get in a swing, only blocking the blows that came his way.

Ivy knew she had to do something. She tried to recall the dream from last night. There had been two people missing. She turned Finn around and pulled him in by the collar. An explosion erupted behind him as she kissed Finn. His mouth tasted like blood and ash. She pushed him away just as he brought a hand to her face. "Keep Correlyn safe," Ivy said.

Finn's face was painted with confusion and then fear as Ivy turned around and ran.

"Ivy, no!" Finn's scream rose over the commotion, but Ivy didn't look back. She couldn't turn back, or she would lose the sudden surge of courage that was driving her. Ivy jumped the wall of her father's knights, *Rayner's knights,* just as a raider slipped through. Some of the knights yelled at her to stop, but she kept going.

She slid in the grass as a raider's sword swung at her throat. She threw up Promise and sliced it across his belly, then jumped back to her feet. She searched the crowd until she spotted him. Ronin seemed to be devoid of anything other than anger as he sliced raiders to pieces. Ivy ran to him, stabbing another raider through the neck who stood in her way. A warm mist covered her face and hair as she jerked her sword from his throat. Ronin spotted her and immediately shifted the look on his face.

His sword found its way through a man's chest and protruded from his back as Ivy reached him. She spun him around to face her and pointed back to the wall of knights where Rayner was still fighting the horned knight. "Help Rayner!" Ivy demanded and started to run again, but Ronin caught her by the wrist.

"Where do you think you're going?" his voice boomed over the thunder of battle.

Ivy snatched her arm free and said through her teeth, "To kill Helvarr." She left Ronin, only stealing a glance back to make sure he obeyed her. He stood there, watching Ivy run off for a moment before slicing his way back to the circle of knights.

Ivy frantically searched the mass of men for Helvarr's black hair. Many of the knights wore helms and could be easily identified. A bloody horse raged past Ivy carrying a man who was slumped over in the saddle. She pushed her way further into the slaughter when a spear landed in the ground just in front of her. Ivy stopped and looked up to see Helvarr, surrounded by knights who carried shields and spears, all pointed at her. A raider bumped into her from behind, and Ivy's attention left Helvarr for only a moment as she pushed the man back and stabbed Promise through his chest. When she turned back, Helvarr was gone, but the knights were marching toward her.

Luna cried out above, and Ivy realized she was circling her. Her massive wingspan cast shadows on the battlefield, absorbing all the light around them. A flock of arrows shot up in the air, and Luna swerved and dove to miss them. Ivy looked back to see Helvarr sitting atop a stark white horse, pulling back an arrow. He let it fly, and Ivy watched as it pierced Luna's wing. "No!" she heard herself scream. Luna dropped like a rock and disappeared into the wave of men in the distance. Ivy ground her teeth together and squeezed the hilt of Promise until her knuckles went white. She knew she couldn't get through the shield wall to get to Helvarr, but she had to try. Ivy knew that her father had sacrificed his life for them. She wasn't sure if Magnus actually thought he could get through to Helvarr, or if he was finally giving in to the mistake he'd made.

She didn't want to believe that her father would willingly give his life or that he knew he was walking to his death the moment he left the kingdom. Magnus always had a reason for his actions, but Ivy couldn't think of any at that moment. Perhaps her father thought he deserved death. That he needed to right his wrongs, and he knew Helvarr would never stop hunting him. Had her father sacrificed himself so that Helvarr would stop trying to harm his family? Ivy felt sick as she thought about it. If that were true, then her father had been wrong. Helvarr wouldn't stop until they were all dead because Rayner was the heir, and he posed a threat to the throne that Helvarr wanted. Their family would never be safe as long as Helvarr was still breathing.

Ivy took in a deep breath and shifted her stance as the shield wall closed in on her. Their spearheads poked through the red wall of shields, edging closer, dying to taste her blood. Helvarr watched from atop his horse. Ivy whispered a silent prayer for her family and Finn, hoping he hadn't come after her. She let herself picture his soft brown eyes and warm smile as the raiders came close enough to jab at her. Her heart was wildly racing, and her palms sweating.

Ivy gripped Promise with both hands and held her sword in front of her, ready to fight to the death. "I'll see you soon, Father," she said softly and let go of her fear as the first raider stuck his spear forward. Ivy chopped the head off with her sword and stepped back, waiting for the next one. The wall opened, and a screaming raider raced through and swung his sword at Ivy's head. She staggered back, almost tripping on a dead body. She threw up her sword against his, but he leaned all his weight into it, forcing her down. Ivy kicked the man in the ribs and threw him off and got back to her feet. He swung again, nearly slicing Ivy's throat as she leaned back.

Promise struck the man in the leg, and Ivy watched the

warm blood watering the ground on which they stood. The raider drew back, but Ivy advanced on him, swinging Promise at his head. Her sword stuck in the man's skull. The shield wall was coming closer.

Her sword wouldn't budge.

Ivy put a boot on the man's head and pulled, but it was lodged deep. A spear thrust forward and sliced Ivy's lower leg. She cried out in pain, still trying to free her sword when she heard an ear-piercing shriek from above. It sounded the way a sword screeches against metal armor, or how rushing water drowns out every sound around it. It was primal and blood-curdling. Ivy craned her neck up, and her eyes lit with fire and grew as wide as the raider's shields. "What the—"

CHAPTER THIRTY-SEVEN

FROM THE ASHES

A wall of fire rained down from the sky and burned the raiders in front of her. The heat shot up to kiss Ivy's face, and she threw up a hand to block the waves. They dropped their shields and screamed as the fire consumed them. They tried to run from the fire while others fell to the ground, screaming in pain. Ivy saw Helvarr through the flames, and his face was that of shock. She followed his gaze up into the sky.

"Luna?" she said to herself. Luna's white feathers were gone, and fiery orange ones took their place. Her eyes burned red, and flames shot out from the ends of her wings and tail as she soared through the sky. "Luna!" Ivy cried to the bird, and Luna tilted her head to Ivy. She took off, running toward the bird as Luna opened her mouth and bellowed out a comet of fire. She flew low to the ground and lit an entire rank of raiders on fire. Ivy couldn't believe what her eyes were showing her. Her father always said that Luna had powers. Ivy thought back to the Whispering Woods and how Luna had saved them. She was able to fly into the woods and lead them all out one by one without being affected by the Wood's power. Ivy never could have imagined that her powers went beyond that.

Luna circled around and flew toward the catapult that was readying another boulder. But this time, her beak stayed shut as she threw her wings out in front of her, stopping her in midair and sending a wave of fire to destroy the weapon. Ivy stopped in her tracks and watched as the fire quickly destroyed the catapult which seemed to explode from the force of the fire. Ivy turned around and sprinted through the armies. Luna could take care of herself.

The wall of knights was still protecting her family when Ivy ran up. They separated to let her in and quickly killed a raider that had been on her heels. Finn ran up to her and threw his arms around Ivy. "Don't ever do that to me again," he cried, his voice trembling. Rayner was bleeding from a wound to his arm, and Correlyn's face was cut up from the horned knight's armor.

"Where's Ronin?" Ivy called to her brother. Rayner pointed with a shaky finger, and Ivy followed it until she spotted Ronin fighting the horned knight just outside their protective wall of men. Ivy didn't know how Ronin managed to get the knight away from Rayner, but she was grateful.

Every other sound seemed to drown out around her save for the two knights' swords clanging against each other. Ivy watched Ronin skillfully slide around the horned knight. His armor was dented from Ronin's blows, but it was too thick for his sword to pierce. He was no longer fighting with anger but with the familiar calmness that always radiated from him.

He was the best fighter Ivy had ever seen, and yet the horned knight seemed to be toying with him. His sword came down too close to Ronin's face, and Ivy took a step forward. She didn't need anyone else's blood on her hands, and if Ronin fell to the horned knight, he would haunt Ivy's dreams forever. A loud crash made Ivy snap her head back. A flaming barrel exploded just outside the circle of men, and Ivy turned her attention to the catapults. They were no longer firing on the walls of Godstone but them.

Finn tightened his grip on Ivy's shoulder as if she might run into battle again. Rayner shouted commands to the knights, but they ignored him. "Get them out of here!" one of them screamed to another. A group of knights broke off from the circle and swarmed Rayner and Correlyn while others went to Ivy and Finn. They were pushing them back toward the gates of Godstone, away from the battle that they were clearly losing. Ivy's breath caught in her throat as the knights pushed her further and further from the battle. From Helvarr. From the promise she made to her father.

"No!" she pushed against the knight. "I need to kill him!"

"It's too late, Lady Ivy!" the knight roared back. "You and your family need to go!" Finn tried to pull Ivy back, but she wouldn't budge.

"I'm not leaving! This is my home!"

The knight grabbed Ivy by the collar and yanked her forward. His breath was hot and laced with fear. "Not anymore." The words cut through to Ivy's soul, and she felt her knees buckle, but the knight held her up. "You want to die here?" he yelled but didn't wait for Ivy to answer before shoving her back at Finn, who grabbed Ivy by the waist and pulled her closer to the crumbling kingdom that had once been her home.

The streets were empty, and Ivy wondered if the people had forced their way through the eastern gate to escape on fishing boats. Buildings were crumbling, and houses were burning. The smoke washed away the light from the sun and filled the air with the smell of burning death. Ivy turned around to see Earl Rorik's family, Lord Kevan's, and Kyatta, with various people of the northern clans following closely behind and killing any raiders that tried to follow. The knight ushered them through the streets, and Ivy broke off into a run when she spotted a swirl of golden hair.

Her mother stood at the entrance to the central tower with an army of knights around her. But her mother didn't look up as Ivy approached, her gaze resting on the king who lay on a bed of woven branches to transport his body. Ivy felt sick at the sight of him. His skin was pale and looked entirely too fragile. Like one touch might make him fall apart, leaving nothing but bones. Ivy let out a loud sob, and only then did Elana look up to her daughter. Her eyes were fiery red from tears.

Luna swooped down in all her orange glory and landed beside her king. Even she looked sad as she pushed her head against his arm, trying to will him to wake. The flames at the ends of her feathers died off, but her white feathers didn't return. "We have to move," a knight said, trying not to sound cruel. A loud crash rattled the earth as another section of the wall came down.

The queen's eyes grew wide at the sight of raiders spilling in through the ruins of the wall.

"We have to go now!" the knight yelled and pushed the queen to start running down the street. Ivy watched as a handful of knights lifted her father's body and followed them. Rayner held his wife's hand and ran alongside the fallen king. Luna took off ahead, her flames returning and sending sparks and ash falling from the sky. Ivy could hear horses charging them from the back, but she didn't turn around. They ran through the streets, as the smoke seared their lungs and burned their eyes.

Ronin appeared beside Ivy, and she noticed that he was unscathed, but something resembling fear danced in his eyes. The eastern gate was open, and Ivy could see the black beach and beyond it—nearly all the boats were gone from the harbor. She almost stumbled as her father's ship came into view. It was massive and sat calmly in the dark waters as the storm of battle went on behind them. It was made from the Blackwood trees, and its sails were the pale purple of her father's eyes. The Blackbourne sigil flew high above the crow's nest of the mast. A Blackwood tree encircled by its own roots. "No, no, no," Ivy muttered to herself. She had seen this ship last night in her dream, but it was in the wrong harbor.

Arrows rained down in front of them, abruptly stopping their escape. Raiders screamed behind them, their horses pounding on the black sands of the beach as more archers nocked back their arrows. Kyatta and Correlyn did the same and dropped a few of them before they could fire. Earl Rorik let out a terrifying cry and barreled into a man, knocking him from his feet and sending his ax through the raider's face. "Go!" he shouted back over his shoulder.

Piotr ran up and grabbed Ivy by the other arm, pulling her

toward the ship with Finn. Rayner called to Earl Rorik, but he was quickly swallowed up by the raiders. His son Grimm yanked his mother by the arm, but she snatched it away and ran to her husband. Lord Kevan ran down the docks and helped the knights carry Magnus's body up the ramp then helped Elana into the ship. More arrows pierced the gunwale just as they got Magnus inside. Piotr let go of Ivy and ran to help his father draw up the anchor.

Ivy stumbled as Finn pushed her along, craning her neck back to see Earl Rorik emerge from the slaughter. He was covered head to toe in blood, but his wife didn't come with him. Grimm screamed and tried to run into the crowd, but the earl grabbed his son and shoved him toward the waiting ship. Ivy's boots pounded over the dock as she ran with Finn, looking back to make sure her brother was following. Rayner wouldn't board until everyone got on safely, and Grimm stood with him. Ivy hadn't noticed Kyatta board the ship, but the white-haired woman was already high in the rigging and shooting arrows at the raiders who stormed the docks.

Ronin stood at the top of the ramp, yelling at Ivy to hurry. A fire arrow landed just below where Ronin stood. It stuck into the side of the ship with a loud *thud* as more came falling from the sky. Ivy turned back just as she reached the bottom of the ramp and saw Luna sweeping down on the raiders and lighting them on fire. Their screams were as sharp as a blade as they dropped to the black sand. Ivy was so focused on Luna, that she almost didn't see the horned knight. He seemed to emerge from the shadows and suck up all the light around him. His midnight stallion tore through the crowd, headed toward—

Ivy's heart stopped beating in her chest. Rayner stood at the edge of the docks with Grimm as Correlyn stood ahead of them in the sand, still firing her arrows into the crowd. "Rayner!" Ivy screamed with everything she had. Her brother whipped his head around and followed Ivy's finger to where the horned knight was charging. But not toward Rayner, toward Correlyn.

Rayner broke off into a run. His voice caught in his throat as he slammed his boots into the sand. The stallion was charging at full speed, and Correlyn was facing the other way, loosing arrows as rapidly as Rayner's heart was beating. "Correlyn!" he managed to scream, but he didn't recognize his own voice. Her black hair swirled around her face as she turned on her feet. Rayner threw a hand out as his feet brought him closer, but the horned knight scooped her up like she was nothing. Rayner nearly ran into the horse's rear as it passed. He'd felt the brush of Correlyn's hair as she was yanked from his reach. She hadn't noticed the horned knight until he already had his armored hands around her. Rayner was too panicked to form any words. He got to his feet and started running after the stallion when a pair of powerful hands grabbed him from behind. "No!" he screamed and thrashed against the grip, not bothering to turn around to see who held him.

Grimm tightened his grip on Rayner and yanked him back, throwing Rayner off his feet. "Let me go!" Rayner scrambled back to his feet. "Correlyn! Correlyn!" he screamed. The horned knight ran his stallion back through the herd of approaching raiders, and Rayner followed with his eyes. Correlyn was thrown over the knight's lap and then tossed to the ground to land at Helvarr's feet. He stood there wearing a smile as the horned knight jumped from his horse and pulled Correlyn to her feet. She punched and kicked, but the knight made no move to stop her. Rayner struggled against Grimm's grip, hot tears spilling from his eyes as he watched his wife grow smaller and smaller.

Grimm pulled Rayner all the way to the ship, Ivy watching her brother fight the whole time. She stood completely still at the top of the ramp. She couldn't make sense of what just happened, and guilt stabbed her in the stomach. Both Magnus and Correlyn had been missing from her dream, and now she knew why. Correlyn may not be dead, but she was gone. Ivy could see Correlyn struggling against the horned knight's grip until he bent down and seemed to whisper something in her ear.

She watched Correlyn back away from the knight before Grimm's body swallowed her vision. He stood in Ivy's path, still gripping her brother in his arms. Rayner's eyes were already red with tears. "We have to go now." Grimm all but threw Rayner into the ship and blocked his path. With everyone aboard, Grimm threw the ramp down and watched it crash against the docks below. Ivy sank down beside her brother, and Finn came up and put a hand on Ivy's shoulder.

"They took her!" Rayner cried. "They took Correlyn." He buried his face in his hands. Utterly defeated.

"I know," was all Ivy could manage, fighting against her tears. No one spoke, save for the knights giving orders to others to raise the sails.

The cloth burst to life in a sudden gust of wind, but Ivy felt her heart being pulled in the direction of Godstone. She stumbled to her feet and watched as her home burned. The raiders swarmed the beach like hungry sharks, and the kingdom fell behind them. Smoke billowed up into the sky, carrying with it the memory of what Godstone used to be. Ivy couldn't believe how quickly everything had happened. She snapped her eyes shut at the sight and tried to bring forth the image of her home when she last sailed away. Her father stood at the docks, watching his daughter drift away on an adventure. Last winter seemed too far off to her now. So much had happened, good and bad, but right now, Ivy only felt the bad.

Finn's firm hand rested on her shoulder, and Ivy leaned back into his chest. This had been his home as well, another home that he'd lost. Ivy turned to scan the faces on the ship. Earl Rorik had left Tordenfall to fight for her father. Lord Kevan and his family left their city to protect Godstone. Kyatta stood with her shoulders slumped over. The people of the Moon Wood didn't usually get involved with other battles, yet she had. Elana sat bent over Magnus's body, her shoulders shaking with the tears that were likely falling, but Ivy couldn't see her face.

Rayner came to stand by his sister, letting his eyes fall on the destruction of their home. Ivy grabbed his hand and squeezed it in hers. "We'll get her back," she said quietly. Finn wrapped an arm around her waist.

"We'll get it all back," Finn whispered against her hair. Rayner squeezed his sister's hand in return but kept his eyes straight. Ivy knew her words weren't empty promises, and neither were Finn's. She could feel it in her bones, the way you feel the strike of a sword. They would get their home back, they would get Correlyn back, and Ivy would fulfill her promise to her father.

They may have lost their home for now, but the battle for the North was far from over. They would let Helvarr think he won, to sit in her father's throne, and keep it warm for Rayner. It was strange to think that Rayner was the rightful king of Godstone. She knew her brother hadn't been eager to take over for their father, but it had been thrust upon him. She knew Rayner would face it with the same level of dignity that their father had. She wondered what kind of king Rayner would make, but already she knew he would be great.

Magnus had been preparing Rayner for years now, almost as if he knew his reign would be cut short and that his son would need to be prepared to take the throne. Ivy turned slightly toward her brother and released his hand.

"What are your orders, Your Grace?" Ivy slightly lowered her head toward Rayner. He turned to face her, his pale purple eyes looking hauntingly similar to Magnus's at that moment. Everyone else gathered around him at Ivy's words. Rayner looked out to the people aboard the ship, who had sacrificed everything for his father. They had no reason to pledge loyalty to Rayner after Magnus's fall.

Yet, one by one, they got down on their knees and bowed their heads. Finn sank beside Ivy, and she did the same, watching her brother's reaction. Any pain that covered his face lifted as he composed himself and set a stern look on his face. He was the image of their father in the way he seemed to stand up straighter as everyone kneeled before him. Their mother rose to her feet with tears still fresh in her eyes, but when she laid them on Rayner, she smiled. Rayner smiled in return and watched his mother give him an approving nod and kneel on the deck of the ship.

In all the chaos and death, the loss and heartache, Ivy felt a swell of pride as she looked up to her brother. This wasn't supposed to be the way it happened, but their fates had been sealed long ago, and nothing could have stopped what had happened. Ivy knew her dreams were now a glimpse into the future, but she wasn't sure if she could change what she saw. The gods hardly ever revealed their plans, but Ivy knew that whatever path they had set before her, she must take it and trust that the gods were leading her to something better. Nothing is gained without a loss. This had been a bad defeat, Ivy knew that, but that didn't mean it was over. They would fight with everything they had left in them to take back their homes and restore peace.

Ivy looked at her brother until he met her gaze. "So, Your Grace," she repeated. "What are your orders?" Rayner stared at her for a long moment, then lifted his eyes to the bowed heads before him.

"We'll go to the only king left who can help us." Rayner's voice boomed over the wind in the sails. Ivy felt her heart flutter in her chest; she knew from her dream already where they were going. "My father died for his kingdom," Rayner continued. "He died trying to undo the mistake he made years ago. I could never live up to King Magnus the Mighty. But I promise this, I will fight for you as he did. I will gather allies, armies, and ships." A few people lifted their heads to look at Rayner.

"King Mashu will help us, and together we'll take back the North." His voice rose as he spoke. "We will take back all your homes, one by one. We will run the raiders out of our lands or kill them where they stand in our way!" A few shouts of agreement rose in the crowd. "We have all lost much in this battle, but it's far from over and those who are lost . . . their deaths will not go unavenged. I promise to lead you, fight for you, and never ask anything of you that I wouldn't do myself. I am not my father"—he looked to where Elana knelt next to the king's body—"and I will never try to be. But I will be a just king, as he was, and carry on the legacy of the Blackbourne name. And may my first promise to you as king be heard loud and clear: we will get our home back." Ivy counted the seconds of silence until the crowd rose to their feet and cheered Rayner's name.

Though there was no ceremony, no coronation, Rayner was king in every sense of the word. The king of Godstone stood beside his sister as his men shouted his name, already assigning a byname.

"King Rayner the Unbroken!" Their mantra filled the air. "Rayner the Unbroken! Rayner the Unbroken!" Ivy joined in the cheer. Rayner turned to his sister and let a broad smile form on his lips.

"Father would be proud," Ivy said as she hugged her brother close. Finn wrapped his arms around them, and the crowd moved toward them. Their arms linked over one another as they huddled around their new king. Elana caught Rayner's eye, and prideful tears lingered in her eyes as she looked at her son. "We will return home," Rayner's whispered in Ivy's ear. "I promise."

EPILOGUE

A dream. It was just a dream.

That's what Correlyn had told herself. Yet her eyes burned from tears, and her face was throbbing from where she'd been hit. She could still hear Rayner's voice calling to her as Grimm dragged him away toward the boat, toward safety. Her heart broke to hear her husband's voice so defeated and panicked. Correlyn had passed out on the beach of Godstone and woke up in what she could only describe as a dungeon. She knew where she was, and instantly panicked the second she opened her eyes. Ivy had been brought here by Meisha, but Correlyn had been brought here by—

No, she couldn't believe it. She stood up from the cold stone floor and paced her cell, looking for anything, but it was empty save for a metal ring in the wall meant for a torch. The room was dark, and Correlyn got on her hands and knees to peer under the door where only a sliver of light illuminated the room. She didn't see anything or hear any voices outside. She sat back on her heels and brought a hand up to her face. It was cut up but no longer bleeding. Correlyn didn't know how long she'd been there, but she could only hope that

Rayner and everyone else had gotten away. They needed to get away because if they hadn't, then Godstone would be lost forever. She recalled everything about the battle. The wall crumbling, Luna burning people, and Magnus . . .

The king had fallen at the hands of Helvarr. Correlyn had watched Ivy drop to her knees with her father and heard Rayner screaming beside her, but she couldn't focus at that moment. She couldn't make her mind believe what her eyes had just witnessed. Correlyn had never known her father, and Magnus had always treated her kindly, more so since she married Rayner. He'd been a father figure to her, and the moment he died Correlyn felt every punch of pain that his own children had. She couldn't imagine what Queen Elana must have felt when they carried Magnus's body back through the gates. It wasn't supposed to end like that. Elana was pregnant with his child.

A child that he would never meet, never teach how to fight, never rock back to sleep from a nightmare. A tear rolled down her cheek as she thought about everything that had been lost. Correlyn wiped it away with the back of her hand and began searching her pockets. Whoever had carried her down here had stripped her of her armor and taken her sword and bow. She fumbled with shaky hands as she dug into her pockets, searching for anything that she could use as a weapon. Correlyn always kept a knife hidden in her boot, and she quickly reached for it, but it was gone. She cursed under her breath and wondered who could have known that she had a hidden knife. Correlyn sat up straight when she heard footsteps descending the spiral staircase. She backed herself into the furthest corner of the room, ready to pounce.

Her heart was hammering in her chest as she heard a set of keys jingling in the lock. This was it. Perhaps her only chance for escape.

Helvarr walked through the door and smiled at Correlyn. She felt her knees shaking beneath her but tried to remain upright and remind herself to breathe. He'd taken off his armor and looked to be clean of any blood that he'd spilled on the battlefield. Helvarr strolled into the room like a cold breeze, dragging a chair behind him. The wood on the stone was the only sound she could hear besides the thundering of her heart in her ears. Helvarr placed the chair in the middle of the room and plopped down with a loud sigh. Correlyn's eyes darted between him and the closed door, but he noticed the panic on her face and smiled bigger.

"I'm not going to hurt you," he drawled. Correlyn stayed silent, observing him. Helvarr pulled an apple from his pocket and held it out to her. Her stomach growled, but she refused to move, to take anything from him. He rolled his eyes and set the apple on the stone floor between them before leaning back in the chair, throwing one arm over the back and looking her up and down. Correlyn narrowed her eyes on him, but he barked out a sharp laugh at her attempt to intimidate him.

"I just want to talk," he said.

"I don't have anything to say to you," she spat back. Helvarr flashed his white teeth at her and continued.

"No? I don't think that's true. I think you have plenty that you wish to say to me." Correlyn stayed with her back against the wall and crossed her arms over her chest. "I saw you fighting on the battlefield," he went on. "You're very skilled with a bow. Tell me, do you enjoy killing?" Correlyn stepped forward to spit in his face before backing up against the cold stone wall. Helvarr's smile faded slightly as he wiped his face with his sleeve. "I wouldn't aggravate me. You're my prisoner, remember?"

"Go to hell," Correlyn snapped at him.

Helvarr only smiled and picked up the apple from the ground, sinking his teeth into its flesh. "Where have the Blackbournes gone?" he asked between bites. Correlyn pushed herself off the wall and took a few steps toward him. He stopped eating his apple to watch her.

"Even if I knew where my family has gone, I would never tell you."

"Your family?" Helvarr mocked. "Interesting. Well, I don't believe you." Correlyn felt her heart flutter but kept her face stern. "I don't want to hurt you, Correlyn." Her name coming from his mouth made her cringe. "But if you don't tell me where they've gone, I'm afraid I'll have no choice."

"Come and try," Correlyn said through gritted teeth. "And we'll see who's the one that gets hurt."

Helvarr chuckled and took another bite of his apple, watching her with those sharp copper eyes. "I like you. You've got a lot of fight in your bones." He stood up suddenly and stood over Correlyn.

She backed away just a step, but he followed her, so close to her face that she could smell that apple on his breath. "Let's see how long it takes to break that." Correlyn shoved her hands into his chest, forcing him to stumble back. He dropped that crooked smile and grimaced at her, throwing his apple against the wall with such a force it exploded. Correlyn winced at the sound but balled up her fists, waiting for him to attack.

Helvarr stood up tall and ran a hand through his black hair and straightened his coat. "Don't tempt me. I don't want to hurt you, but I will if you push me." Correlyn spit at him again, and before she knew what was happening, he was across the room, pinning her up against the wall. She tried to kick him, but he leaned his body into hers, forcing her back against the wall. Helvarr pinned her arms above her head, squeezing her wrists until she stopped squirming. His breath was hot in her ear and his chest like the stone wall that pushed into her back. He tried to catch her eye, but Correlyn kept turning away, not wanting to see that face that had taken so much from her. "If you cooperate," he whispered. "Perhaps I won't need to bind your wrists."

"Go ahead. Perhaps it will be enough to make a noose," Correlyn sneered, running her eyes down his neck. Helvarr flashed his teeth and let out a restricted growl. "And if you hurt Rayner . . ." She made herself look at him. Look into those empty golden eyes. "I'll kill you before Ivy has the chance."

Helvarr eased himself away but kept her wrists pinned above her head. His eyes shifted, and if Correlyn didn't know any better, she would say that he almost looked hurt. "I don't doubt that," he said in a quiet tone. "But, little Ivy won't have the chance unless you tell me where they went. I don't like surprises."

Correlyn felt a surge of anger rising from her belly. Helvarr had *surprised* them on every account. He'd ambushed Magnus's forces, sent raiders after Ivy, and an assassin after

Rayner, yet he dared to tell her that he didn't like surprises. "Do whatever you want to me, I'll never help you hurt them more than you already have. You're a rabid dog that needs to be put down," Correlyn growled at him.

Helvarr let go of her wrists and stepped back, and as soon as Correlyn was free, she threw a punch. He caught her wrist and twisted it back, forcing her to her knees. "I asked you not to do that," he said calmly as he released her. She ignored his warning and kicked her leg out, catching the heel of her boot in his shin. He grimaced from the blow and reached down to grab her, but Correlyn rolled away and got to her feet. "Fine," he said, the anger returning to his face. "You want to play games? Then let's play." Helvarr pulled a knife from his boot, and Correlyn's eyes widened as she spotted it. "Don't worry, I won't kill you. But maybe I'll give you a scar to match the ones that bird gave me." He ran the knife down his face against the scratch marks from Luna's talons.

Correlyn started sweating; there was no going back now. She'd angered him to the point of fighting, and she wasn't sure who would win. Her eyes grew even wider as she realized it was her blade that he held in his hand. Correlyn felt sick at the thought of his hands on her, searching for weapons while she lay unconscious. Helvarr lunged at her, and Correlyn quickly stepped from his path and around the chair. He twisted around and swung the knife too close to her face. She stumbled back into the stone wall just as he ran at her. She ducked as Helvarr thrust her blade into the stones, dirt, and pebbles falling on the top of her head. She kicked him again and tried to get to her feet, but his hands dug into her hair and pulled her back.

Correlyn's head slammed against the stone floor, and white lights danced in her vision. Helvarr tried to straddle her, but she kneed him in the ribs and grabbed hold of the hand that held her blade. They struggled over the knife, and Helvarr sat on her chest, all of his weight pushing her ribs into her lungs. She fought to get in a full breath when he threw a punch at her ribs. Correlyn let go of the knife and coughed at the pain as he got off her. Helvarr's breathing was heavy as he got to his feet and switched the blade to his other hand.

"You're strong, I'll give you that," he said, returning to a fighting stance. Correlyn got to her feet, clutching her ribs and trying to steady her breathing. "The way I hear it," he hissed, "your husband barely fought for his life. To give up so easily," he tsked. "Such a pity, you could do better."

Correlyn's hands were shaking, and her face grew hot. Rayner had fought with everything he had, and he almost died. Correlyn didn't know what she would do without him, without this new family of hers. She had to fight with everything she had just as her husband did. She had an idea of where they might have sailed, but she would never give them up, no matter how he tortured her or how many bones he broke. Helvarr grinned at her, waiting for her to attack, and she obliged him.

Correlyn ran at him, and as he brought up his knife, she ducked under the blade and drove her elbow into his back. The blow was enough to get a small cry of pain from him, but he didn't go down. Before he could turn around, she kicked him in the back of the knee, forcing him down, and leaped on his back. She clawed at his face as he twirled around, trying to throw her off. Helvarr stumbled back and slammed her into the stone wall. He slammed her again and again, but Correlyn wasn't giving up. She reached for the knife in his hand, but he yanked it away, slicing her forearm. The warm blood trickled down her arm to cover her hands, but she didn't stop. This is what he wanted, he pushed her to violence, and she was going to give him everything she had left.

Helvarr bent down and threw her over his shoulders. She hit the ground and rolled a few feet until her back was against the chair. She quickly stood up, grabbed the chair, and flung it at him. He threw up his arms to block it, and Correlyn ran. She burst through the door and tripped on the first step of the spiral staircase. She could hear Helvarr cursing her from behind and hear his heavy footfalls chasing after her. Correlyn's heart was racing as she took the steps two at a time. The door at the top of the stairs was open, and Correlyn ran through it, closing it behind her.

She was on the ground level of the central tower, where she'd waited all night with Magnus and Elana for word on Rayner. He'd come back so bloody and beaten that even Magister Ivann thought he was dead at first. Correlyn shook the image from her head and grabbed the first chair she saw. She jammed it under the handle of the door just as Helvarr's fists pounded against it. Correlyn stumbled back and scanned her surroundings, looking for a weapon, but there was nothing in the room. There was no time to search anywhere else. She had to run. Helvarr pounded on the door again, and Correlyn swore it cracked the wood. She poked her head out the main entrance, and before her courage could leave her, she bolted from the tower.

Her eyes couldn't take in all the destruction whizzing past

her, it was too much, and right now, Correlyn had to focus. It was starting to get dark outside, and she guessed that Helvarr had only had her down there for a few hours. At least that meant Rayner and Ivy were a good distance away by now. A tear escaped as she ran through the streets of Godstone, and headed for the beach. She didn't know if there were any boats left, but she didn't care. She would swim into those cold black waters to escape him if she had to. Smoke still filled the streets, and it stung her eyes as she ran. Correlyn could see the burnt structures of houses and crumbled buildings in her peripherals. Helvarr's raiders were sprinkled throughout the kingdom, and some started to chase her as she passed.

"Get her!" Helvarr's voice chased her down the main street. A raider stepped into her path, and Correlyn threw her shoulder into his chest, knocking him from his feet. The pain rattled her bones, but she tried to ignore it. She dared a look behind her—Helvarr was catching up, and with him, a handful of raiders had their swords drawn and ready. Correlyn ran faster. She mustered up every bit of strength she had left and sent it to her legs. They screamed at her to stop, but she ignored them. "Correlyn!" Helvarr screamed at her. She rounded a corner and slipped in a pool of blood. Helvarr almost caught her by the arm, but she quickly shot away from him.

The back gate of Godstone was open, and she could see the black beaches. The air was salty and fresh against her cheeks, the gulls circled above, and Correlyn felt herself half-smile at the sight of freedom. No guards stood at the gate, likely because they didn't expect anyone to come through them. Helvarr was still calling to her from behind as Correlyn ran through the open gates and into the sand. Her eyes darted in every direction, but she couldn't spot a boat. Her heart sank a little, but she kept running, looking for any way out. The Shadow Sea would be freezing even if the spring weather was warm.

She could see the black waters lapping against the stones and decided she would try and swim to the nearest cliff and scale the wall. Helvarr's raiders wouldn't follow her into the sea, and if she was quick enough, maybe she could get back on land before they had a chance to rally their horses. Then she would head south, as far as she could run until she found somebody, anybody who could get her a horse or put her on a boat. She thought she had a decent plan working in her head when suddenly it went blank, and a steel hand grabbed her by the shoulder.

She was thrown to the ground with such a force her arms were half-buried in the midnight sand. The horned knight stood above her, yanking Correlyn to her feet just as Helvarr was running up. Correlyn struggled against the knight's grip, and tears swelled in her eyes as she looked past the knight to the sea that would have taken her away, in one way or another. Helvarr was out of breath and stormed right up to Correlyn and cracked her across the face with the back of his hand. She went down in the sand again, her cuts from earlier reopening and her split lip was leaking blood into her mouth. She spit the blood at Helvarr's boots and glared up at him with her cold grey eyes. "You little . . ." Helvarr reared back to strike her again, but the knight caught his arm and yanked Correlyn to her feet.

Correlyn wiped the blood from her face and stood back,

but the knight grabbed for her shoulder to make sure she wouldn't try to run again. Correlyn struggled against the knight's grip, kicking and screaming but to no avail. "Quit squirming," Helvarr ordered. The knight grabbed hold of both her shoulders and squeezed until Correlyn thought her collarbones might shatter under the skin. She dropped to one knee, and the knight released her.

Correlyn couldn't let them break her. She wouldn't allow them to use her to get what they wanted. She would die before she let that happen. They could hurt her all they wanted if it meant they never got their hands on Rayner or the rest of her people. Correlyn felt a stab of guilt at the thought of sacrificing herself for Rayner. She knew he would do the same for her, but it would kill him. Correlyn said a silent prayer in her head for Rayner and rose back to her feet. Helvarr grinned at her, but anger danced in his eyes like firebugs in a dark field. She stood up tall and tried her best to keep her face stern and hateful as she turned to the horned knight and spit blood on his helm.

"I'm going to kill you first," Correlyn hissed.

Helvarr laughed, and Correlyn snapped her head at him. He composed himself and said, "I don't think you want to do that, Correlyn dear."

"And why not?" she snapped back. Helvarr didn't answer but gave a strange look to the horned knight who stepped toward Correlyn before reaching up to remove his helm. Correlyn thought her head might explode, her heart would stop beating, and her eyes would burn inside of her skull when she spotted flowing black hair that fell out of the helm. Correlyn stepped back a pace, not believing what her ears had heard earlier that day when the horned knight spoke to her. There was so much commotion around her and in her head that Correlyn thought she must be going crazy. Yet, when the helm was lifted, Correlyn was staring into a mirror. Her black hair was as dark as the beaches, and her smoky grey eyes somehow looked darker than they had last time. Correlyn stumbled back another step, tears spilling from her eyes. She shook her head as if that would make the image disappear. This had to be a nightmare, this couldn't be real. "Now, is that any way to talk to your mother?" Lady Oharra asked.

ACKNOWLEDGMENTS

Didn't I just write one of these?

Well, I've got more people to thank for this book. Let's switch up the order of thanks— gotta keep you people on your toes.

First, I have to thank my husband, Vaughan. You've been so supportive and patient through this process, and let me ramble on and on about this series. You continue to support this dream and I can't thank you enough for everything you've done.

To the woman this book is dedicated to— thank you mom for loving my stories, and helping me in any way you could throughout this publishing process. Anytime I call you with news about my books, you're always excited to talk about what's next in this journey. Thank you, Dad, for everything. I'm glad that Ivy's story has opened the world of fantasy to you, and keep that spoon handy because I'm not done writing stories. April, you've been amazing with keeping up with my latest books, and I'm so grateful to have you in my life. Love you all.

Okay, now for the heroes behind this book. Coco, you

continue to amaze me with your beautiful artwork and I'm so honored to work with you on this series! Thank you so much. To Sarah, my amazing editor. Thank you for your time and patience, and for helping me polish my book baby. To Franzi for again creating a beautiful book design to compliment the cover, your work is outstanding! I look forward to working with you all in the future.

To all my readers: Maureen and Amanda, thank you for believing in me. To all my ARC readers, there's too many to list but thank you all for your feedback and love for this series. I love the play-by-play messages I get as you're reading the book, even if they are angry messages after a character death! Sorry. (But not really). Arleta!! You're in this book, can you believe it!? I had so much fun incorporating you into a scene with Finn. Thank you for all the support you show my books! To Corbin, Megan, Katie, and every other fan of this series, I can't thank you all enough for hyping up this book and for how deeply you love (and hate) my characters! And to my map maker, Sheridan. You took my original map and gave it a much-needed face lift, and it's just gorgeous. I'm so happy we connected through this process and I look forward to working with you again. Thank you all!

Crystal!! You didn't think I'd leave you out, did you? You continue to be such a great supporter and an amazing friend. Every time I have even the slightest news about my books to share, you're the first person I message. You love these characters like they're real, and your excitement fuels me to keep going. Crystal, you are amazing and forever my #1 fan! House Blackbourne for life.

To my professors at MCLA who supported my book, and

helped me grow and challenged me as a writer. To all the local bookstores that carry my book, it's been such a humbling experience to walk into a store and see my book on the shelf. So, thank you everyone for the part you played in this series. I couldn't have done any of it without you.

Until next time, from a heart as cold as Helvarr's, thank you all so much!

ABOUT THE AUTHOR

Brittany is a self-published author, and "The Girl Destined to Rise" is her second novel. She's currently finishing her BA in English/ Creative Writing at MCLA, and looking forward to graduating and focusing her time on her books. Brittany currently lives in a small town in the Berkshires with her husband and her many unread books. When she isn't writing, Brittany enjoys searching her bookshelf for a new read, picking them up and putting them back before heading to Barnes and Noble to buy more. A writer can never have too many books.

CPSIA information can be obtained
at www.ICGtesting.com
Printed in the USA
BVHW042139081122
651516BV00001B/7

9 781662 929175